Redemption

By

Derick Parsons

The persons and events described in this book are fictitious; any resemblance to real persons or events in entirely coincidental.

Text copyright © 2012 Derick Parsons
All rights Reserved

For Eimear, for Everything

Prologue

William Henry Akima strolled easily along Foster Road, slowly rolling his broad shoulders in simple enjoyment of the warm September sunshine through his thin white cotton tee-shirt. Today was the first day he had ventured forth so lightly clad on this trip, for he was used to a harsher sun, and a higher, bluer sky, and what passed for sun-bathing weather amongst the native Dubliners seemed to him cool, even chilly. Even today's unseasonably good weather –which had the locals gasping and sweating as they went about their daily business- was to him scarcely warm enough for such light attire, but he was determined to enjoy it nonetheless. If nothing else life had taught him to suck the good out of every day, and not to waste time with comparisons between what is and what could be. Particularly as things can always be very much worse as well as better. That was a lesson he -in common with most of his fellow Africans- learned early, and well.

He turned left into Sarsfield Place, heading for his apartment in the heart of Phibsboro's residential desert, a broad smile on his face as he walked, and little on his mind beyond the pleasure of simply being alive on a warm, sunny day. Willie's face, like all descendants of Nguna-based tribes, was very round, very black, and very prone to smiling on the smallest pretext, and his shaven head made his face seem even more moon-like. His ancestry was almost pure Zulu, though he was not aware of this and would not have much cared if informed; in the ghettoes of Soweto where he had been raised only the pure-bred first or second generation 'country boys' cared about their lineage. Everyone else was too busy trying to force a living from a hostile world to care much about their antecedents, particularly as many of them were of mixed or unknown parentage. Willie was a bastard in the literal sense of the word, a fact which bothered him not one iota; snobbery, at least, was not one of his faults. During his formative years there had never been any time for such foolishness; an upbringing that had seen him lose three of his four brothers to violent death, and both his sisters to drug addiction and prostitution, had imbued him with a very clear and simple philosophy on life that left no room for such nonsense.

He had little interest in the politics of his homeland either, and even less in the still-simmering hostilities between the ruling ANC and the Zulu Inkatha to which he, by blood at least, should have belonged. Throughout the massive upheavals which years before had not just rocked but totally restructured South Africa he had remained aloof, disinterested even, save where he could turn a profit from the chaos. For he was a man with a single goal in life, a mission to which he totally dedicated himself; Willie's ruling passion was for making money, and he was more than ordinarily skilled at this craft. He was already rich and every passing day saw him richer, a fact which -quite apart from his generally sunny disposition- gave him a good reason for the broad smile currently wreathing his face. Another was the fact that he genuinely liked Ireland, and always thoroughly enjoyed his visits there. He travelled to Dublin three or four times a year and had done so for the past twelve years, which was ample justification for him to own his own apartment in the city. And indeed this apartment was another reason he had to smile; the now-exploded property bubble had affected him far less than most, and in spite of the collapse in house prices his home was still worth far more than he had originally paid for it, all those years ago.

As he sauntered down the street he encountered more than one malicious glare, and even the occasional muttered imprecation, but these he paid no attention whatsoever; Dublin's growing hostility towards immigrants -refugees or otherwise- caused him a touch of regret but not an instant of worry; he came from a country where dislike was expressed with machetes or AK 47 assault rifles, so a few hard looks or insults were to him about as significant as the warm breeze currently playing about his body.

Even one with his massive *sang froid* had registered the recent change in attitudes, however, and now he wondered a little at this change, viewing it with sorrow rather than anger. On his very early visits, when he was barely out of his teens, his black face had still been something of a novelty in this almost entirely white country, and people had quite often stared openly at him in the streets. Willie had not minded. He came from a curious people himself, and where he grew up any stranger -regardless of their colour- was an object of intense interest. Besides, he had sensed that the overt interest in him was by and large not unfriendly. Not so anymore. The past twenty-five years or so had changed Ireland almost beyond, and now there were a great many black people in Ireland. And when people stared there was no curiosity but often anger in their eyes, and a smouldering resentment which he did not understand. Times were hard but was there not enough wealth in this land to feed the hungry people who flocked this way, often fleeing from terrible hardship or the fear of sudden, violent death? He, of course, needed no charity but his colour saw him ranked alongside the neediest refugee, and he found it hard to understand the depth of the rancour aimed at foreigners. Not that he took it personally, for how could anyone know that he brought wealth rather than seeking it? But the mean-mindedness behind the glares saddened him. Nonetheless he would continue his still enjoyable -and of course profitable- trips to the Emerald Isle, and even occasionally flirt with the idea of one day retiring there for good. Not that he ever would, of course; it was far too cold and damp, and the people were much too pale and anaemic for his taste. When he had finally amassed enough money to satisfy even his craving, Jamaica or Barbados would perhaps be his last port of call, or even Africa, to bask in the hot beauty and begin collecting the very different but equally important wealth of children. Many children. Children who would never understand what it is to truly hunger, who would never have to fight merely to stay alive from day to day. Children whose earliest memories would be of light and love and joy; rather than fear and misery and want. To such a man as he family-building might not necessarily be the most pleasant of tasks but Willie, in spite of his obsession with cold hard cash, understood clearly that the man who left behind only money was one who died a pauper. Such a fate was not for him. His grin deepened as he walked; but he would not raise them in Ireland! Not unless global warming worked an unlikely miracle on the climate, that is.

As he turned into the driveway of his apartment block a group of young boys ran past him, screaming into his face, 'Fuck off, nigger! Fuck off back where yeh belong! Ye black bastard, yeh!'

Willie stared after them in surprise and anger, his smile temporarily in abeyance as he wondered why they were not in school, and where ones so young could have garnered their hatred for an unknown face, simply because it was black. From the parents, no doubt. His face was sombre as, bypassing the communal front door, he passed through the gate at the side of the red-bricked building and entered the back garden. Yes, things were much changed, and it was in the nature of things that as a man grows older change always seems to be for the worse. His bleak mood quickly lifted, however, for the taunts of foolish children could not really hurt him, and coming home always filled his heart with a quiet warmth. As the only ground-floor resident Willie had sole use of the small back garden -complete with a stone flagged patio- and in the riotous blooms of colour therein he took enormous pleasure, and no little pride. He employed a gardener to come in two days a week all the year round to care for it, whether he was in Ireland or not, and the little garden was generally immaculate, a haven from most of life's cares. Willie's smile slipped again as he noted that today, however, some of his prized shrubs and ornamental trees were looking decidedly bedraggled; battered even. The plants in the front garden were always so, with the constant comings and goings from the various flats, to say nothing of careless or rowdy passers-by, but who had intruded on his private garden? Children, perhaps, from the school that bordered the bottom of his garden; they often climbed the dividing wall between their playground and his garden in search of errant balls, and even occasionally used his garden as a short-cut to the bus stop on the main road. And this in spite of his frequent complaints to the Headmaster. Not that she cared; the kids in the local school were pretty wild, and almost everyone living within a mile of the school had complained about them at one time or another, without satisfaction.

He sighed heavily; this was turning out to be a less pleasant day than it had earlier promised. Tomorrow he would have to speak to Juno, the gardener, and insist that he attend more closely to his duties. After all, it was only two days before that he had supposedly spent the entire day tending to these plants. Willie shook his head as he unlocked the patio door, his usual beam now just a memory; could no one be trusted these days to fulfil their duties properly? And must every joy turn so quickly sour? Or was such a thought merely a sign of advancing age? A mental picture of himself as a cantankerous old man presented itself to his mind, instantly restoring both his mood and his smile; he was neither yet. No, he would not let anything destroy his peace of mind on such a glorious day. Especially as he was still aglow from making love to his new, young and very beautiful lover, and faced the prospect of an equally pleasurable evening ahead.

He unlocked his patio door and stepped directly into the sitting-room of his flat, heading for the kitchen and a soothing mug of tea; enough of the local culture had rubbed off for him to regard this as a universal panacea for all of life's woes. He froze in the kitchen doorway, however, his eyes suddenly enormous and very white in the dim light as his gaze fell on a man sitting at the kitchen table waiting for him. A man he had never seen before. A man wearing black leather gloves even in the summer heat. His mind racing wildly, driven by his conscience, Willie's mouth fell open and he feebly uttered, 'Who... What... What do you want?'

Then, as anger joined the fear in his heart, he demanded in a rough, louder voice, 'Who are you and what do you want with me?' He took a threatening step forward, 'Well? What are you doing in my home?'

The man at the table made no reply but slowly got to his feet. Slowly and quietly but with infinite menace. He was tall and massively built, with the overblown limbs of the dedicated bodybuilder and an aura of barely suppressed violence. His face had the flat planes of a boxer, and his lifeless gaze and lack of expression were far more intimidating than any grimace of anger or hatred could have been.

Willie saw all these danger signs but felt no fear; rather his nostrils flared as his fighting blood boiled over, his usual smiling expression hardly even imaginable as his lips twisted into an angry snarl. With real menace of his own, his powerful body coiled to attack, he hissed, 'I shall not ask you again, man. Who are you and what are you doing in my home?'

He received no reply and was about to launch himself across the kitchen at the intruder when a slight noise behind made him whirl around, sudden fear flooding over him. Quickly though he reacted, however, he was not quite quick enough. Two other strangers had crept out of the bedroom behind him and were closing in on him fast, upraised baseball bats clenched in their black-gloved hands. The larger of the two men reached Willie first, and without hurry clipped him on the side of the head with the wooden bat as he turned to confront them. Clipped him without any great effort but with devastating effect as Willie instantly collapsed backwards into the kitchen and sprawled bonelessly on the gray stone tiles, unconscious even before he hit the floor.

The man in the kitchen lifted a baseball bat of his own from the counter-top behind him and without haste rounded the table to join his companions. They formed a semi-circle around Willie's prone body and began hitting him about the head and torso, lazily swinging the baseball bats in an easy, concerted rhythm reminiscent of experienced lumberjacks hewing at a fallen tree. In spite of their apparent lack of effort Willie's body quickly sustained fearsome injuries, and in less than a minute he was dead. The killers seemed somehow to sense the moment he died, because at that instant all three paused for a split second, their rhythm failing for the first time. The lapse was only momentary, however, and they immediately resumed their remorseless assault. Long after Willie was dead –long after, in fact, his own mother would not have recognised his battered, bleeding corpse- the three men finally came to a halt. They paused for a instant above the body of the man they had just killed, the way men will when they have just completed a task together, taking a moment to share the accomplishment instead of immediately departing.

The spell was broken by the leader of the three killers bending to fumble in the dead man's pockets for a moment, removing a mobile phone and tucking it into his jacket. Then he stood up, produced a can of red spray-paint from the pocket of his black leather jacket, and quickly daubed a slogan onto the wall. He stepped back to admire his handiwork, then the three men threw their red-stained bats into a corner of the room, each throwing his bat into the same spot in an almost ritualistic gesture. Then they quietly left the apartment, peeling off their black leather gloves and dropping them into a plastic bin-liner as they went. The leader pulled a balaclava down over his face too, lest a neighbour spot them, and they left the way they had entered, slipping through the sliding patio door before brushing carelessly through the shrubs and bushes onto the lawn. Unheeding of any observers in the apartments above they quickly scaled the low wall at the bottom of the garden and jumped down into the playground of the school beyond, knowing that it would be deserted at this time of this particular day, a Bank Holiday. They had a car parked some two hundred yards from the school, out of sight of any of the apartments, and knew that even if spotted they would be long gone before the police could arrive. Within minutes they were far away, without ever having impinged on the consciousness of any of the locals.

Back in his apartment Willie's dead body was cooling slowly in the warmth of the sun-flooded kitchen, his blood congealing on the tiles and forming a stain that would never lift. Above his body, in an equally vivid crimson splash, the blood-red paint was drying unevenly on the wall, but the letters were still perfectly legible. They read: *NIGGERS GO HOME. IRELAND FOR THE IRISH.* Underneath, in smaller letters, was written, '*The Sons of Cuchuailainn*'.

Chapter One

The instant his alarm-clock started shrieking Detective Chief Inspector Jack O'Neill stirred, half sitting up to slap off the alarm before rolling over and burying his face back into his pillow. His out-flung right arm encountered only empty space on the other side of the bed, however, and he awoke fully as awareness of the void beside him pierced his foggy brain. Trying to ignore the odd sensation that the unoccupied half of his bed was somehow a vast, empty space rather than just a strip of mattress a few inches wide, he rolled reluctantly and somewhat unsteadily out of bed. Fighting a sense of nausea, his eyes bleary and still half closed with sleep, he padded into the bathroom and fumbled his way into the shower cubicle, on some level half-believing that he would emerge alert and refreshed, like the guys in the television ads. He didn't. When he finally gave up and emerged dripping wet and clutching blindly for a towel, he was certainly wide awake but still tired, just as hungover, and no readier to face the day. The advertising execs were lying to the world. Now there was a surprise. At fifty-six he really should be more inured to life's little disappointments.

After brushing his teeth he shaved with hands that hardly trembled at all, which meant that he didn't cut himself once. Which made a pleasant change, these days. Not so long ago he would have used Murine on the aching orbs confronting him in the mirror but now he simply ignored the tell-tale red eyes and returned to the bedroom to dress. His white shirt was crumpled from the dryer but clean, and although his dark blue suit was years out of fashion it was well-cut and of decent quality material, and still imparted to its wearer at least a degree of respectability. His tie, of course, was black. Even after eight years deep mourning was, to Jack, a statement of fact rather than a social convention.

He grimly surveyed the finished ensemble in the bedroom mirror, dismayed by what he had let himself become. He was a tall man and powerfully built, but he was thinner than he should have been and his thick crop of black hair sprinkled with gray had lately become gray hair sprinkled with black. His dark blue eyes, now permanently bloodshot, were slightly hazy rather than piercing, as they once had been, and his haggard, deeply seamed cheeks told heavily against him. The fissures and broken-veined marring his skin showed clearly that the more bottles a man empties into himself, the more life the bottles empty out of him.

With a slight, resigned sigh he went downstairs to the kitchen and made himself a mug of black coffee, still in thrall to the ad-men to the extent of hoping that this would help his hangover. It might have, except halfway through bolting down the scalding drink he reached into a cupboard and refilled the mug to the brim with whiskey. Six months before, when he had started this habit, he had made various excuses to himself for beginning the day in this way, everything from a 'hair of the dog' helping his hangover to needing a nip to 'keep out the cold'. Now he just drank in the mornings without bothering with excuses.

Jack set the burglar alarm and left his house, quickly walking the half-mile to Glenageary Dart station as a token gesture to the vow he had made in his youth to always exercise and always stay in shape. Alcohol had eroded all his life's aspirations thus, until only shadows remained. And even this pretence at fitness would have long ago dissolved in whiskey if he had not deliberately sold his car once the boozing started to get out of control; to become a drunk driver would have been just too bitterly ironic. He still had resolve enough not to become another Rollo Walker, the man he hated most on this Earth. Rollo Walker was the man who had killed Jack's wife and only child. Suzanne, Jack's wife, had been forty-four at the time of the accident, and as vibrant and humorous and earthily alive as any woman could be. A big, zesty woman with an appetite for everything life had to offer, she had also been clever, loving, and mostly understanding about his obsession with his job. For years they had watched the marriages of friends and colleagues shatter or simply wear out, and this had made them treasure their own fundamentally happy union all the more. Sue had been far from perfect, in spite of what his roseate memories now whispered, but he had loved her, and been happy with her, and although all too aware of his own faults he had never doubted that she felt the same about him. But it was his daughter Martina that Jack had lived for, Martina who had put the magic into his life. She was the reason he had arisen every morning with a smile on his face, and slept contentedly at night no matter how rough his day had been. Just fifteen at the time of her death, she had already been possessed of a transcendental beauty far removed from her quite ordinary parents. Waif-like, blonde and green-eyed, Martina had possessed the ethereal beauty of an angel, and every time he looked at her Jack's heart had stopped in his chest. Every single time, every single day of her life, from the moment she had been born. And, more importantly, her temperament had matched her looks. She was sweet, loving and affectionate, rarely throwing the tantrums that marked the teenaged children of most of his colleagues, who seemed to delight in making their parents' lives a misery. On the contrary, Martina had generally fussed around him when he came home at night, and worried about him when he was particularly late. In the face of his constant boasting about her his envious colleagues had often joked that he should make the most of it while he could, that she was too good to be true, and so she had indeed proven to be. But it was not hormones or teenage rebellion that had taken her from him; a drunk driver had wiped her and her mother out, had ploughed at speed into their car as they returned from their regular Friday night grocery run and killed them both instantly.

Instantly was what Jack had been told, and what he devoutly hoped was true. It was not a subject he ever dared delve into deeply. Were he still a praying man he would daily have offered a heartfelt plea for it to be true, for he had seen the mangled victims of car crashes all too often, had seen the massive trauma inflicted on their fragile bodies, to even contemplate the alternative. In fact it was his nightmares about Martina lying helpless in the wreckage of their car, calling fruitlessly to him for help as she died by agonising inches, that had started him drinking in the first place. Without whiskey Jack watched them suffer and die every time he shut his eyes at night. Or rather, he watched *Martina* suffer and die. Jack had loved his wife, but his daughter had wholly owned his heart. Much as he had loved Sue, it had sometimes occurred to him that he might eventually have recovered from the blow of her death. Maybe not totally, but enough for him to have some sort of life again. Who knew, perhaps even to attain some sort of happiness again, in time. But without his little girl there was no hope of joy, no chance even of peace. Life, and everything it held, had lost all value and meaning when he lost her, with only pain remaining.

Jack jostled his way onto an already crowded Dart electric train and stood staring sightlessly out of the window at the gray, choopy sea passing by the window, adrift in his own private hell. A hell in which vast quantities of whiskey was the only thing that could dull the pain. The drinking had started almost by accident, had crept into his life by small, almost unnoticed degrees. Certainly for a year or so after his bereavement he would have scoffed at the notion that he was an alcoholic. Sure, he drank a lot; he always had. Many detectives did. It went with the territory, with the lives they led and the sights they were confronted with every day, and especially murder detectives. A few stiff drinks every night helped them to get to sleep. Thus it had always been for Jack. *Excessive* drinking had really started with a reluctance to go home to an empty, silent house. On any given night there was always someone from the Squad going out for a pint, and whatever pub they frequented was always bright and cheering and *alive* in a way that his silent house no longer was. So he had started going for a couple of drinks almost every evening. It was easy, it was comforting and it stopped him from being alone. And from thinking. That was important; his thoughts were not such that any man should have to endure. He had few close friends and no family, but in the pub there were always other detectives, other lonely men who understood his professional life, at least, and with whom he could communicate. The problem was that every night it got harder and harder to go home, and he found himself staying later each evening. Instead of two or three drinks every night he found himself having five or six. Then eight or nine. And then at last the real slide down the drain, when he no longer kept count; *could* not keep count. There was no one to keep him in check, no one to say him nay. He got into the habit of working seven days a week, just to be out of the house, and of course he would pop into the boozer on the way home every night.

In the beginning the booze hadn't affected his work much, and in fact his success rate had actually risen for a while, simply because he had no other distractions and could give all his time to his job. But before long the drink had taken over to the extent that he no longer worked weekends, preferring to spend his days as well as nights in the pub. That was when his career had finally started to slide. But by then he no longer cared. The sun no longer shone in his life so what did his job matter? Alcohol dulled the pain, temporarily at least, but it also told him that all was futile, that nothing counted but nothing itself. For nothing is the eventual destiny of us all. This thought troubled him not one iota. If anything it provided comfort, telling him that one day his suffering would end.

He got off the Dart at Pearse St. Station and began the second leg of his daily exercise; the walk up to Harcourt Square. This was a harder slog than the easy stroll to Glenageary Dart station, but he nevertheless stuck with it every day. Not so much because of his promise to his younger self as because there was an early house on the way in which he called every morning for a couple of double whiskies. He quickly walked there now, his jangling nerves forcing him to push himself until he began to sweat lightly in spite of the cold. And when he reached the pub he slipped inside without as much as a glance over his shoulder to see who might be watching him; much he cared, these days. The pub was hot and reeked of stale booze and staler conversation but the feeling Jack got on entering this fug was as close to a sense of home-coming as he ever got these lonely days. The barman knew him well and put a tumbler under the Jameson dispenser the instant he opened the door, meaning that Jack was soon drinking, in company with a mixture of other desperate people, and with revellers from the night before who refused to give up and go home. On the whole he thought he preferred the quiet, purposeful drinking of life's casualties to the forced gaiety and noise of those who wouldn't admit that the party was over.

Fortified by two large whiskies, he backtracked to the old Garda Metropolitan HQ in Harcourt Square, now an administrative centre, where he was so well known that the guard at the front door simply waved him through without any identification check. And in fact he rarely bothered to carry his warrant card with him these days; after all, it was not as if he ever used it. Not now that he was in the Central Records Office. He couldn't honestly say that he *worked* there, merely that he was *in* it.

He got a coffee from the machine just outside his tiny basement office before entering the room itself, which was hardly more than a large cupboard and was painted a depressing, institution yellow. He slid in behind his desk -which, with a filing cabinet, pretty well filled all the available space- and sat down to drink the coffee, though without a stiffener this time. Those early liveners would enable him to keep going until lunchtime. And at lunchtime... Well, he would slip out for a non-existent bite to eat and simply not return. That was the reality of his life now, with not even a pretence at working, and as he was by far the most senior man in Records there was no one to stop him. And even if he were ever reported no action would be taken. The Gardai look after their own, and Jack had once been amongst the best they had. Besides, no one likes to bring down even a tarnished legend.

Even after he had stopped caring about his job he had still done just enough to coast along as a Murder Squad detective for a while. And even when he had reached the stage of being dead drunk every night it had not ended his career; it had merely caused it to stagnate. It was when he had begun drinking at lunchtime that his career had truly been over, even before he started taking 'curers' for breakfast. Because when he took a drink at lunchtime nothing could make him go back to work; he became consumed by a blind, unthinking thirst that would not be denied. The final straw, as far as his place in the Murder Squad was concerned, had been when he had attended a press conference dead drunk. Luckily for him the assembled reporters, hard drinkers themselves in the main, had been more amused than anything and -knowing of his loss- had charitably let the matter rest. Most of them, in any case. But even the few snide digs that were eventually published in the dailies were far better than the full-scale witch-hunt which could so easily have ensued.

There had never been any question of his being sacked of course; not at his level. Aside from loyalty to a comrade the Garda took pains to avoid scandal wherever possible, and would gladly whitewash even the blackest sheep to preserve the shining image they –not without some justification- liked to present to the public. He had politely been offered early retirement, which he had very impolitely refused. He would have been given a full pension, of course, because 'they' would have allowed him to retire on the grounds of ill health, but that was not the point; he was not clinging to the remains of his career for the money. He no longer cared about his work but at some level a part of him knew that if he had no formal structure in his life, and not even the pretence of order and routine, he would very soon disintegrate. Without even the ghost of the discipline his job had once demanded he would swiftly have drunk himself into the gutter and then death, and he was intelligent enough to know this. And stubborn enough to still not want to succumb just yet.

Pressure had been brought to bear to make him retire, of course, but he had resisted, and the issue had not been forced; the bad publicity attendant on holding a full disciplinary inquiry was the last thing the hierarchy wanted. In any case his superiors –some of whom he had walked a beat or ridden patrol with in their youth- were largely compassionate men and had not the heart to dismiss an old comrade, and moreover one who was clearly suffering. He had been shuffled from department to department, refusing offers of treatment and help, an encumbrance and an embarrassment to all, until finally, when the rest of the Metropolitan Detective branch had relocated to the Phoenix Park, he had been left behind, shoved into Central Records to moulder in the basement. Technically he was supposed to be reviewing old cases, checking for procedural errors that could be used as warning examples in the Detective Training Manual -and in his early days he had actually contributed a few pieces- but in reality he had been shuffled off to decompose quietly and out of sight. And this he was now doing, for since being dumped in there with the clerks and secretaries his drinking had finally reached its current heights. Or depths. The problem was that he knew it must end soon, one way or another; no one could drink at the level he had reached for long without killing themselves. And even if he survived he was coming up to the age where he could retire on a full pension without need of disability, and he knew that this time his superiors would insist on his going. He had few friends left amongst them now, and their initial -genuine- sympathy had gradually turned to impatience with what he knew many of them viewed as his self-indulgence.

Even thinking about retirement made him break out in a cold sweat, and after a brief inner struggle he took his emergency bottle of Jameson out of his desk drawer and added a stiffener to the dregs of his coffee, abandoning his resolve to drink that one straight as easily as he had abandoned a thousand other such promises to himself. The problem of what to do with his time after he retired would just have to wait for another day. And no doubt booze would play a large part in the eventual solution to that problem too. He leaned back in his chair and thought without humour; *the* final *solution?* Perhaps.

The phone on his desk rang, startling him, and he glared at it almost suspiciously; very rarely did it ring these days. A wrong number seemed the obvious solution and it occurred to him to simply ignore it, but few people can listen to the ringing of a phone at close quarters for long, and Jack's nerves were not what they had once been. He quickly caved in, snatching up the receiver and snapping, 'Yes, what is it?'

After a pause a slightly dubious voice said, 'O'Neill? Jack? It's Eamonn Rollins here. I was wondering if you could pop up to see me, please?'

Surprise flooded Jack's mind, to be quickly replaced by dread. No summons from on high was ever to be welcomed; was today to be the day they finally kicked him out of the Gardai? Eamonn Rollins had once been a friend of sorts -had been junior to him, in fact- but now he was the Assistant Commissioner for Crime (Metropolitan Division), and as Jack hadn't spoken to him in years a summons to his office was unlikely to be a social affair. On the contrary it was likely to be extremely unpleasant, and could only have one outcome. With his heart sinking Jack gathered together the sodden shreds of his once considerable courage and said, 'Of course. When would be convenient?'

'I had right now in mind,' replied Rollins dryly, 'If, of course, you're not too busy.'

'Right,' said Jack dully, 'I'm on my way.' He put down the receiver and sighed. Not heavily, and with no particular emphasis or pathos. Just a gentle sigh of resignation. Then he got to his feet and squared his shoulders, refusing to feel any self-pity; he had wallowed in that long enough. And after all, he had known that it had to happen some day.

There was a toilet next door to his office and into this he now proceeded on an errand he had not pursued on behalf of a senior officer in quite some time; he used the toothbrush and mouthwash he habitually kept in the filing cabinet next to the whiskey. Perhaps a vestige of self-respect lingered, after all. Then, sucking an ancient extra-strong mint he had also found, he reluctantly got into the elevator and made his way up to the corridors of power on the top floor. As he tapped on the door of Rollins' palatial office he was girding himself mentally to take it like a man, to show no weakness and to seek no pity. His reputation might be long gone but he still owed it to himself to go out with whatever shreds of dignity he could muster.

He entered on the great one's command and closed the door, hardly daring to look at the man who had once been a friend. Rollins, a very tall, thin balding man with a pointed jaw and small brown eyes, got to his feet and held out his hand, smiling in welcome. In the too-hearty tone of a healthy man talking to an invalid he cried, 'Jack! Long time no see. *Too* long! You're looking well, I must say.'

Jack gave him a perfunctionary smile in return, his heart thudding so loudly in his chest that he wondered for a moment if the other man could hear it too, could *see* the violent tremors shaking his chest. He also thought that if Rollins believed he looked well it was time he took a trip to an optician. He gripped the proffered hand briefly and then sat down uninvited on the visitor's side of the vast desk that dominated the room, sinking deep into the plush leather upholstery that was usually reserved for more important buttocks than his. He settled wonderingly into the unwonted comfort, not bothering to reply to the inane small talk. Eamonn could act like a salesman if he wished; Jack wasn't going to play games, or make this any easier for him. He did, however, cast a slightly cynical glance around his old mate's office, which was twenty times the size of his own and better furnished than his house. Aside from being luxuriously appointed it had an immense window and a view of Dublin, which his converted cupboard certainly did not. Not that Jack was jealous –he couldn't have cared less- but it was nice to see that the Garda bureaucracy had its priorities right when it came to apportioning out its ever decreasing budget.

Rollins unwrapped a mint humbug and tossed it into his mouth before leaning back in his chair to observe his subordinate in silence for some time, studying him from head to toe. Jack was a six-footer, and broad with it, but his clothes hung loosely on him, and Rollins wondered when he had last eaten a good meal. Though at least his suit was clean, and had been pressed in the not-too-distant past. The chin was still firm but the lines etched in his cheeks and the red tinge in the slightly watery blue eyes told their own tale. All in all though, he was in surprisingly good shape for a man who for years had been determinedly drinking himself to death. But then, he had once been a fine athlete, and traces of this still remained. But by God in other ways he was a wreck. Having finished his silent appraisal Rollins smiled, showing teeth that were yellowed by his compulsive sweet-eating, and said brightly, 'You must have enough time served to get your full pension by now, haven't you? God, how time flies. It only seems like yesterday we were a couple of raw coppers pounding the beat. In fact, you must be pretty close to mandatory retirement by now, Jack. What is it, another two years or so left?'

Jack gave him a grim little smile, 'Four. Nearly. Unless they lower the compulsory retirement age for us senior men again. There are rumours of it.'

Rollins shook his head dismissively, 'It'll never happen. We still have *some* friends in Leinster House, thank you very much. Which is part of the reason I called you up here, incidentally. But you could go now with no loss of benefits, is my point. If you wanted to. Are you still as enamoured of the job as ever or are you looking forward to retirement?'

Jack's smile broadened and he replied as lightly as he could, 'Oh, I'm looking forward to it. I've lots of plans. I've been neglecting the garden terribly, for a start, and my golf has gone to hell. I'm looking forward to putting both back in order. And don't laugh, but I've been thinking of getting into breeding and maybe even showing pedigree dogs.'

Rollins raised his eyebrows, visibly surprised that the other man had any interests at all beyond the next bottle, 'Really? I didn't know you were an enthusiast. What breed?'

Jack smiled again, amazing himself with the glib lies flowing so easily from his tongue, 'Bulldogs, of course. I've always had a passion for them, and what other dog would an ex-copper be interested in? Who knows, I might even get to Crufts one day. That's the dream, anyway.'

Rollins nodded, his lips pursed thoughtfully, 'I'm glad to hear you have outside interests to occupy your time. Too many cops go to pieces once they retire because they've no real life outside the job. Especially murder detectives. It takes a hold, becomes an obsession. And if they've no family or hobbies they go downhill fast after they leave.'

A short uncomfortable silence fell, during which Rollins opened his bag of humbugs and unwrapped another one. Jack watched him pop it into his mouth with a touch of amusement. Rollins had been an inveterate chain-smoker in his youth, but by a superhuman effort had managed to quit twenty-odd years before. There had been no patches or nicotine gum in those days and Rollins had kicked the habit by sheer will-power, but somehow in the process he had transferred all his passion for the weed to his crappy humbugs. And passion it was; Jack had never seen him without a bag. In fact, one night on their way to a surveillance job Rollins had dragged him from shop to shop for over an hour until he had found a place that carried his particular brand. And when he *had* finally found one that stocked them he had bought their entire supply rather than risk running out again. It wasn't so much a habit as an obsession, albeit a relatively harmless one. However, on that score Jack didn't feel qualified to criticize anyone, and compared to whiskey mints seemed a pretty innocuous sort of addiction.

When he had dragged out the suspense for long enough -and finished his sweet- Rollins gave what he probably thought was an encouraging smile and said slowly, 'However, you haven't retired yet. Which brings me to the reason for this little chat. You aren't exactly covering yourself with glory down in Records, now are you, Jack? Nor are you worked off your feet. In fact, as far as I can discern your last contribution to the Manual was two years ago. So I thought perhaps you might be interested in taking on one last real case before you hang up your boots. How do you fancy investigating another murder before you go?'

Chapter Two

Jack stared at his one-time friend in stunned disbelief. *God Almighty, had he heard him right?* 'You want me back in the Murder Squad?' he said in stupefaction, knowing it could not be true. He was light-headed with relief merely at not being forced to retire early, but to be offered a real job again seemed an impossible dream. Then he caught hold of himself and took a deep, calming breath, almost as amazed by his own reaction as he was by the news itself; he hadn't realised that he missed the job so much.

Eamonn shook his head and said positively, 'No, certainly not; there's no room for a man of your seniority in the Murder Squad. You've been supernumery to establishment for years, you know. I just want your help dealing with one particular case. You'd still be working out of your present office down in Records, and I'm afraid I can't spare a big team to support you. In fact, I can only give you one assistant. It'll be just like the old days, Jack, a bit of real old-fashioned detective work. Just you and a youngster wearing your shoes out, knocking on doors and asking questions.'

Jack rubbed his forehead, wishing for the first time in years that he had not had a single malt breakfast as he struggled to think clearly. At last he said, 'Real detective work is right. And the first mystery to solve is why you're offering me a murder case. We go back a long way, Eamonn, so let's not arse about; we both know I'm mouldering away down in Records because of the booze. You must *also* know that I still drink, so why the sudden recall?'

Rollins made a wry face and said, with a show of frankness, 'Yes, I know about your drinking, Jack, though you've always seemed to keep it under control. Well, more or less. And yes, it's true that you wouldn't be my first choice to head up a murder investigation. Unfortunately it's also true that I'm desperately short of men. You're very much a last resort in this matter.' Here he gave a rueful smile but his words still stung.

Jack gave him a bitter twist of the lips in return that could just about pass for a smile and swallowed a pang of anger. It was true, after all, and who ever heard of a proud drunk? Yet still it burned.

Still wearing a smile Rollins continued smoothly, 'There's been a huge upswing in the murder rate all around the country in recent years, as I'm sure you're aware, and all my people are up to their eyes in it. Worse, I've seconded every senior detective I could get my hands on from other divisions, so much so that *they're* all getting short-handed, and complaining upstairs about it. It isn't just murder that's on the up, all serious crimes have quadrupled in the last few years, fuelled by the river of drugs swamping the country. We've promoted everyone we could find with the slightest vestige of talent but it still isn't enough. We're way understaffed, and in these recessionary times our budget is forever tightening. And now I've got another murder, committed yesterday, and no one to put on it. And I do mean *no one.*'

Jack silently stared at him, flabbergasted but still suspicious. All manner of wild thoughts ran through his mind, with one prevalent above the others; *here was an escape from the deadly, grinding boredom, from the prison his life had become. A chance of...what?* Atonement? He didn't know, exactly, but here was an opportunity to achieve something, to make a difference again. Even if it was just for his own personal... What, satisfaction? Pride? He couldn't think of a suitable adjective to please his mind, but his heart knew exactly what he meant. Yet still he hesitated, not wanting to get carried away; something didn't feel right about the whole situation. Aside, that is, from the sudden, niggling fear that he might not be up to it any more. At last he said slowly, 'I might be a drunk but I'm not a fool. And neither are you, Eamonn. So stop bullshitting me. Being undermanned and overworked is nothing new. We always have been, since the day I joined. And it isn't a good enough reason to dig up a drunken has-been like me and give him a *murder*. Now, why do you really want me to look after this case?'

Rollins gave him a very frank, open smile and said patiently, 'I'm *telling* you the truth, Jack. Mind you, it's a very low-profile case. *Very* low-profile. A black man was murdered yesterday in Phibsboro. A South African, as a matter fact, who has...*had* residency here. You know my job is mostly juggling and yes, politics, and there have been other, higher profile killings recently. There have been fourteen murders in Dublin alone over the last *month*, and three of the families involved have political connections. I'm under intense pressure to come up with results and I just can't spare any men for this case.' He smiled apologetically, 'I'm not a racist, I hope, but nobody cares about this guy, Jack. He hasn't even got any family, much less political pull, and although I hate to admit it that leaves him very low down on my list of priorities.'

Jack frowned, 'I wish you hadn't told me that, Eamonn. I liked you better in the old days, when you were just another cop. But you know what? Although I can *hear* the sincerity in your voice I still don't believe you. You're still not telling the truth about why you're digging me up out of my professional grave. I'm a leper, an untouchable, and we both know it. Like we both know you could find *someone* somewhere to deal with this if you really tried. And if you don't care about getting this solved it doesn't have to be anyone good. So why am I sitting in your office discussing it?'

The smile was gone from the Assistant Commissioner's face and he delved into his bag of mints again, seeming to derive comfort from just touching them as he continued in a cold tone, 'Every word I spoke was the truth. Either accept that, and accept this case, or go back to rotting in your basement. To be honest I don't much care which you choose.'

Jack made no reply, merely gazing at him steadily and wondering why his old team-mate was still lying to him, until Rollins finally threw up his hands in defeat and admitted, 'Alright, alright! Everything I said holds good but I admit there is another reason as well. The other reason is Seamus Carr, an independent T.D. from Carlow. An independent who just happens to hold the balance of power in the present coalition government. If he withdraws his support the government loses its majority and could be forced to hold a general election.'

Jack shook his head, 'I still don't see where you're going.'

Rollins smiled ruefully, 'You will. Carr has a list of demands for the government in return for his support but only one of them concerns us. He has a nephew in the Gardai, one Frank Carr. Apparently this nephew is some sort of black sheep of the family, choosing the Gardai over the family business. Not to put too fine a point on it, the doting Uncle Seamus told me he was a bit weird. Which is why the family are keen to see him settled into a good career. After bumming around the world for a few years as some sort of hippy, young Frank stunned his family by returning home and joining the Gardai. He joined three years ago almost to the day. After *exactly* a year pounding the pavement down in Carlow he was transferred to the Detective branch, Metropolitan Division. And now Seamus Carr wants him in the Murder Squad. Most of his time up here has been spent behind a computer but Uncle Seamus believes he should be investigating murders. *Jesus*! The bad news for us is that I'm under pressure from the bloody *Taoiseach* himself to keep Carr sweet. So I want to give young Frank this murder, to ease him into the Murder Squad proper.'

Jack nodded, 'But you can't because he's only a wet-eared kid with no experience and there'd be an outcry if he was let anywhere near a murder on his own. So, to prevent any scandal you want me as a figurehead, a token senior detective. I suppose it'll look better if some nosy journalist takes an interest, too.'

Rollins cleared his throat and shook his head firmly, '*No.* Don't be so hard on yourself. You were a damned good cop and I would never ask you to be a mere figurehead. *You* will be the boss; *you* will run this investigation. I just want you to break young Carr in; show him the ropes, as it were. Teach him some of the wisdom you've accrued over the years and give him a bit of experience before we have to let him into the Murder Squad itself and turn him loose on cases of his own.'

Jack laughed sardonically, 'And since the victim is just some nigger with no family it doesn't matter if he screws it all up, right? A result preferred but not essential. I get you. And to think you used to be a copper once. God, you make me sick.'

Rollins went white with anger and half-rose from his chair, 'Watch your *mouth!* Who the hell do you think you're talking to? Every case I deal with is important to me, regardless of the victim's colour, and unless you want to be suspended immediately you'd better remember that! Okay, some cases are more important than others, but so what? It's always been that way, we've always had to prioritise our resources. But don't you ever dare to suggest that I don't care about a man's life just because he was black!'

He was panting with rage, but after several fraught seconds he calmed down a little and some colour returned to his cheeks. 'And another thing, with all the hysteria over the recent tide of immigration these are sensitive times, O'Neill, and I will not have any of my officers using that word! Got it?'

'But it's all right to *think* it, is that it?' asked Jack cynically, disgusted but not much surprised; Rollins had always had a reputation as being something of a racist. Nor was he the only one on the force, unfortunately.

'This is a hand up out of the gutter for you, O'Neill!' snapped Rollins abruptly, refusing to answer, 'A chance for you to redeem your career and retire with some semblance of dignity, rather than being forced out in disgrace as a washed-up old drunk! Will you take it or not?'

Jack shrugged, not caring either way, 'Sure, why not? I've got nothing better to do. You know I don't exactly work a full day anymore?' There was no answer and he nodded, 'Of course you do. But then, you don't care if this case is solved or not.'

Rollins opened his mouth to blast him but Jack forestalled him with a raised hand, 'It's all right, I understand. Sure half the promotions every year are a result of family influence rather than talent. It's always been that way and I suppose it always will be. And I've no right to judge you, because I care no more about the outcome of this case than you do. What's one more death in a world of six *billion* people, where *millions* die every single day? It's nothing, that's what. I just want to have everything clear and in the open, so we all know where we stand. Your boy gets a crack at a murder where his mistakes won't matter, the political heat is off you, and I don't get kicked off the force just yet. And my rank makes everything look kosher to anyone interested. So everyone's happy. And the victim has no family to complain if we don't get a result.'

Jack shrugged again, trying to banish the hot, sick fury boiling in his stomach, 'Fine, what do I care. I'll keep an eye on him, in the mornings at least, and give him the odd word of advice. Make sure he's at least doing the basics right. Good enough?'

Rollins nodded, 'Fine, that's all I want. Though I prefer to see it as an older, experienced man mentoring a raw youngster. A fully *trained* youngster, mind. Here's the file on the corpse, though God knows there isn't much in it. Take it down to your office for a read and I'll have young Carr sent down to you. You can give it to him there, along with a few lessons on how to run a murder investigation.'

Jack took the folder and left the room without another word and without slamming the door, carefully preserving his indifferent attitude. But inside he was boiling; *just what kind of prick had Rollins become?* Or had he always been so callous and self-serving? A man was dead but simply because he was black there would be no real attempt at an investigation, just a half-arsed fumbling about by some wet kid being fast-tracked to promotion because he had connections. And a *quarter*-arsed fumbling about by a washed-up old drunk, of course, let's not forget him. And all to keep some fat politician happy. *God almighty!*

Refusing to ask himself why he had agreed to front such a charade, he made his way back down to his subterranean domain and fixed himself an Irish coffee, or rather, a large whiskey with a splash of coffee in it. In spite of everything he could not help feeling a flicker of dejection; so now he was a babysitter, by God. Being marooned in Records these past few years had been bad enough, but teaching some wet-behind-the-ears young culchie how to wipe his own arse was still a step down for him. Worse, he wasn't even a rising young star whom he could mould and train in his own image, someone who would benefit from Jack's experience, but some halfwit who had only attained the rank of Detective through blatant nepotism. And who sounded distinctly dodgy into the bargain. What the hell had Rollins meant by calling him the black sheep of the family? He didn't much care for the "hippy" part either; that usually meant drugs, and Jack hated drugs almost as much as he hated drunk drivers. Exactly what sort of cop was this Carr, for God's sake?

He didn't have long to wait to find out. Not ten minutes after he sat down there came a soft double tap on the office door. From force of habit rather than because he actually cared any more Jack returned his bottle of Jameson to its hiding place in the filing cabinet before growling, 'Come in!'

A tall young man entered and said pleasantly, if diffidently, 'Chief Inspector O'Neill? I'm Frank Carr. Mr. Rollins told me I'll be assisting you in a murder inquiry.'

'Oh he did, did he?' Jack replied sardonically, sourly eyeing him up and down and mentally noting the barely-suppressed excitement in the young man's voice as he said the words "murder inquiry". 'Well, that's one way of putting it, I suppose. Shut the door and sit down, for God's sake.'

Carr did as he was bid, though with the second chair occupied the little room was now filled to capacity, and the two men silently regarded each other across the top of the desk for a long moment. Jack was a bit surprised by what he saw, but not displeased. Frank Carr was tall and well built, with black curly hair and even, regular features. His skin was suspiciously soft and smooth looking but he didn't strike Jack as being weak or effeminate. But what impressed him most were the eyes. They were large and clear, bright blue, and they looked back at him calmly and openly. They were transparently honest, but what Jack liked best was the light of intelligence gleaming in them. Weird the boy might well be; stupid he almost certainly was not. Which was a relief, at least. All in all the lad was a big improvement on what Jack had expected. Or rather, *feared*.

Frank for his part studied the middle-aged man in front of him with interest coloured with more than a touch of awe. In spite of his fall from grace O'Neill had a record second to none in the Detective branch, and stories about him still circulated even so long after his glory days. To meet even a fallen legend face-to-face can be daunting, but Carr was not easily cowed. Nor was he so awe-stricken that his sharp eyes didn't note the telltale signs of the heavy drinker on Jack's face, in his watery red-tinged eyes and slightly shaky hands. The smell of raw whiskey was pungent in the air, too, and with a touch of sorrow Frank reflected on the more recent, less inspiring stories he had heard concerning his new boss.

To break the lengthening silence Frank finally coughed and said, 'Er, I'm not too sure about this case we're supposed to be handling, sir. Could you fill me in on the details?'

Jack broke out of the slightly melancholy train of thought he had drifted into and replied, 'I'm not too sure of the details myself, son. I haven't looked at the file yet.' He opened the folder lying on his desk and grunted, 'Like a note to the milkman; short and to the point. Name; William Henry Akima. Address, blah-blah. Date of birth, blah-blah-blah. That's interesting; he had no job or recognised source of income but didn't claim any benefits. In fact, according to this he employed a part-time gardener. Apparently it was this gardener who found the body this morning and rang 999.' He glanced across at Carr to make sure he got the point and said, 'He had a gardener even though he lived in an apartment. Interesting. The Gardai called to the scene reported that Akima had suffered a violent death and appeared to have been dead for some time, probably since yesterday. Hmm; no listed next-of-kin. According to Rollins he had no family but that's not mentioned here; I wonder how he knew that? This also says that he's been investigated by the Inland Revenue a couple of times for not showing a visible means of support. Hmm, that might explain it; he lived and worked in his native South Africa, and only stayed in Ireland for a few months every year. On a sort of extended holiday-come-business-networking trip, it seems. He must have liked it here.'

'If he only came here on holiday, and had no job, how did he get residency, sir?' asked Frank.

'Good question. Answer...I haven't a clue. Immigration might tell us, unless the answer is a brown envelope to a official, which is hardly unknown with that lot. There really isn't much to go on here, is there? According to this report Scene-of-Crime-Officers are there at the moment, gathering the forensic evidence. I suppose all you can do is have a look at the scene, talk to this gardener and the neighbours, and see if anything shakes loose while you're waiting for the Post Mortem and forensic results.'

Carr nodded, 'Very good, sir. Should we take my car?'

Jack shot him a hard look; was he being funny? It didn't appear so. He asked dryly, 'What's this 'we' business? Who said I was going with you?'

Carr blinked in at him amazement, 'Er, well, I just assumed you... I mean, I can't... I mean, I've never... Er, sorry, sir, but I wouldn't know where to start on my own.' Frank dropped his gaze in visible confusion. Obviously Rollins had not told him at least that O'Neill was to be simply a figurehead in this affair.

Jack thought about it; the preliminary investigation at a crime scene could take hours, and lunch-time wasn't all that far off. And it had been some time since he had failed to show up in his local by one o'clock. On the other hand it had been even longer since he had visited any sort of crime scene, let alone a murder scene, and he had been a detective too long not to have a highly-developed sense of curiosity. Or, to put it another way, he was naturally nosy. And, more to the point, he had a hip-flask in his drawer that he could fill and bring with him.

At length he said, 'As it happens, I will go with you, though I can tell you right now that you're going to be doing a lot of the leg-work in this case on your own. And as I don't possess a vehicle; yes, we will take your car. What do you drive?'

'A Ka.'

'I know you drive a bloody car, you just said so! What *type* of car?'

Frank grinned, 'I didn't say car, I said *Ka*. K-A. I have a Ford Ka.'

Jack's eyes widened, 'Jesus, what the hell for? Why not get a real car?'

'It's a great little car,' protested Frank defensively, 'Nippy, easy to park, reliable. Perfect for the city. And perfect for two people, provided you've no kids.'

'Two people? Are you married, then?'

'Well, no. But you know what I mean.'

Jack was beginning to see why Rollins had described him as weird. 'I do know what you mean. You mean it's big enough for two people to jaunt around in, but too small to do any courting in. Right?'

Frank gave a slightly embarrassed cough, 'Well, I wouldn't call it *courting* but yes, it's too small to...I mean, no one could... Not in a Ka. Anyway, I have a flat for that sort of thing. Hey, leave my car alone! It's all I could afford, what with the cost of rent in Dublin and everything.'

Jack stared at him without speaking for a long minute, which did nothing for the younger man's peace of mind; nothing he had seen so far of Frank tied in with Jack's preconceptions, and he was pretty sure he was going to have to re-evaluate him. He was a lot more than just some greasy politician's nephew, and Jack realised that in spite of himself he quite liked the boy. He drained the cold remains of his fortified coffee and got to his feet, 'Right, then, let's get out to Phibsboro. You can show me just how wonderful your bloody Ka is on the way.'

Chapter Three

In spite of O'Neill's reservations, and complaints about lack of room once they were in the *Ka*, they arrived out in Phibsboro in one piece, and in reasonable time. The unmarked but to policemen unmistakable white vans outside Akima's apartment block showed Frank as clearly as a sign post where to stop, and he demonstrated just one of his precious Ka's advantages by parking in a space left vacant simply because very few other cars could have fitted into it. Jack greeted this exhibition of the benefits of a small vehicle, and of his new assistant's driving skill, with a non-committal grunt as he slowly -and with pretend difficulty- climbed out.

As the two detectives approached the entrance to the small apartment block two reporters, with photographers in tow, hurried across to intercept them, firing a volley of shouted questions on the way, each determined to get his questions in before the other. Jack eyed them sourly, wondering who had tipped the buggers off and how best to handle them. Even two of the brutes was two too many. After thinking quickly he assumed a friendly smile and raised his hands, saying jovially, 'Boys, boys! Take it easy. I can't hear a word with the two of you shouting over each other!'

The reporters paid no attention, simply repeating their questions in even louder tones, and with a sigh Jack said, with a great show of frankness, 'Look, here's the deal; we got a call that there's a dead man on the premises so we're on our way to take a look. We don't know anything about him yet, not even who he is. We haven't seen the body yet so we don't even know if foul play was involved. Give us a chance to catch our breath and find out what's what and we'll fill you in later, okay?'

The reporters paid Jack no mind but rather eyed each other venomously; there was no real story here but the two had been bitter enemies for years, and neither could bear the idea of the other even having his question answered before him, much less being scooped by him, and almost simultaneously they began asking their questions again. With a noise that sounded suspiciously like 'Bah!' Jack abandoned his policy of appeasement and simply started walking determinedly towards them. They gave way along the path reluctantly, still shouting questions into his face as they had no doubt seen reporters do in movies, and felt they should too, but eventually they parted and allowed the policemen to go by. Frank showed his warrant card to the Garda at the front door of the flats, feeling a strange mixture of pride and embarrassment as he did so for the first time ever at a murder scene.

The uniformed Garda nodded and said, addressing Jack only, 'Don't forget to write down the time of entry when you sign the Crime Scene Entry Log, sir. It's on the hall table beside the phone. And the technical lads are still there so put on gloves and booties. There are boxes of them beside the logbook.'

The two detectives followed these instructions before entering the apartment together, both feeling an identical, anticipatory tightening of the gut as they crossed the threshold. There were busy men in white overalls and surgical gloves everywhere, bustling about with a careful, practiced haste that left Frank feeling awkward and out of place; an outsider rather than one of the initiates. Jack too was a little hesitant, though this was due to the fact that he didn't know any of the Technical team, the Scene Of Crime Officers. Not one. Of course, they were all quite young but obviously he was even more out of touch than he had realised.

They made their way through the spacious living room –a plain, cold room which was lit up only by a warm yellow and orange suite of furniture- to the kitchen, where the body still lay on the floor, surrounded by busy SOCO's and a photographer. Jack sombrely read the message written on the wall, his face grim. Then he looked down at the battered, blood-covered figure and felt his stomach clench; the head was so badly crushed it was hardly recognisable as human any more. It was not a sight for the faint-hearted and he took a deep breath, forcing down his rising gorge. Some aspects of the job hadn't changed, and when it came to viewing corpses, absence definitely did not make the heart grow fonder.

He looked sideways at Frank; the boy's face was carefully expressionless but just a little too pale and set. An ancient memory of the impact viewing his own first corpse had had on him stirred in Jack's mind and he said softly, 'When I was a youngster we tried to show how tough we were by making jokes about the corpses, and by pretending that we weren't fazed by even the most terrible sights. The horrors would always come back in the night, though, and as I grew older such things affected me more and I hid them less. If sights like this upset you...well, good. They should. If you stop caring you stop being a good cop.'

Frank nodded distractedly and mumbled, 'I've seen dead bodies before, on traffic duty, just never a murder victim. I've seen *photos* of murder victims, of course, but not one in the flesh. It's hard to believe that someone could have done this deliberately. He looks so small and alone, so pathetic. And just think, if he didn't have a gardener he might not have been discovered for weeks. It's sad. *A flower trampled, a life fore-shorn/ Into pain and suffering, mankind is born.*'

Jack had no ready response to this and gave Frank a sidelong look. He disliked indifference to suffering, or the pretence of indifference, but a cop who quoted poetry over a corpse at a crime scene? *God Almighty, what have I been landed with here?* He nodded towards the message scrawled on the wall and said, 'What do you make of that?'

'That doesn't make me feel sad,' Frank replied grimly, 'That makes me want to indulge in a little violence of my own.'

Although a touch relieved by this more prosaic reaction, Jack shook his head, 'That isn't what I meant. I don't like the look of that message at all; it suggests we're dealing with an organization rather than an individual. Some sort of Nazis or something. It hasn't been written in the victim's blood, has it?'

'No,' said a voice from behind them, 'Of course not.'

They turned and faced the speaker, who added rather pompously, 'I'm the Assistant State Pathologist, Dr. Henry Ryan.' He was a small, wizened man with thick glasses, thinning hair and a face that seemed to be permanently sniffing an unpleasant odour. He also had the air of a man who habitually emphasised the *doctor* in front of his name. 'It's just red paint, from a spray-can by the look of it. The SOCO's have taken samples for analysis.'

'Who's the forensics officer?' Jack asked.

'O'Halloran. But he's been and gone already. Busy day, don't you know. I did the death cert, photos and a preliminary exam, and there's an ambulance on the way from the morgue. Will you release the body so I can do the autopsy? Not that the cause of death will be hard to establish, with his brain smeared all over his kitchen floor the way it is.'

'Sure, I'll release it,' said Jack heavily, 'No point in leaving him lying there. There isn't much to see, anyway. The murder weapons aren't hard to spot, and as there were clearly at least three attackers I doubt he put up much of a fight. So we can forget about checking the hospitals for a wounded assailant or anything like that. Have you found anything else?'

Ryan snorted, 'Oh yes, the SOCO's found lots of hairs and fibres and fingerprints, I believe. But I doubt if they belong to the killers. It looks like they knew what they were doing. We got footprints from where they entered and exited through the garden, though, and they might help. Three of them, as you said, to match the baseball bats. All men, to judge by the shoe-sizes. I'm sure O'Halloran will send you a profile of the tracks, along with all his other findings. All he has to do is spend a few weeks eliminating the things that belong here from those that don't and he might have something for you. I don't know him well but I hear he's very good, and very quick. I should have the autopsy report long before that. But then again I might not; O'Halloran's not the only one who's worked off his feet.' He gave Jack a very sharp glance, 'You're O'Neill, aren't you?'

Jack nodded but said nothing.

The little man sniffed, 'Thought I recognised you. From an *old* photo, I might add. Well, don't bother asking me to rush the results through because for one thing I'm already up to my eyes, and for another I always work as quickly as I can.'

'I don't doubt it,' said Jack gravely, 'I've heard nothing but good of you.' In fact he had never heard of the man, but a little sugar can sometimes go a long way. And the gentle flattery did the trick because the little man swelled visibly with pride and said, 'I should hope so.' He gave a little smirk and added, 'I wish I could say the same about you. Still, you never know; I might be able to give you a preliminary report in the morning.'

Jack shrugged, suddenly disinterested again as his mood changed, 'Don't knock yourself out. I've been assured from on high that this case is very low priority indeed. It seems that an unknown, unconnected foreigner -and a black one to boot- is of no great interest to the great and the good.'

Ryan sneered cynically but before he could answer Frank burst in hotly, 'Well, he's of great interest to *me*! And I'll get the bastards who did this if it's the last thing I ever do!'

O'Neill looked at him with eyes that had seen too many horrors for such open displays of emotion and asked, 'How old are you?'

Frank flushed, in anger and a touch of embarrassment, 'Twenty-six! What's that got to do with anything?'

Jack looked at him with a touch of cynical amusement, but also warmth. That kind of passion for the job he understood, and liked. Allied with his sense of outrage it might make a decent copper out of Carr yet, however odd he might be. But Frank's obvious passion also left Jack a touch sorrowful for the loss of his own youthful fire. Once he had cared so much; now he cared not at all. Because with every human being on earth destined only for death anyway, what did it matter?

His pensive mood changed abruptly and he walked out into the back garden, where a uniformed Garda showed him where the SOCO's believed the killers had forced their way through the damaged bushes. He peered through the gap in the shrubbery to the school beyond, mentally noting that it would have been shut the day before. The killers had clearly known where Akima had lived and had made their plans accordingly, even down to picking a day when they could use the school grounds as cover to slip into his garden unobserved. Not a random killing then, but carefully planned. These "Sons of Chuchailainn" must have known Akima, and targeted him deliberately.

He walked back into the apartment and said to Ryan, 'I suppose there's no question of the victim's identity? I mean, the corpse *is* the guy who lived here, Akima?'

Ryan shrugged, 'As far as we know. O'Halloran found a passport upstairs and the description matches, though the face is too battered to id him from the photo. The bone structure is the same, and he is in his flat after all. Don't worry, he took fingerprints in case Akima had a record somewhere, and dental impressions too, to compare with the records on file with Akima's dentist in South Africa. Assuming he had one, that is.'

'Hmm,' mumbled Jack. He turned to Frank and said brusquely, 'Right, I'm off. I've seen enough here. Things for you to do, Frank, after I've gone. Number one is to talk to the neighbours. *All* of them. Don't assume that because no one phoned the Garda no one saw anything. Apart from not wanting to get involved, you wouldn't believe the things people can explain away to themselves. Besides, something trivial in itself could lead us to the killers. Aside from the events of the weekend, grill them to find out everything there possibly is to know about this guy. About his friends, social life, sexual habits...everything. Got it?'

'Got it.'

'Next, find and talk to the gardener. Since he called in the body and failed to mention tripping over the killers on his way in we can assume he doesn't know anything about the death itself. So concentrate on finding out every single little thing he knows about his employer. Sorry, ex-employer. And I do mean everything, but particularly the social aspect. He had to have friends, and family somewhere. Got it?'

'Got it.'

'He can also formally identify the body once it's in the morgue if you can't turn up a relative. Actually, before you go looking for him go through this place with a fine-tooth comb. Bank statements, letters, photos, a diary; look hard enough and you'll learn everything we need to know about the unfortunate Mr. Akima. When you know everything about him you'll know *why* he was killed, which will lead to *who* killed him. Got it?'

'Got it. But...'

O'Neill made an irritable *moue,* 'But *what*?'

'The writing on the wall, sir. I mean to say, *Niggers go home? Ireland for the Irish?* Surely that indicates a racial motive for the killing? Shouldn't we also investigate some of these anti-immigrant groups that have sprung up in Dublin recently?'

'You can investigate anything you want, laddie,' replied Jack balefully, 'But as far as I'm concerned this guy knew his killers, racists or not. And doesn't it strike you that the graffiti is a bit of a bloody giveaway? Like maybe it was left there to make us look towards some of these loony groups? Mark my words; most people know their own killers, and there was probably a damned good reason for this murder! And I personally don't think his colour was a good reason.'

'Me either, but others might,' offered Frank softly, but Jack ignored him. He started towards the front door but something made him turn back. Perhaps it was natural curiosity, perhaps it was the look of contempt Ryan was aiming at him. For whatever reason, he turned back to the little doctor and said, 'You say there were footprints in the back garden?'

Ryan nodded, 'The assailants forced their way into the garden through the bushes at the back. They might have known the victim, as you say, but they certainly weren't invited.'

'Were there any signs of a break-in?'

He shook his head, 'Not the slightest trace. Why?'

'Well, how did they get in, then? If men force their way into your garden you don't open the back door and let them into your home. Not when they're carrying baseball bats. And even if you're stark raving mad and you *do* let them in, once they attack you, you don't flee from them into the kitchen, from which there's no exit, no escape.'

'Do you have a point?' asked Ryan coldly.

'They were here already, waiting for him,' replied Jack impatiently, eyes, combing the room. 'Probably in one of the bedrooms, so they could trap him in the kitchen. Breaking in without leaving *any* signs and then waiting patiently for him to come home -possibly for hours- without wrecking the place doesn't sound like drunk or drugged-up skinheads out for a bit of nigger-bashing, now does it? How did they know a black man even lived here? And the fact that they came on a bank holiday and gained access through the school yonder points to it being premeditated. Racist attacks are generally spontaneous, aimed at some poor sod in the wrong place at the wrong time. This sounds more like a carefully planned and executed murder to me. In fact, execution is probably the right word for what happened here.'

'Maybe,' sniffed the pathologist, unimpressed.

Jack stuck his chin out at him belligerently, 'Course it was. You said yourself they knew what they were doing. Can you imagine a neo-Nazi thug hiding quietly in here, perhaps all day? Without making any noise or even smoking in case the smell frightened his victim off? Without doing *anything?* Of course not. If it was an ordinary bunch of thugs they'd have got bored and wrecked the place after ten minutes. And let's face it, vandalism is more their style than murder, anyway.'

'Maybe,' was the reply for the second time.

Jack snorted, his rusty brain starting to warm up, 'Okay then; these footprints. What kind of shoes are they from? Doc Martens, runners, what?'

Ryan paused, thinking furiously and obviously unwilling to answer. 'I can't tell for certain,' he stalled. 'I'm not forensics. I just took a look out of curiosity.'

'Oh, come on! Were they boots or runners?'

'It doesn't look that way,' the doctor admitted.

'Were they the impressions of ordinary shoes?'

'I couldn't say for certain but' -reluctantly- 'I would have to say that the tracks *appeared* to have been made by shoes with heels rather than boots or runners.'

'Exactly!' said Jack triumphantly, 'And the skinhead hasn't been born who will wear ordinary shoes. And three of them? No way!'

Frank was hanging on his every word yet it was he who burst Jack's bubble. In a diffident tone he said, 'I'm sorry, sir, but most of these new groups aren't comprised of skinheads and the like.' *Who's even seen a skinhead in twenty years?* 'Most of the new ones are made up of ordinary people, of all ages and classes. A lot of them believe that immigrants are going to destroy the country economically, while others are simply scared of them. Afraid of increased crime and drug-pushing and the like. And, of course, some are just blatantly xenophobic or racist.'

'And where does "violent murderer" and "expert burglar" fit in among those groups?' asked Jack sarcastically, 'Since there's no evidence of a break-in, no broken glass, *nothing*? Mark my words, this Akima guy was dodgy. He was mixed up with professional criminals and they turned on him.'

'I think you're confusing professional criminal with 'professional person',' Ryan said sweetly, 'Or do you really think habitual criminals wear shoes as opposed to trainers? Some might, but three out of three? Hardly. And even white-collar workers can pick a patio lock, for God's sake. It's not like there was an alarm to disable or anything. And wouldn't criminals have robbed him? He was wearing a Rolex, though you might have missed it, and he had a couple of hundred Euros in his pocket.'

'What, you don't think neo-fascists would have stolen his watch?' sneered Jack, who had indeed noted the garish timepiece on the victim's wrist, 'If anything it proves my point; he was killed by people who knew him, for a very specific reason!' Jack turned and again set off towards the door, before once again turning back, and this time addressing Frank, 'And another thing, those bats look bran new. Ring every sports outlet in Dublin and get details of every baseball bat purchased within the last two weeks. Particularly multiple purchases. Got it?'

Frank nodded, 'Got it, sir.'

Jack stamped off, and this time did not return. They heard him give his name and a very brief, not to mention bad-tempered, statement to the reporters waiting outside and then silence fell once more. When it was clear he was not coming back Ryan sniffed and said, 'Gone haring off to the nearest pub, no doubt,'

Frank gave him a cold look, 'Perhaps. On the other hand, can you think of anything he missed before he went?'

Ryan looked startled, 'Almost everything, I would have said. I thought you agreed that the killing had a racist motive?'

'It's a possibility, nothing more. Most of what the Chief Inspector said had merit too. But even if he's wrong he left no stone undisturbed.'

'You mean he left *you* to turn over every stone.'

Frank had conceived a degree of liking of his own for Jack and, more important still, Ryan was not a policeman and therefore was allowed no adverse opinion on policemen or police matters. So there was hostility in his usually soft voice as he said, 'Yes, but he pointed out each stone for me, didn't he? That's the important part. Any fool can flip over a rock when he's led to it by the nose.'

Ryan muttered something unintelligible and returned to his work, leaving Frank victorious. Revelling in the freedom Jack had given him, and now comforted rather than intimidated by all the experts busily working around him, he banished any flutters of self-doubt and got to work. First he enlisted the help of the uniformed Garda at the door and together they began quizzing not just the victim's neighbours in the block of flats, but everyone living nearby who might have been able to glimpse the killers as they entered the garden or the flat itself. And he learned absolutely nothing, though this was partly because many of the neighbours were out at work. Still, he thought it strange that none of the people he managed to interview knew anything about their neighbour; most hadn't even known his *name,* for God's sake. But perhaps that was a result of his living in an apartment block. Or perhaps just city life. Certainly Frank, though hailing from a small town where everyone knew their neighbours intimately, couldn't have named any of his new neighbours in his Dublin flat.

Undaunted by this setback, he obtained from the Gardai Central Office the address of the late Mr. Akima's gardener -who bore the melodious if unlikely name of Juno Malabu Wren- and phoned that gentleman's home, only to discover that he was not at home. Strike two. After ringing the police and breathlessly reporting how he had just discovered the dead body of his employer, Mr. Wren had disobeyed instructions to stay put and had vanished before a mobile unit had reached the scene. But wherever he had gone it clearly wasn't home. Yet surely he was not a suspect? Not when it was obvious that three men had perpetrated the killing? *Too* obvious? Could one man have used the three bats to throw them on the wrong scent? Or perhaps Wren had been involved in some way and had later panicked and fled. But somehow that just didn't feel right. But then, according to Jack *nothing* about this felt right.

Still optimistic, Frank muttered to himself, *'In the weave of my life's essence, I bare to you my soul,'* and began searching the dead man's home and possessions in search of some trace of Akima's soul. But he began his search of Akima's weave after his own fashion, initially at least. By this time he was the only person left in the flat and he wandered through the four rooms with his eyes half-closed, examining nothing closely and indeed hardly even glancing at any particular object. Later he would go through every item minutely but not just yet. What he wanted was to try and get a *sense of* the dead man, trying to smell him or taste him, trying to feel his essence in his own home. In this he failed. He paused, puzzled; what was missing? *Ambiance,* that was it. And he suddenly realised that there was no sense that this was *anyone's* home. It was as soulless as a hotel room. It was not just that it was so neat and tidy; it was bare of any personal effects. No paintings or knickknacks or photographs or letters...nothing. It was fully, even comfortably, furnished, but there was no clue in any of the objects as to who had lived there. Apart from the strong, even garish colour of the sitting-room furniture there was nothing even to hint that he had been an African, for God's sake! *Why not?* Frank applied himself to the problem for some time but no solution presented itself.

With a sigh he gave up and began a more traditional, and extremely thorough, search. In some ways Frank might have been an unusual policemen but in some matters he was very old-fashioned indeed. He even had a verse to match his philosophy; *where inspiration fails, perspiration oft prevails.* But in spite of his efforts he found what he was by now expecting to find; nothing. No clues to friends or family, no hints at a personal life, none of those things that reveal a person for who and what they truly are. Nothing intimate. No books, no diaries, not a damned thing to suggest that a man had lived there and not a robot. He did find details of a current bank account, containing just over sixteen thousand Euro, and more mundane papers dealing with direct debits for the utility bills, but he could not find as much as a personal letter from even the most distant friend or relation. The closest he came to success was in finding an old envelope with a scrap of paper inside. Written on the piece of paper was an address in Foxrock. No name or phone number; just that address, which probably meant nothing at all. Frank had gotten to know the victim at least to the extent of believing that he never kept anything that might provide the slightest clue as to who he was. Which in itself was a clue of sorts, if he could only figure out what it meant.

He sighed heavily and looked at his watch; dinner-time. Except tonight dinner time meant it was now time to call once again on all those people who had been absent from home earlier. And yet the thought did not dismay him. For the first time in his life he was filled with a sense of purpose, a sense of certainty. Destiny, even. In University he had often struggled with the philosophical ideals of right and wrong, only to finally conclude that neither exist, that even the most basic tenets of right or wrong are simply a matter of opinion, of viewpoint. Sometimes, indeed, of fashion. He no longer believed this applied to every situation, or to every deed. Universal right or wrong might not exist, but for him increasing maturity was bringing certainty in at least some aspects of life. Here today he had seen graphic evidence of an absolute wrong. To bring the perpetrators to justice would be an absolute right. Some people might disagree with his viewpoint, but simplistic or not this philosophy was enough to satisfy Frank. It also confirmed for him that, in spite of the protests of his family, who had all foreseen a more lucrative career for him in business circles, he had been right to join the Garda. In the search for those who take the lives of others he had found his life's work, his mission, and this knowledge pleased him.

Chapter Four

Jack could not have been described as being enthralled with the mystery of this, his swansong case, -particularly as he was little more than a glorified babysitter on it- but he was a little more interested than he had pretended back at the dead man's apartment. Interested enough to spend much of that evening thinking about the victim, if only sporadically. He even moderated his alcohol intake a touch, partly because he was lost in thought, fashioning and then abandoning scenarios in his mind, but at least partly to ensure that he was functioning a little better than usual the next morning. He still drank enough to leave many men comatose, but for Jack it was barely enough to ensure he fell asleep that night. And not quite enough to keep the nightmares at bay.

To rise without a struggle when the alarm sounded -in spite of his uneasy sleep- was an experience he had almost forgotten, and to his surprise he found himself humming softly as he took his shower. This could only be good, and the revolution was completed by his hesitating before adding whiskey to his morning coffee. He lost the brief struggle, but at least he had *considered* setting out for work dry, and in the end had added less Jameson than was his wont. And this was very nearly a victory in a lifetime of lost battles.

The trip into town was not quite as unpleasant as usual either, as the rocking motion of the DART was on that morning soothing rather than sickening. And even being crammed in alongside hundreds of other commuters was for once on the right side of bearable...just. All in all it was such a pleasant beginning to the day that he very nearly smiled at the ticket collector in Tara Street station. It was after he exited the train station that this bright new regime stumbled and almost tottered to a fall. It had been at least two years since he had missed his early-morning bracers in the early house, and now he hesitated on the corner of Stevens' Green, unsure whether to pursue his usual course across the park or to make straight for Harcourt Square. The dryness of his tongue and a sick feeling in the pit of his stomach sang a siren song for established routine, but he was distracted by a mental image of young Carr sitting in his office waiting for him, an expression of eager anticipation on his face. What expression would replace it if he walked in late, stinking of whiskey and not totally sober at even that early hour? It had been a long time since Jack had cared what others thought of him but evidently a shred of self-respect remained for, after a brief struggle, his better side -aided no doubt by thoughts of the half-full bottle of whiskey in his filing cabinet- won the day.

He marched into the building feeling refreshingly virtuous and swept down to his basement cubbyhole like Caesar returning in triumph to Rome. When he entered his office - having picked up a plastic cup of coffee from the dispenser on the way- he found, to his complete lack of surprise, Frank sitting there waiting for him, an eager look of anticipation on his face. And when the youngster smiled brightly up at him in greeting Jack suddenly felt very glad he had for once resisted temptation.

'You're here early, aren't you? Ah, the energy and impetuosity of youth!' he said, with a mocking causticity he didn't truly feel.

Frank grinned slightly shamefacedly, 'Well, you know how it is, sir.'

'Oddly enough, I do,' Jack replied as he sat down and took a noisy slurp of his coffee. 'It's been a while but I still remember how I felt when I first became a detective. It would be a poor lookout for the future of the Garda if a youngster like you *wasn't* enthusiastic about his first murder enquiry. It's like sex; you never forget your first. Unfortunately, you can all too easily forget how your first sight of a murder victim made you feel. Don't let that happen to you, Frank, try not to become hardened to the sights you see. I've watched too many men become bitter and cynical in this job, and they were the poorer for it. And not just professionally.'

Jack had never spoken like that to another copper before, not sober at any rate. Apart from his own embarrassment at revealing such thoughts and emotions, few enough would have understood or cared. The young, idealistic and even poetic Frank Carr was another kettle of fish altogether. He was different. Or perhaps it was Jack who was different; perhaps old age and booze together had mellowed him.

Jack's body, if not his mind, was missing its usual alcohol intake and, with the old thirst an urgent whisper in the back of his mind and his hands trembling slightly, he suddenly said, 'Nip outside to the fax machine and see if anything's come in from Forensics or the Pathologist's Lab, would you, Frank?'

His new assistant leapt to oblige, and while he was gone Jack took the opportunity to put a little iron into his lukewarm coffee, wondering bleakly to himself as he did so how long he could keep this charade up. And whether there was any point to it; did he really care what his very junior assistant thought of him?

When Frank returned the older man slammed the drawer of his filing cabinet shut and slugged down half his coffee in one draught. Only then could he relax back in his seat and say expansively, 'Right, what have you got for me?'

'Nothing from Forensics or the lab yet, sir. And nothing from my inquiries yesterday either, I'm afraid. None of the neighbours saw or heard anything out of the ordinary over the weekend, and none of them knew Mr. Akima at all. *At all,* even though he had owned that apartment for years. As far as any of them are concerned the flat might just as well have been unoccupied.'

Jack laughed aloud at Frank's disapproving tone and said in amusement, 'You're in the big city now, farm-boy, where people stay out of each other's business. Get used to it. Hang on, did you say he *owned* the apartment? Even though he had no job?'

'Yes, sir. He bought it for *cash* nearly twenty years ago, just as the boom was starting, which is a bit unusual. I checked with his bank and they told me so; they're holding the deed for him. Well, for his next-of-kin now, I suppose, assuming they can establish one. They gave him a clean bill of health financially, though he was anything but an ordinary customer. He had no regular monthly deposits or anything, he simply transferred large sums of money from a South African bank into his account here every time he came over. This year he transferred fifty thousand Euros.'

'Holy shit!' spluttered Jack, sitting up straight abruptly and spilling some of his fortunately cold coffee over his hand, '*Fifty grand*? This year alone?'

'Yes, sir. Last year it was forty-five. It's a lot when you consider that he only stayed for a few months at a time. And had no mortgage to pay, nor a car loan or credit cards. He didn't drive, by the way, as far as I can discover. But he spent it on *something*, because what was left over from his *last* visit was barely enough to cover the direct debits for his ESB bill and phone rental and stuff. It's odd that he didn't simply get all his services turned off when he wasn't here but there you are. Maybe he didn't plan his visits, maybe they were spur of the moment trips and he liked everything ready in case he popped over on impulse.'

'From Africa?' said Jack sceptically, 'that's a long way to bloody pop!'

Frank shrugged, 'Well, I can't think of any other reason to keep his services and stuff on. Unless he let others use the flat when he wasn't here.' Jack simply grunted and the younger man continued, 'Oh, and he had a monthly standing order for five hundred Euro payable to the account of his gardener. But that's not a lot out of fifty thousand.'

Jack brightened momentarily, 'Ah, the gardener! What did he tell you?'

'Nothing so far, sir. I'm afraid I haven't been able to speak to him yet. He wasn't at home yesterday afternoon or evening.'

'Odd. And perhaps suspicious. What did you find in the flat?' Jack asked impatiently, 'in his personal effects? I told you that was where you'd find the man, and solve the case.'

'That's the weird thing, sir. I didn't find *anything*. No personal effects of any sort. No letters, no photos...*nothing*. The place might as well have been a show-flat; fully furnished but devoid of any individual imprint, of any *personality*. Perhaps the killers removed all his personal stuff; certainly his mobile phone was missing. The closest I came to a personal effect was his passport and an old envelope with a Dublin address on it. A *Foxrock* address, no less, though there's no name to go with it.'

'Foxrock, eh? Well, he seems to have been loaded himself so it's no surprise if he had wealthy pals.' Jack swallowed the remains of his coffee and said thoughtfully, 'But it's odd that you found no personal stuff in the place. Though the apartment was only a sort of holiday home, of course, so I suppose all his personal effects could be in his permanent home in South Africa. But it almost seems as if he was trying to leave nothing of himself here, to put down no roots and form no attachment to the place. Which begs the question *why*? What was he hiding?'

Frank nodded, 'Exactly, sir. Because unless he was deliberately keeping his place free of personal effects *something* would slop over from his real home. His real *life*. Even if it was just photos of his kids or parents or whatever. I've always been one to travel light myself but I'd always have photos or a letter from home with me. I'm sure he was concealing something; surely no one could naturally be such a minimalist?'

'Such a what?'

'Minimalist. Er, one who is not interested in goods and possessions, who focuses on life's essentials and ignores the frills.'

'The fifty grand per trip would seem to preclude that,' said Jack dryly, 'to say nothing of the flash watch and his owning his own flat.'

'I didn't say *communist,* sir. A minimalist doesn't object to money or property, merely to clutter. To inessential details. Though really nowadays the term refers to a type of art rather than a personal philosophy.'

'Really?' said an unimpressed Jack, 'Where the hell do you get this stuff?'

'U.C.D. I did an Arts degree, I'm afraid.'

'Jesus, what for?' Jack caught himself, 'I mean, what subjects?'

'English and Philosophy, with a little Greek and Roman civilisation thrown in by way of light relief.'

'Hmm,' uttered Jack sardonically, 'The perfect education for a cop, don't you think?'

Frank grinned, unabashed, 'Broke my father's heart. He considers anything but a law or business degree to be not just heresy but tantamount to devil worship.'

'I see. A bit of a black sheep, in fact,' mused Jack thoughtfully.

Frank nodded, 'I suppose. And refusing to enter the family firm afterwards was the icing on the cake. I know it upset him, but after three years in University the idea of selling carpets for a living just didn't do it for me, even at corporate level. I'd had my mind opened and was hungry for more.'

'More what? Education?' asked Jack, not without the vaguest hint of a sneer.

'Of a type. Life education, if you will. The kind you get from travelling the world and experiencing new peoples and cultures. When I came home I considered going back to college, to do a degree in Criminology or Psychology, but after the freedom of travelling for so long I just couldn't face the grind of all that study. Nor the restrictions of being a student. So here I am.'

'Indeed. Well, never mind the autobiography,' said Jack sourly, 'Where does all this leave us? Nowhere, that's where!' He paused for a moment, 'What about the baseball bats?'

'I'm afraid I haven't had a chance to inquire yet, sir. But all the shops should be open by now. Do you want me to start ringing around sports suppliers?'

Jack shook his head, 'We'll get one of the clerks to do it. Rollins might not have the manpower to stretch to a full murder team but I doubt he'll complain if I borrow one of the typists now and then. God knows, most of them do little enough around here anyway.' Awareness of just how little *he* generally did around there sprang into his mind, causing his cheeks to redden even more than usual. To cover his embarrassment he coughed and growled, 'Who knows, we might even get a beat Garda for some of the legwork.' He gave the younger man a baleful glare, 'And you know what you've forgotten, don't you?'

If he was expecting Frank to become flustered under pressure he was disappointed, for the young man replied in a sanguine tone, 'The address on the envelope turned out to be a dud. It's the derelict site of a house that burnt down a couple of years ago.'

Jack snorted sceptically, 'A derelict site in Foxrock? Bloody Hell! I knew the housing market had collapsed but I hadn't realised things had gotten *that* bad!'

Frank shook his head, 'They haven't, and I suppose derelict is a bit of a misnomer; it's nearly complete. The place burnt down a couple of years back and the owner started fixing it up but abandoned it before it was fully refurbished.'

'Who owned it?'

'That's interesting, actually. Remember Michael Riordan, the government Minster who was involved in that big scandal a year or so ago?'

Jack nodded, 'I remember. Current affairs don't interest me much, and politicians even less, but I remember *him*. Murder is our game, after all. Riordan's wife was murdered, wasn't she?'

'That's right. In fact, the house in Foxrock was the murder weapon, in a way, since she was burnt to death in it. Anyway, Riordan owned that plot of land, but he hadn't finished rebuilding the place when he resigned from the government and relocated to Switzerland.'

Jack chewed his bottom lip thoughtfully, 'What's all this got to do with our victim? Do you think there's a connection?'

Frank shrugged, 'Between Akima and Riordan? It doesn't look like it. Akima doesn't *appear* to have had any business connections in Ireland but he must have done, otherwise why come here at all? It wasn't for the weather, that's for sure. But Riordan has a daughter, Grainne, and Akima might have known her. She's only twenty or so but I suppose it's possible she was his girlfriend or something. Anyway, he must have had *some* reason for having that address written down, and since it's the only thing I found I thought we'd better follow it up.'

'Later. If Riordan's out of the country it's hardly urgent, especially as his daughter's probably with him. First we'll go talk to the gardener. Surely *he* must know something about Akima's personal life? But the address thing isn't what I meant when I said you'd forgotten something. There was something else.'

'On, no, I didn't forget that either, sir,' replied Frank coolly, 'But because of the time difference I haven't received a police report back from Johannesburg on Mr. Akima yet. And I have to say they didn't seem particularly anxious to help.' His smile showed just the faintest trace of self-satisfaction, 'I presume that *is* what you meant, sir? A background check on Mr. Akima in his own country? And, of course, they're looking for a next-of-kin to inform about his death.'

Jack merely grunted, pretending to be displeased at his assistant's foresight. 'Well, you seem to have thought of everything. So far. Let's see if you can stay one step ahead, smart-arse. What's our next move, then?'

'Er, a trip to see Akima's gardener?'

'Close, but no cigar. Before we go anywhere I have to introduce you to the bane of any policeman's life; paperwork.' He pulled open a drawer in his desk and produced a grey ring-binder folder. 'This is our Murder Book.' He printed this title on the folder, adding underneath *William Henry Akima*. 'It is now our Bible. Into this we will place every report sheet, every note, every transcribed interview and conversation, and every piece of official paperwork like the Autopsy Report and the forensics report from the Technical Bureau. *Everything* goes in it. Including any random thoughts, theories or flights of fancy we might have. You've done the courses and received the training; do I need to stress how important it is to make sure nothing gets left out?'

Frank shook his head vigorously, 'No, sir. I've heard the horror stories in training; the convictions lost, the guilty parties who walked because some vital piece of evidence was mislaid or misfiled. They couldn't have stressed the importance of good records any more strongly and believe me, it stuck.'

'Good,' nodded Jack, 'And on a more personal note I can promise you that I solved about half the cases I've closed by reading through the Murder Book over and over again until something struck me that I'd missed the first twenty times. Okay, lecture over. Just one other thing; from time immemorial it's been the custom that the junior officer types up the daily log of all incidents and all actions taken.' He gave a slightly slantwise smile, 'This custom we will of course continue.' He produced a sheaf of assorted forms from his desk and said, 'Right, let's get to it; we need to fill in these forms and write up the log from yesterday. The first rule of police work is to stay on top of the paperwork. Otherwise it'll bury you. And since I'm something of a dinosaur I'm afraid I only have this old typewriter to work with.'

Frank carefully refrained from rolling his eyes as he said in a neutral voice, 'Er, everything is electronic these days, sir. The murder book, all the forms; everything. We can just log all the data onto the computer. It's quicker, nothing can get lost, and of course it's much easier to store. And to access later.'

'I'm not *that* out of date!' snapped Jack, 'I know all that, and you can open a file and record everything on Julie's machine every evening. But in addition to the computer records I like to have the actual paper reports in my hand. I like to touch them, shuffle through them, spread them all out on a table and skim my eyes over a dozen reports at once. You'd be amazed how often you can spot a discrepancy in testimony or eyewitness statements that way, how you can make a new connection between two disparate reports.'

I also, he did not add, *like to bring the murder book home and read it at night, with no distractions and nobody about, to commune with the dead and seek answers to my questions.* He didn't know Frank well enough to say something like that, and so the younger man set it down to his being old and irritable and stuck in his ways. But all Frank said aloud was, 'Whatever you prefer, sir,' and the two men got to work.

It took almost two hours to type up all the preliminary reports but at last it was done and Jack got to his feet and stretched stiffly, 'Right, I think that's it for now. In future we update this book -and our daily log- every evening before we go home. Or rather, *you* do. Come on, let's go see the quaintly named Juno Wren.' He threw open the office door and apprised Julie -the clerk who occasionally doubled as his secretary- of what he wanted her to do regarding the baseball bats. At the end he added, 'We're expecting an important fax from South Africa too, so watch out for it. I'll ring if we get a lead and decide not to come back today.'

Frank, who very much liked that "we", interjected, 'No need, sir, I'll just leave my mobile number.' He offered Julie a dazzling smile and a cheap business card, 'Here, my number's on this. Can you ring me as soon as the fax arrives? It could be important. Thanks.'

Julie was a big, busty bottle blonde with a kind heart, flawless skin, and a soft spot not just for Jack but for policemen in general. At almost forty she was also a childless singleton who –almost deafened by the last loud ticks of her body-clock- was becoming desperate for a mate. In her heart she knew she had been born to be a mother, but time was fast running out and there was still no sign of a prospective father for the children she so badly wanted. In practical terms this meant that every man she met became a candidate for the vacancy, and thus had to be vetted by means of some very ponderous flirting. The Women's Liberation movement had pretty much passed Julie by, though even this had not aided her in her quest for a husband. Or, more accurately, her quest for a financially solvent sperm donor; Julie had her priorities straight. Though, as it happened, this attitude was one of the main causes of her problem. Right now she smiled back and said, with what was intended as an alluring look in her big blue eyes, 'Is your home number here too? No? Not to worry. You be sure to keep your mobile on at all times, and I'll ring you if I ever desperately need a big strong man to rush to my rescue in the middle of the night.'

'Er, okay,' replied the mortified Frank, suddenly as red as beetroot and more than a little nervous, 'Though I think dialling 999 might produce quicker results.'

Julie, with a slight pout, said in her best Marilyn Monroe, 'Oh, but I'm sure *you* could satisfy *all* my needs.'

The scarlet Frank swallowed hard but did not -could not- reply. Fortunately Jack rescued him by saying irritably, 'Jesus, pass me a sick-bucket! For God's sake stop slobbering over the boy, Jools! You're old enough to be his mother, you silly old fool, and we've got work to do! Come *on*, Frank!'

He stamped off and Frank, with an apologetic look towards the furious Julie, gratefully trailed in his wake. And Jack filed away in his brain the fact that his hitherto unflappable assistant seemed to lose his self-assurance in the presence of women. Well, older predatory women, anyway. In the stressful and often dangerous world of crime investigation it is vital to know all your partner's weak as well as strong points. Cases, and occasionally even a life, can depend upon such apparent trivialities. And, of course, such knowledge means that much innocent fun can be gleaned in the ancient art of persecuting one's assistant.

Juno Malubu Wren lived close to his deceased master physically but a whole world away in almost every other respect. There are many nice parts of Glasnevin, and there are some not so nice parts; Juno lived in a block of Council flats in one of the not so nice parts. When they arrived outside his front door Frank looked at the surrounding flats with distaste; they were dirty, dilapidated and smeared with graffiti. The whole place stank, but it was the metaphorical odour of poverty and crime that revolted the young man, the birthright that many of the myriad children swarming through these flats would inevitably inherit. With such a breeding- and training-ground, what hope was there for them for the future? Frank shook his head slightly as he rang the bell, saddened by the needless waste of so many young lives. Jack's face remained impassive; his view of the locals was equally jaundiced but less sympathetic. He had been dealing with scum for too long to pity them overmuch, and in places like this the scum predominated over the unfortunate few trying to lead a decent life against the odds. *C'est la vie.*

Juno opened his front door in a manner Jack liked; throwing it open welcomingly, and with no trace of apprehension. The policeman immediately marked him down as an honest man. Or, more to the point, one with no recent guilt staining his conscience.

'Mr. Wren? Good morning, I'm Detective Chief Inspector O'Neill of the Metropolitan Division, and this is Detective Garda Carr. We'd like to talk to you about Mr. Akima, if it's convenient.'

Juno took a step forward, blocking the doorway. He was short and stocky, with a shining black moon-face not dissimilar to that of the dead man, and close-cropped curly hair. He looked up at Jack with apprehensive brown eyes and said defensively, 'What do you want of me? I have done nothing wrong. I told the policewoman on the phone that I know nothing about Mr. Akima's death. All I have done is lose my job. A very good job that I depended upon for my livelihood.'

'I appreciate that, Mr. Wren, but you only spoke to an operator, not a policewoman, and we still have some questions to ask you. May we come in?'

Juno sighed and seemed to deflate, and he said resignedly, 'If you must, you must. Please, come this way.' He led them in to a sitting-room that was far neater and cleaner than the outside of the flat presaged, and which was redolent with a heavy, musky scent that instantly transported the two policemen to Africa. It was no more than the spices Juno used in cooking and perhaps a little incense yet this, along with a few carved wooden artefacts, was enough to ensure that no unsuspecting visitor would be left in any doubt as to the occupant's antecedents. Which provided a telling contrast to his ex-employer's sterile home. No, not home; domicile; Akima's apartment was too impersonal to be truly called a home.

Juno waved them onto a long sofa aglow with blazing yellow and orange cushions that had in fact once belonged to his employer, and sat in a battered old leather armchair facing them. He stretched out his hands in front of him and said, 'There is really nothing I can tell you about this terrible crime. Mr. Akima was dead when I arrived to begin work. I saw his body through the French windows when I went around the back to get the some tools from the shed. At first I could hardly believe what my eyes were saying to me, but I have seen dead bodies before so I rang the police on my mobile telephone. I don't have a key to the flat so I could not go in to him, even if I had wished to do so.'

'You didn't try the back door?' asked Frank, 'See if it was open?'

Wren shook his head, 'I was afraid to go near the place in case I left fingerprints or something. I saw nothing, heard nothing. I *know* nothing. I did not do this thing, and I do not know who did. I cannot imagine anyone wishing Mr. Akima harm. He was a very good man, very reasonable and polite. Providing I carried out my duties satisfactorily, of course. If I neglected my work he could become quite stern, as of course was his right. But I think I may boast a little and say that he rarely had cause to complain in all the time that I worked for him.'

'And how long was that?' asked Jack, settling down into the comfortable sofa and wondering if Wren could be trusted to make a Christian cup of tea. Probably not; Jack had been to Africa on holiday, many years before, and the locals' idea of tea had been aromatic but bloody awful to taste.

'More than four years.'

Jack nodded, 'We haven't been able to discover anything about Mr. Akima. Any personal details, I mean. What do you know of his social life, of his family and friends? Of his business?'

'Nothing,' replied Juno in wide-eyed surprise, 'I just tended his garden. What should I know of him? He was my employer, not my friend. I had no *social* contact with him.'

Jack regarded him thoughtfully; surely even in these multi-cultural days Africans were not so plentiful in Dublin that their relationship was just a coincidence? Or were they, and he had just been so deep in a bottle that he hadn't noticed?

'Did you know Mr. Akima in South Africa?' he finally asked.

'No, no, no! I am not South African. I am from Burkina Faso. I never met Mr. Akima until I began working for him. I was a refugee, you know, not an immigrant.'

'Oh yes?' said Jack dubiously, far from sure of the difference. 'And do you have residency here?' he asked idly.

'I am a citizen.' said Juno proudly, 'I am Irish now!'

Jack couldn't help smiling at the incongruity of this statement, as well as the evident pride and pleasure behind it, 'Well, congratulations. I think. How did you meet Mr. Akima?'

'Through the African Peoples Support Group,' replied Juno promptly. 'There are many groups in Dublin designed to help immigrants and refugees, but the APSG is the only one run *solely* by, and for, people from Africa. He contacted them some four years ago and said he needed a new gardener, his old one having left Dublin. I was one of several men needing a job and I was given his number. After a short interview he deemed me suitable and gave me the post. Now that he is dead I do not know how I will manage. I have other clients now as well, you understand, but Mr. Akima's regular payment was the core of my little business.' He smiled deprecatingly and stretched out his hands, 'That is what I call it, though it is not really grand enough for the title *business*. A gardening round would perhaps be a more accurate description. And now, without him, it is ruined, alas.'

Jack made a sympathetic face, 'I see. Unfortunate for you. But even more unfortunate for Mr. Akima as he lost everything, not just a client. So are you quite certain you know nothing of his private affairs? He never mentioned a wife back home, or what he did for a living? Brothers and sisters, friends in Ireland? Nothing at all?'

Juno considered briefly before shaking his head. 'Mr. Akima was a pleasant gentleman but I was in his employ, and he was not the kind of man to forget that. We never spoke except on business matters. We rarely spoke at all, in fact, after the first few weeks. Once I proved myself reliable he left me very much to my own devices. I'm not sure how much interest he took in the garden for its own sake, actually. So long as I kept it looking well he cared nothing for what plants I used, and certainly he never chose any of them or made requests for particular flowers. He simply desired it to be neat and colourful. During the year I paid for whatever was necessary, new plants and fertiliser and the like, and when Mr. Akima returned from Africa he reimbursed me.'

'Really? Wasn't that inconvenient for you?' said Frank in surprise.

Juno shrugged, 'Yes, very, but he added ten per cent to the total, by way of compensation and as interest. And in any case he was too good a customer for me to risk offending him with a refusal on so small a matter.'

Jack looked at him for several long moments; he would have been willing to swear that Wren was telling the truth, though it seemed almost inconceivable that anyone could work in a man's home for four years without learning *anything* about him. Though of course he had only been in his garden, not his home. But still. After a moment's thought he asked, 'Why did you leave the scene of the crime yesterday? The operator told you to remain there until a policeman arrived.'

Wren smiled apologetically and raised his hands in a placatory gesture, 'I am truly sorry for that; I fear I panicked. In Africa it is often unwise to remain too close to the scene of a crime. Sadly, in my homeland if the police cannot find the real criminal they will often simply arrest the person closest to hand. And sometimes such people are beaten until they confess. Of course things are not done so in Ireland, but I am afraid I lost my reason and ran away. Old habits, as they say, die hard.'

That seemed fair enough, though Jack did not share Wren's touching -if naive- faith in the probity of the Gardai Siochana. Not all of them, anyway; Jack could have told him a few hair-raising stories of his own. However, the interview was getting them nowhere and Jack decided it was time to end it. He leaned forward and said, 'Listen, Mr. Wren, if we are to discover who murdered your employer we need to know more about him. I want you to think long and hard over the next few days, and if you think of *anything* about him, his friends, or his family, hobbies or clubs he might have been in, please give me a call.'

Right on cue Frank produced a business card that -magically, it seemed to Jack- already had his office phone number printed on it as well as Frank's mobile, and handed it to the little man. 'Don't be afraid to call no matter how trivial it seems. The slightest clue could help. A person's name he mentioned, or a place name, a pub he drank in, a restaurant he frequented regularly...*anything.*'

Juno took the card but said dubiously, 'I will try but really there is nothing I can tell you. If we spoke at all it was only concerning the garden, or my pay, perhaps.'

Jack nodded resignedly, 'Fair enough. But please try, anyway. Something might come back to you. You realise that you will have to make and sign a formal statement? My office will contact you to arrange a convenient time. While we're at it, I don't suppose you know the name of your predecessor? The gardener before you?'

Wren shook his head regretfully, 'I'm afraid it never came up. Perhaps the APSG would know; he may have recruited him there too.'

Jack nodded and looked at his assistant, 'Anything else?'

Frank thought for a moment before asking, 'Do you ever return home, Mr. Wren? To Burkina Faso?'

Juno shook his head, 'I am afraid not. My homeland is very troubled and most of my family are dead. Nothing remains there for me but danger, and even if it were not so I could not easily afford the fare.' He made an effort and smiled broadly, 'Ireland is my home now, for which I am very grateful.'

Frank smiled back, 'Except for the weather, eh?'

Juno exploded with laughter and slapped his thigh, 'Ye-es! It is very much too cold! Even in summer! And the rain! Eee-eee! I wear thermal underwear all year round! And in winter *two* layers!' He sobered suddenly and, as if afraid of giving offence, quickly added, 'Of course, this is a very small price to pay to live in peace and safety.'

'Do you ever suffer racial abuse?' asked Jack curiously, reflecting to himself that peace and safety were not things Akima at least had found there.

Juno shrugged, 'Some bad looks sometimes, little more. Sometimes insults from groups of teenagers, but always said as a joke between themselves rather than said directly to me. It is worse for women; I know two women who have been attacked and beaten but most of these hooligans have not quite the courage to attack a man. The local children often shout names at me, but what is that to a man who has seen civil war? Being showered with bad words is preferable to being showered with bullets, yes?'

'Well, yes,' agreed Frank, his face going red as he got angry on Wren's behalf, 'But you don't have to tolerate abuse of any sort, you know. If you lodge a complaint with the police action will be taken, I promise you.'

Juno showed his dazzling grin, 'If children insult me I tell them that I am a cannibal and will eat them! That sends them running home to their parents, screaming with so delightful fear!'

Jack laughed and got to his feet. 'Maybe that's the best way of dealing with the little buggers, at that. But please don't ever be afraid to go to your local police station and make a complaint; we take racism very seriously these days, and anyone who abuses you on the basis of your colour can be charged with incitement to hatred.' He looked at Frank, 'Right, time to go, unless you can think of anything? Okay then; thank you for your help, Mr. Wren, and please remember what I said. *Anything* you remember, however trivial, might prove helpful.'

Looking doubtful but nonetheless agreeing politely, Juno showed them out of his little piece of Africa, beaming with relief to be rid of them so easily and painlessly, and shutting the door perhaps a little more firmly than strictly necessary. Once back in the car Jack said glumly, 'Well, that was no bloody help whatsoever. A complete waste of time.' He shook his head in disgust. 'By the way, what did you have in mind when you asked him about trips back to Africa? You think he was a courier or something for Akima?'

Frank looked at him in surprise. 'God, no; that never occurred to me. I was just wondering if he ever got homesick. It must be hard to be alone in a strange land. I felt sorry for him. *Hard-torn from native soil, upturned roots clutching fragments of rock; unsatisfying momentos. Alone, the transplant dies.*'

Jack looked at him in silence for several long, pregnant seconds before shaking his head in disbelief and turning to stare blankly out of the opposite window.

Chapter Five

The journey back to Harcourt Square was achieved in a fraught silence that was partly the result of a sense of failure and partly due to the growing urgency of Jack's need for a drink. He had brought with him his small pewter hip-flask filled with whiskey, and it was burning like a hot coal in his jacket pocket, but he left it to burn. As yet the desire was still weaker that his reluctance to expose his frailty to Frank, but the battle was purely a rearguard action within a general retreat, and his self-respect was fast nearing the always inevitable surrender. When they finally reached HQ Jack, with an unintelligible grunt over his shoulder, vanished into the visitor's toilet behind the foyer, unable to wait even the extra minute or so that would see him down to the bathroom beside his own office. Every nerve in his body was screaming for the release that lay in his inside pocket, and he had the flask out and was drinking deeply even before the cubicle door had swung fully shut behind him, sending liquid fire on a burning path to his knotted but eager stomach.

Frank hesitated in front of the reception desk for an uncomfortable moment, unsure as to whether or not he was expected to await his lord and master's calls of nature. But he hesitated only a moment before heading for the basement, curiosity easily defeating deference to his superior. He descended the stairs to the Records department two at a time before slowing sharply as he nervously approached Julie, agog to find out if she had received the South African fax but a smidge afraid to ask.

Julie was no longer a danger to him, however, now that Jack had blown her cover as to her age...in her mind, at least. Her friends had assured her so often that she didn't look a day over thirty that by now she either truly believed it, or else pretended to even to herself. However, even she couldn't force herself to hope that Frank would disregard Jack's comment about her being old enough to be his mother and she had reluctantly crossed him off her list of possible mates. Now that another potential father for the children within her crying out to be born had been warned off she relaxed and was simply friendly in a natural way that, if she had only realised it, was far more attractive than her clumsy attempts at vampishness. And far less frightening. She gave Frank the fax and a rather perfunctory smile and said, 'Yes, it arrived. Here you go. I didn't ring you because it only arrived a couple of minutes ago.'

Frank took the report eagerly, and in his impatience a touch impolitely. It comprised only a single sheet of paper and his eyes swiftly devoured the entire contents. They were disappointingly meagre; William Henry Akima was a wealthy businessman with no criminal record, though a few discreet inquiries had revealed that he did not have a good reputation in Soweto business circles. However, there were only unsavoury rumours against his name; no dark revelations, no secrets that would explain his murder. As far as anyone could tell he was a more or less ordinary, albeit successful man. He was also, Frank mentally added, a large and frustrating enigma.

At that point Jack made his appearance through the basement door. He marched past the rows of clerk's desks into his office without even pausing and Frank hurried after him, glumly sharing the bad news with the back of his head. Once Jack got to his magic cabinet and popped a couple of breath-mints into his mouth he felt fit for human consumption again and hence able to communicate once more with his assistant. Sitting down behind his desk he grunted, 'It's disappointing but I wasn't expecting much anyway. I was far more hopeful of Mr. Wren. *His* lack of information was the real blow.'

Frank nodded agreement and offered him some others, *'Dearth of knowledge forms a bitter cup, a poisoned chalice filled with sin/ Not death, no, what awaits...is the deeper misery of what might have been.'*

Jack gave him a sour look, 'Spare me, please. The only good thing about all this is that our Mr. Akima is final proof that poets are full of it.'

Frank seemed to take this as a personal insult and arched his eyebrows as he asked, 'And how do you make that out? Er, sir.'

'Well, William Akima was one man who *was* a bloody island, wasn't he?'

The innocent -or, to the cynical, mindless- optimism of youth made Frank confidently reply, 'Something will turn up. It's just a matter of looking hard enough.'

'No,' said Jack heavily, 'It isn't. It's matter of looking in the right place. *Always.* And we aren't doing it. Any next of kin listed in that fax?'

Frank nodded, 'A cousin. The rest of his family are dead, apparently; parents, siblings, the lot. The South African police are informing her of his death.'

At this point Julie entered the office and said without preamble, 'Right, that's every sports shop in Dublin accounted for. Considering that no one in this country even plays the stupid game a lot of baseball bats are bought every day.'

Jack gave her a pitying look, 'People in Ireland don't buy them to play baseball with; they buy them to use as weapons. What did you find out?'

'Marathon Sports in Blanchardstown sold five bats of the right type last Saturday, the day before the killing. Three of them to a single customer.'

Criminals make enough stupid mistakes to keep a flicker of hope alive even in an old cynic like Jack and he said, though without any great expectation, 'Cash or credit card?'

It was Julie's turn to give him a pitying look. 'Anyone daft enough to buy his murder weapon on a credit card is more than likely in prison already. Or some sort of home. They were paid for in cash, of course.'

'Was the shop-girl able to describe the guy who bought them?'

Julie gave the hollow laugh of one who has spent many profitless hours trying to extract even the faintest gleam of intelligence from shop assistants, 'Of course not! The guy I spoke to was the one who actually made the sale, and he had no recollection of it whatsoever! You wouldn't believe it possible, would you? It was only by looking up the computer receipts that he could even tell that anyone bought bats that day at all, or that the transaction was made in cash. It's the MTV generation, computer games have left them all with the attention span and memory of a goldfish.'

'Three seconds,' put in Frank helpfully.

'Yeah? Then how could he tell that *he* made that particular sale?' nit-picked Jack irritably.

Men! Honestly, they remained children forever. With a contemptuous sniff Julie replied, 'His code was on the till receipt, of course. With the new electronic registers you have to key in your personal code every time you make a transaction. How else would they keep track of who gets the commission for each sale? Or bonuses?'

Jack looked speculatively at Frank, 'Perhaps if we called in and spoke to him? Or rather, if *you* called in and spoke to him. It might jog his memory.'

'Right!' said Julie derisively, 'These kids spend their entire day in a trance, not seeing or hearing anything around them. It's like they're on auto-pilot or something. Or on drugs. It took him ten minutes of agonising to tell me that the buyer was a man. He thinks. Well, he's pretty sure. No, wait, could it have been a woman? No, it *was* a man. Or was it? He couldn't even tell me if the guy was clean-shaven, dark or fair...nothing! These kids don't even look at you when you're buying stuff from them; they're miles away, and usually listening to music on their earphones. Good luck!'

Jack cocked a twinkling, if rather bloodshot, eye up at her, 'Turning detective, Jools? Frank must really have made an impression on you for you to ask so many questions; you've never taken such pains over any of the tasks *I've* ever given you.'

'That's because collecting your laundry or paying your bills over the phone never really struck me as vital police business!' responded Julie tartly. And with that she flounced out of the room, thus ensuring that she got in the last word.

Jack laughed, 'What a woman! It's a great shame for some man that she never married. If I was a bit younger I'd marry her myself!' He sobered quickly and said, half to himself, 'Though I don't think she's quite *that* desperate.' He shook himself, 'Right, so until we find out if these particular bats were the murder weapons we've bugger all to go on. In all my years I don't think I've ever seen such a blank canvas as our Mr. Akima. Without knowing anything about his business or personal life where the hell do we start? We really need the Forensics Report or the autopsy to throw us a bone. Until we get them, any thoughts on our next move?'

Frank was spared having to confess to being stumped by the arrival of a young female detective, who stuck her head into the room and said in a frigid, disapproving tone, 'Sorry to disturb you, sir, but I have a report here that Mr. Rollins said you were to have as soon as you returned. He also said he wants to see you afterwards. He said you'd know what he meant.' She placed a single sheet of paper on the desk before disappearing once more into the more wholesome upper regions of the building where the air was cleaner and careers still flourished.

Jack studied the report, his face growing gloomier by the second. At last he said heavily, 'Oh, *shit.*'

'Sir?'

Wearily Jack handed him the Incident Report sheet. Frank drank in the details greedily before echoing his superior, 'Oh shit!'

At ten am that morning the body of a young black man named Daniel Wistarra had been found in a builder's skip in an alleyway off Abbey Street. Preliminary examination indicated that he had been brutally beaten to death. Spray-painted on the side of the skip was the legend; NIGGERS GO HOME! IRELAND FOR THE IRISH. THE SONS OF CUCHUAILAINN.

'What do we do, sir?'

Jack appeared to have aged, and some of the new life his association with Frank had infused in him seemed to shrivel away. At length he replied, 'First of all you say, *I told you so.* Then you say that I was wrong about criminals or professional muscle killing Akima, and am obviously past it. Feel free to mention alcohol having addled my brain and, if you like, you can then drop in a casual reference to my listening to you in future. Also, a knowing look and a smug smirk wouldn't go amiss.'

Needless to say Frank offered none of these things. Instead he said awkwardly, 'The points you raised yesterday were all valid. Don't be so hard on yourself. Anyone can make a mistake.'

'Clearly. But I shouldn't have been so *blasé,* so dismissive of the evidence in front of our noses. It's just that the whole gang thing seemed like a herring as red as the spray-paint it was written in. It all just looked too easy to be true; racists kill black man for kicks. Life's rarely that simple.' He sighed wearily, 'I guess I was trying to show off a little in front of Ryan, too, trying to show I still had what it took, no matter what he might have heard.'

There was no reply Frank could make to this remark so he sensibly ignored it, saying instead, 'So what now, sir?'

Jack shook his head to clear it. 'It says here that the body's still in place, that the SOCO's are examining the scene at this moment. So now we go look at the poor bastard, and let Doc Ryan have some fun at my expense.' He looked up at Frank, and, strangely, he no longer looked so old, or defeated, as a look of bitter resolution had ironed away some of the lines on his face. 'Then we start looking at some of these anti-immigrant groups.' A glint of anger showed in his eyes as he said softly, 'We're going to get the pricks who did this, Frank. Count on it.'

Chapter Six

When they arrived at Abbey Street they found Potter's Alley cordoned off at both ends, with the lines of blue and white Garda tape being manned by two grim-faced Gardai at either end, all of whom were stolidly ignoring the efforts of the assembled reporters to elicit details of the crime. There weren't two reporters this time; more like ten or twelve, not including a TV3 camera crew. As soon as the assembled hacks saw O'Neill ducking under the tape they converged on him with a barrage of questions, which he ignored. Deriving a certain savage satisfaction from this he said quietly to one of the uniformed Gardai on the barricade, 'Have any outsiders been near the crime scene?'

The Garda, a sergeant, shook his head, 'As far as we know only the workmen who found the body have seen it. The reporters didn't get wind of it until we called HQ, and we already had the alley sealed up tight by then.'

O'Neill nodded in satisfaction, 'Good. Now listen, anything you or your men saw is to remain strictly confidential, understand? They're to speak to no one about it, including members of their own families. Particularly concerning anything written on a wall near the body, if you get me.'

'I understand, sir. There is a message, but it's not on a wall. It's written on the side of the skip the body's in. Don't worry, I can imagine how important it is that word doesn't get out, specially about the gang's name, and I'll make sure none of the lads talk about it.'

'Good man.' O'Neill turned back to the newsmen and said loudly, 'Gentlemen, your attention, please. Sorry, and ladies too. I know you're all desperate for information but all I can tell you right now is that the body of a man was found in an alley off Abbey Street early this morning. A Gardai Technical Team is currently examining the area, but I'm afraid that's about all I can tell you at this stage.'

One of the reporters shouted out, 'Who are you?'

O'Neill eyed him coldly; it was a fair question, given his recent inactivity, but the lack of recognition still stung. It hadn't been *that* long since every crime reporter in Ireland, much less Dublin, would have recognised him from a hundred yards away. He took a deep breath and said evenly, 'Sorry, I forgot to introduce myself; I'm Detective Chief Inspector O'Neill and I am in charge of this investigation.'

A female reporter shouted out, 'What's the victim's name, Mr. O'Neill?'

Jack rolled his eyes and said contemptuously, 'Come on, you know better than that. No name until the next of kin has been informed.'

One of the others shouted, 'Is it true the victim is black, Chief Inspector?'

Jack hesitated for a moment, 'If he is a victim; no cause of death has yet been established. I haven't seen the body yet, but yes, my understanding is that he is black and his death is being treated as suspicious. Now, please excuse me, but I have work to do.'

The same reporter shouted, 'So do we! Tell me, is there any connection between this murder and the killing of that black man in Phibsboro over the weekend?'

O'Neill hesitated again before saying carefully, 'Not as far as I know. Why should there be? Sadly, there are murders almost every day in Ireland nowadays.'

'But are you investigating both cases? And if so, *why*, if they aren't connected?'

Jack hesitated again before saying, 'I *am* investigating both but there are so many killings in Dublin these days that detectives often have to double up on cases.'

The same reporter said, not without satisfaction, 'Even so, don't you think it's significant that two black men have been murdered in Dublin within two days?'

'I *told* you,' intoned Jack, trying to contain his impatience, 'I haven't even seen the victim yet, but even if he is black I see no reason for there to be a connection. Dublin has a large multi-racial population, and unfortunately people of every race, creed and colour are killed here every day. Now come on, that's enough for the moment. We only just got here and we still know next to nothing. Give me a couple of hours and I'll call a press conference, and try to answer some of your questions then.' With that he turned and proceeded up the alley, swiftly followed by Frank, resolutely ignoring the myriad extra questions fired after him by the ever-hungry reporters.

As they walked Frank said quietly, 'If there is some sort of lunatic gang murdering black immigrants, don't you think the black community should be informed of it? *Warned?*'

O'Neill grunted, 'Perhaps. On the other hand I don't want other half-wits joining in with racist attacks of their own, clouding the water with red herrings. Our job is going to be hard enough as it is without having to investigate every fool who fancies joining the new Nazi party, and who chucks a brick through a black man's window. Besides, the way things are since the recession started the publicity might gain the buggers more recruits.'

Frank compressed his lips and shook his head in disagreement but offered no further argument; it could wait until later. The idea that it was not his place to argue with his vastly senior boss never crossed his mind, nor Jack's, oddly enough; the Gardai was far from being a democracy but Frank was like no other assistant he had ever known.

Dr. Ryan, along with a three-man SOCO team, was already there when they reached the end of the narrow alley where the body had been found, and he did indeed enjoy himself at Jack's expense, though fortunately his sense of humour was limited. As soon as he saw the two policemen approaching he said, in a puzzled tone, 'Here's a strange coincidence, O'Neill. The same guys who had it in for Mr. Akima seem to have had a grudge against this boy too. Funny that, considering they were professional criminals. Of course, the fact that this guy is black too, and even African, has nothing to do with it. Oh dear me no!'

Jack had no defence and so was forced to take it, with just a mental; *Up yours*. Aloud he merely said, 'How do you know he was African?'

'He had his passport with him. From Rwanda, by the way. He was just a kid, barely twenty years old.' He nodded towards the Gardai at the end of the ally, 'The cop who answered the 999 call already called immigration, seeking the next of kin, but it seems our dead friend's family were all murdered in Africa long before he got here. Poor little bastard.'

Mentally echoing this sentiment but keeping his face impassive Jack stood on his tip-toes and craned his neck to take a look inside the big yellow skip, the contents of which two of the forensics men were carefully sifting. In spite of his years in the Murder Squad, and the foul sights he had seen, he could not help wincing at the sight of the crumpled, savaged figure lying huddled amongst the rubbish and building site detritus. *Poor little bastard indeed.* With a face of thunder he turned back to Ryan, 'Any idea when it happened?'

'Hard to say yet. Judging by the liver temperature I'd guess he's been dead somewhere between eight and twelve hours, which ties in with what the builders said.' Ryan nodded towards three scruffily dressed men standing near the skip, cigarettes in their hands. 'The boys there say he definitely wasn't in the skip at six last night, because they dumped stuff in it just before they went home.'

Jack glanced in their direction, 'They discovered the body? Frank, get a statement from whoever found it first, will you? Doc, what else did you find in his pockets?'

'Apart from his passport? Not much. Twenty-odd quid in cash, a set of keys, and a couple of letters from the Social Welfare. They give his address as a flat in Pearse Street, by the way. I'll send it all down to your office after they've been analysed.'

'Alright. What's the address?'

'Flat 7, 18 Winter Gardens, Pearse Street.'

From one of the builders Frank was questioning Jack caught the words, '...thought it was a doll or something at first. It didn't even look human, all twisted up like that.' Jack made a *moue* of distaste and blocked the voice from his mind. 'Is the M.O. the same as in the Phibsboro killing?'

'No. If it was the same men they didn't use weapons this time. Fists and feet, at a guess, though I won't be certain until I do the autopsy. At least, no weapons have been found yet. And of course I can't say how many attackers there were, though I doubt if one man alone could have inflicted such damage.'

Jack nodded and looked around at the dingy surrounding buildings in disgust. 'Offices, for the most part, and half of them empty. I don't fancy our chances of digging up any witnesses if he was killed last night; they'll all have been empty by six or so. Still, we'll get some uniforms knocking on all the doors, asking questions. And we'll put an appeal out on the radio and on Crimeline. Sometimes you get lucky.'

Ryan gave him a look that clearly indicated his belief that Jack needed all the luck he could get, but made no audible reply.

Jack turned to survey the alley, his lips pursed and his hooded eyes raking the walls and ground, though more for inspiration than because he thought the SOCO's might have missed anything. There was a diesel generator providing electricity and standing floodlights were set up all around the crime scene, trailing thick black cables everywhere and bathing the whole alley in a bright yellow glow and making it look like a movie set. Or at least, his idea of what a movie set looked like. He slowly turned in a circle, a puzzled look on his face, before saying, 'This alleyway is a dead end. Where the hell could the victim have been going? Or coming from?'

Frank rejoined them in time to hear the question and he replied, 'Unless he was walking up Abbey Street itself and they dragged him up here, where they could... Well, where they wouldn't be disturbed.'

'Mmm, could be, I suppose. He could have been coming from one of the pubs on Capel Street. Or going *to* one of them, depending on the time. The problem is, why drag him so far up the alley? The skip must be a hundred yards from the main street, yet even without the white tape around them you can clearly see the blood-stains there in front of it. Why bring him so far up before attacking him?' He took another look around, seeking a legitimate reason for anyone to be in the alley at night. And then it became clear to him; the victim had tried to escape his killers by fleeing up the alley, not knowing that it was a dead end. No doubt he had tried to double back past them once he realised his mistake, and had been trapped near the skip. That was the narrowest point of the alley and the logical place to trap him as he tried to dodge past. Assuming they *were* the same assailants who had murdered Akima there would probably have been three of them, more than enough for the job against a skinny little chap like this one.

Jack thought about this scenario for a moment before nodding to himself, confident he had the answer. There was no way of proving it, of course, but it *felt* right.

Curiosity had gotten the better of Frank and he had peeked into the skip, an act he seemed now to be regretting. He took a step back, drew a deep breath, and began examining the writing on the side of the skip with exaggerated attention. 'Best take a photo of that, eh, sir? To compare it with the writing on Akima's wall?'

Jack opened his mouth to blast the younger man but, on seeing his pallor, refrained from pointing out that such details were the duty of the SOCO's, and had in fact already been done. Being confronted with two such terribly battered corpses in two days might test even a veteran, much less such a rookie as Frank. He closed his mouth again and turned back to Ryan, 'Did you find anything interesting when you examined the body? Anything that might give us a headstart while we wait for your report?'

Ryan shook his head, 'Not a sausage, I'm afraid.'

Jack sighed, 'Why am I not surprised? When is there ever? Speaking of reports, when can we expect the results of your post mortem on Akima?'

'Tomorrow, with a bit of luck. Don't get too excited, mind. I didn't find anything earth-shaking in my preliminary examination.' Here Ryan gave an unpleasant little chuckle, 'The contents of his stomach were interesting, though. Best wait for the Forensics boys; they might have more for you.'

Jack made an impatient gesture, 'I'll be retiring in a few years, you know. I was kind of hoping to solve this before I go.'

Sergeant Peter O'Halloran, the leader of the Technical Team both here and at Akima's flat, looked up from his scrutiny of the blood stains on the ground. 'I heard that, you know. There are better ways of being put to the bottom of my priority list than showering me in personal abuse, but not many.'

Jack reluctantly smiled at him, 'Name one.'

'Screwing my little sister, for a start. That puts you on my ten-year waiting list.'

'How about screwing your wife?' asked Ryan, his lips twisted in the sour grimace that with him was meant to pass for a friendly smile.

O'Halloran grinned, 'That's a different matter altogether. For that you get same-day service, and all the beer you can drink. I'm been trying to get someone to take that bitch off my hands for years.'

They all laughed, a little too loudly, grimly defying death with a little humour, however inappropriate, as men will when surrounded by fate's bloodier handiwork.

Jack didn't know O'Halloran, a deficiency he was beginning to regret, and he now approached him and asked, 'I know it's early days but is there anything I should know?'

'Not yet. No sacks of drugs or money, no discarded weapons. Not even a piece of cloth torn from the killer's hand-made jacket and still clutched in the dead man's hand, ready for you to track down the tailor. Who of course only made one such garment in his entire life, and who has the purchaser's name and address on file.'

Jack had to laugh, 'Jesus, Colombo has a lot to answer for.'

'Colombo my arse! Sherlock Holmes was the man for me. He wasn't a detective at all, you know, but the very first forensic scientist. And at least his murderers always left *something*, some tangible evidence, unlike those pursued by our friend in the shabby raincoat, whose arrests often seemed to depend on rather unlikely confessions.'

'I could use some of that myself,' admitted Jack. 'Evidence, I mean. And the more tangible the better. Though by God I wouldn't turn down a confession either, however unlikely. Have you finished your prelim on the Akima case?'

O'Halloran rolled his eyes, no trace of humour remaining. 'Give me a break, we only scanned his apartment *yesterday*. Do you know how many crime scenes I visit per day? All being run by coppers who think I've nothing else to work on but *their* case?' He sighed before saying gruffly, 'Nothing unusual leaped out at me, I can tell you that, so don't build your hopes on what we gathered. How about if I try and get you the fingerprints by tomorrow, and a preliminary report by Friday?'

Jack grunted, 'If you're looking for teary-eyed gratitude, forget it! No detective is ever going to admit it when you're quick. He'd be too afraid you'd take twice as long next time. We all know you lot like to make your job look difficult.'

'No bloody appreciation,' muttered O'Halloran darkly, 'that's the problem. It's like working for my wife.'

'It could be worse,' said Jack with a grin, 'At least I don't expect sex as well.'

O'Halloran shuddered and furtively looked over his shoulder, *'Don't,* please! I'd hate to give the bitch ideas.'

Jack had an idea he could stand there all day and not get the better of him so he just shook his head and turned back to Frank, calling, 'Come on, there's nothing else for us here.' He waved his hand, encompassing the high, commercial buildings surrounding them with the gesture, 'There's not a sinner living around here so there's not much chance of us finding a witness to anything that occurred outside working hours. Still, we'll send a few lads around to make inquiries; there might have been the odd workaholic working late or cleaners tidying up or something. And if Rollins still won't give us a few extra bodies even though it's now a dual murder, we'll do it ourselves. I was thinking we could put out an appeal on Crimeline, too. Talk to the Press Liaison Officer about setting it up, will you? And check with the local station, see if anyone reported seeing or hearing anything in the area last night. Check for 999 calls as well.' He shrugged, 'It's unlikely but you never know your luck.'

Frank nodded brightly, 'Okay. What are you going to do?' He caught himself, 'Er, I mean, what else do you want me to do?'

Jack gave him a sidelong look and on impulse changed his plans for the afternoon, 'I'll go back to the office with you. We should be taking this guy's flat apart but it'll have to wait. That girl said Rollins wanted to see me this afternoon and I just bet he does; I could write the script of what he's going to say right here and now. I'm surprised he even let us view the crime scene before dragging me into his office. Anyway, this guy…what was his name? Wistarra? Jesus. His flat will have to wait because I don't want you going there alone. Plus, I've got the delightful task of dealing with our friends in the Press; I'll have to decide how much to tell the buggers, and either issue a statement or call a conference. While I deal with Rollins you can track down our victim's next of kin and send a Ban Gardai to break the sad news to them. Then I'll start to do what I do best. Think, that is.'

Although he was being wholly –and bitterly- ironic Frank nodded and said, apparently seriously, 'I understand; *Wring the fevered brow, harvest the thought-born pearls/ precious as an angel's tears are they, and harder won.'*

'Yes,' said Jack, simply giving up on him. 'Now do you think you can drive me back to the office rather than simply up the bloody wall?'

Chapter Seven

As the two detectives rather glumly entered the building in Harcourt Square the receptionist caught Jack's eye and said, 'Mr. Rollins wants to see you, sir. He left word that you're to go straight up to his office the instant you return.'

'I *know* he wants to see me,' said Jack sourly, 'we got his message earlier. Jesus, does he think I'm going to emigrate or something?' In truth he was not looking forward to the interview, though it was only to be expected; their nothing little killing was now a campaign of murder and hatred by a neo-Nazi gang, which put it somewhere in the stratosphere in terms of Press interest. And if nothing else he had learned that once a Garda gets to executive level he spends half his time worrying about public relations and the other half shovelling blame for anything that goes wrong onto his subordinates; shit might indeed roll downhill, but hurling it that direction removes any uncertainty in the matter. And if the gauntlet they had had to run from reporters after leaving the crime scene was anything to go by, public scrutiny on -and interest in- his quiet little swan-song case was going to be intense. He turned to Frank, 'Go on down to the office. You can start on the appeal for Crimeline. Keep it simple, a "were you in the area and saw anything" type of thing. Do you know who's in charge of the whole Crimeline thing these days?'

'Chief Inspector Hart, sir.'

'Oh? I can't say the name rings a bell. Anyway, get the appeal over to his office if I'm not back by the time you've finished. And don't forget the next of kin.' He started towards the lifts but then turned and shouted after his assistant, 'And none of your flights of fancy! Keep it short and simple! And no bloody poetry!'

With a grin and a wave of assent Frank vanished down into the basement, leaving Jack to make his way up to Rollins' office with leaden footsteps. He was not looking forward to this interview, nor the prospect of facing a ravening pack of reporters afterwards. But tempting though it was he knew he couldn't fob them off forever, nor could he ignore them as they would then simply print rumours and half-truths that might be even more damaging to public morale. He could already imagine the outraged editorials the papers would all be printing on the morrow, to say nothing of the screams of protest that would soon emerge from the immigrant support groups, and from anxious black citizens. And that was *without* them knowing about the "Sons of Cuchuailainn" malarky. When *that* became known they'd have a field day with it. And if there were more attacks –and Jack had a horrible feeling that there would be- it would all get very much worse. Morbidly hoping for a nice disaster or sex scandal to divert the jackals, or for the Americans to attack yet another unfortunate Third World country for their gas or oil, Jack knocked twice on Rollins' door and entered without waiting for an invitation.

'You wanted to see me, sir?' he said glumly.

Rollins was studying a thick sheaf of papers, which he threw down onto his desk before saying heatedly, 'What the hell is going on, Jack?'

Resisting a suicidal impulse to start a discourse on the state of the world economy, Jack walked over and took a seat without waiting to be asked. He looked Rollins in the eye and said flatly, 'Our quiet little case is proving to be a touch more complicated than we anticipated. And much higher profile.'

'Clearly. My phone hasn't stopped ringing because the press are slavering with delight at the thought of a racist mass-murderer on the loose. *Are* the two killings connected?'

'Yes, definitely.' And Jack quickly explained about the "Sons of Chuchailainn".

Rollins shook his head, 'Jesus! And how close are you to an arrest?'

'Give us a chance!' protested Jack in astonishment, 'Do you think these buggers have taken out an ad out in the Times or something, giving their address? We only just viewed the second crime scene, from which the body hasn't even been removed yet! All we know about this second guy is his name, for God's sake!'

'And the fact that he's black.' Rollins pointed out. 'And that "Ireland for the Irish" shite. Make sure you sit on *that* information, Jack. *Hard.* I don't want this racist thing getting out of control, and I don't want other arseholes joining in the fun. This has to be resolved quickly. There are plenty of bleeding-heart liberals out there just looking for a crusade to follow, and they'll scream blue murder if we don't get instant results. If you don't arrest someone quick, and you're not seen to be putting in the effort, you'll be off this case and forced into retirement before you know what's hit you. Got it?'

Jack went first hot and then cold with anger but kept his temper enough to say evenly, 'I've got it, all right. And you'll get a result, provided I get the support I need. After all, we wouldn't want the press finding out how low profile and unimportant this case really is, now would we?'

'Don't you dare threaten me!' roared Rollins, rising to his feet and turning crimson with anger, 'Who the hell do you think you are? And don't try to blackmail me either, or by God I'll break you!'

Jack blinked at him in surprise; he had been doing both, of course, but this wasn't how the game was played at all. Rollins was supposed to have ignored the threat and given him some more backup as a personal "favour". As if Jack would ever willingly talk to the Press about anything, much less complain to them about his superiors! What the hell was wrong with Rollins? As a political animal he should know better.

'It wasn't intended as a threat,' he lied slowly, 'but with only two of us working the case some bright spark might make an issue of it, accuse the Gardai of not caring and not putting in the effort because the victims are black. And we already have a bad reputation as being a bit racist.'

'Bullshit!' sneered Rollins, slamming his fist down on the desk, 'I know what you were getting at!' He sank slowly back down onto his seat, 'I told you at the start; you're on your own with this one! If I had anyone to spare you wouldn't be handling this damned case at all and you know it! That was the whole point of dragging you out of your basement in the first place! So how the hell I am supposed to find you a team now? I *might,* if you're lucky, find you a uniform or two to help with the legwork for a couple of days, but that's your lot!'

He reached for one of his eternal humbugs, putting it in his mouth without even realising he was doing so before continuing, in a slightly muffled voice, 'And talking to the Press is a double-edged sword, Jack. You try to embarrass me with this whole Carr thing and by God I'll crucify *you!* Now get the fuck out of my office!'

Jack went quietly, stone-faced in front of his superior but secretly not entirely displeased. He had been afraid –half convinced- that he was about to be replaced, now that the case had cranked up more than a few notches in terms of importance, but for the moment at least he was still in the saddle. And if nothing else he had shown Rollins that he wasn't prepared to be made the scapegoat if it all went pear shaped. He grinned to himself in the lift at the thought of a war of words fought via the press; much he'd care what Rollins said about *him*. The Assistant Commissioner, however, was a very different kettle of fish; he still had a career and was still ambitious, and really couldn't afford the sort of embarrassment Jack could heap on him if accusations started to fly. TD's and their nephews indeed! He wondered for a moment if he should have put in a written request for more help on the case before dismissing the idea; he didn't want to push Rollins so far that he actually followed up on his threat to take him off the case. And his superior seemed more than a little on edge. *Well, I guess it's tough at the top.*

He made his way downstairs to his office and, finding it empty, took the opportunity to take a quick swig of Jameson to settle his nerves. When Frank returned, having delivered his Crimeline appeal to the Media Relations Officer in person, the older man leaned back in his battered old swivel chair and said slowly, 'We all have sex, right?'

Frank, taking his seat, made a rueful face across the desk, 'If possible. It's not always as easy as all that, even in these liberal times. Not if you have standards, that is. Why?'

'Because I'm wondering what our friend Akima did to to...er, satisfy his urges in that area. Assuming he had any, of course; nothing else in his life seems normal. Among his things there was no hint of a family or a girlfriend, either here or in South Africa, right?'

'There were no hints of *any* relationships, personal or business.'

'Well, that's a bit odd at his age, isn't it? Especially with him being an African. Most Africans consider children a gift to the future and have as many kids as they can, as soon as they can. So why not him? It's not like he couldn't afford them.'

Frank pursed his lips thoughtfully, 'You think he could have been gay?'

'Well, it's a possibility, isn't it? If he was just between girlfriends he certainly kept any signs of an ex well hidden.'

'He might have had a girlfriend we don't know about yet,' suggested Frank, 'She might ring us when she can't contact him, or if she finds out he's dead. Though if he was seeing someone surely she'd have to leave *some* trace of her presence in his flat. Maybe he did one of those cleansing things and deliberately emptied all trace of her from his life, which is why his flat seems so barren.'

Jack raised his eyebrows and Frank smiled, 'It was meant to be a joke. Some women, when they're getting over a bad break-up, ritually go through their home and eradicate all traces of their ex.'

'Joke or not, you never know; maybe that's just what he did,' said Jack heavily, 'Certainly his place was empty enough. Personally I think he was getting ready to leave Ireland for good, and that's why there were no traces of anything personal in his own place.'

Frank nodded, 'That's a well-known phenomenon, particularly among criminals getting ready to take a powder.'

Jack shrugged, 'These are all possibilities we'll have to explore but they're not getting us any closer to a killer. I wish we'd found an address book, or a mobile phone; it would make our job so much easier.' He paused, 'That's strange, isn't it? We know he had an African mobile phone but the killers took that and left the Rolex. Maybe there were numbers in it they didn't want us to find. But until a girlfriend surfaces -and I think if he had one there would have been signs of her in his flat- the gay thing is worth looking into. How's your knowledge of the Dublin gay scene?'

'Minimal, but I've a feeling it's about to improve dramatically,' Frank replied humorously, 'You want me to trawl through our gay bars and clubs with Akima's photo, questioning barmen and looking for ex- and/or current lovers?'

'Can't do any harm,' nodded Jack moodily, staring off into space; all this talk about sex had led him to some fairly depressing thoughts about his own life and the lack of any such activity therein. Not that the whiskey had left much in the way of desire. Which was the most depressing thought of all.

'Except to my reputation, of course,' suggested Frank whimsically, '*that'll* be ruined.' A thought struck him and he said, 'If he *wasn't* gay and had no girlfriend there's a chance he might have used prostitutes. We could ask Vice to help us there, get them to show his picture to some of the local working girls. There are a lot more black people in Dublin nowadays but even so one of them might recognise him, especially if he was a regular.'

Jack nodded, 'We'll give it a go, though really we're clutching at straws. With the way things are today a strapping young -well, fairly young- chap like Akima wouldn't have needed to use prostitutes; even without a steady girlfriend he needn't have gone short of sex. Not with slappers waiting to be picked up in every pub and club in Dublin for free. And let's face it, even if he used prostitutes most of these girls are too whacked out on drugs to recognise a photo of themselves, much less one of their customers. And the gay thing's probably a waste of time, too. Those gay clubs and what-not are so dimly lit that one black man would probably look much like another. To the staff, I mean, not the customers.'

Frank gave him a sidelong glance and Jack said, somewhat defensively, 'Well, it's true. Don't look at me like that; I'm no racist. Why would staff at a nightclub pay more than superficial attention to a customer, black *or* white? Besides, most nightclubs are so dark you can hardly see your hand in front of your face, anyway, and many black men are at least superficially alike. At least in the bloody dark!'

Frank shook his head disapprovingly, 'They really aren't, you know. Aside from their colour –which varies a lot- black men differ far more than white men in their features; it's just that white people rarely look beyond their colour. And even if they really were all alike you shouldn't talk like that. You'll have the Racial and Intercultural Liaison Officer after you if you're not careful.'

'You have got to be bloody joking!' exploded Jack, 'Tell me there's no such person! *Please!*'

Frank laughed, 'There is, I assure you! The Garda have gone very politically correct since the immigrant boom began. We had to; there were a lot of complaints against us in the early days of the influx, apparently, claiming we were all racists. With, I have to say, some justification. So we now have an Intercultural Office, and all sorts of guidelines for dealing with foreigners, as well as Irish citizens of foreign extraction. Haven't you read any of the memoranda on these issues, sir?'

He asked the question innocently but Jack wasn't fooled and refused to rise to the bait, contenting himself with shooting his assistant a sideways look from under his brows before saying, 'I know, I know, I'm a cliché. A crusty, reactionary old dinosaur, yes? Not a cool, modern hep-cat like you. But that doesn't make me a fool, or a racist.'

'No, sir, just a bit old-fashioned and possibly set in your ways. Though I imagine the phrase "hep-cat" went extinct even before the dinosaurs.'

Jack responded only with a rude gesture and Frank laughed and got to his feet, 'I'll blow up some copies of Akima's passport photo, and pass one on to Vice.'

Jack sighed, 'Fine. I'll try and talk to this Racial Officer while you're gone.'

Frank paused in the doorway, 'What did the Assistant Commissioner want, sir?'

'Just to kick us up the arse and tell me we should have solved the case yesterday. What do his type ever want?'

Although he hardly knew Rollins at all, Frank grimaced and left the room, muttering, *'Walk soft in the corridors of power, lest the dread beast 'Authority' you devour!',* leaving the senior man to take another quick nip of whiskey before beginning his search for the Racial and Intercultural Officer, God help us all. He eventually tracked him down by phone, and very soon wished he hadn't.

In many ways Inspector Gerry Mangan was about the least likely Garda ever to walk a beat; so much so that many of his compatriots believed he in fact never had, that he had somehow sprung to life a fully-fledged Inspector, like a flower that blooms overnight. He was soft-spoken and self-effacing to a fault, though the merest hint of prejudice of any sort aroused the lion in him. He was also an advocate of the theory that criminals do not, in fact, exist, that when a crime is committed all of society is to blame; a view that might appeal to sociologists but not to many policemen, whose *raison de etre* was locking up bad guys and who could ill-afford the guilt and sense of futility such a philosophy would necessarily entail. He also believed, with more justification perhaps, that prisons were an utter waste of time and money, and that criminals were in need of help rather than punishment. Not really a typical cop. Jack had never met him and now, hearing his voice on the phone, pictured him as a thin, limp-wristed dreamer who loved all God's creatures equally and refused to condemn anyone, lowlife or not. In the physical description at least he could not have been more wrong. Although Mangan was softly spoken and even gentle, he was a huge, powerful, red-faced Kerryman, who did indeed love his fellow men, the exception being those specimens from Cork, and even that animosity was solely reserved for the duration of the Munster Football Championships. GAA was a religion with him so he wasn't too keen on Dubs either, having been raised on the intense rivalry between the two sides in the seventies. Mind you, since Dublin's fall from football greatness he found them less objectionable, and in his softer moments could almost pity them. *Almost.* At least they weren't Man Utd fans, whom he totally despised; as far as he was concerned soccer was a foreign game, and an effeminate one at that. Not limp-wristed then, though possibly a daydreamer in that he had a vision of the Ireland of the future being one being big racial melting pot, with a mixture of races and colours and religions all co-existing happily together. Except soccer fans and except, of course, when the All-Ireland football championship rolled around.

When Jack eventually tracked down his number and phoned his office Mangan proved only too willing to help, and heartily damning of anyone who disapproved of the foreign invasion of recent years. He truly believed that borders and frontiers should be consigned to history, and that people should have the right to live anywhere they please, race or country of birth notwithstanding. And he persevered with this view in spite of the fact that most of Ireland's immigrants came from soccer-mad countries.

'Sure, O'Neill,' he replied to Jack's query, 'there are one or two anti-immigrant groups in Dublin, though I have to say none are particularly militant, much less violent. And to be fair there are a lot more *pro*-immigrant groups out there, as well as refugee welcoming committees.' Mangan was very much a man who liked to be fair. 'But I can't imagine any of the anti-immigrant groups being involved with violence, and they certainly wouldn't be rabid enough to *kill.* There have been a lot of racially motivated attacks by half-witted individuals, but no *organised* violence.'

Jack was silent for a moment and then said doubtfully, 'What do you mean, a *lot* of racially motivated attacks? Just how many are there?'

'Less than any other country in Europe,' said Mangan defensively, 'but still quite a few. Quite a few *incidents,* that is; abuse, name-calling and the like. Actual physical attacks? A dozen a year maybe, countrywide, with the number growing fast as the recession bites deeper and resentment of foreigners grows. Like I say, *far* less than any other country in Europe. Though still too many, of course. There were only two incidents in 2004, with the number rising each succeeding year to sixteen last year.' He paused, then continued reluctantly, 'Actually the *rate* of incidents each year is rising faster than in any other country in the EU.'

Jack puffed out his lips in a soundless whistle; where had he been hiding these past years? The answer was simple, of course; in a whiskey bottle. But even so, he had never considered the Irish people even faintly racist. It had simply never occurred to him that the Irish were – in the main- anything but the friendly, welcoming stereotypes the whole world recognized; how had Ireland changed so much without his noticing? He shook his head, thinking that being lost in a whiskey-fog was not a wholly bad thing. At last he said, 'So the idea of a neo-Nazi group murdering blacks isn't as far-fetched as I thought?'

'Well, it still sounds a bit unlikely,' said Mangan doubtfully, 'Most of the people who are anti-immigrant are decent enough citizens too, you know. They're just concerned that now the housing bubble has burst Ireland will be left with thousands of deadbeats that *they* have to pick up the tab for. And with the Celtic Tiger as dead as the Dodo there are hard times on the way for all of us. Actually, the hard times are here but they're going to get even worse. As well as unemployment they're also worried about future crime levels, and racial friction. Most of their prejudices come from ignorance and fear rather than malice. What these people are not, generally speaking, is thugs.'

This was not what Jack wanted to hear; it would be bad enough if your generic mindless thug was prejudiced, without ordinary citizens feeling that way too. He stuck his lower lip out in a pout before saying, 'So you've never heard of a gang in Dublin that specifically targets and attacks immigrants? Or even just blacks? Or Africans?'

'I'm afraid not,' was the reluctant answer. 'Most of the fools who've been arrested for racial attacks were doing it off their own bat, or were part of a group of idiots who were boozed-up and fancied a bit of aggro. I'm not sure they cared what colour their victims were, to be honest. Though black faces are easy to pick out, and pick on.'

Jack sighed. 'Alright. Tell you what, give me the names of the more vocal of the anti-immigrant parties and I'll take a look at them, see if any of them have become enamoured of Hitler's final solution.'

'Okay,' replied Mangan doubtfully, 'but I think you're wasting your time; the vast majority of the assaults reported were drink-related, or part of an argument about something else. We've seen no signs whatsoever of anything shall-we-say organised or co-ordinated. Still, I'll keep my ear to the ground and see if I can pick up anything. Plus, I doubt if even the most outspoken of the anti-immigrant organisations would keep quiet about an actual *murder* campaign.'

Jack wrote down the short list of names and addresses that Mangan called out, and then hung up with a word of thanks followed by another sigh. No doubt there were nutters among their members, but were any of them savage enough -*demented* enough- to kill people just because of their colour? And kill them with such violence? He didn't think so, and certainly hoped not. God knows he had seen many killings committed for the stupidest of reasons, including simply looking crooked at the wrong person at the wrong time, but he still found it hard to stomach the concept of Irish neo-Nazis plotting a deliberate campaign of murder. The mere thought of it revolted him. Still, when you came down to it murdering people on the grounds of religion was really not so different, and that was an old Irish tradition. Well, among northern Protestants it was, anyway.

Frank's return to the office interrupted his thoughts. 'Right!' said the younger man briskly, 'I talked to Vice. That's a few more wheels set in motion. Let's hope they churn something up.'

Jack nodded gloomily, 'Yeah, because I can't see us having much luck with the anti-immigrant groups. I have a list of them here. We'll take a look at them tomorrow. The Inter-whatsit Officer doesn't believe any of them would do something like this, and I have to say I agree with him. If there is a neo-Nazi group lurking in Dublin -which I doubt, by the way- it'll be very small and very secret, and we'll have to winkle it out the hard way.'

'Such as spending our evenings in gay bars?'

Jack, not deigning to answer, looked at his watch and started in surprise; it was almost four o'clock! This was the closest he had come in to putting in a full day's work in years. And he had hardly had a drink at all. Well, for him. This oversight, however, was easily rectified. It was nearly time to wrap it up for the day. But perhaps he could give it another hour. He rubbed his hands together, banishing all thoughts of booze with a violent effort of will, 'Right, our next step! What's it to be?'

Frank hesitated, 'Well, I just got the Crimeline appeal off, so what about interviewing people in the properties around Abbey Street? We need to chase them up.'

Jack shook his head, 'They're all offices; the people working in them will be heading for home soon. Besides, Rollins promised me a couple of uniformed lads for that sort of thing. Well, as good as promised. I'll get on to him in a minute about that. What else?'

'Er, what about chasing up Akima's autopsy report? That might turn up a few pointers for us.'

Jack waved a dismissive hand, 'Hardly! We already know how he died, and more or less when, and we have the murder weapons. What else is it going to tell us? Anyway, Ryan promised it for tomorrow, not today. The forensics report might help but it could be days yet before we get that. Besides, forensics are really only useful when you already have a suspect...we still need to dig up background on our victims. What else?'

'Not much,' said Frank apologetically, 'Though there is that address we found in his flat; we still haven't checked Riordan's daughter yet, to see if there's a connection. I did a little background research on her last night, sir, and it proved quite interesting. There's a police file on her as long as your arm, even though she's so young. Drugs-related, for the most part, though nothing recent. Seems she's a bit unbalanced. Up until a few months ago she was a resident in a private mental hospital here in Dublin. I contacted them but they refused to divulge her new address, just referred me to her therapist.'

'And?' said Jack impatiently.

'Well, I don't think the girl was involved in Akima's death but she has a long record so she must know some criminal types. And what was Akima doing with her address?'

Jack shook his head and said moodily, 'You're clutching at straws, lad. Still, I suppose we'll have to talk to her. Did you get her shrink's number?'

Just then they were interrupted by Julie, who bustled in without bothering to knock. 'Envelope from the State Pathologist's office,' she said breezily, slapping it down on the desk and adding knowledgeably, 'The Akima Autopsy, no doubt.'

'No doubt,' said Jack sourly, one eye on the clock and his temper deteriorating in direct proportion to the growth of his thirst, 'Do you think you could knock in future?'

'Of course!' said Julie brightly, 'In fact, from now on I won't disturb you at all! I'll just leave all reports lying on my desk until you come and damn well get them yourself!'

In spite of his mood Jack smiled and said, 'Get out of here, woman, we're working!'

'Well, thank God I'm not a criminal!' retorted Julie as she left the room, 'I'd be frightened to death by *that* news!'

Jack shook his head in pretend disgust as he opened the large brown envelope, 'Bloody women! Why do they always have to get in the last word?' He scanned quickly through the type-written pages of the report before saying, 'Fair play to Ryan, he was faster than he let on. Unfortunately it's of no use to us at all, save to confirm that it *was* murder and not a heart-attack or something, brought on by the fear and stress of the attack. Massive cranial injuries, sub- and epidural haematomas...Jesus, it's nearly as bad in print as it was in the flesh. That bloody Ryan's a ghoul.' He paused, 'There's a hand-written note here from Ryan; he particularly recommends the contents of the stomach to my attention.' He flipped over the page and read briefly before glancing balefully at Frank, 'It seems you will be delving into the gay scene after all. Apart from a Big Mac, fries and Coke, Akima's stomach contained traces of human semen. Trust Ryan to emphasise the *human*. Not his own, I'm relieved to say. Ingested after the Big Mac and very shortly before his death. Which, I might add, he confirms as being on Monday, somewhere between eleven in the morning and three in the afternoon. The Big Mac would point at early afternoon, I'd say.'

'So you were right about the gay thing,' mused Frank thoughtfully, 'I would say well done but it was just a lucky guess. One of my friends in college was gay; I'll ring him tonight and get a list of likely bars and clubs in the city centre. Not being a native Dub myself I wouldn't know where to start.'

'No,' said Jack dryly, 'Though I'm sure you could give guided tours of the gay scene back home in Carlow. You going to start touring these clubs tonight?'

Frank nodded, though without any great enthusiasm, 'I'll make a start, anyway, though of course it depends on just how many gay places there are. I'll do my best but you know, if he was in a relationship rather than cruising the clubs regularly, we still might not find out anything.'

'And even if we do find a boyfriend it'll probably lead nowhere,' added Jack, 'Unless the boyfriend's a violent psychopath. Still, we can but try.'

'The result matters not, if the quest be worthy/ Of success or failure, only time is the jury.' Frank agreed.

Jack carefully ignored this, saying instead, 'This therapist woman, did you get her phone number?'

'Yes, sir. I took the liberty of ringing her while you were with Mr. Rollins but she wouldn't divulge the girl's address or even number over the phone. She wants to talk to us first, to find out what we want with Grainne Riordan and what we're going to ask her.'

Jack stuck out his lower jaw, 'Bloody cheek! Who the hell does she think she is?'

'She says the girl is still mentally very fragile, and not up to being interrogated. She seemed a very er, *determined* person, sir, and the girl *is* under her care, medically speaking, so I think we'll have to talk to her before conducting an interview.'

'Alright,' said Jack, giving in with bad grace, 'She work in town?'

Frank shook his head, 'She's at home, apparently, on leave.'

'Ring her and make an appointment to see her.'

Frank coughed, 'Er, I already have. We're to call in to her house in Killiney tomorrow at nine am, sir.'

'Oh, is that so?' asked Jack balefully. He brightened suddenly, 'Well then, you can pick me up at a quarter to. My place isn't far from Killiney. You know my address?'

'Yes, sir.'

Jack didn't ask how he had found out; the boy was supposed to be a detective, after all. Instead he said, 'I'm going back up to Rollins to see if I can squeeze a couple of men out of him to knock on doors around Abbey Street and ask if anyone saw anything. You ring the Press Liaison Officer and whip up a statement with him about these two killings. He can release it in my name as soon as it's ready. I know I said I'd deal with the reporters but I just can't face a Press conference today, so let's try and fob them off till tomorrow. You know what I want the statement to say?'

Frank nodded and said, with a half-smile, 'Nothing at all, as far as I can gather. Two deaths, unconnected, and no mention of the "Niggers go home" thing. Or the "Sons of Cuchuailainn", obviously.'

'That's about it,' agreed Jack. 'Violent society we live in, changing face of Ireland, sign of the times, you know the drill. And make it *apparently* unconnected, though a possible racial motive is being considered, along with other theories. It won't hold the Press off for long but even a few days without every half-wit in Ireland copying them, or trying to join them, is a gain.'

'Yes, sir. *Fight the inevitable, hold off the bitter end/ For the moment of Grace, hope still can send.'*

'I like that,' said Jack unexpectedly, 'Hope *is* a state of Grace, isn't it?'

'It can be,' replied Frank, 'If it's realised in the end. Otherwise it only makes eventual disappointment all the more bitter. Dickens put it best in Bleak House when he wrote of "the sickness of hope deferred".'

'Did he, indeed?' said Jack, whose knowledge of Dickens was limited to the name. 'Well, personally I'd rather hope forever than give in to despair, but who am I to argue with Dickens?' Apparently seeing no irony or contradiction in this remarkable statement –in spite of his recent history- he continued, 'Anyway, after you've issued the statement start trawling through the records for assaults on blacks and foreigners over the past few years. Just in Dublin, mind, for the moment. See if you can find some sort of pattern, or a multiple offender or something. You never know your luck. I'll probably go home after I send the uniformed boys out to Abbey Street so I'll just see you in the morning. You can ring Vice and tell them to concentrate on male prostitutes. And don't bloody forget to write everything up in the Murder Book before you go home.'

He stood up and stretched before adding, 'Christ, I forgot the most important thing! You still need to dig up Wistarra's next of kin; I'm sure *he* had a family and they need to know what happened to him ASAP.'

Frank nodded without enthusiasm; this was one area of being a murder detective he was not looking forward to. 'I'll take care of it, sir.'

Jack came around the desk and was halfway out the door before suddenly stopping and giving him an evil grin, 'And...good hunting tonight, lad! Have fun! And if you're not above taking a little advice from one older and more experienced than you; keep your back to the bloody wall! And if you drop anything; leave it on the floor!'

'Yes, sir,' murmured Frank sadly, thinking that comparing his superior with a dinosaur was a little unfair to that unfortunate animal. He shook his head as Jack marched out of the office in rare good humour. He even made as if he was going to goose Julie as he went, with the pretence enough to elicit from that lady a squeal of mock fright, followed by a very real and resounding slap.

Chapter Eight

Next morning it was a tired and red-eyed Frank Carr who picked O'Neill up outside his little house in Glenageary. Jack, while not exactly bright-eyed and bushy-tailed himself, nonetheless managed a malicious grin when he settled into the passenger seat of the little *Ka* and caught sight of Frank's pale face, and the dark shadows under his eyes. As they drove away from the kerb he said casually, 'Morning, Frank. Any luck last night?'

In spite of having had only a couple of hours sleep Frank managed a smile at O'Neill's artless tone, 'Well, I didn't score, if that's what you were getting at. And what's worse, I didn't find anyone who recognised Akima's photograph either. Of course, I mostly questioned bar staff and bouncers and the like, but I also spoke to more gay men than I would have believed existed in the whole of Ireland, much less Dublin. And more than a few lesbians, too. To no avail, I'm afraid. Not one of them recognised our Mr. Akima.' Tired as he was, he managed to come up with, *'The bitterest of all fruit ripens, toil reaping a harvest bare/ the purse remains empty, like a child's hungry stare.'*

Jack was getting used to this sort of thing and simply replied, 'Quite. Well, I suppose it was always a bit of a longshot.'

Frank nodded, concentrating on not scything down a horde of uniformed schoolgirls who had chosen that precise moment to dart across the road in front of him. After a tense pause he said, 'I left a copy of Akima's photo in every bar and club I visited, along with my phone number. You never know, I might have just picked the wrong night; another night half the people there might have recognised him. One guy I got talking to promised to make up a "Do you know this Man" sort of poster and put it up in every gay bar in Dublin. Another long-shot, I know, but sometimes you get lucky.'

'Keep telling yourself that,' muttered O'Neill sourly, repressing a flicker of private amusement; how naive did a copper have to be before he admitted to a colleague that he had left his name and number at half the gay bars in Dublin? Frank was was lucky it was just the two of them; if they were in a fully staffed team the whole of the Garda Siochana would soon hear about it, and the ribbing might never end. However, he let it pass; friendly banter was not really his thing, especially at this time of morning. He stared moodily out the window for several minutes before grumbling, 'I don't know, from television and stuff I got the idea that gays were rampant sexual predators, with all of them shagging each other in an endless merry-go-round of casual partners. Not this guy, though. There's another of my illusions shattered.'

'Well, AIDS is still around,' Frank suggested, 'And although it's no longer a hot topic to the general public I imagine gays still take it pretty seriously.

'And even if we find any of his...ah, conquests,' Jack continued, ignoring him, 'they still might not lead us anywhere. Not if he was targeted at random by a racist group, which will be the focus of our investigation from now on if his personal life doesn't throw up a suspect or two PDQ.'

Frank shrugged, 'At this stage I'd be grateful for any sort of lead. I spoke to Carter yesterday after you left, by the way. You know, the Chief Inspector in charge of Vice? I gave him Akima's photo, for him to circulate amongst Dublin's prossies, but when I rang him first thing this morning we drew another blank. A few of his men showed the photo to all the tarts they came across last night but none of them recognized him. I know it wasn't really on, unless he was bisexual, but I thought we'd better cover every angle, just in case. Anyway, it's just another dead end.'

'Hmm. Still, what would you expect? Prostitutes aren't likely to volunteer information about their clients to Vice Officers, now are they?'

'You'd be surprised, sir,' Frank contradicted him, 'A lot of these girls are actually quite friendly to the police. They hold no grudges about being arrested so often because they look upon it as an occupational hazard, and most of them like to see policemen around their areas in case they get into difficulties. And it's hard to blame them. After all, whores have been targets for psychos and perverts ever since the days of Jack the Ripper. And very likely even before then.'

Jack had never worked vice and had no interest, professional or personal, in prostitutes. So he just grunted, 'No doubt. What about rent-boys? I though I told you switch Vice's attention to them?'

'I thought we'd better check out both,' said Frank, 'but according to Carter there aren't a huge amount of male prostitutes in Dublin anyway. For one thing the gay scene isn't that big and, like you said, many gay men are promiscuous so maybe there's less demand. He rang me late last night to say he'd spoken to the few he knows without success, but he's going to chase down some more tonight. But unlike the girls these boys are *really* uncooperative; they tend to run from the cops and refuse to talk to them if caught, so even if Akima used them we might not discover a thing.'

O'Neill nodded but made no reply, and both men lapsed into a somewhat gloomy silence until they reached Military Road in Killiney. When they turned into the driveway of Kate Bennett's home Jack said, in an envious tone, 'Bloody hell! Nice house!'

Frank contented himself with a non-committal noise as the *Ka* crunched its way up the white gravel driveway but he agreed that it was indeed a nice house. It was a very large, detached red-brick sitting in an even larger, well-groomed garden. It had a great many wide bay windows, and six white stone steps leading up to the black double front door. A house so big would have to contain five or six bedrooms at least, and in this area would undoubtedly be worth at least two million Euros, recession or no.

All of which combined to make Jack whistle softly and remark, 'We're in the wrong bloody business, lad, if shrinks live in houses like that.'

'She's not your average shrink, sir,' Frank put in, 'She's had a successful career as a writer too, and her husband has his own building firm. I know that doesn't mean much nowadays but however he's managed it my enquiries indicate that he's one of the few builders making money right now. Though in point of fact she's a psychologist, not a psychiatrist.'

Jack had simply been acting to type, having in fact little interest in his own material possessions, much less those of others, and he made no reply. In truth they could have been driving into Buckingham Palace and he wouldn't have been truly envious, and he wondered briefly why he felt obliged to say these things to maintain the curmudgeonly character that was settling more firmly upon him with each passing year. A character he didn't particularly like but which he seemed powerless to prevent developing. Perhaps it was the effects of incipient old age and very current loneliness creeping up on him.

They parked the *Ka* in the driveway -which could comfortably have accommodated a couple of dozen more like it- and made their way up to the big, imposing front door. Jack rang the bell and they waited in a suitably impressed silence for an answer. In less than a minute the door swung inwards, opened by a very attractive, medium sized, dark-haired woman who coolly eyed her visitors up and down before saying, in a not terribly welcoming tone, 'You must be the policemen.' She did not say this in a tone which indicated that meeting policemen was one of her greater joys in life but at least she stood aside and added politely, 'Please come in.'

She showed them into a book-lined study and seated them in antique leather chairs before ensconcing herself on the other side of a vast walnut writing-desk almost buried in stacks of paper. She took a deep breath and said, 'You'll excuse the mess, I'm sure. The fact is I work from home, and because I've a lousy memory I'm constantly shuffling back and forth through paperwork looking for a name or a date or something. It makes me appear rather disorganised but...' She paused briefly before continuing, 'Well, the fact is that I *am* rather disorganised. Strange that I feel the need to make excuses for it, particularly in my own home. Surely I'm entitled to be a messy pig if I feel like it? Why should I be embarrassed by something that's none of your business anyway? I wonder what that says about my character?' Her face relaxed into a smile, which suffused her face with so much life and sudden warmth that the eyes of both men widened at the unexpected radiance thus revealed. Still smiling faintly she said, 'Let's start at the beginning. I'm Kate Bennett, and I'm Grainne Riordan's therapist. And friend, I may say. She's still undergoing intensive treatment and is not yet fully well, so before I approve an interview I have to ask you exactly what is it you wish to speak to her about?'

Jack blinked for the first time since setting eyes on her, for once lost for words. The psychologist didn't appear to be more than thirty or so and was extremely attractive, particularly when she smiled. Apart from a great mass of dark hair and full red lips she had a thin, intense but pretty face, and enormous hazel eyes no man would easily forget. Intelligence and determination were written in every line of her face, but there was also a well of emotion in those huge eyes that bespoke either vulnerability or great empathy. All in all she was one of the most intensely *alive* and charismatic people either man had ever met and glowed as if she were actually luminous. And, aside from apparently being able to conduct a conversation all by herself, she was also hugely pregnant, which only increased the rather intimidating first impression she created.

'Er, well,' muttered Jack, abandoning the unfounded hostility he had conceived for her the day before and gathering his thoughts, 'let me explain the reason for our visit. We're investigating a recent murder and your patient's old address cropped up among the dead man's effects. So we don't really want to interview this girl; we just want to ascertain if she knew or had any dealings with the victim, and can tell us anything about him.'

Kate frowned in puzzlement, 'Why?'

This rather stumped Jack so Frank, with a disarming grin, put in, 'Because we have absolutely nothing else to go on at the moment. The home of the victim, Mr. Akima, was as bare as an egg of personal effects, and he doesn't seem to have had any friends or family in this country. None that we can locate, anyway. Your friend Grainne is the only sniff of even an acquaintance that we've found for this guy. So I'm afraid we're rather clutching at straws.'

Kate laughed and leaned back in her chair, placing her hands flat on her distended stomach, 'Well, you're honest at any rate. But I still don't see what you want with Grainne. I mean, she's hardly a suspect in this murder?'

Jack smiled, 'Of course not. It's simply that we haven't been able to find out *anything* about Akima, neither his personal nor his business life. Which, as you can, imagine is seriously impeding our investigation. But if Miss...er, your patient, knew him, she might in turn be able to lead to us to other friends or acquaintances.'

Kate gave him a hard look, 'Or lovers?'

Jack shrugged; he wasn't about to apologise for hoping that the girl knew something about Akima, no matter where it led. Though if the autopsy report was telling the whole story it wasn't likely that this girl had numbered in their ranks. 'Or lovers, yes.'

Kate pursed her lips and said, 'Grainne has had a, shall we say, *checkered* past. As I'm sure you're already aware. She's trying very hard to come to terms with her life, past and present, but she's still quite fragile and I'm not sure raking up any of her previous...*liaisons*, will benefit her.'

Jack's expression hardened, 'Checkered past or not, fragile or not, we're talking about a *murder* enquiry here. In fact it's two murders now, which means that right now your patient's welfare is a very low priority with us. You must be aware that you have no legal right whatsoever to withhold information about this person's whereabouts, and I'm quite prepared to charge you with obstructing the Gardai in the course of their duty if you refuse to divulge her current address.'

Kate's expression also hardened, into obstinacy, and Jack, seeing this, suddenly altered his approach before she could speak. He leaned forward and, giving her a half-smile, said reasonably, 'However, I can sympathise with anyone who has suffered hardship and trauma in their lives, and I can assure you that I'll treat Miss...er, Riordan with the utmost gentleness. Also, we have reason to believe Akima was gay so there's not much chance they were lovers. In all probability she knows nothing whatsoever about this man, and I have no intention of browbeating an innocent girl for information she doesn't possess. If there is a connection it's probably with her father, anyway, and even if she knew Akima it's extremely unlikely she knows anything about his death. I basically just need to know if she ever knew him, and if she can point us towards any mutual friends or business associates. Or, as you say, lovers. But it won't be an interrogation, I promise.'

Kate weakened visibly, this softer approach taking effect where his threats had signally failed. At length she sighed and said, '*If* you talk to her I would have to supervise the interview, with the power to stop it if she becomes in any way distressed. Grainne has had a very difficult life, and even though she's now well on the road to recovery she's still very vulnerable emotionally. If she knew this man in her dark days the pain of a previous, unpleasant association might prove too much of a strain for her new-found wellbeing.'

Jack held up his hands, 'Just a few general questions, all very low-key.'

'*A fair word wins more than any threat,*' said Frank seriously,' *As the sun blooms more flowers than the frost.*'

Jack glared at his assistant for this intercession, while Kate gave him a distracted and slightly suspicious look. But she nonetheless said, 'Very well, I'll allow you a short interview. If you promise you'll immediately stop questioning her on my say so.'

Jack hesitated at the proviso and then shrugged, 'Agreed.'

Kate smiled, her whole face lighting up again as she said sweetly, 'As a matter of fact Grainne is living here with me at the moment. If you'll excuse me for a moment I'll ask her to speak to you.' She hauled herself to her feet and waddled rather than walked out of the room, radiating benevolence.

Jack shook his head in disgust and muttered, 'Bloody woman! I can't believe the girl was here all along!' He glared at Frank and snarled, 'And no more bloody poetry or dodgy quotes from you! Got it?'

'Sorry, sir,' said Frank sheepishly, 'It just sort of slipped out.'

'Well, don't do it again! She probably thinks we're nuttier than the girl!'

At that moment the door opened and Kate returned, leading by the hand the single loveliest girl either man had ever set eyes on. She was tall and slim, with long golden hair and big green eyes that would have been hypnotic save for the apprehension in them as she surveyed the two strangers awaiting her. Her skin was the colour of pale honey, and her sculptured features and full lips left both men suddenly speechless and a little short of breath. The only jarring note in her appearance was the old, baggy, ill-fitting clothes she wore, which ensured that little could be seen of the figure beneath. And, while nothing could detract from the astonishing beauty of her face, this raiment no doubt offered pointers to the current state of her mind.

Frank opened his mouth, possibly to offer some ode of admiration to her beauty but, mindful of his superior's admonition, closed it again with an audible snap. Jack, being old enough to be at least partly immune to the effects of such a vision, cleared his throat and said, though not without an effort, 'Pleased to meet you, Miss Riordan. Er, sorry to disturb you but we have one or two questions we need to ask you.'

Grainne sat on the opposite side of the desk and said, in a deep, slightly husky voice, 'Yes, Kate told me. She said I might have known some man who has just been murdered. Is that correct?'

Jack nodded, 'We found your old home address written on a piece of paper in his apartment, and thought that perhaps he had some connection with either you or your father.'

It might have been imagination but Frank thought he saw her flinch ever so slightly at mention of her father and, to his horror, he only just managed to restrain himself from reaching out and patting one of her slim, pale hands; hands she was wringing together furiously. He also noted that Kate, seated close to her patient, did indeed reach out and clasp one of those elegant members in a comforting grip. If Jack noticed anything he showed no sign of it as he leaned forward and said gently, 'Does the name William Henry Akima mean anything to you?'

After thinking for several moments Grainne shook her head blankly, her huge, liquid eyes far away but showing no signs of recognition. Jack recoiled in disappointment, though in truth he had already resigned himself to failure. It was all on a par with the rest of the investigation and he bit his lip in frustration; Akima might as well have been the invisible man for all the impact he had made in life. It just wasn't possible, for God's sake! A man *couldn't* move through life without impinging on any one else at all. What was he, a ghost?

'I'm sorry,' Grainne said softly, 'I don't recognise the name at all.'

Jack sighed, defeated, but Frank here offered the girl one of his photos of Akima and said, 'He was a medium-sized, powerfully built black man of forty years of age. From South Africa? Owned an apartment in Phibsboro?'

As she stared at the photograph Grainne's face was still blank but suddenly her eyes opened wide and her mouth fell open in shock. Her lower jaw worked soundlessly for several seconds and then she gasped, 'Willie! Willie-boy!'

The two policemen exchanged hopeful glances and then Jack, suddenly purposeful again, said sharply, and with burgeoning hope, 'You knew him.' It was not a question but he was nonetheless demanding an answer.

Grainne's eyes were *enormous* and awash with unshed tears as she stared blankly into her past. And she said softly, in a remote voice, 'Willie... I... I remember...' Her face suddenly went blank and smooth, and although floods of tears spilled down her cheeks her expression was curiously unemotional and her great eyes were blindly staring inward.

'Right, gentlemen,' said Kate crisply, hauling herself to her feet with an audible grunt of effort, 'End of interview.' She put her arm around Grainne's heaving shoulders and said with irritation, 'This is precisely the sort of reaction I feared. And warned you about. I'm afraid you'll have to leave. Now.'

Frank automatically rose to his feet, horrified by the girl's collapse, but Jack glared at the psychologist and said coldly, 'It's obvious that she knew this man and I'm afraid that changes everything. She could have vital information about Akima and we need to learn whatever she knows. *Now.*'

Kate's lips thinned in anger and her hazel eyes were hard and sparking fire as she snapped, 'No, not *now*. Can't you see the poor girl is in no fit state to be questioned? Apart from the fact that you have no warrant or court order you promised to leave on my say so and I'm holding you to your word. Kindly leave my house this instant.'

Jack, spitting mad but bound by his word, slowly and reluctantly got to his feet, 'Very well, but we *will* be back. With a warrant if necessary.'

'Bring anything you please,' replied Kate coolly, 'Grainne is a mental patient in my professional care, and my treatment of her supersedes your investigation. *Legally.*'

As neither of them was sure whether or not this was actually true the two policemen left the house in reluctant irritation, shepherded out the door by an equally angry Kate. Jack stamped away down the path but Frank paused on the doorstep and quietly said something to the psychologist. She shook her head angrily but he persisted, talking low and persuasively for a minute or so. After a moment's hesitation she finally gave a curt nod and closed the door with a bang, leaving Frank to belatedly follow his superior to the car, a half-smile on his face.

When he climbed in beside him Jack, breathing fire and fury, said angrily, 'She *knows* him! She knows *something,* otherwise why would she get so upset? And that bloody woman...' Words failed him and he tailed off for a moment before saying grimly, 'She's the only lead we have, and we're going to find out what she knows if it kills her! And us! And her bloody psychologist!' He glared suddenly at his assistant, 'What the hell are you looking so smug about?'

Frank slammed the car door and said cheerfully, 'Well, we finally got a break, for one thing; we've found someone who actually knew Akima. And for another, the good doctor just agreed to let me talk to Grainne again tomorrow. If she's recovered from her upset, of course.'

Jack blinked in surprise, 'How the hell did you get her to agree to that?'

Frank grinned, 'I only had to ask nicely. And, er, promise not to bring you along.' And with that he started the engine, trying not to giggle.

'Most amusing,' growled Jack, jerking angrily at his seatbelt. He clicked it into place and sat in silence for several seconds, reluctantly putting the girl and whatever she knew to one side for the moment as he pondering their next move. After Frank had pulled out of the driveway onto the main road he said, 'I don't suppose you have that set of keys they found on Daniel Wistana's body with you? No? Pity. Right then, we'll swing by the office to collect them and then go take a look at his apartment. And we'll go in silence, if you don't mind. I've had just about enough of your yap for one morning.'

Pearse Street was always one of the less salubrious streets in Dublin, and Winter Gardens was one of its least attractive components, although during the housing bubble an influx of city workers disinclined to commute, and willing to buy, had raised the general tone of the area a touch. Gaudy modern apartment blocks rested cheek-by-jowl with seedy old tenements in an uneasy marriage that benefited only the local burglars, of whom there was no lack. When they arrived at Wistarra's address both policemen pursed their lips and exchanged knowing looks; the cheap, tatty apartment block, the graffiti-ridden walls and filthy street outside; the whole seedy, run-down atmosphere reeked to them of crime and criminals. Yet this did not colour their opinion of the dead youth adversely, knowing as they did that with Dublin's chronic housing shortage many immigrants had of necessity to live in areas few Irish people would care to even walk through, much less reside in.

Frank was careful to lock his car after they got out, which made Jack grunt, 'I wouldn't bother if I were you. If the little bastards around here want a car, they take it, locked or not. And your alarm's not much use either; it only takes them a few seconds to make off with a motor these days. Right little professionals, these kids.' He jerked his thumb over his shoulder, 'Though I can't see anyone bothering to steal *that* thing.'

Stung by this jibe against his pride and joy, Frank gave him a sidelong look and said innocently, 'I suppose a touch of the cat o' nine tails would be the way to treat them, eh, sir?'

Jack snorted in amusement; in spite of everything he wasn't quite Victor Meldrew, thank you very much. Not yet anyway. 'You won't wind me up that easily, lad! I'm wise to you! Though I have to say I wouldn't object to flogging the little bastards. Joy riders my arse! It's little joy they bring to the world.'

Frank laughed, shaking his head in mock-despair, and the two men walked up the steps and into the apartment block together in near perfect accord. Both were a touch eccentric, in their own way, but although polar opposites in almost everything both were finding that working together was surprisingly easy, and even enjoyable.

Daniel Wistarra had lived on the ground floor, for which Jack uttered a silent prayer of thanks when he saw the "Out of Order" sign on the lift; climbing a few flights of stairs would not have markedly improved his mood. Although the call to immigration the day before had indicated that he had no family Frank rang the doorbell long and hard before finally using the keys to gain entry, feeling disquietingly like an intruder as he did so. Inside the flat was dark and dim and musty, and devoid of occupants. It even *felt* dead, as if affected by the decease of its occupant. It also contrasted wildly from William Akima's home. Instead of neatness and bare sterility the younger man's home was a messy jumble of mixed possessions and dirt, with piled CD's and magazines jostling for space with discarded clothes and old pizza boxes, overflowing ashtrays, and empty coke cans.

O'Neill looked around with distaste and muttered, 'What a dump! Didn't he ever clean up in here?' He shook his head, 'Teenagers don't differ that much, do they? Background and culture notwithstanding. None of the buggers will clean up after themselves.'

"He never will now, either.' replied Frank quietly, a sombre expression on his face, refraining from pointing out that Wistarra had in fact turned twenty, though not long before.

The two men moved quickly through the apartment, sorting the rubbish from personal effects and piling anything that might prove useful onto a newspaper that Frank spread out on the grubby coffee table. Unlike Akima, Daniel Wistarra had hundreds of photographs and letters scattered all around, although most of the letters were of an official nature and were from the departments of Immigration and of Social Welfare. And the more personal correspondence was exclusively addressed from Africa, which would hardly help them in their search for suspects. When they had gathered everything that might prove useful the two men sat on the grubby old sofa and began sifting through it, partly searching for clues and partly trying to garner an impression of the dead man from his possessions. For they had already half marked down his killing in their minds as a random act, brought about by bad luck. He had simply been in the wrong place at the wrong time, and no clues to his killers' identities were likely to be found here. However, it wasn't in the nature of either man to be anything less than thorough and they proceeded with a painstaking search.

At last O'Neill sat back and said, 'Apart from the fact that he liked pop music and fashion magazines there really isn't much here. Nothing that will help us, anyway.'

Frank sighed in frustration, 'No, sir. Just a lot of meaningless clutter. Life dandruff. And there are actually *too* many photos for them to be of any practical use. Can all these people have been friends and family, do you think?'

'It doesn't seem possible, does it? Maybe he was interested in photography or something. We'll have to talk to his social worker to find out what sort of a lad he was. Strange that there's a million photos but no camera.'

'Maybe he had it on him when he was murdered, and the killers took it,' offered Frank.

'Hmm,' grunted Jack, to whom this had already occurred, 'See any sign he was working?'

Frank shook his head, 'He seems to have been getting some sort of Assistance payments, and a weekly "Socialising Grant". Whatever that is. No sign of a work permit or residency papers or anything like that. There are a lot of photos of this white family, sir. More of them than anyone else. I assume they're the foster family, the Mulallys.'

Jack shot him an angry look, 'What bloody foster family?'

'Er, sorry, I forgot to tell you this morning. Yesterday you told me to try and trace his next of kin? Well, I found out that he was an orphan when he got here as a ten-year-old, and was fostered to a family in Ranelagh. He only moved in here a year or so ago. Sorry, sir, I should have told you. They were informed of his death last night by a Ban Garda team trained in trauma management.'

Jack grunted noncommittally, feeling a touch of relief that someone had carried out the dirty work for him, mixed with guilt over same; dealing with grieving relatives was one of the worst aspects of the job. Mind you, they were going to have to interview the family anyway, and sooner rather than later, but there was nothing worse than seeing people's faces at the moment they heard they had lost a loved one. Aloud he only said, 'Any sign of Akima in any of those photos?'

Frank looked up in surprise, 'No, sir. You don't think they knew each other, surely?'

Jack shrugged, 'Probably not but it's possible, isn't it? There aren't *that* many Africans in Dublin, are there? Though I suppose it would be pushing coincidence too far if they knew each other, assuming that they were just killed at random by some bunch of nutters. Especially if Wistarra came here when he was only ten.'

Frank pursed his lips, 'When we went to Akima's place your first impression was that it was a cold-blooded, premeditated job, not the work of thugs or random loonies at all.'

Jack grimaced at the memory, 'Don't remind me. Ryan enjoyed throwing that back in my face yesterday, didn't he?' He shrugged, 'And even if they were professional muscle there's no law to say they weren't hired by neo-Nazis. The only reason I'm not keen on working the racist angle is that it'll be like looking for a needle in a haystack. A haystack we can't bloody well find.' He looked around disinterestedly, 'Come on, we might as well go. There's nothing else for us here. We'll talk to his social worker, and perhaps the foster family, and I suppose we'd better try that club or whatever it is that Akima's gardener told us about. What was it called?'

'The African People's Support Group,' said Frank absently.

'Right.' Jack paused, 'What about the search I asked you to do yesterday? For thugs with a habit of attacking immigrants? Did you get around to it?'

Frank nodded, 'I found a few repeat offenders but I'm not sure if any of them are going to be any use to us. Three are in prison for their racist attacks, one has now left Dublin for London, and another is dead, stabbed in the throat by a crony during a drinking binge.'

'Nice,' observed Jack sourly, and with no great sympathy, 'though there seems to be a stabbing or shooting in Dublin every day now so I suppose shouldn't really be surprised.'

'That leaves three names,' continued Frank, 'none of whom seem the type to found a neo-Nazi organisation, to be honest. Drunken fist fights are more their mark. Still, they could be foot soldiers for someone with a brain so I brought their names and addresses with me if you want to check them out.'

'Later. We'd better talk to young Daniel's social worker first.'

'We should check up on those anti-immigrant groups, too.' said Frank, half apologetically.

O'Neill stood up and stretched, 'We will, laddie. We'll turn over every stone, for all the good it'll do. A case like this was always going to be a nightmare. Where there's no motive there are no suspects, and with no motive there's nowhere to start the investigation. I bloody well hate random killings!'

Frank got to his feet too, and said optimistically, 'Oh, I don't know, sir. It's a bit early for despair. *When the way is dark and clouded, with nothing as it seems/ The patient seeker's rewarded, with fulfilment of his dreams.*'

Jack turned away with a sigh, 'God help me!' And then, with a shake of his head, for the first time in years he said to a colleague, 'I need a bloody drink!'

Chapter Nine

When they reached the pavement outside Daniel Wistarra's flat Jack stopped and said, 'Look, we'd better split up for the rest of the day if we want to get anywhere. We have to interview some of these anti-immigrant people but we should also talk to Social Welfare Services about our young friend; find out what sort of lad he was, make lists of his friends and acquaintances, that sort of thing. As an orphan he must have had a Social Worker, at least till he hit eighteen.'

'Yes, sir,' Frank agreed before hesitating, 'But, ah, if we're agreed that these are random killings by racists, is there really any point? I mean, how will investigating Wistarra's background help us catch a gang who basically target strangers on the basis of colour alone? You said yourself that you thought Wistarra was just in the wrong place at the wrong time, which is why these "Sons of Cuchuailainn" guys used their fists and feet on him. Wasn't that your point; that if he was a specific target they would have brought weapons with them?'

Jack shrugged, 'Yes, but they had a spray-can of scarlet paint with them, didn't they? So they planned to attack *someone*. And he wasn't big-built like Akima, he was only a skinny lad; maybe they knew they didn't need weapons to deal with him. Or maybe they didn't know where he lived and knew they'd have to attack him in public. They wouldn't want to carry weapons around in full public view, now would they? Anyway, random or premeditated, I just *want* you to talk to the Social Welfare people about Wistarra, okay? Humour me. I like to cross every "t" and dot every "i". You can never have too much information, and you never know until afterwards what trivial little fact will lead you to the killer, so let's find out everything we can about this guy.'

'Okay,' agreed Frank, unconvinced but swallowing any further reservations he might have had, 'I take it in the meantime you'll be talking to the anti-immigrant brigade?'

Jack nodded, 'They're our best lead to unearth a secret racist group, no question, and I'd prefer to tackle them myself. That's a job for someone with experience, if you don't mind me saying so. Give me that list of names you have, of people convicted of racist attacks. What do you think the chances are of someone on it being a member of one of these anti-immigrant groups?'

Frank smiled as he handed it over, 'I don't think we're that lucky, sir, do you?'

'We haven't been so far.' Jack checked his watch, 'It's not far from lunchtime now but I suppose we'd better keep at it. We can meet up at the office later.' It occurred to him that his days of knocking off at one seemed to be over and this thought very nearly made him smile; whatever he might have tried to make himself believe, this was better. He shook himself and continued, 'I don't know how long it'll take to talk to these people so we won't set a time. I'll just see you when I see you.'

Frank produced one of his cards like a conjuror pulling a rabbit from a hat, 'Here, in case you want to get in touch with me. My home number's there as well as the mobile, by the way, in case you ever need me at night.'

Jack, not mentioning that he himself was possibly the only man on earth not to possess a mobile phone, stuffed the card into his pocket without looking at it and said, with a grin, 'I'm not Julie, you know, I rarely awake in the night needing the services of a big strong man! Anyway, just make sure you find out everything there is to know about Wistarra while I see if

I can track down Ireland's answer to Adolf Hitler, God help us all.' He rummaged through his pockets until he found the short list Mangan had given him and added, 'The first of these mobs has an office near Mespil Road. How about a lift in the crapmobile?'

The headquarters of the Concerned Citizens Against Immigration was a suite of offices within an old converted house, and when Frank dropped him off outside the big, rather shabby Georgian building Jack gave it a long, considering look before climbing the steps to the front door; not unlike himself, the old building was fraying at the edges and had seen better days, but he still thought it deserved better than this. The front door stood ajar so he marched inside, surveying the rather dusty vestibule with interest. Black and white marble floor tiles, oak-panelled walls and high moulded ceilings were all very fine in their way - though in this case these articles were tatty with age and neglect- but they certainly didn't speak to him of Nazism. He would have expected something darker and more gothic, perhaps with a more martial feel.

There was more than one tenant occupying the building, but the ground floor was solely given over to the CCAI, as a small wooden plaque on the nearest door testified. In fact, it also bore the legend 'Head Office', which surprised Jack; did that mean there were other, regional branches too? Hatred between orange and green was endemic in Ireland, it seemed, but was prejudice and bigotry against *foreigners* so widespread that they needed subsidiary offices? He doubted it but it was a nice touch, and more than made up for the lack of military regalia; maybe someone here suffered from delusions of grandeur after all. Idly reflecting that there was nothing you don't see eventually, if you only live long enough, he banged loudly on the door. When this produced no response within three seconds or so he tried the handle, throwing the door open and marching in.

The inner office had been painted recently and seemed surprisingly modern for such a faded old edifice, though the high ceiling and ornate plasterwork gave the room a touch of old-world style and elegance no modern office could boast. There were no less than six large desks crammed into the middle of the room -and God knew how many filing cabinets- and at four of these desks sat men looking at him with expressions of surprise and mistrust. The other two desks contained women, with expressions even more severe and accusatory than those of their male counterparts.

No one spoke so O'Neill jerked a thumb over his shoulder and said gruffly, 'I knocked but no one answered. I'm Detective Chief Inspector O'Neill, Metropolitan Division. Exactly who is in charge here?'

Hasty looks were exchanged, with more than one glance being directed at another door at the back of the room, before one of the women said pleasantly, 'I'm Moira Breen, Inspector, the office manager. What can we do for you?'

'*Chief* Inspector,' said O'Neill coldly, and pointedly, 'You're the head of this organisation, are you, Madam?'

'Well, no, not exactly; I just run the office. I'm in charge of admin. What is it that you want?'

'To *speak* to whoever is in *charge,*' replied O'Neill, enunciating each word distinctly and with an edge to his tone, 'Am I not making myself clear?'

More glances were exchanged before Breen said cautiously, 'Our Chairman, and spokesperson, is Cecil Dalton.'

'Good, I'll speak to him, then,' said Jack, giving her a smile as bright and artificial as the bunch of plastic daffodils on her desk. He couldn't believe these people; all that was missing was a sign saying "You don't have to be a Nazi to work here, but it helps". Jack's smile became genuine; or maybe a mug printed with the legend, "World's Greatest Dictator".

More glances. Then, diffidently, 'Er, if I might ask, what did you want to speak to Cecil about?'

'I'll tell *him* when I see him,' rejoined Jack, beginning to feel irritated and allowing it to enter his voice, 'Which will be round about *now,* thank you.'

Breen got to her feet, 'I'll just see if he's available at the moment.' And she slipped through the door at the back of the office, closing it carefully behind her.

Jack sighed loudly, already bored and angry and developing an even more marked dislike for these people than he had anticipated. She returned in less than a minute, pushing the door to the inner sanctum wide and saying, with a rather strained smile, 'Please come this way, Inspector.'

Jack, not deigning to correct her this time, swept past her contemptuously, one lip curled in unconcealed disdain and anger bubbling up inside him. The lair of the great panjandrum himself was considerably smaller than the main office, and contained nothing beyond a large, battered old desk and several of the ubiquitous steel filing cabinets. It also contained Cecil Roderick Dalton, possibly the most nondescript human being the detective had ever set eyes on. Of average height, average build, and with an average, nondescript face, Dalton was the most instantly forgettable person Jack had ever met. From his mousy hair through the neat gray suit and down to the worn but still good black shoes, Dalton was a police photofit artist's worst nightmare, whose only distinguishing feature was a pair of gold-rimmed glasses. One thing he was not, Jack instantly decided, was a killer. At least, not of the violent type; Jack could see him slipping rat poison into his wife's cocoa but not beating a man to death with a baseball bat. Always supposing, that is a woman could be found who was charitable enough to marry such an object. On the other hand Himmler had been an equally unimpressive specimen, and muscle was not hard to hire, so he could yet be a killer by proxy.

Dalton was on his feet, one hand extended in greeting and a rather nervous smile on his thin face. 'O'Neill, was it? Please come in and sit down, Inspector, and tell me what we can do for you.'

Jack rather reluctantly gave the outstretched hand the briefest of touches and took a seat with a sigh, 'I worked very hard for my promotions, Mr. Dalton, but it seems the fair Moira doesn't think I deserve them. At any rate she keeps taking away my last one.'

The little smile remained in place but Dalton looked a touch bemused as he said, 'Sorry? I'm afraid I don't follow you.'

'It's *Chief* Inspector,' said Jack wearily, 'Not that it's important. I'm here on a sort of fact-finding mission, to find out more about your organisation. Part official business, you understand, but also part private curiosity. Who knows, I might even want to join up?'

He had decided on this ambiguous approach on the spur of the moment and it paid immediate dividends as Dalton promptly replied, 'Good! I'm glad to hear it!' He rubbed his hands together enthusiastically and continued, 'We've had more than our fair share of negative publicity so I'm only too pleased to have the chance to set the record straight. First of all, and contrary to what you might have heard in the media, we are *not* fascists.'

Jack had never heard of them prior to his chat with Mangan, and doubted if anyone else in Dublin had either, but he was willing to play along with Dalton's overblown sense of self-importance if it kept him talking, so he offered him an encouraging, 'Really?'

'Oh, indeed,' said Dalton, nodding vigorously, 'We are, it's true, opposed to wholesale immigration into our country by undesirable elements, but to hear the mud that's been slung at us you'd think we were trying to establish the fourth Reich.'

Jack nodded and drummed his fingers on the desk in front of him, starting to feel sick of the jumped-up little toad already, 'So if you're not Nazi's, what are you?'

'Exactly what our name says we are,' responded Dalton instantly, 'We're concerned citizens, people who care about the future of this country. The culture of the Celtic Tiger spawned a generation that cares only about money and material possessions, and nothing about their culture and traditions, their heritage and their race. Yet in spite of their obsession with material things this new generation fail to grasp a few simple economic realities.'

'Such as?'

Dalton made an impatient gesture, 'It's obvious, isn't it? The good times are over and a long, bleak winter has arrived. Over the coming years it's going to be a struggle to look after our own poor, our own disadvantaged, let alone the hordes of foreign freeloaders clogging up our social welfare system. And not just the poor; half of the ordinary working people in the country are in dire financial straits, losing their jobs and even their homes. Add to that vast swarms of migrants to care for, the majority of whom have no training, no education and no skills, and we have a huge problem for the future. That's a *fact*. A few of these people are genuine asylum seekers but most are just opportunists, looking for a soft tit to suck on, and they offer no benefits of any sort to this country. They come here and demand homes, food, money and education for their swarms of children, and every cent of the millions being spent on them is money *not* being spent on needy Irish people. The simple truth is that Ireland cannot afford to carry these freeloaders. Not with the Celtic Tiger dead and buried.'

Jack was tempted to ask if Dalton had only founded his group after the recession had begun or earlier, after immigration had first started, when immigrants were actively needed to fill vacant jobs but were still not always welcome. But he managed to hold his tongue. He was still trying to appear neutral and in any case he already knew the answer; people like Dalton would object to foreign immigration even if everyone in the country were a millionaire. But he contented himself with saying mildly, 'Oh, come on, things are bad, yes, but surely a few thousand refugees won't break us, no matter how many kids they have!'

With pursed lips Dalton coldly said, 'What about a million? There are already at least a half-a-million Poles alone here. At *least*, and probably more. And that's just Poles! There are another quarter of a million foreigners of other nationalities in Ireland at this minute, and a total of a million foreigners on these shores is only a year or two away! It was bad enough when the building trade was booming and there were jobs for many of them, but what about now that the building trade is in recession? These Eastern Europeans will work for far lower wages than Irish tradesmen, and I needn't mention how money grubbing all businessmen are. If it comes to a choice between hiring some Polack on minimum wage and an Irishman on twice as much, who's going to end up on the dole? While half the Polack's wages get sent out of the country? The dole queues are long enough but because of the foreigners living here tens of thousands of *extra* Irish men and women will end up unemployed. And this, apart from ruining our economy and social structure, can only lead to tension, resentment, and eventually open confrontation and hatred. Which may well lead to violence.'

Having finished this declamation Dalton glared at Jack, daring him to contradict. Jack shrugged, 'With the economy going down the toilet maybe the influx will dry up.'

Dalton smiled at him for the first time, though still with an intense look in his eyes; the look of a man flogging his hobby-horse. 'That's certainly the hope, Chief Inspector,' he replied, finally promoting Jack to his proper rank, 'but what about the swarms already here? We need to send them back where they came from to save not just our economy but our entire society. For we're not just paying a financial price. As a policeman you must have noticed the *explosion* in criminal activities since wholesale immigration started; would you care to see crime figures concerning ethnic minorities in Britain, France and America? Among the children of immigrants? Aside from the racial tension and disharmony, I assure you that every country in the world with a significant immigrant population suffers terribly at their hands, crime-wise.'

'No, I would not like to see your statistics!' said Jack emphatically. He was tempted to ask Dalton where the *thousands* of native heroin junkies in Dublin alone fitted into the crime figures but he refrained, still bearing a faint hope of gleaning something useful from the man. He was feeling a little glassy-eyed and punch-drunk from the tirade washing over him, but still retained enough will to live to try and direct the conversation by asking, 'But what about those who are here already? What should be done about them?'

'Make a one-off payment to each and every one of them to go back where they came from!' replied Dalton promptly, 'It was Leo Varadkar's idea in the first place and he should be the first one deported, bloody Polack like him.'

'But what about those who still won't go?' Jack persevered.

'Cut off their dole,' said Dalton, who had evidently given the matter considerable thought, 'No more education or healthcare, and no houses either. They'd take the payment then, quick enough.'

'Not those who have jobs, and privately rented accommodation,' persisted Jack with unwonted patience, 'How do we deal with them?'

Dalton snorted, 'Force the employers to sack them! Laws can be passed to give Irish people priority in the workplace, which they should have anyway, and *would* have if employers weren't so short-sighted and greedy. I'm afraid we'll never get rid of them all but' -he sniffed audibly- 'I suppose every dog must carry its share of fleas.'

'So you wouldn't be in favour of more, shall we say, *direct* methods?' suggested Jack delicately.

Dalton's face darkened. 'You're just as bad as all the others!' he accused bitterly, his lips tightening into a thin white line, 'You're only pretending to be interested in our views! In fact you think we're some sort of Nazi's too! Don't bother denying it; it's true!'

Jack hadn't intended to deny it, as it happened, but with a mental roll of the eyes he decided to tough it out and said soothingly, 'No, of course I don't think anything of the sort. I have to say you've presently your case lucidly and logically, and in truth you've impressed me quite a lot. It simply occurred to me that there must be others of similar sympathies, but less forbearance. Others who, perhaps, might let their feelings get the better of them and turn to less democratic, less peaceful ways of discouraging immigration. And, as you said, *forcing* those already here to go back where they came from.'

Dalton shrugged and said with bad grace, 'Of course there are people like that. Look in just about any pub in Ireland at closing time and you'll find some, I should think.'

'Yes,' persevered Jack patiently, 'but are there people in your organisation who favour a more aggressive approach?'

Dalton frowned and his lips thinned, 'No, there are not! How many times must I say it? We, and myself especially, are totally opposed to any sort of violence! *Totally!*'

Even a cynic like Jack could not doubt the sincerity in Dalton's voice, and he sighed as he saw another of his slender leads petering out. He perked up again, however, as Dalton continued unwillingly, 'There were one or two such, in the beginning, but I can assure you that we weeded them out pretty swiftly.'

'Oh? And can you give me their names?' asked Jack, fishing for a pen and notebook.

Dalton frowned, 'I see no necessity for that. You have no warrant and our membership is, of course, confidential. In fact, I think I should have been asking you some questions, Chief Inspector, like what it is you actually want here?' Although Dalton was far from quick on the uptake, even as he asked the question the penny finally dropped, along with his jaw. 'Those two blacks that have been murdered!' he said incredulously, 'You're looking for their killers and you think... You're looking here! You think...' Words failed him and he subsided into an angry, disbelieving silence.

'I can get a warrant,' said Jack coldly, gladly abandoning appeasement in favor of intimidation, 'but do you really want us poking through all your files? These murders are going to generate a lot of publicity, you know; do you want it broadcast that the Gardai raided your headquarters, looking for the killers? Maybe brought the whole lot of you in for questioning? I can't see that doing much for your credibility, or your recruitment figures.'

'I told you we aren't some sort of fascist organisation, and we don't seek recruits, but political support,' retorted Dalton acidly.

Jack waved a hand in silent dismissal of the distinction and after a pause Dalton finally nodded and turned to one of his filing cabinets, 'Very well, I won't have it publicly said that we refused to co-operate with the police. And, if I'm honest, I'd rather not have you back here. With or without a search warrant. Hmm, let's see; there was a chap called Michael Halloran, for a start. I have his address here somewhere. And a friend of his, a guy called Francis' —he paused while rummaging through a file- 'ah, yes, Francis Connarton. Both men had to be expelled from the CCAI quite early on.'

'And why was that?' asked Jack, writing the names in his notebook and noting that neither were on the list of convicts that Frank had given him.

Dalton gave him a cold look, 'Because they were racists.'

Jack's mouth dropped open in astonishment, 'You have got to be bloody joking!'

'I'd never joke about such a serious issue!' the little man snapped angrily.

Jack had no trouble believing that; Dalton struck him as the type who had never told a joke in his life, and in fact wouldn't recognise one if it bit him on the arse. But even so this was just a little too much. He waved his hand, indicating the offices, 'And all this, Mr. Dalton; what's it all about if you're not a racist yourself?'

The little man bridled instantly, 'I am opposed to the vast swarm of immigrants currently infesting this country and straining its limited resources! And to them polluting our heritage, and culture and society! Where those immigrants come from and what their colour, race or creed is, is a matter of complete indifference to me! White freeloaders are just as unwelcome as black ones in my book! And indeed white workers taking jobs from Irish people are even *more* unwelcome than freeloaders in these straitened times!'

Once again Jack believed him, paradoxical though his words seemed, and suddenly he felt old and worn out. Great harm was done to humanity by evil men, of course, but no more than was done by well-meaning little tits like this, who honestly saw no wrong in their actions and who genuinely believed they served a just cause. And Jack suddenly thought he had an insight into how Nazism had arisen in Germany in the first place, and for a split second he wondered how many other civilised peoples would have succumbed in precisely the same fashion the Germans had, if subjected to the same pressures. He shook his head in silent sorrow for all humanity before saying, 'I'm going to need a full list of all your members and ex-members. Names and addresses.'

Dalton opened his mouth to automatically protest but Jack forestalled him with a raised hand, 'If you prefer I can get a court order. Given the current sensitivity of the issue, and the headlines in the papers, I don't think any judge is going to protest too much, do you?'

Dalton thought better of arguing and, lips pursed, said judiciously, 'Okay, but it could take some time. I'm afraid most of our records are on paper rather than on computer. We'll have to go through them all by hand.'

Jack's lip curled, 'You can't have *that* many members! Make a list. Tonight. Someone will be in touch tomorrow to collect it.' He got to his feet wearily and said mechanically, 'Thank you for your time, Mr. Dalton, you've been very helpful.'

'Glad to be of help,' responded Dalton in an equally wooden and unconvincing tone, sounding anything but, 'I'm happy to do anything that might repair the damage that adverse publicity has done to this movement, and to our cause.'

Jack thought that Ireland had suffered enough from causes over the years and needed no new ones but he just nodded without replying and was about to exit the room when a thought struck him. He searched his pockets for the paper Mangan had given him and said, 'What do you know about the… hang on, the Ireland First Party?'

Dalton hesitated before saying sourly, 'They might be more the kind of people you're after, Inspector.'

Jack ignored his latest demotion and said interestedly, 'Oh yes? And why's that?'

Dalton continued reluctantly, the words seeming to soil his mouth, '*Superficially* they appear to share our aims and beliefs, but I'm afraid they are very different people to us. A very different type -and class- of person. And I fear violence might not be beyond some of them. As a matter of fact, the Ireland First Party was founded by Halloran and Connarton after we expelled them for their rather extreme views.'

Jack nodded in satisfaction, 'Well, we'll just have to have a chat with them too, won't we? See if they can be of any help.' He paused in the doorway before suddenly turning back and saying, loudly enough for those in the outer office to hear, 'And by the way; I'm a bloody *Chief Inspector* you bitter, jumped up little racist twerp! Join you lot? I'd rather cut off my own genitals than have anything to do with you and your band of petty-minded little bigots!' And with that he stamped out of the office, taking care to slam the door loudly behind him.

God Almighty, what an unmitigated little swine! After listening to him Jack felt as if his mind had been sullied, as if he needed a shower for his brain. He marched down the steps onto the street below thinking; *swine, yes; murderer, no.* No one knew better than Jack that murderers came in all types, shapes and sizes, but even so he would bet his pension on Dalton being sincere in his opposition to violence. Though he had met murderers who had sounded just as believable on first acquaintance. Jack sighed and fumbled for the flask in his coat pocket, suddenly depressed; aside from not being much further on with his investigation, if ever he needed a drink to wash the bad taste of life out of his mouth he needed one now. Dalton and his ilk revolted him, and indeed seemed to him more foreign to the Irish ethos and spirit than any immigrant could ever be. *Cead Mile Failte, my arse!*

Chapter Ten

After dropping Jack off in Mespil Road Frank had driven back to Daniel Wistarra's local Social Welfare office, which was actually on Pearse Street itself, only a few hundred yards from where the unfortunate youth had lived. Parking was not an option so close to the city centre so Frank simply pulled up on the double yellow lines outside the Welfare Office, knowing that he could get a ticket waived if need be; the real problem would be if he were clamped. With a silent prayer to the god of motorists -a notoriously unreliable deity- Frank locked his Ka and hurried into the new, yellow-brick office block, resolving to bring a blue bubble-light with him in future; set on the dashboard it might deter even Dublin's famously rapacious and unsympathetic clampers.

When he entered the Social Welfare building the sight of several hundred applicants, predominately African couples bobbing about in what appeared to be an absolute ocean of children, crowded into the inadequate waiting room and adjacent corridors gave him momentary pause, but Frank was made of stern stuff and refused to be discouraged. After a minor struggle to get through the throng he presented himself at the front desk and, with his most charming smile, requested an immediate interview with Peter Lawlor, whom the letters found in the flat named as Daniel Wistarra's Social Welfare Officer. On hearing his request a strange expression crawled across the receptionist's face, as if she was unsure whether to laugh or cry. Or possibly scream. With a despairing gesture towards the crowded waiting room and corridor she warned him he was in for a long wait.

Frank, who had not yet learned the ancient police art of throwing his official weight at minor functionaries, hinted feebly at his official status and the importance of his errand, but the receptionist, soured by years of dealing with a demanding and ungrateful public, was unimpressed: she had quickly taken his measure and was not to be bullied by such a tyro. With a sigh he took a seat and resigned himself to the inevitable, vowing to in future make himself more demanding and less diffident.

As it happened the receptionist -perhaps not wholly immune to Frank's good looks and better manners- managed to squeeze him in after a very minor wait of only an hour and a half. Which was, as she took pains to inform him, not just a huge personal favour but very nearly a miracle.

When Frank -after checking for the fiftieth time to make sure the Ka had not being clamped or towed- was finally ushered into the tiny inner office a tired and harassed-looking man of perhaps thirty-five stood up to welcome him with a handshake and a brusque but not hostile salutation of, 'Can we make this as brief as possible, please? I've got a lot of irate and needy people waiting to see me.'

'And I've got a *murderer* to catch,' rejoined Frank sharply, sitting down without waiting for an invitation; the long wait had left him in just the right mood to deal with bureaucrats. 'And I really don't think a few minutes of your time is too much to ask for if it helps to catch a killer before he takes another innocent life. Do you?' He glanced around with distaste; the office, though new like the building itself, was pokey and dusty, and crammed to the ceiling with thick files. It was also windowless and painted a particularly vile shade of institution green. He gave an inward shudder and thought; *Thank God I don't work here.*

Lawlor made a face as he sat back down, 'I appreciate that, Mr. Carr, which is why I'm seeing you at all today. But my work is important too, so I'm simply asking that we make this as brief as possible.'

Frank was immensely proud of being a detective but let the "Mr." go and nodded, 'Fine.' He took a notebook and pen from his inside pocket and said, 'I want you to tell me everything you know about a young African immigrant named Daniel Wistarra,'

'Wistarra, Wistarra,' muttered Lawlor, a faraway look in his eyes, 'Yes, I know Daniel quite well.' He scooped up a file seemingly at random from a vast pile heaped on the unbelievably crowded desk. 'There we are. Daniel Wistarra, Winter Gardens.' He glanced up at Frank through unfashionable, heavy-rimmed glasses, 'What do you want to know about him? You can't suspect *Daniel* of being a killer?'

'I want to know everything about him,' replied Frank simply. 'And no, he's not a suspect. In fact, if you were close to him I'm afraid we have some very bad news. Far from being a suspect, I'm afraid he was the victim of a murder.'

'*Murder?*' The social worker closed his eyes in dismay and Frank continued awkwardly, 'You may have heard that a black youth was murdered just off Abbey Street the other night? Well, I'm sorry to have to tell you this but that was Daniel. That's why I'm here; we're investigating his death and the more we know about him the better chance we have of catching his killers.'

Lawlor looked at him sadly, 'So that was Daniel? I heard about the murder but they never gave any name on the news.' He shook his head and sighed, 'I wouldn't say we were close, our relationship was purely professional, but I liked him. He was a nice lad, though very shy and gentle. What a damned shame.' He darted a sudden, suspicious look at Frank, 'Is it true it was a racist attack? That's what it said on the news last night.'

Frank gave him a rather strained smile; dissimulation, much less deceit, was simply not in his nature. But he gave it his best shot by saying, 'Do you believe everything you hear on the news, Mr. Lawlor? A *suspected* racial motive is only one of several lines of inquiry we're pursuing. However, at this point we don't know for sure why he was killed, which obviously makes the *who* almost impossible to establish.'

'So in a murder case it's motive that leads you to the killer? Always?' Lawlor frowned, 'By that line of reasoning, if it *was* a racial murder, you might *never* find the perpetrators? Since there's no direct link, I mean?'

Dissimulation was one thing, outright lying quite another, and Frank made no reply. After a pause Lawlor continued, 'I see. Well, I can't tell you much about him from a *personal* perspective, I'm afraid, since he was in the care of Child Services until he turned eighteen, whereupon he came to me. According to his file his juvenile case worker was Valerie O'Donnell, whose number I can give you, by the way, as she's something of a friend of mine. I *can* tell you that he has -had- been in Ireland since the age of ten, *without* being granted citizenship. Residency only. I couldn't tell you why.' He sniffed disparagingly, 'Such is the world-famous hospitality of the Irish people, and State. He was fostered with a family called Mullaly in Ranelagh until he was eighteen, whereupon he signed on the dole and got himself a flat. With my help, of course. He did the Junior and Leaving Certificates, I may say, but failed them both rather badly, which meant he had no qualifications and hence little in the way of job prospects. And that's about all I know, I'm afraid. It's tragic, really. His life was only just beginning.'

'Yes,' said Frank, a touch sadly. 'Never really had a chance, did he?' He gave himself a mental shake; he was supposed to be a professional here. 'What about on a more personal note? Any idea if he had a girlfriend, close friends, anything like that?'

Lawlor gave him an incredulous look, 'You've seen the queues here. We do our best but do you really think we have the time to delve into our clients' social lives? Like I told you, when he was younger he had his own case worker dealing with him, making sure he was happy and integrating well and the like, but once he turned eighteen that sort of thing ceased to be the State's problem. My job was simply to make sure he received all the allowances and benefits he was entitled to. Talk to Valerie in Child Services; she'd have forged a closer personal relationship with him over the years. And his foster parents will obviously be able to give you a better, more personal insight into his life.'

Frank sighed; another dead end. *Big surprise.* He asked idly, 'And do you know off-hand if he *was* happy and integrated?'

Lawlor shrugged, 'More or less, I suppose. I always got the feeling he expected a lot from life, that he had big dreams in spite of his lack of qualifications. And, if I'm honest, his lack of *brains*. The academic sort, anyway. But then, everyone wants to be famous now, don't they? In general I think he was happy enough. Mind you, there was one incident that upset him rather badly, and soured him against Irish people. When he was sixteen a group of teenagers beat the shit out of him on O'Connell Street. And then set him on fire.'

Frank looked at him in disbelief, shocked out of his growing lassitude, 'You can't be serious?'

Lawlor's face was red and his eyes furious, 'Oh yes I can! A group of our fine young citizens hospitalised him because his skin happened to be darker than theirs. Makes you proud to be Irish, doesn't it? You lot never caught them either.' He shrugged, the sudden, unaccustomed fire leaking away in weariness, 'Just another tale from the naked city.'

It was clear that such occurrences were far from unusual in his life, and were no longer capable of raising more than a momentary outburst of passion, as he continued in a neutral tone, 'I suppose he was lucky it was just his clothes they doused in lighter fuel, and not his face as well. A passer-by helped extinguish the flames with an overcoat so his skin wasn't actually burnt but obviously the whole thing still made a deep impression on him. Left him feeling insecure and vulnerable and with no sense of place, of belonging, which of course is immensely important to the young.'

Frank was silenced for a moment, shocked and sickened and distracted from his enquiries. He tried to focus; that attack was undoubtedly a coincidence. The chances of there being a connection were so small as to be laughable. Talk about unlucky, though. *Jesus.* He sighed, searching his mind for further avenues of exploration before saying, 'Do you know anything about his childhood in Africa? About his birth family?'

Lawlor gave him a grim, humourless smile, 'I know he was from Rwanda. He was from the Tutsi tribe, and he saw his entire family butchered in front of his eyes by rampaging Hutus. He only escaped by playing dead amongst all the dismembered bodies. Red Cross workers found him huddled between the butchered corpses of his parents and older siblings.'

'God Almighty,' muttered Frank, derailed out of his professional mien again. It was more a prayer than a blasphemy. He had called the boy unlucky but that had to be the understatement of the year. He shook his head, trying to remain objective. Without much success. *What had he not asked?* 'Did you ever happen to hear him mention a man called William Akima, by any chance? Or Willie-boy?'

'Was he the other murdered black man? It said on the news that two Africans had been killed in the last few days?' Frank made no reply and Lawlor thought for a moment before shaking his head and saying, 'To the best of my knowledge I've never heard that name before. Sorry.'

Frank nodded in resignation, 'Well, I wasn't expecting much. Luckily.' A thought struck him, 'Have you ever heard of the African People's Support Group?'

'Of course,' nodded Lawlor, 'I know the name, at least. A wonderful idea it is too. Daniel was a member, you know. That much I *do* know about his personal life. With him it was more a social thing than anything else, though they do offer legal advice and help with finding jobs and homes and the like. It also gives people with a common background, living in a foreign land, a chance to get together and make new friends. I think that's what Daniel was looking for when he joined; a sense of *belonging*, of community. I doubt if he ever really felt Irish but after being attacked that time he certainly didn't, so I think he tried to find a new identity amongst other native Africans. Though it's hard to believe that he could have been nostalgic for the place when he'd spent half his life here. And especially when you consider what happened to him over there.'

Another understatement. Frank gave him a thoughtful look; here, finally, was a piece of good news. Well, a connection, at least. Akima had hired his gardener though the APSG, and now it transpired that Wistarra was a member too. But did it mean anything? Apart, that is, from yet more people to question, probably without result. Being a detective reminded him of what his philosophy professor in UCD had told him about education, about how every answered question led to six more questions, with the net result being that the more one learnt the more one realizes just how little one really knows. Or ever *could* know.

You didn't know the bloody half of it, professor, thought Frank glumly, *and you used "one" a little too often in your discourses for my liking.* He got to his feet, 'Well, thank you for your time, Mr. Lawlor, I know how busy you are and I appreciate your seeing me.' He produced a card, 'And if you think of anything at all, please don't hesitate to ring me.' These words were becoming routine, Frank realised, and every time he uttered them it was with less and less hope of a response.

By the time Frank got back to the Harcourt Square office, having stopped off on the way for a quick bite of lunch at a sandwich bar, he found Jack already there, and in no very pleasant mood. Frank filled Jack in on what he had learned at the Social Welfare Office, which was pretty much nothing, whereupon Jack returned the favour by relating the details of his meeting with Dalton and the CCAI, which wasn't much more. His interview with the CCAI had left Jack filled with a vague, formless anger that he could not even properly define, much less articulate, so he allowed it to manifest itself as anger that Cecil Dalton had believed him when he had suggested that he might wish to join their organisation.

'Bloody cheek!' he snorted, 'Do I strike you as a paranoid xenophobe? As a damned racist?'

'Well...' hedged Frank in a doubtful tone. Jack shot him a dirty look and the younger man laughed, 'No, of course not. Strange, though, isn't it? The way people assume that the Gardai are naturally predisposed to racism? Must be the uniforms. Association of ideas, I suppose.' A gleam that Jack was coming to recognise entered his eyes and, sensing the onset of poetry, the older man swiftly cut in, 'I checked out another of our three xenophobic groups on my way here; their office is only around the corner.'

'Any luck, sir?'

'Of a sort. It turns out that the Celtic Purity League actually consists of just one nutter and his equally cracked wife. I haven't got to the last name on our list yet, the Ireland First Party, but they seem a bit more promising.' And he explained how the group had been founded, and by whom. 'But to be honest I'm not holding out a great deal of hope; this lot will probably turn out to be another bunch of blowhards, all talk and no action. I mean, if you were going to go around murdering blacks, would you really advertise your racist tendencies by starting a *public* organisation aimed at booting out all foreigners and keeping Ireland "pure"? Advertising your agenda, and your bigotry?'

'No, sir, but racists are not generally known for their towering intellects, sir,' suggested Frank optimistically.

Jack sighed, 'Neither are policemen. And I suppose it could be like Sinn Fein being the political face of the IRA, back in the bad old days, legally raising money and support for the cause while the other lot dealt with the violence in the background.' He shook his head, 'We really aren't making any progress here at all, are we?'

'No, sir,' said Frank reluctantly, 'Not much. Except we now know that Wistarra was a member of that African Support group. That might lead somewhere. After all, Akima recruited his gardener there so it's not impossible that he met Daniel there too.'

'Hmm, I suppose.' Jack sounded less than convinced, 'But even if they knew each other there's surely no connection between their murders? Aside from the racist angle, obviously. I mean a separate connection? Unless these "Sons of Chuchailainn" wankers got a list of their membership or something. Though if that was the case, surely they'd have attacked Wistarra at home too? For safety, and privacy? Well, we'll check it out. We can get a list of all their members or associates or whatever and warn them to be extra vigilant until we get to the bottom of all this.' A sudden thought struck him, 'Here, you don't think Wistarra was gay too, do you?'

Frank shrugged, 'It's possible, I suppose. There was no hint of a girlfriend among his stuff, was there? Nor of a boyfriend either, mind. Why?'

It was Jack's turn to shrug, 'I dunno. Just a thought. The sperm in Akima's stomach; any chance it could have been Daniel's?'

'Again, it's possible, if a bit unlikely,' replied Frank cautiously, 'But there's nothing at all to suggest they even knew each other, apart being connected with the African Support group. I suppose they could have met there. But even if they did know each other, even if they were lovers, what does it mean?'

'Damned if I know,' Jack shrugged again, 'Mind you, their deaths couldn't just be a coincidence if they were lovers, now could it? I can believe that their both being members of the APSG was coincidental, but if they were lovers and if both of them were murdered within a couple of days of each other, surely that would *have* to mean that there was another, non-racial motive for killing them?'

He sighed, 'I'm clutching at straws here, aren't I? We had those anti-immigrant groups pegged as a likely source for fanatics and now they're a bust. At least, the first two were. I'll check out the other one, the Ireland First Party, later; their office is just off Baggott Street. If they *have* an office,' he added moodily, 'The headquarters of the Celtic Purity League turned out to be a one bed-roomed flat.' He scratched his head, 'While I'm there I'll get a list of their members' names and addresses too. If they'll hand them over without a warrant, that is. I asked for one for the CCAI earlier, but it won't be ready till tomorrow; have it picked up, will you? Not that I think it'll lead anywhere; after all, Dalton should know the extremists among his members, and I *think* he was co-operating. But these Ireland First lot are supposedly more extreme so we'll have to trawl through their names and check them against our files.'

'Looking for...?' prompted Frank without thinking.

Jack gave him a look, 'Membership of the Black Panthers, of course. What the hell do you think? Anyone with a record of violence against blacks or other immigrants would do nicely, wouldn't you say? Though anyone with a history of *any* sort of violence will bear closer examination.'

Frank's blushes were spared by the arrival, unsolicited, of Julie, bearing two cups of coffee. 'I thought you could do with these,' she said, adding tartly, lest they quite correctly peg her as a softie at heart, 'to lubricate those mighty brains.'

Jack gave her a hard look that was akin to a glare and she quailed just a touch; she had never seen him like this before. Not just sober and clear eyed but focused and determined; aggressive even. 'Sorry. Just thought you could do with a cuppa.'

Jack's face relaxed into a more familiar, if somewhat defeated, smile, 'Thanks, Jules. We certainly need some source of inspiration. Has the autopsy report on Wistarra come in yet?'

'I rang the Lab; it's due this afternoon,' she responded smartly, 'Five o'clock by the latest, according to pathology.'

Jack eyed her with sudden approval, impressed with her sudden change in attitude; how come he had never noticed before just how efficient she was? The answer to that was obvious, if painful: because he had never had much in the way of work for her before, of course. He noticed something else too; for today at least she had abandoned her tight cut-off tee shirts and mini-skirts, and was looking more her age in a simple blue trouser suit. She also, he realised, looked a damned sight more attractive now that she was no longer trying to look eighteen. Perhaps she had taken his words the other day to heart. Though not, he hoped, too much; he quite liked her perennial clinging on to her vanished youth, and her eternal optimism that Mr. Right was just around the corner, wedding ring in one hand, nappy-changing bag in the other. Or maybe he liked her because she conformed, more or less, to his old-fashioned views of what a woman should be like. He shrugged mentally; what could be more natural than for one stereotype to be attracted to another? *Attracted? What the hell am I thinking?* He took a drink of the hot, fresh coffee and drew his wayward mind back to business, 'Good. Well, let us know as soon as it arrives. And do me a favour, would you? Ring the Lab and ask them to run some tests and find out if the sperm found in Akima's stomach is Daniel Wistarra's.'

She made a revolted face but ventured no comment. 'Right away,' she said briskly, sweeping out of the office. Things had certainly changed around here, and very much for the better. She had always liked Jack, and now she was surprised to find she was starting to respect him a little too, which made working for him far more satisfying. And helping with a murder enquiry was certainly more interesting than the usual run of her duties, which were mostly comprised of typing and filing.

Jack was less pleased with recent developments and growled at Frank, '*Can* you check a dead man's sperm? For its type or whatever?'

'I don't know, sir. I would imagine so, even assuming it...er, *they* were dead too. Anyway, I'm sure they can do a DNA test to find out if it's his or not.'

'Hmm. Well, we'll find out soon enough, I suppose. Right, what now?'

'Well, I still have to talk to Grainne Riordan again, that still might lead somewhere.' Frank paused for a moment, 'This sperm thing; if they were lovers the killings might have been the result of a love triangle rather than racial attacks.'

Jack shrugged, 'Maybe. Are any gays violent enough to gather a few like-minded friends and kill two men over sexual jealousy? When they're always shagging each other anyway? I mean, most of them are pretty promiscuous, aren't they?'

Frank gave him a patient, if slightly fixed, look, 'We've been through this, remember? That's the popular view of gay men, certainly. Popular and patronising. It could be just a myth; any gay guy I've ever met seemed to have a boyfriend. I'm afraid having one gay friend, and one night spent trawling through gay bars and clubs, doesn't really make me an expert on the culture, now does it, sir?'

'Compared to me it does,' growled the older man, 'I've never even met a gay man. Or rather, a man I *knew* was gay, which is probably a very different thing.' He shot a glance at his assistant from under his brows and smiled, 'Yes, yes, I'm just an old dinosaur, aren't I? The curse of aging, laddie. The world is constantly changing but as you get older you find it harder and harder to change with it. And you youngsters sneer at us old fogies, never realising that one day you'll be just like us. Will *be* us, after we're gone.'

Frank nodded sympathetically, '*The wheels of time grinds men to dust; first heart, then soul, then body rusts.*'

Jack gave him a look of his own, 'I might have known you'd have the apposite quote. Where the hell do you get them from?' He raised his hand abruptly, 'Never mind, I don't want to know. I'm too old to start poetry appreciation classes.'

'You're not as old as you've let yourself come to *believe* you are,' said Frank earnestly, 'And one of the best ways of staying young is to continually seek new interests. And new cultures, new points of view.'

'Right now the only thing I'm interested in is finding the bastards who are killing people because of the colour of their skin,' said Jack sombrely, 'Nothing else seems worthwhile, compared to that. That's why, once you've been a murder detective, you can never do anything else. Never *be* anything else.' After a moment's pause a thought struck him and he asked, 'Have we ever had either body officially identified?'

'No, sir, we still haven't found any next of kin for Akima, but Daniel Wistarra's foster family have agreed to formally identify him. They're going to the morgue tomorrow morning, I think.'

Jack nodded, glad he would not be there to see it; he had escorted many a grieving relative to the Dublin City Mortuary at its Marino site, and it was not a task he had ever gotten used to. Nor did it help that the new mortuary had still not been built and the state pathologists worked out of a collection of pre-fabs on the site of a fire brigade training ground. He shook his head to clear these thoughts away and looked at his watch, 'Look, I'm going to go talk to this other anti-foreigners group. You get Juno Wren to come in and identify Akima, though whether or not that'll satisfy the coroner I don't know. And try to get a photo of Akima out to the Mulallys, see if they recognize him. But for God's sake tread carefully in case Wistarra *wasn't* gay. No sense in upsetting them needlessly.'

Frank rolled his eyes, 'Well, *duh*! I wasn't going to say; is this a picture of your fosterchild's middle-aged gay lover!'

Jack shook his head sadly, 'I don't know what appals me more, your lack of respect to a superior or your weird idea that Akima was middle-aged at *forty*.'

Frank laughed, 'Forty is practically senile when you're twenty-six, never mind middle-aged! It might as well be a hundred. *Sir*.' He turned his mind back to business, 'What about the African People's Support Group? Shouldn't I talk to them, too?'

'If you have time. You obviously aren't planning on going home tonight,' said Jack dryly, 'but I am.' He got to his feet, 'You won't have time to do everything today so just do your best. Time for more Nazi-hunting for me. I feel like yer man in that movie. That Jewish guy. And don't forget to write everything up into the file before you leave.' He walked out of the tiny office and headed for the stairs, winking at Julie on the way.

'You're looking good today, Jules,' he called out as he passed, 'I'm glad to see you've stopped dressing like a teenager. It's about time you started acting your age!'

'You too,' she instantly riposted, 'Instead of acting like a ninety-year-old!'

Jack gave her a mocking smile and blew her a kiss as he approached the stairs; Julie's reply to this, though unspoken, had at least the merit of being succinct, involving as it did just a single finger.

Chapter Eleven

Frank's one bedroomed flat in the centre of Dun Laoire was small but comfortably furnished, and almost unnaturally neat for a young man living alone. Years of travel had taught him the value of simplicity and order, and ingrained tidiness made any mess or disorder abhorrent to him. Besides, he had early on learned the hard way that housework is much easier if you clean as you go rather than allowing a backlog to accumulate. That evening he was in his tiny kitchen, cooking a simple meal of pasta and cheese-covered garlic bread, and humming cheerfully as he worked. For perhaps the first time since childhood his life felt in total harmony, settled as he was in a job he thought he could grow to love, with his own place, -small though it was, and rented- and a still smaller car, which at least he owned. Right now the food smelled delicious, a pretty girl was on the way over for dinner, and white wine was chilling in the fridge. Could life get any better? Not much, in his opinion. Particularly if his girlfriend elected to stay the night, which he was pretty sure she would. His mobile rang and he scooped it up with a cheerful, 'Hello, Frank here!'

'Hi, Frank, it's Linda.'

'Linda, hi! I was just thinking about you. I hope you're hungry because I've enough food here to feed the five thousand.'

An exaggerated sigh drifted out of the earpiece, 'I'm sorry, Frank, but I won't be able to make it for dinner. I'm afraid I have to work an extra shift tonight. You know how short-staffed we are at the moment.'

As she was a perennially overworked nurse in St. Vincent's hospital he did indeed know, and hid his disappointment as best he could as he replied, 'Oh well, not to worry. Some other time, eh?'

'Sure.'

There was a pregnant pause as he waited for her to continue, a pause that stretched out uncomfortably and made his stomach sink; he had been expecting her to suggest a more concrete arrangement. When it became clear there was no more to follow he said diffidently, 'Well, how about Saturday night?'

There was another hiatus, followed by another loud sigh. 'I'm not sure that's a good idea, Frank.'

Frank felt a stronger stab of disappointment as he recognised the signs of an impending brush-off but he persevered manfully, 'Well, when are you free then?'

Another exaggerated sigh, 'We're so busy I really don't know when I'll be off again.'

It was Frank's turn to sigh and he had a momentary impulse to sweat the words out of her, to make her suffer a little, but he was naturally soft-hearted and let her off lightly by saying, 'Perhaps we should just leave it at "sometime" then.'

There was unmistakable relief in her voice as she gushed, 'Perhaps that *would* be best. I mean, I like you, Frank, but with the pressure of work and everything...it's just so hard to have a relationship.'

'Sure,' he sad lightly, 'Don't sweat it. I'll see you around, yeah?' He put the phone down with another sigh; *Oh well, easy come, easy go.* Although not exactly lovelorn he *had* liked her, and couldn't help making a rueful face as he tried to push aside a hollow feeling in the pit of his stomach; so much for the delightful evening he had planned!

He returned to his cooking, reflecting that none of his relationships seemed to last longer than a few weeks for some reason. Was there something fundamentally wrong with him? He didn't think he was ugly so was he boring or somehow repellent to the opposite sex? Or was he perhaps just unlucky? He grinned to himself; *maybe he was just crap in bed!* His naturally optimistic nature quickly reasserted itself and he told himself that it was just a matter of time, that the right girl was out there somewhere, looking for *him*. He was young, and there was no great rush. He looked at the food he had prepared and shrugged philosophically; Linda cancelling at least meant that he now had dinner for the next night as well. Pre-cooked, at that. *Silver linings, boy, silver linings. They're everywhere if you only choose to look for them.*

He sat down to his solitary dinner at the breakfast bar, thinking that if he ever bought a place of his own his first purchase would be a table and chairs; sitting at a counter on a high stool just wasn't the same at all. Indeed, perhaps now was the time to buy an apartment or a little house; now that he was on a detective's salary he should just about be able to afford it, particularly with the housing market still in the toilet. Well, he could *maybe* afford it. If he confined his interest to places the size of rabbit hutches, that is. As he sat there he thought about almost anything, in short, except the fact that another girl he had liked had not felt the same way about him. But although disappointed he recognised deep down that she had done the right thing; they weren't right for each other, and as he knew that she was only looking for a serious relationship there wasn't much point in their wasting time with each other, however enjoyable that might be. And if he was honest he would admit that rather than missing *her*, what he would mostly miss was having sex with her.

The phone rang again and he picked it up with less alacrity this time, and with less ebullience in his voice as he said, 'Hello?'

There was no mistaking O'Neill's whiskey-roughened growl, 'Frank? It's me, Jack. Did you see the news tonight?'

A whimsical picture of the lead story on RTE news being Linda's dumping him flashed into Frank's mind and he suppressed a laugh as he replied, 'No, sir, I'm afraid I didn't. Should I have?'

'Yes, you bloody well should! Those bastard bloody vultures ran a big piece on the two killings, trying to tie them together into a conspiracy. They said that "sources" revealed that "evidence" found at the scene linked both murders. They had a picture of Wistarra lying in the skip, Frank, and the writing on the side of it. Some wanker in one of the surrounding offices took it with a camera-phone. By the grace of God the "Sons of Cuchuailainn" bit can't be made out, but he got the "Niggers Go Home" and "Ireland for the Irish" shite. The reporters went to town on it, talking about "pogroms" and a "campaign of hatred". Which it is, of course, but we didn't want to give the buggers publicity! That's what they want, that's the whole point of it all! The news people even drew comparisons with those mental Russian skinheads; remember the dirtbags who murdered nineteen immigrants in Russia that time? Then they showed our Press Officer making the official statement playing down any racist connection, just to make him look stupid. You'd think half of Ireland was out attacking black people! This is all we sodding need. After this every skinhead and closet Nazi in Ireland will be out on the streets attacking every dark face they come across. *Bastards*! This is exactly what I *didn't* want to have happen!'

Frank clucked sympathetically, though he was by no means convinced that public awareness about the murders -especially amongst the black community- would be a bad thing. And skinheads had gone out with the Indians, for God's sake. 'Still, look on the bright side, sir,' he said optimistically, 'There can't be *that* many racists in Ireland. Not the rabid, violent type, I mean. At worst we might have one or two isolated incidents. And at least they haven't been able to leak the name the gang is using.'

O'Neill raised his voice to the point where Frank winced and held the phone away from his ear. 'That isn't the point! From now on everything we do is under the microscope. This is now officially a media circus. Don't you see? We're going to have the pro-immigrant groups on our backs, screaming for action and denouncing the entire country -including the Gardai- as racist murderers, and the anti-immigrant lot screaming just as loudly that this was what they were afraid of all along; foreigners bringing violence and death into the country! And all the politicians in the middle afraid to say anything definite either way but demanding results from us. Preferably yesterday! This whole thing is going to spiral wildly out of control, Frank, just you wait and see. I'm already dreading tomorrow's papers. Can you imagine the headlines?'

Frank could indeed, but saw no good purpose in saying so; Jack was manic enough as it was. Instead he said, 'If the news stories makes these killers more circumspect, and black people more cautious, they might serve a useful purpose. They might save lives. It might work out a good thing, in the end.'

After a heavy pause O'Neill sighed and said, 'I hope so. As long as it doesn't make matters worse by inspiring copycats. Oh well, no point in crying over spilt milk, I suppose. And I may be overreacting.'

'Well,' said Frank cautiously, afraid of provoking a storm, 'I do think you're blowing things a *little* out of proportion.'

There was a long silence and then Jack said, in a rusty voice that showed how difficult the admission was, 'I suppose the truth is that I'm scared.'

No such notion had occurred to Frank but he was not short of insight, and suddenly it all became clear.

'I've been mouldering away in my quiet little basement for years,' continued Jack slowly, 'with nothing much asked of me and nothing mech expected. But now the pressure will *really* come on; from above, from the press, and from the public. And I'm scared I might not be able to deliver anymore. Before' –*before my life went down the toilet*, he thought but did not say- 'it was just part of the job and the pressure never bothered me but now... Well, it's been a long time since I headed up an investigation. If I'm honest I was only supposed to be breaking you in and showing you the ropes on this one, training you to be a detective on a case no one cared about. But now this second murder, and the publicity, has changed everything.'

Frank knew well he should keep his mouth shut; in this situation it was best to say nothing at all. So he surprised even himself when instead he took a deep breath and said simply, 'I believe in you, Jack. I know you've had some problems but you're still basically the same man you always were. That means you have the same qualities that made you a top detective in the first place. By rights you should be pretty ring-rusty but I haven't seen many signs of it, and I have no doubt that you'll crack this case.' Frank was no cheerleader and he cringed in embarrassment even as he uttered these words but, lame or not, he meant what he said, and his sincerity rang in his voice.

There was another silence and then Jack replied, albeit in an unconvinced voice, 'Thank you, son. But it's *we*. *We'll* crack the case. If only because I don't think Rollins believes we can. He never did, you know; he only assigned me to it as your babysitter. And I do still have *some* pride, you know. Ignoble, perhaps, when people are dying, but I can't help it. Quite apart from the other lives at stake here I just can't bear the thought of *failing*.'

This was a minefield into which even Frank feared to venture so he contented himself with saying, '*The motive matters not, if the act be pure/ Take a gift from the devil, if cancer it will cure.* The motive doesn't matter as long as we get the result, as long as we put these bastards away. And we will. So, what's the plan for tomorrow morning?'

'Well, the first thing I have to do is hold a Press conference. There's no putting it off now; every reporter in Ireland will be after us like slavering hyenas. How do you fancy appearing on telly with me?'

A horrified Frank instantly cried off -he could imagine few worse ordeals- and Jack lapsed into a moody silence, wishing he could swerve it too. How did all these jungle and Big Brother people stand it? Where was the bloody attraction? So many clowns desperate to get their stupid faces on telly while the mere idea of facing the cameras filled him with horror and dismay. After a few moments he asked, 'Did you get round to seeing that African support lot? Ha, didn't think so! I'll go talk to them first thing in the morning while the Press Liaison Officer is rounding up the reporters and telly people. Meanwhile you go see Lady Muck and that girl. Don't let her push you around, and stick at it until you dig up something about Akima. *Anything.*'

'Right you are,' agreed Frank, looking at his watch, 'It's only seven o'clock now, I'll give Ms Bennett a ring now and arrange a definite time. It was left pretty open when I suggested it to her yesterday.'

'When you begged her, more like,' replied Jack caustically. His heart-to-heart with Frank had calmed him down considerably and he was more like his old self as he said mildly, 'Anyway, there's no rush to be in early since I won't be there. How did you get on with the other stuff I left you to do?'

'Okay. I got Wren's statement, and he formally identified Akima's body, though by rights it should be a family member. Plus I called out to Wistarra's foster parents, the Mulallys, with Akima's photo. I'm afraid they didn't recognise him at all.'

'Big bloody surprise!' grunted Jack, 'That Ireland First group turned out to be a bust too, by the way. The head guy, Halloran, is a bit of a scumbag but I don't see him as a murderer, and there are only four others in the whole group.' He laughed suddenly, 'He wasn't keen on telling me that but eventually he had to, when I bullied a list of his members names out of him. They've no office or anything, the address was his flat. And while he has extreme views I don't see him having the balls to do anything about them. And beating men to death is no light thing. Still, I went back to the office and left the list of names and addresses on my desk; run them through records in the morning, will you? If you get there first, that is. We'll interview them all but not yet, not unless we find one of them has a bit of previous form.'

'No sweat, I'll do it first thing, before I talk to Grainne Riordan. Unless Ms Bennett will let me see her at the crack of dawn, in which case I'll get her out of the way first. I live in Dun Laoire, you know, so there's no point in tracking into town through the traffic only to head back out an hour later.'

'Yeah, well, suit yourself. Just try not to break your spine bending over backwards to please her.'

'What about the rest of the concerned citizens mob?' asked Frank hurriedly, anxious to change that particular subject, 'Are you going to interview any of them?'

'I don't think *so,* unless we get desperate. If Dalton's anything to go by they're just a bunch of nobodies, you know what I mean? Impotent little men who amount to nothing and need someone to look down on, to blame for their own inadequacies and failures. After all, they chucked Halloran and Connarton out of their organisation as being too bad and dangerous to know, and they're a pair of rancid little pouffes, about as tough as a pair of two-year-olds.'

'I know what you mean, Jack,' replied Frank thoughtfully, *'The grey will hate the vibrant red, and say his life should be bled/ Of colour, force...'*

Jack hurriedly cut him off, 'I forgot to tell you; when I went back to the office I got the report from the two uniforms I sent out to Abbey street looking for witnesses. No one saw or heard a bloody thing that night. Another big surprise, eh? And Rollins has taken them back off us again already, says we're back on our own tomorrow.' His sigh rattled down the phone, 'Listen, I need some food, and a drink, so I'll let you go. But Frank, just one other thing before I go; it's bloody *sir* to you, *not* Jack. Alright, sonny?'

Frank laughed, unfazed, 'Yes, sir! Sorry, sir! See you in the morning, sir! Have a good night, sir!'

Jack hung up the phone, muttering something about "punk kids" and sounding not unlike Grandpa Simpson, but clearly not really angry. Still grinning, Frank hunted in his notebook for Kate Bennett's number, feeling the warm glow of contentment that Linda had temporarily extinguished rekindle itself inside him. He found himself liking the older man more as each day went by, in spite of his faults, and was glad that Jack had opened up to him about his self-doubts. It wasn't until he had dialled Kate's number and was listening to her phone ring that Frank realised that, in spite of the relatively late hour, there had been no trace of a slur in Jack's voice. Which realisation made the glow all the warmer; the old boy really was taking the case seriously. Now, at least. And maybe in return the case was dragging him out of the mire he had let himself slip into. When the phone was finally answered, by a very deep male voice, he said uncertainly, 'Mr. Bennett? Detective Garda Frank Carr here. Could I speak to your wife, please?'

'Ah, Detective, Kate told me about your visit,' rumbled a deep voice down the line, 'Are you the cute youngster or the rude old man? I'm under orders to screen all police calls, you see, so I need to know.'

Frank laughed, 'Oh, I'm young and cute, never fear. Though I have to say your wife hid her admiration extremely well when we met, Mr. Bennett.'

'*Yes,* that's just one of her many talents. I'll go and get her, though perhaps I should mention that my name is not Bennett; it's Howitt. My wife kept her own name after we married.' His tone was resigned as he said this but there was a touch of amusement there too. 'Women's lib, don't you know. I keep telling her that it's going to cause endless confusion once the baby's born but, well, you've met Kate. Very much her own woman, shall we say.'

Frank kept a diplomatic silence and Howitt continued, 'Hold on a minute and I'll get her for you.'

'Thanks.'

After a slight pause Frank heard the clicking of heels on a tiled hall and then Kate's cool but not unfriendly tones saying, 'Kate Bennett here.'

'Ms Bennett, this is Detective Frank Carr here. I called to your house earlier with a colleague?'

'Oh, I remember you, Mr. Carr, don't fret about that. Considering the effect you two had on my patient I'm hardly likely to forget you, now am I?'

'Er, no, I suppose not. Sorry. Well, that episode *was* a little unfortunate but I hope the girl suffered no lasting ill effects from our visit?'

'The *girl* had to go to bed for most of the day, under sedation. *Light* sedation,' she added, clearly reluctantly, 'She's still there now and is, I hope, asleep. Anything else?'

Frank sighed, 'Ms Bennett, it isn't our intention to upset or hurt anyone, and in spite of your obvious concern for Ms. Riordan I think you must be well aware of that. The people we're looking for have already murdered two men, and we'd like to prevent it becoming three, or even more. So if we have to upset a fragile, innocent girl to catch these scumbags; well, that's regrettable but so be it. I personally don't think the price is too high.' He also thought, but did not add; *So snap out of it and join the real world!*

'That might console me,' came the acid reply, 'if I believed for one minute Grainne could help you find your murderers. But if she can't she'll have been upset, and possibly emotionally destabilised, for nothing. Won't she?'

'I'll be as gentle as I can,' said Frank patiently, 'But we have to follow wherever the trail leads, whether we get a result or not.'

It was Kate's turn to sigh, and say, in a somewhat gentler tone, 'Of course I know that you meant no harm. And I certainly don't want to help a *murderer* by obstructing your investigation. Apart from it being my civic duty to help, a Garda saved my life not long ago, very nearly at the cost of his own. It's just that Grainne is far more than just a patient to me. She's also become a very dear friend.'

'Er, I know a little of your -and her- history,' said Frank carefully, reluctant to upset her again, 'So I can understand that. But you must realise that we *have* to speak to her again, even if it means going to court to gain access to her. Although,' he added honestly, 'I've no idea what the legal position is.'

'Very well, you may interview her,' said Kate abruptly, 'But I hold to what I said yesterday; only you can see her, not that other man. And only under my supervision, and not for very long. Agreed?'

Frank kept any trace of triumph of his voice as he replied, 'Of course. Frankly, I doubt if she knows much anyway, so it shouldn't take very long.'

'Don't bullshit me. The mere mention of his name upset her quite a bit last time, so she must know *something* about him...that's your whole point, isn't it? I'm afraid I'll have to reserve the right to terminate the interview instantly if I feel it detrimental to her mental health,' warned Kate.

'Hmm.' This was not quite so good. Thoughts of his cancelled date were still not far from Frank's mind, which prompted him to say, 'Would it help if we made it a bit less formal than a police interview? I mean, the three of us could meet for coffee or lunch or something, somewhere informal? Then perhaps Grainne would feel less pressure, and if she's nice and relaxed she may remember more than if she's in the middle of a full-blown panic attack. And even if she can't remember a thing, at least the experience will be less traumatic for her.'

'Okay,' Kate decided instantly, 'That's a good idea.' The open, rather insulting surprise in her tone made it unnecessary for her to add; *for a policeman.* But then, Gardai are not famed for their sensitivity, nor are they trained for it. 'To be honest I don't much care whether she remembers anything or not, but as you say, an informal setting will make the whole ordeal less stressful for her. Particularly if you're gentle, and tactful. And you *will* be. When would be good for you?'

'How about tomorrow?' suggested Frank promptly, 'After all, the sooner we get it over with the better for all concerned.' *And the killers could strike again at any time while we pussy-foot around your ward!*

'Okay,' said Kate again, 'But I think it'll have to be on home ground. We have taken Grainne out to a few restaurants and the like recently, but the added stress of your presence, and your questions, might make it all a bit too much for her on this occasion. Come out to my house tomorrow at twelve o'clock and we'll have lunch here.'

'Great,' said Frank cheerfully, 'I'll look forward to that.'

'Oh, me too,' said Kate dryly.

Frank laughed, unfazed by her lack of enthusiasm, and suggested, *'Gird up your loins, buckle your brace/ A dark knight cometh, cold death on his face.* I'm not the bogie man, you know.'

'That,' returned Kate, unperturbed, 'remains to be seen.'

Frank gave up, merely saying, 'Until tomorrow, then.' He hung up, a tingle of excitement running through his body. *Calm yourself, you fool,* he told himself, *the girl probably knows nothing.* But his ever-sanguine heart refused to allow such negativity. From her reaction to Akima's photo the girl had certainly known him, and hence must know *other* people who had known him. This, with the knowledge that he was gay, meant that Akima was finally starting to assume form, to take on at least a little flesh. Not for much longer would he be just a shadow, a maddening enigma who passed without trace and touched no other lives. They would finally have something to work on, to work *with.* He could feel it. He sought for the apt quotation and as usual found it almost instantly; *Victory, the balm for weary toil/ Only grows in hard-worked soil.*

Kate's heart was anything but singing as she replaced her receiver, and her turmoil showed on her troubled face. Her husband Peter, a veritable giant of a man, stood propped against the door frame of the sitting-room, a frame he pretty well filled. With open concern in his dark eyes he asked softly, 'What's wrong?'

Kate shook her head, unaccountably near tears. 'We're so close. After so much work and so many disappointments we're so close to freeing her from her past, to giving her a new life and a chance of happiness. And now I'm afraid that her past is going to reach out like a great big hand and drag her back down again. You didn't see her; she was worse than she's been for ages.' She looked at him with huge damp eyes stripped naked by emotion. 'Can no one ever break free from their past?'

He went to her and enfolded her in his arms, a warm feeling filling his heart as her massive, bulging abdomen pressed against him, reminding him of how blessed he was. 'You did,' he reminded her gently, 'And so will Grainne. But remember, you had to confront your past to defeat it, and so will she. You can't protect her forever, you know. Not from her own life, her own memories. And with *her* past there's a lot of bad stuff for her to wade through. She has to deal with all of it and *you* have to let her. Talking to this cop, reliving some of the bad stuff, might actually do her some good. In a way, it's not so different to the therapy you've been doing with her this past year, getting her to face her demons, and her own past actions.'

'Wow,' she managed a smile, 'When did you become so insightful?'

He smiled back, 'Not bad for a big, hairy-arsed builder, eh? I guess some of the old psychology must have rubbed off on me over the years.'

She hugged him tightly, finding ineffable comfort in his presence and his touch rather than his words, for he had said nothing she did not already know, in her head if not her heart. But in spite of the reassurance of his flesh, of his love, her heart was cold with dread, for in her mind her own recovery, her own well being, was inextricably linked with that of Grainne. And she feared for her young charge, for her *friend,* as she had not for many months past.

Chapter Twelve

Checking the list of names that Jack had left on his desk took Frank no more than an hour the following morning, and produced a big fat zero, leaving him time to kill before he set out for his interview with Grainne. Jack had still not arrived for the Press Conference - which had the Press Rooms upstairs in an uproar of camera- and sound-men setting up their myriad pieces of equipment- so Frank called the offices of the Concerned Citizens Against Immigration and asked for the list of their membership to be faxed across to him. They were reluctant to part with it, even to the Gardai, but Frank's utter loathing for them and their beliefs and aims made it surprisingly easy for him to turn nasty and flex a little official muscle. A threat to call around to their offices with a few uniformed officers and drag them all down to Store Street Garda Station if they didn't cooperate ensured that the list was duly faxed across, though with no good grace. He set to work checking through it for anyone with a criminal record, a little shocked at how easy it had been to assume the part of a bully. At least he hoped he was just playing a part; using his position to browbeat members of the public did not quite fit in with his mental image of himself, nor of the man he wanted to be. And he was not one to trot out that old chestnut of the ends justifying the means; he considered that a poor excuse for the abuse of power, and the first step towards totalitarianism. However, he pushed self-doubt from his mind and started work on this second, far longer list, though more in hope than expectation; he set great store by Jack's opinion and doubted that someone like Dalton could pull the wool over the old man's eyes.

When his task -fruitless as it happened- was complete he set out in his little car for Killiney, nursing an unwontedly bad mood. He was unused to failure in anything he undertook and the lack of progress in this, the most important task of his life to date, had deflated his hopeful mood of the night before. Youth and innate optimism soon restored his temper, however, and by the time he arrived at the Bennett -or rather, Howitt- household he was his usual cheerful self again. He found Ms Bennett in much better spirits than on their previous meeting too, and in fact she greeted him with a dazzling smile and flung the door wide for him to enter. 'Mr. Carr, good of you to be so punctual. Please come in.'

Wondering a little at the unexpected warmth of her greeting Frank followed her into the dining-room, -which was more or less the same size as his entire apartment- where he found a great bowl of salad and three places laid at one end of the huge oak dining-table, but no sign of his quarry.

'Grainne will be down in a minute,' Kate forestalled him, bustling about with glasses and a jug of ice-water, 'She's just getting ready.' She laughed, 'Girls will be girls, eh? Especially when there's a man coming to lunch. I'm afraid Grainne has contact with almost no one but my husband and I so your visit, semi-official or not, is a welcome break from routine for her. Do please sit down.'

Frank obeyed, looking at her in some amazement; the change in the hitherto rather forbidding psychologist was astonishing, and a little unsettling. There were hectic spots of colour on her cheeks and her eyes were shining, but the main difference was in her personality; she was not just friendly but apparently bubbling with joyful energy.

Kate noticed his wondering look and laughed gaily, 'Do I seem a little agitated? Well, there's a good reason…my contractions have started!'

Frank got to his feet in alarm, unspeakable horror contorting his usually even features into something that resembled a Halloween mask. He began stuttering out questions but Kate just laughed again and waved him back to his seat, 'Relax, detective, they're still ages apart. I doubt if I'll be going to the hospital until tonight or even tomorrow morning. I rang Harcourt Square to try and put you off but you'd already left.'

'There's a radio in my car,' stammered the totally unnerved Frank, 'and I have a mobile. You should have had them call me. I wouldn't have dreamed of...'

Kate made a dismissive gesture, 'I thought it would be as well to get this over with; I don't want you bothering Grainne while I'm in hospital. Besides which the contractions are mild, a long way apart, and haven't stopped me from getting hungry and wanting my lunch. And, if I'm honest, I was hoping your visit might help keep my mind off the ordeal I'm about to undergo. For a while, at least. And Grainne's too; the poor girl is in a worse state than I am. As with most ordeals in life, the waiting is worse than the reality. I hope.' Kate grimaced, 'Though labour is probably an exception to *that* rule. I'm afraid my knowledge of childbirth is entirely theoretical.' She sighed, 'And right now I kind of wish it would stay that way.' She waved a hand, 'Please, begin your lunch.'

Almost dizzy with the sense of unreality surrounding him, Frank picked up a slice of bread and mechanically buttered it, reflecting that he had thought conducting an interview over lunch *outré* enough as it was, and wondering bemusedly if any other police interview had ever begun in such unorthodox circumstances. He preferred not to think at all about how it could end.

The door opened and Grainne entered, looking so astonishingly beautiful that Frank almost choked on his mouthful of bread; real girls in real life didn't look like this. Ever. She was like some exotic alien or something, as if she belonged in a zoo or a hothouse for rare blooms. He instinctively rose to his feet and held out his hand in mute greeting, wishing that he did not look quite such a fool, chewing as he was on a chunk of brown bread and goggling at her like a fat kid in a sweet shop.

Grainne was dressed very simply in black jeans and a white blouse, but a figure like hers needed no *haute couture* to set it off, and with her cloud of fine golden hair and perfect face, even without any makeup she seemed to him dazzling, a match for even the most glamorous of movie stars. She gave Frank a white-toothed smile and looked directly -if nervously and briefly- into his eyes, which she had not done on their previous meeting. She took his proffered hand and said in her husky voice, 'Nice to see you again, Inspector.'

She took a seat and the dazed Frank practically fell back down into his, almost overwhelmed by the triple whammy of her perfect looks, low throaty voice and enormous green eyes. He shook himself angrily; what the hell was wrong with him? Apart from being unprofessional he was acting like a complete fool; he really needed to get a grip on himself. He cleared his throat, 'Er, it's just plain detective, actually. And I've only just reached that rank so Inspector is still a long way off, I'm afraid. But please call me Frank.'

Grainne smiled again, causing his breath to catch in his throat; her whole face came alight. 'Of course, Frank. I should have realised you're much too young to hold such high rank.'

Frank smiled bemusedly in return and resumed his meal, thinking that perhaps it was just as well that Grainne didn't get out much; without making the slightest effort she was capable of causing riots anywhere she went. She was certainly causing havoc with his professional gravitas; what would she be like all dolled up and out on the warpath? He ate in silence for a few moments, oppressed on one side by the girl's exquisite beauty and on the other by her guardian's gravidity. He stole a glance at Grainne; she seemed more animated, more *there*, than at their first meeting, but whether this was temporary or permanent he had no way of knowing. And with his knowledge of her history he could not help wondering how stable she was, and how his questions might affect her. If he ever got up the nerve to ask any, that is.

'I'm glad to see you so much better today,' he said to Grainne, rather shyly, 'I'm afraid we upset you yesterday.'

Grainne gave a throaty chuckle that made the hairs on the back of his neck stand on end and looked him full in the eyes –making his heart skip a beat- before replying, 'You mean I freaked out! I'm sorry about that. The past few years have an unreal, nightmarish quality for me, and when a memory from that time breaks into my mind in a…a *real* way it invariably throws me.' She darted a glance at Kate, who was watching her intently, 'But I'm learning to cope with my past, and my own fragility.' She smiled and shrugged in a slightly weary fashion, *'Slowly.'*

Frank smiled back with an effort, trying to stop those massive, liquid green pools from hypnotizing him completely, *'The chains of the past, fetters that will not let go/ Only with pain are they cut, with the work grim and slow.'*

The girl blinked in surprise, 'Yes, I suppose so.' She smiled again, 'I've never thought of my past as a fetter, holding me back, but of course that's exactly what it is. And every misdeed is a link in the chain. As are the past crimes of others against us. Are you a poet?'

Frank blushed deeply, to his intense irritation, and he wondered briefly just when was the last time he had made such a complete fool of himself. Almost certainly *never*. 'Er, well, I try to be, in a small way. I'm a dabbler, I suppose.'

'No,' replied Grainne instantly, gazing at him raptly, 'that was *good*. Have you ever tried to get published?'

Frank's blush intensified, if possible, and he mumbled, 'Well, as a matter of fact I've had one or two pieces printed, in magazines and anthologies. No collections, though. There isn't that big a market for poetry, and I can't afford to self-publish.'

Grainne raised her eyebrows and leaned forward over the table, saying intensely, 'Ah, but can you afford *not* to publish your work? Art needs to be published, and every artist needs an audience. Otherwise what's the point?'

'Well, I hadn't really thought about it like that, or of myself as an artist. And to be honest I'm really not all that good. I do have dreams but that's all they are, dreams. I know my limitations, whatever my ego might whisper.' He shrugged, 'Besides, poetry alone wouldn't sustain me even if I were published. Physically or emotionally; I have a strong need to be *doing* as well as writing.'

Kate, who had been watching this growing love-fest with a mixture of alarm and reluctant amusement, at this point interjected, 'And does being a *policeman* sustain you in both ways?'

Frank considered for a moment before replying, 'Being a Garda pays the bills pretty well, and offers the chance of a career, but aside from that I suppose it also fulfils another need in me.' He smiled, 'The law can be slippery, and justice often fails, but surely righting wrongs and punishing evildoers must appeal to any romantic? It appeals to my sense of justice, to feelings of my *outrage* every time a crime is committed. And especially when that crime is murder.'

The instant they were out he regretted the words; both women had murky pasts and he feared they might mistakenly apply his words to themselves. But, to his relief, neither took his words in a personal context but rather smiled at him; Grainne radiantly and with a touch of admiration, Kate with grim irony.

'Were you a fan of the Lone Ranger as a child?' she asked sweetly.

Frank laughed, 'A bit before my time, I'm afraid. Though as a child I had a soft spot for old Clint Eastwood movies.'

Kate raised her slender, perfectly arched eyebrows, 'I *see*. Do you see yourself more as a Dirty Harry type, then? An outsider, a loner doing whatever it takes to punish evil, even if it means breaking rules, and even the law itself?'

Frank shook his head, 'Trying to psychoanalyse me, Doctor? I think I'll keep my mouth shut from now on, thank you very much.'

Kate laughed and got to her feet, 'No one's that easily analysed, I'm afraid, or that quickly. If they were my job would be a hell of a lot easier. Even the most seemingly simple person is really a seething mass of often contradictory thoughts and feelings and instincts. To say nothing of strange impulses and compulsions. That's what makes my work difficult and frustrating and utterly fascinating.'

Frank nodded, 'Not unlike being a detective, in a way.'

She shot him a look that showed how much he kept surprising her, and how she had to continually re-appraise him, before replying, 'I guess we both have a mission in life. The main difference is that mine is to repair life's victims, yours is to avenge them. Now, if you're both finished I'll wash up while you ask Grainne your questions.' She gave him a slightly stern look before saying to her ward, 'The kitchen door will be open, though, and I'll only be an instant away.'

Frank jumped to his feet and said in horror, 'Please, don't move about! You might...er, don't trouble yourself! You just sit there while I tidy up. If Grainne helps me I can ask her my questions over the washing-up.'

Kate said dryly, 'I haven't even told my husband about the contractions yet because I hate fuss so please, relax.' She sat back down, however, and said, 'Still, if you insist I'm willing to forego the pleasure of doing the dishes. For once.'

With an affectionate smile that showed she knew her friend's acerbic exterior to be largely a front Grainne began gathering the dirty dishes before moving through the connecting door to the kitchen. Behind her back Kate, to his surprise and even alarm, winked at Frank and said, 'Good psychology, detective, allowing your interrogatee a simple physical outlet while you question her; by having something else to focus on apart from your questions she won't feel so pressured, or trapped. Makes it all less formal, too. But be gentle, and remember; I'll be listening.' She gave him a slightly grim smile, 'So less of the flirting, and the poetry, too.'

A flustered Frank gathered the rest of the crockery and followed Grainne into the vast, gleaming kitchen, reflecting that if this was Kate in a good mood he would hate to get on her bad side. He also formed a high degree of respect for her absent husband; the thought of actually wooing such a tough subject quite unnerved him; how had the man ever worked up the courage to even ask her out in the first place, much less propose? *He must have balls of bloody steel.* Though no doubt she had been softer and meeker when young. Probably.

For a few moments he and Grainne worked in silence, scraping off the plates and stacking them in a neat pile. Only when the sink was full of soapy water and his lovely helpmeet was busy plying the scrubber did Frank, drying cloth in hand, say as casually as possible, 'So, can you tell me how you knew William Akima?'

Grainne immediately flushed bright red and began scrubbing the plates she was holding hard enough to remove the pattern, much less any dirt. After a pause she said carefully, in a flat monotone, 'I knew a lot of people in those days. Particularly men. I'm afraid I was a bit wild. Drink, drugs, sex; I was a real party girl. Willie used to frequent a lot of the same bars and clubs as me, and we became pretty friendly, though we weren't actually *friends*.'

There was an uncomfortable silence where she failed to elaborate before Frank decided to be honest with her. He said gently, 'Look, I know a little of your history, and please believe me when I say I have the utmost sympathy for what you endured as a child. You need feel no embarrassment or shame for your actions during your...er, *wilder* days.' He laughed suddenly, 'People always feel awkward discussing delicate matters but policemen are like doctors; there really is nothing we haven't seen before. Besides, your behaviour all stemmed from your being the *victim* of an horrendous crime when you were a child. Believe me, I have nothing but sympathy for you.'

Grainne nodded, her eyes on the sink full of suds, and replied painfully, 'I've never discussed my past with anyone but Kate, and no matter what anyone says I shall always feel shame about the way I was back then. Or at least embarrassment. There were reasons for it, of course, but reasons can so easily become excuses. But there's nothing embarrassing about my relationship with Willie-boy; we were friends, nothing more. Our friendship wasn't meaningful or intimate, we never arranged to see each other or anything. We just travelled in some of the same circles and had fun together whenever we met up. Partly because Willie usually had good dope on him and partly because he loved to laugh and dance and have a good time.' She smiled sadly, 'Both were very attractive qualities to me back then.'

She fixed her eyes back on the sink as she said, in a would-be casual tone, 'I tried to seduce him, of course, as I did most of the men I met back then, but he wasn't interested. He told me from the start that he preferred men. He told me the only woman he would ever touch would be the mother of his children, sometime in the unspecified future. And he made it clear that even that would be a duty rather than a pleasure. He always said he intended to have at least ten kids, after he retired from business.' She looked him in the eye for the first time since they entered the kitchen as she said, with a gleam of quiet humour, 'I guess he didn't consider me the maternal type.'

Being on the receiving end of a blast of those huge green eyes at such close quarters left Frank wondering how even a gay man could resist her but he kept this observation to himself, contenting himself with saying, 'Did you ever meet any of his boyfriends?'

Grainne reflected for a moment. 'I don't think so. I really can't remember ever seeing him with the same man twice. I think he just played the field. He was only interested in sex, you see, not relationships. He was very old-fashioned in his own way, like one of those closet gays from years ago, with a wife and kids for the public to see, but secretly meeting men in toilets for sordid sex. The idea of marrying a man and building a life together, adopting kids or anything like that, was totally alien to him. Perhaps because of his upbringing in Africa, which of course is macho central. I don't think the word *tolerance* is even in the dictionaries over there.'

She turned to give him another blast with those eyes, which were now slightly watery, 'But you must realise, Frank, that I remember very little from those days, and what I do recall may not be accurate. I was generally either drunk or stoned. Or both.' She turned back to her task, 'And the little I do remember is painful for me now. Drugs change people, and the things I did at that time seem more like a nightmare to me now than actual memories. While on drugs, or to get them, I would have done *anything*. And I pretty much did.'

No immediate response to such naked honesty sprang to Frank's mind so he remained silent for a moment, fighting a horrifying urge to put a comforting arm around her, or at least pat her on the back. Then he said, 'Your impression seems pretty good to me. We haven't been able to turn up any sign of lovers, past or present, or even friends. And from trawling through his stuff I got the impression he was something of a loner. *Did* he have any friends?'

Grainne frowned in concentration, 'At that time I was pretty much obsessed with my own problems -or rather, with trying to avoid them- so I'm afraid I didn't pay close attention to the people around me. But you're right about Willie being a loner. I used to meet him in clubs and at parties but now that I think about it he generally arrived -and left- on his own.' She smiled with sudden radiance, causing Frank to catch his breath, 'It was only a few years ago but even so there were less black people in Dublin then, so Willie was my only black friend. I remember him better than most of my friends from that era, yet see how little I recall? But I was genuinely fond of him, and I think I would have remembered if he had been seriously involved with anyone.' She frowned and bit her lip, 'I remember seeing him with Jimmy quite a bit, but *he* certainly wasn't gay.' Her tone made it clear she had firsthand knowledge of this and she darted a sideways look at Frank before saying, 'Er, Jimmy Shiels, that is. He was my boyfriend and probably the closest thing Willie had to a friend back then, but he's dead now, I'm afraid.' Once more she had to steel herself before saying, 'He was murdered by...'

Words failed her and Frank, acting on impulse, reached out and took one of her sud-covered hands in both of his, 'Look, you aren't responsible for the actions of other people, family or otherwise. You have *nothing* to be ashamed of.'

She lowered her head and Frank thought she was weeping. Certainly her voice was choked as she softly replied, 'So Kate keeps telling me. And I try to believe it. But deep down it isn't easy to escape the shame. The *guilt.*'

'You have to keep trying, though,' he said softly, 'And gradually it will get easier. Inch by inch. *Perseverance in spite of pain, grows the soul true gain.'*

Grainne uttered a forced laugh and pulled her hand away to resume her labour, 'Perhaps. Anyway, I'm afraid Jimmy is of no use to you. And I can't think of anyone else Willie was close to. Not in my circle, anyway.' She paused, 'There was one guy I used to see him with now and then, though he wasn't a friend of mine. He was involved with Jimmy in some way, too.' She gave Frank a droll sideways glance, 'Jimmy wasn't exactly a model citizen, and even when I was with him I kept well clear of his business dealings. And this guy was *scary*. He certainly scared Jimmy. But what the hell was his name?' She shook her head in frustration, 'I almost had it there for a moment but it's gone, I'm afraid.'

Frank sighed; this was not what he had hoped for. As the only known associate of the victim he had had great hopes of Grainne. But on this particular case her lack of useful memories was pretty much par for the course. After all, so far nothing had been easy so why should it change now? Still, he had to keep trying, and he said, 'Will you keep thinking about it? I know it's painful for you to think about those times but please try; it's very important. Plus the names of anyone else Willie knew even on a casual basis.' He sighed again, 'We really haven't been able to find any...'

'Crilly!' interrupted Grainne triumphantly, giving him a start, 'That was his name! Like Father Ted! That's how I remember. But what was his first name?' She frowned in concentration, and the rapt Frank studied her, mesmerized by her beauty in spite of himself, until her brow smoothed back to alabaster perfection and she smiled in triumph, 'Sean, that was it! *Sean Crilly.* He was about as close to Willie -and Jimmy- as anyone. He was no friend of mine so I never paid him much heed, but I don't think I ever set eyes on him unless Willie was around. Willie never said anything about him but I got the idea that they were more business acquaintances than friends.'

Frank beamed at her, resisting the impulse to kiss her on the cheek, 'Well done!' At last a bit of luck. Was it too much to ask for this Crilly guy to still be around? Or would this lead vanish in the same way as all the others on this case? 'That's terrific, Grainne. I don't suppose you know anything else about this guy? Where he's from or anything like that?'

'I know he was a Dub because he had a really strong accent but that's about it,' she said doubtfully. She shook her head and he continued cheerfully, 'Not to worry; I'll find him.' He paused for a moment, 'Is that the lot? Can you remember any other particular friends of Akima's? Male or female?'

She shook her head regretfully, 'Not offhand. I think that's about it. He really didn't seem to have many friends.'

You're telling me, was Frank's unspoken thought. 'Still,' he said optimistically, his normally upbeat personality reasserting itself, 'it's a start. Actually, it's more than I expected. And you never know where this guy will lead us. Thank you.'

Grainne blushed and lowered her head. 'Willie wasn't a *close* friend but I liked him. Jimmy and that Crilly guy were scum, so between knowing them and always having drugs on him he was probably a crook too, but I'd still like to help catch whoever killed him.'

'And I appreciate it,' said Frank, delighted to hear that Akima's friends were scum; he just hoped they had criminal records too. But would he be able to locate them? With a start he realised that she had been running around with Shiels and Akima only two or three years before at most. Grainne's habit of talking about her past as if it had all happened many years before had distorted his own perspective; this Crilly guy should certainly be still around, which made him not only the only business assocate of the victim they had found, but also a very viable suspect. This thought cheered him immensely and he said, 'Thanks for making this effort, for talking to me at all. I know it was difficult for you.'

'You made it easy,' she replied, almost inaudibly. 'It's part of my therapy to face my past, to talk about these things, but you've been very patient, and very kind.'

Frank was rather at a loss for a response to this but was spared the trouble by Kate's dry tones saying from the doorway behind them, 'If you've *quite* finished the washing-up, Detective, I've got another little job for you.'

Frank turned to her gratefully, 'Of course. Just name it.'

'I'd like a lift to Mount Carmel hospital, please; I'm afraid my contractions are speeding up at quite an alarming rate. Unless, of course, your Garda training included a course in delivering babies?'

Chapter Thirteen

Frank was specifically trained to deal with crises in a cool, professional manner, without fuss or panic. Thus he was not proud of how he reacted to this emergency; namely, first by almost having a heart-attack, and then by scuttling about like a headless chicken, causing a lot of confusion but not achieving anything useful. Later on, mulling it over in mortification, he couldn't swear that he hadn't actually clucked while he was at it. However, he eventually recovered from his panic and rose to the occasion sufficiently to drive the equally frenzied Grainne and Kate -who never turned a hair- to the hospital. He even phoned Kate's husband at work and gave him the glad tidings, albeit in a slightly breathless voice. When Peter Howitt arrived at the hospital Frank happily surrendered Grainne to his care and shamefacedly fled to the predominantly male sanctuary of Harcourt Square, thankful that his muse had never inclined him towards the medical profession.

When he entered their little office he found Jack in remarkably good humour; remarkable because he was almost free of any taint of alcohol and didn't seemly overly troubled by the lack. He hadn't had a completely teetotal morning, of course, but by his extremely elastic standards he was practically dry.

'Well?' he caustically greeted his junior as Frank entered the office, 'And how was your *date* with the fair Grainne? And the lion-tamer, of course.'

'Bizarre,' said Frank feelingly, giving him a rueful grin, 'And not something I'd care to repeat. I've had a few disasters in my love-life over the years, but even my worst date never ended like this one.'

Jack frowned in puzzlement, 'What the hell are you talking about? And what, if anything, did you discover?'

Frank took a deep breath and gathered his scattered thoughts, 'Actually, I learned the name of an associate and possible business partner of William Akima. Well, two associates really, but one of them is dead so he won't be much use to us. Though I suppose friends and family of his might point us to *other* friends of Willie-boy. The other associate I'm going to check out on our computer files now. A guy called Sean Crilly. A *scary* guy, according to Grainne, and probably a criminal. Ever heard of him?'

Jack frowned and shook his head, 'Can't say I have. Should I?'

Frank shrugged, 'The only people Grainne Riordan saw with Akima on any sort of regular basis were this Crilly fellow and a guy called Jimmy Shiels. Grainne's impression -which I admit might not be very reliable- was that Shiels and Crilly were probably more business associates than mates, and since I already knew from delving into Grainne's past that Shiels was a thief and a drug-pusher I thought that Crilly might have a record too. Grainne described them both as scum, though...' He stopped, not wanting to finish, *Though that didn't stop her sleeping with Shiels for drugs.* He had conceived a fondness for the girl, and felt a protectiveness toward her that he had never known before.

'I see,' said Jack, noticing the abrupt halt but not pursuing the cause of it, 'Well, look them both up.'

'Er, Shiels is dead, sir,' said Frank apologetically, though he had nothing to be sorry for, 'He was murdered a year or so ago.'

'Well, run a check *Crilly* then!' said Jack crossly, 'I've never heard of him but that doesn't mean a lot these days.' He gave Frank a sharp look, 'I take it you're hoping he *has* a police record, so we might just have ourselves a suspect as well as an associate, eh?'

Frank smiled apologetically, 'I daren't hope too much on this case but you never know. I was thinking that if Crilly was a crook then Akima might be too. They might have fallen out and Crilly might have killed Akima, and invented all this "Sons of Chuchuailainn" malarky to throw us off the scent. It's probably just wishful thinking but even if Crilly didn't kill him at the very least we should get some more information from him on Akima, maybe get a few more names of friends and possibly colleagues. *Anything.* Provided we can trace him, of course.'

Jack nodded, 'Right, let's get to it. Though since I'm not exactly computer literate I'll let you take care of that. That all sounds promising, so why did you say lunch was a disaster? Quite productive, I'd call it.'

Frank laughed aloud at that and then said, in a musing tone, 'Yes, I suppose you could call it productive. *Something* was certainly produced!'

'What the hell are you laughing at?' asked O'Neill suspiciously. A thought struck him, 'Here, you didn't upset that psychiatrist woman again, did you?'

'She's a psychologist, actually,' said Frank, refraining from pointing out that it had been Jack, not he, who had upset her the preceding day. He assumed a pensive look, 'And do you know, I just might have.'

Jack frowned at him, 'What makes you think that?'

'Well, sir, when I left she was giving birth.'

For a moment Jack's eyes bulged with astonishment, then he laughed, 'No, not really?'

Frank nodded, 'Honest. At least, she was pretty close to it. And remarkably cool about it all she was too. Hardly turned a hair. You'd never believe it was her first baby. I didn't exactly cover myself with glory at first but after I calmed down a bit I managed to give her a lift to the hospital without crashing.'

'You didn't take her to the hospital in that bloody *Ka?*'

Frank looked at him in genuine surprise, 'Of course. What else could I do? I was a bit worried myself that she wouldn't fit, mind you, but we *were* in something of a rush. And she fitted in perfectly in the end. You'd be surprised.'

Jack shook his head in disbelief, 'God Almighty, surprised isn't the word. Well, what was it, boy or girl?'

'I didn't wait around for the finale. After all, it wasn't really my place.' Frank showed a shamefaced grin, 'Also, I bottled it.'

'Better men have done that before you,' replied Jack slowly. With a smile tinged with sorrow he added, 'Watching the birth of your own child is a gift from God, but watching the birth of someone else's must be a nightmare from hell. Seems you've had quite a day of it already. But it's early yet and you're not going home until we've checked out this Crilly guy. Come on, we'll use Julie's machine.' He got to his feet and walked out of the office.

'How did the Press conference go, sir?' asked Frank, hurrying after him.

'Better than the last one,' muttered Jack over his shoulder. Seeing Frank's uncomprehending look he explained, 'I was drunk at the last Press conference I held. This one was better than that, at least. But you know what reporters are like; for every question you answer they have another ten. They're insatiable, and they wouldn't leave the racist angle alone. Not that I blame them, obviously, but it's going to make our job a lot harder. Anyway, I explained why we wanted to tone that aspect down and appealed to them to help us out.' He shrugged, 'So you can imagine tomorrow's headlines "Racist Gang Out To Murder Every Black in Ireland".' He shrugged again, 'Like I say, I don't really blame them; from their point of view it's a bloody good story. But we're going to be the ones dealing with the backlash from black *and* white pressure groups, the politicians, and the copycats. And copycats there will be; you wouldn't believe the calls we've had today. I've had a ton of calls, a lot of them supporting the killers and saying blacks deserve to be killed just for being here!' He shook his head in disbelief, 'I would never have believed the Irish were as racist as some of them are proving to be, I can tell you. It just goes to show.' He stopped at the secretary's desk and, with a jerk of his thumb, demanded impatiently, 'Beat it, Jules, we need your computer.'

Julie shot him a glare of outraged surprise, but instead of exploding she took several deep breaths before saying through gritted teeth, 'How *dare* you! Say please, you narky old beast.'

Jack's scowl softened to a half-smile that was tinged with admiration -no one *ever* got the better of her- and he said, 'Fine; *please*. This is important, Jules, and we won't be long.'

'Yes, and of course my work isn't important; it's just meaningless make-work!' In spite of her words Julie swivelled round in her chair and got to her feet, pleased with this minor victory. Though he had never been hard to work with Jack had always portrayed himself as cynical and hard-bitten, readier with a snarl than a smile. However, Julie, along with her fellow workers, had very quickly realised that his bark was considerably worse than his bite. And lately he hadn't even been able to keep up a credible *pretence* of being a curmudgeon. It seemed she only had to turn snappish and brook no nonsense to bring him immediately to heel. This naturally made her heart warm towards him, and the knowledge of her dominance over him made her toss her head as she walked away, and put the suspicion of a wiggle into her walk.

O'Neill found himself watching her walk away approvingly before he caught himself, shocked by his own behaviour; he'd be flirting with her next, for God's sake, supposing such a thing possible. And him a married man.

Frank, who had outwardly shown no cognizance of this unseemly byplay by a pair of ancients who ought to know better, hid a grin as he accessed the Garda Criminal Database; he personally thought that Jack flirted with Julie all the time, if unconsciously, and was far fonder of her than he realised. Than he *let* himself realise. He also reckoned that no woman with such a soft heart as Julie -and such powerful maternal instincts-could fail to have a *tendre* for a man so obviously in need of TLC as O'Neill. Not with his past. In fact, he privately thought that Julie's earlier, faintly ridiculous attempt at vampishness was designed to attract O'Neill's attention, and maybe even spark a little jealousy in him. He also thought that, whatever his secret feelings, Jack had grown too comfortable in his crown of thorns to easily lay it aside. He shook his head, reflecting that, sad or not, it was all none of his business, and punched the name Sean Crilly into the Gardai criminal records search engine. He sat back, certain that without an accompanying address he faced a long wait as the computer trawled through the myriad names in its data banks. But in a surprisingly short time information began scrolling onto the screen, causing him to whistle softly and say, 'Look at this, Jack! There's only one Sean Crilly on file in Dublin, and his record is as long as your arm!'

Jack leaned over his shoulder and began reading, 'Armed robbery, ABH, GBH, drug-pushing, extortion...Jesus, it's the Godfather part two! This swine was into everything!' In sudden good humour he slapped Frank resoundingly on the back, 'Does he sound like a vicious murderer to you, son?'

'Certainly does, sir!' spluttered Frank, trying to catch his breath, 'Or at the very least, certainly the kind of man who'd *order* a murder. According to this he's the leader of a Finglas crime gang that's suspected of being a major heroin distribution network. So he has no shortage of muscle behind him. And if his gang is anything like him they'd be just the boys you'd pick to beat a man to death with baseball bats. But how could someone like *this* be connected to Akima? We still haven't found a sniff of criminality about *him,* apart from what Grainne Riordan said about him often having drugs on him.'

'No, but the only people we've managed to associate him with so far are two criminals, if you include Shiels, which suggests he was far from squeaky clean,' Jack pointed out. 'Big-time drug dealing means big-time money, and all that ill-gotten cash needs an outlet. And the South African police report seemed to indicate that Akima's reputation was a bit dodgy, though he'd never actually done time. Perhaps he was laundering drugs money or something for Crilly and they fell out over it.'

'Could be, I suppose,' agreed Frank excitedly, 'And if...oh, shit!'

'What? What is it?'

Frank's shoulders sagged with disappointment, 'You won't believe this but the bastard's dead. *Fatally shot two months ago outside his home in a suspected gangland shooting. DOA at Beaumont Hospital...* I don't bloody believe it!'

Jack shook his head without replying, momentarily crushed into silence. Every time they thought they had something solid to go on in this damned case it dissolved in front of them like so much early morning mist. He turned and slowly walked back into his office, pursued by a suddenly dejected Frank. They sat together in silence for some moments, with Jack suddenly feeling the need for a drink more than he had in days. Only the resilience of youth finally allowed Frank to finally ask, in a tone not totally devoid of hope, 'What now, sir?'

'Good bloody question,' muttered Jack, resisting the impulse to answer; *a trip to the nearest pub to get blind drunk.* 'Wish I knew the answer. There doesn't seem to be much else we *can* do.'

'No, sir,' agreed Frank, 'It's just one dead end after another. *Literally* dead ends.'

Silence descended again before Jack said thoughtfully, 'Literally is right. There's a sight too many dead people turning up in this case for my liking. Do you think that could in itself be significant?'

After a minute's thought Frank shrugged, 'Not really, sir. We know for a fact that Jimmy Shiels' death was nothing to do with Akima; the case was closed on that ages ago, with no question of a mistake. And I don't see how Crilly's death could be tied to Akima's.'

'If they were both in the drugs business their murders wouldn't be *that* unusual,' mused Jack, 'It's a dangerous game, after all, and the buggers kill each other every day. There's *too* much money in it, and after all, they are all bloody crooks so they're constantly ripping each other off, and then killing each other. I don't think Crilly knowing Akima was a coincidence, and there's a good chance that Akima knew Daniel Wistarra. And we know there's a link between *their* deaths because of the "Niggers go Home" thing at both scenes.'

'Yes, sir,' said Frank dully, 'but what's the link between the death of a major Irish criminal and the murder of two Africans with *no* criminal record? One of them just a kid? Aren't we just clutching at straws because we've nothing concrete to go? I mean, I know you've pretty much ruled out those anti-immigrant groups but maybe there's a new one we don't know about? A more militant lot? Or something less formal, like a few like-minded psychos who've just linked up together somehow?'

Jack shook his head in frustration and confusion, 'None of this makes any sense. We find out that Crilly and Akima knew each other socially, and possibly business-wise. Both are murdered within a couple of months of each other, yet there's no connection between their killings? Surely that's too much of a coincidence? Is it possible that the motive for Akima and Wistarra's deaths isn't racial at all? That the whole *"Sons of Cuchuailainn* thing is just a red herring?'

'I don't know,' said Frank in a bemused tone, 'You never liked the racist angle in the first place so now we've come back full circle. *An ever-decreasing circle, that winds down to despair/ Where confusion reigns supreme, and the ugly seems so fair.* But there *could* be another, more violent group of racists we don't know about, sir. You said yourself you were surprised by the outpouring of hate calls we received, by the sheer level of racism amongst ordinary Irish people; there could easily be other groups we don't know about. And if so, how do we go about *finding* them?'

Jack shook his head gloomily, 'I dunno. We just keep looking, I suppose. Until we find *something*. I was on to the pathologist's office this morning, by the way, but no joy there. They got nothing useful from Wistarra's body. Traces of boot polish embedded into the skin of his face from the attackers' shoes but, of course, it was all the same type. Want to guess what type that was?'

'Kiwi?' asked Frank resignedly.

'You got it. Probably the most popular brand around. I was hoping for skin samples, since he was beaten with fists rather than clubs, but no go; from patterns within the bruises Ryan reckons they must have used gloves. Real leather gloves if that's any help.'

'Terrific. Still, it might lead somewhere if they can identify the make of glove?'

'Hmm. They're working on it. Trying to trace the dye in the leather, apparently. The wonders of modem science, eh? Well, let's see if they actually come up with anything.'

'Did you get anything from the African People's Support Group this morning, sir?'

'Not much,' replied Jack heavily, 'Apart from confirming that Wren and Wistarra were both members. Akima wasn't, though the guy in charge said that he used to pop in occasionally, and of course we know he hired Wren there. But he couldn't tell me if Akima and Wistarra knew each other at all. It's a support group rather than a social network, and not all of the members become friends.'

This engendered a silence that dragged on until Julie stuck her head in the office and said crossly, 'You could have told me you were finished with my computer, you know. I *do* have my own work to do too, you know, whatever you seem to think!'

Jack raised a weary hand as if to ward off her anger, 'Sorry, Jules. We got distracted.'

She pursed her lips but didn't pursue it, instead saying, rather reluctantly, 'Pathology have just phoned with the results of that cross-check you ordered. The traces of semen in Akima's stomach *were* Daniel Wistarra's, apparently. Does that mean anything to you?'

The two men exchanged amazed glances in which confusion was quickly replaced by burgeoning hope.

'Does that help?' asked Frank cautiously.

'Thanks, Jules, that's all for now,' said Jack with what he thought was a winning smile and, tossing her head at being thus dismissed from the inner circle, Julie vanished. After she had banged the door Jack shook his head and said firmly, 'Right, we're through chasing our own tails. And looking for bloody neo-Nazis. I never believed they existed in the first place but this is the last straw. If Akima and Wistarra were lovers their murders *couldn't* be just a coincidence. Not when you factor in Crilly's murder too. I know he was a drug-dealer but it's asking too much for it to be coincidence that he knew Akima and he was also murdered; there *has* to be another, non-racial link. *Has* to be.' He paused for a moment, struck by a thought, 'It couldn't have been a love triangle, could it? A jealous boyfriend killing them both, then painting the slogan on the wall to distract us from the truth?'

'I don't think so,' said Frank dubiously, 'After all, we know for certain that more than one man carried out the murders.'

Jack made an impatient gesture, 'He could have rounded up his mates or, more likely, hired a few thugs to do the job for him.'

Frank shook his head in disbelief, 'They'd have to be some mates! Though I suppose muscle isn't hard to hire, if you know where to look. Well, *maybe*, but I think your instinct was right in the very beginning; that we're dealing with an organised gang of professional thugs, and that the whole racist thing is just a blind.'

Jack grimaced, 'My instincts have been somewhat dulled of late. Either way we'll still have to check out every angle, just to be certain. That is, if we can *find* any boyfriends, past or present, aside from young Wistarra.' He eyed his assistant judiciously, through half-closed eyelids, lower lip pushed out, 'These guys *were* professional though, weren't they? They certainly didn't make any mistakes. If they *were* hired we'll never track them down so we're going to abandon jealous lovers -and Nazis- and follow the money.'

'Sir?'

'Aside from crimes of passion almost all killings are for money,' said Jack patiently, 'And since Akima had no family to murder him in order to inherit, the only money floating around in this case revolves around Crilly. There are sackloads of money in drugs, more than enough to kill people for. Jesus, not a week goes by in Dublin alone without a gangland killing or two. Crilly was a known dealer, and he knew Akima, whom your girlfriend said was constantly awash with drugs.'

Ignoring the "girlfriend" crack Frank protested, 'There's a difference between having a supply of recreational drugs -which he probably bought from Crilly or Shiels anyway- and being a drug dealer himself!'

Jack shook his head stubbornly, 'Akima was a wealthy, successful man with no business interests in Ireland. So what was he here for, the weather? To fish for bloody salmon in the Liffey? Apart from Miss Riordan herself the only two people we've ID'd as friends of his were both known criminals, and one was a major drug dealer. So we're going to abandon all the bullshit and wild theories and assume there's a connection between their deaths, based on drug money. Now all we have to do is find that connection.'

Frank pulled at his nose and said dubiously, 'Well, maybe, but what about Wistarra, sir? You don't think he was involved in the drugs business too?'

Jack shrugged, 'He must have been. I know he was only a kid but if he was Akima's boyfriend he must have had *some* connection with it. Otherwise, why kill him? Unless it was because he knew who killed Akima, and they were afraid he'd shop them.'

Jack suddenly shook his head and scrubbed his face vigorously with his hands, 'Let's keep this simple! Someone in Crilly's life -maybe even *his* murderer- is responsible for *our* killings; all we have to do is find him. Liam O'Malley from Organised Crime is an old friend of mine.' He paused and, half to himself, 'At least, he used to be. I'll give him a call and find out what he knows about Crilly, and his enemies. *And* his friends; with criminals they're often the same people. One or the other will be behind all this, mark my words.'

'Yes, sir.' With the resilience of youth Frank was perking up again already, momentary despair forgotten, 'And what about Jimmy Shiels? He was a criminal so we should check his erstwhile friends and companions too, and make a list of *their* known associates. You never know, it might throw up another suspect or two.'

Jack gave a wry smile, 'What were you saying about ever decreasing circles? We're going round in so many circles we'll be lucky not to vanish up our own arses! No, Shiels has been dead for ages, and we know who killed him anyway, and why, so we can forget about him for the moment. Sean Crilly is the key to it all. He has to be. Though I suppose you'd better check Shiels' known associates in case any names overlap with those of Crilly.' He heaved a sudden sigh, doubts creeping in, 'Unless he was killed by someone we know nothing about. We're putting a lot of reliance on your girlfriend's word, aren't we? I just hope Akima didn't have some friends she *didn't* know.'

He paused before looking at Frank from under his eyebrows, 'We're clutching at straws again, aren't we? But even straws are better than nothing. We're not giving up on this case.'

'No, sir,' replied Frank staunchly, 'Not until we've solved it.'

Jack nodded slowly, 'Not until we've solved it.' It had something of the feel of a solemn oath when they both said it aloud like that, a sacred pact, but inside he was thinking; *Or until we get kicked off it in disgrace.* He sighed again, then said, 'Right, run a check on Shiels' known associates while I have a chat with my old mate O'Malley. If nothing else sheer bloody persistance might get us somewhere. *Once more into the breach,* and all that.'

'See, poetry is catching,' said Frank as he left the pokey little office, laughing aloud at the disgusted expression that suddenly appeared on the older man's face. 'Before long we'll have you writing your own!'

'Shows what you know!' riposted Jack with grim glee, 'That wasn't poetry, it was from one of Shakespeare's plays. Smartarse!' And, having suitably crushed his assistant, he swept past him and made off before Frank could ask him exactly *which* of Shakespeare's plays it was from.

Chapter Fourteen

Jack tapped on the office door and opened it without waiting for an invitation. At this intrusion Detective Superintendent Liam O'Malley looked up from a vast pile of paperwork and froze for an instant before dropping his pen and leaning back in his seat, a grin slowly spreading slowly across his large, red face. 'Well, well, well!' he uttered with apparently genuine pleasure, 'Look who it is! I heard a rumour you'd crawled out of your bottle back into the land of the living! How are you, Jackie-boy?'

'Not too bad,' admitted Jack, closing the door behind him and accepting both O'Malley's outstretched hand and a chair, in that order. 'Put it this way; I've been a hell of a lot worse. How are you keeping, Liam? You're certainly looking well.'

O'Malley made a face and patted his protuberant stomach ruefully, 'Don't give me that, Jack, I know exactly how I look! Too many good dinners washed down with too many pints of Guinness. And you're no oil-painting yourself, I have to say.'

Jack laughed, 'Your personality hasn't changed, at any rate. Liam the Liar we used to call you, seeing as how you didn't know how to tell one.'

O'Malley smiled back, 'I remember. I was quite proud of that, in the old days.' He paused for a moment before shrugging and saying, a touch sadly, 'I suppose it's better than my kids' name for me; "that fat old bastard" they call me behind my back.' He shook his head in disgust, 'I dunno, teenagers; they break your bloody heart, really they do.' He realised that this was insensitive even as he spoke and shot Jack an anxious look.

Jack managed a smile, albeit a grim one, 'You don't have to tread on eggshells around me, Liam. I'm not going to burst into tears or kill myself in front of you.'

'No? You've been killing yourself in front of me for years,' said O'Malley softly, 'and no matter how hard I tried I couldn't stop you. None of us could.'

Jack shrugged, 'You tried. That counts for a lot. Tried harder and for longer than most of my friends. But there are some things you have to experience yourself to understand, which is why none of you could reach me. None of you had any idea of what I went through.'

'No,' said O'Malley heavily, 'perhaps not.' He looked Jack over furtively, 'You seem to have regained a bit of your old sparkle, though. Are you finally over it, Jack?'

Jack thought about this for several seemingly endless seconds before slowly replying, 'Some things you never get over, Liam. *Never*. But I think I'm finally starting to realise that my life can carry on without them. If I want it to.'

O'Malley eyed him thoughtfully, 'And has the jury returned a verdict?'

Jack smiled, 'Not yet. I'm afraid they're still debating the issue.'

O'Malley nodded, 'But in the meantime you're sober and more alert than I've seen you in years. More *alive*. Being back in harness could be the saving of you, Jack. If you let it.'

O'Neill shrugged, 'Maybe, though God knows that's not how it feels at the moment. The case I'm on at the moment is driving me nuts, to be honest. I can't get anywhere with it, I just keep going round in circles.' He found himself on the verging of quoting, *Ever decreasing circles, that lead down to despair/* and shut his mouth with a snap; *Jesus, I'll be as bad as Frank next!*

'How can I help?' asked O'Malley briskly.

Taking a deep breath, Jack gave him a brief resume of the case so far, ending with his speculation that the deaths of William Akima and Sean Crilly were linked, possibly by the drugs trade. He finished by saying, 'So I want to find out everything you know about Sean Crilly and his associates. I'm sure there's a murderer lurking in there somewhere.'

O'Malley laughed at that, 'There's more than one, boy, and they aren't lurking; murderers are everywhere in *his* background! Or rather, *foreground*! And, of course, someone topped *him* a while back, though no one seems to know who, or why.'

He leaned back in his swivel chair, a frown of concentration on his face as he gathered his thoughts. 'It's a bit odd, actually; usually we have a fair idea why these hits take place, and who orders them, even if we can't prove anything. But we haven't a *clue* who shot Sean Crilly, or why. He wasn't feuding with anyone -for a change- and no one was trying to muscle in on his territory. Not that we know of, anyway. And we never heard of his mates going after anyone to avenge his death either.' He shrugged, 'Rumour has it that his own people did it but you just never know. It certainly wouldn't be any great surprise if it *was* them; these guys are more like sewer rats than human beings, and loyalty is just a word to them.'

Jack mulled this over, wondering how any of it fitted in with his case. The short answer was that it didn't. He sighed and said, 'What can you tell me about Crilly's background?'

'Ah, he was never any good from the beginning,' said O'Malley instantly. 'He was dragged up on the backstreets of Finglas by a drunken slut of a mother and a violent thug of a father who was also a criminal. He was more or less constantly in trouble with the law from the age of about seven. All he ever wanted was to be a criminal, like his Da, and he spent most of early his life first in reform school and then in prison. He never amounted to much, to be honest, but he was cunning enough, and vicious enough, to become leader of the gang he ran with.'

'When was this?' asked Jack interestedly.

'Oh, about five or six years ago, I suppose. He'd always been ambitious, and when the old boss was put away -to serve three consecutive life sentences for a series of gangland killings- he saw his chance and took over. He did a good job too; tightening up security and only using proven hard men for his jobs, old pros like himself who'd never squeal. He never used junkies or anyone like that; too unreliable. And since then we haven't been able to touch him or any of his gang for as much as a parking ticket. Turns out he had a few brains to go with his natural cunning. And viciousness, of course. I'll make a list of his cronies for you, if you like.'

'Sure,' said Jack distractedly, 'Jimmy Shiels wasn't one of them, was he?'

'Shiels? *There's* a blast from the past. But you have to be joking; he was strictly small-time, young Jimmy, hadn't the brains or the balls to be anything more. He might have pushed for Crilly sometimes but it would have been on a very small scale; he was never an integral part of his gang. He's dead too, you know; he got croaked a year or so ago.'

'Yeah, I know. It's just that we have a witness who says they were together quite often.'

O'Malley pursed his lips, 'Maybe, but he wasn't close to Crilly, I can guarantee you that. Jimmy Shiels was a rat, and no one in their right mind would have trusted him an inch. He wasn't up to anything more complicated than a bit of street pushing, and Crilly didn't even use him for that very often. Not according to the street gossip, anyway. You have to understand, everything I'm telling you is just rumour and conjecture. But it's no secret that Crilly went almost totally into drug-smuggling when he took over the West Finglas crew, and very profitably too. For some reason he and his crew more or less gave up on the robberies and extortion and the like, though I heard they opened quite a few brothels.' He shrugged, 'Maybe they made so much money from drugs they didn't need to do the other stuff anymore.'

'And where did they get these drugs? Any idea?'

'Zaire was the rumour, though no one knows for sure. Most of the poppy originates in Afghanistan and then goes on to be processed in factories in Africa, South America, Turkey...' he shrugged, 'Take your pick. The whole world is awash with that shit.'

'My victim, Akima, was from Africa,' said Jack hopefully, 'which gives us another connection with Crilly. Mind you, he was from South Africa, not Zaire.'

'Is that so?' said O'Malley, 'Well, we know that Crilly had business interests in South Africa, though we don't know exactly what or how much, since his name never appeared on paper and he never went near the place. Never left Ireland even to go on holiday, our Sean. Probably afraid we wouldn't let him back into the country. If only it were that simple. We know for sure he had several bank accounts over there at the time of his death, though, containing over two million euro, so he must have had people working for him there. But I've never heard the name Akima before. Or rather,' he corrected himself, 'I hadn't till I saw it in yesterday's paper.'

Jack whistled softly; two million quid! 'What happened to all that cash after he died?'

O'Malley laughed, 'Well, that's how we found out about it. His wife tried to claim it but the Criminal Assets Bureau got there first. She had no way of explaining where it came from so they wouldn't give it to her. And the house she lived in was in Crilly's name so they took that too, since Crilly had no legal source of income, and she couldn't show where the money came from to buy it.'

O'Malley laughed again; a rich, heartfelt sound. 'Maggie Crilly wasn't best pleased about that either, let me tell you! She refused to leave at first but they managed to evict her there a few weeks ago. She's back living in her mother's place now, trying to get the money and the house back through the courts. She's very bitter about it all, apparently, and no wonder.'

'And will she get them back?' asked Jack idly, not much caring either way; given his choice he'd happily see all criminals and their wives sleeping by the side of the road. His sympathies were reserved entirely for their unfortunate victims.

'Not the money, anyway. She has *no* chance of getting her paws on that. And she won't get the house back either unless she can show a legitimate source for the cash they bought it with. And even then she'd have to pay tax on it, since he never declared any income in his life, and never paid anything to the revenue.' O'Malley chuckled with satisfaction and shook his head admiringly, 'I love these new tax laws! Just thinking about CAB warms the cockles of my heart, I tell you! We've got criminals so they don't know whether they're coming or going. Some of the biggest crime lords in Dublin live in Council houses and drive old bangers for fear of having everything they own confiscated! Unfortunately, most of them are now buying legitimate businesses where they can, just to have a declarable source of income. They spend half their time inventing receipts and stuff to account for where their cash comes from, because none of these businesses make a penny!'

Jack smiled politely back at his grinning friend but his mind was elsewhere, wondering how he could dig up a connection between the two dead men. 'Can you give me a list of the members of Crilly's gang? Including who has taken over now he's dead?'

'Sure,' replied O'Malley, scribbling busily, 'The new gang boss is a guy called Mike Sheehy, another long time scumbag and general no-hoper. He always had the name for being reliable but stupid, so his promotion was a surprise. We couldn't believe he had the brains or the ambition to take over but he seems to have managed it, though it's still early days.'

He shook his head in amazement, 'Who would have thought it, old thicko Sheehy taking Sean Crilly's place? Hard to believe anyone that stupid could be a boss. But then, if crooks were smart, old fools like us would never catch any, would we?'

He roared with laughter, to which Jack offered another polite smile as he surveyed the list his old friend had made. 'There aren't any addresses here, Liam?'

O'Malley stopped guffawing to protest, 'What am I, Marvo the bloody Memory Man? They're all well known, Jack, don't worry about that. Every one of them is logged in the computer files. Just look them up.'

'Fair enough.' O'Neill got to his feet and held out his hand, 'Thanks, Liam, this should help a lot.'

O'Malley took the outstretched hand but shook his head in disagreement, 'I doubt it, to be honest. These are all lifelong professional crooks, Jack, hand picked for loyalty. None of them are going to tell you a thing unless you have them by the balls.'

'Maybe not,' said Jack, opening the office door, 'but they were supposed to be his mates; if even one of them is unhappy about Crilly's death they might throw me a hint as to who was behind it.'

O'Malley shook his head, 'They'd be more likely to take revenge themselves. These are not the kind of guys who tell the Garda anything. I don't even see why you care, to be honest. What has Crilly's killer got to do with your case?'

'The murders are connected,' said Jack positively, though perhaps more to convince himself than his old friend, 'The same guys might not have carried out the actual killings but there's a connection somewhere. And I'm going to find it.'

O'Malley shrugged, 'Best of luck, my son, but I think you're wasting your time. These boys are major league, hardened criminals; none of them will tell you shit. Not unless you've got them facing about a hundred years in jail, of course; in that case most of them would rat out their own mothers.'

Jack banged the door shut behind him without replying, partly to cut off O'Malley's endless flow of chatter, and partly in petulance because he feared that his old friend was right. But the truth was he had few enough other avenues to explore; he *needed* Crilly's death to be connected with his case or he was never going to solve it.

He had spent over an hour with O'Malley, and when he returned to the basement he found the whole floor deserted, with everyone else having already departed for home, including Frank. Jack was a little disappointed, having assumed that the youngster would wait for him, but he put this feeling aside after checking that Frank had at least updated the daily log before leaving. And in fairness the youngster *had* had a trying day.

After a brief internal struggle against the lure of Dublin's pubs, their lights warmly inviting against the cold dark evening, he finally compromised by catching the DART straight home but having a drink there. Though not a particularly large one. If he wanted to keep functioning as a detective –and for the moment at least he absolutely did- he knew he had to radically cut down on the booze. With the small whiskey radiating fiery rays from his stomach, spreading comfort as well as heat, he rang Frank at his flat, neatly disturbing him about two mouthfuls into his early dinner. 'Frank? Jack here. I think I might have something for us.'

'Oh?' mumbled Frank, frantically swallowing his hot food, 'Good, because I didn't find anything. It looks like Jimmy Shiels *had* no friends. At least, no one of interest to us. What did you find out?'

Jack told him everything he had elicited from O'Malley, finishing by saying, 'So, what can we conclude from all that?'

'Er, sir?' stalled Frank, unwilling to disappoint –and irritate- his superior by giving the honest answer of *not much.*

'Oh, come on!' snorted Jack impatiently, 'Isn't it obvious? Someone in his own gang snuffed out Crilly, probably this Mike Sheehy guy!'

'I'm afraid I really don't see...'

'Well, who else stood to gain by killing him?'

Frank thought quickly, 'Someone he cheated out of money, perhaps? Or a rival gang trying to take over his business?'

'Not likely, since his old gang still rule the same territory,' argued Jack, 'O'Malley told me there was no feud, no gang war, and no clue as to who offed him. His own crew never kicked up any fuss when he was killed, for God's sake! So it must have been done, or at least ordered, by a rival *within* the gang! And who gained most by his death? The guy who took his place. Sheehy.'

'But he could have cheated a supplier or something.'

'Frank, this guy was a millionaire,' said Jack patiently, 'He'd had a sweet deal going for years, with no fuss or trouble, raking in the cash. Why would he suddenly risk it all by cheating someone dangerous enough to kill him?'

'Greed? Allied to stupidity? That's why these people become criminals in the first place. Or maybe he just jumped into the wrong bed; you said yourself sex was the other great motive for murder.'

'Stop looking for objections!' said Jack impatiently, 'It's Occam's Razor; the simplest solution is usually the correct one. And that's the assumption we're going to work on until proven wrong! Anyway, we've nothing else to go on. We'll work on the basis that Sheehy was behind his death, at least until we prove to ourselves that he wasn't.'

'Okay, I suppose you're right,' conceded Frank, by no means convinced but impressed that Jack had even heard of William of Occam and his theory. His interpretation of it was a little skewed though, and Frank was on the cusp of pointing this out when some deep seated instinct for self-preservation caused him to shut his mouth with a snap.

'Of course I'm bloody well right!' said Jack with a confidence he didn't entirely feel, 'Crilly was killed for money, and the man who made the most money out of his death was the guy who took his place. Therefore he probably killed him. Stands to reason.'

'Perhaps, but, er, don't you think we've rather wandered off the point?' asked Frank diffidently, 'I mean, we're supposed to be looking for the killers of Akima and Wistarra, and now all of a sudden you're trying to solve a killing that's nothing to do with us?'

'Rubbish!' said Jack dismissively, swallowing his own doubts along with a slug of whiskey, 'There's a link between our murders and that of Crilly. *Trust* me.'

'It's a bit of a leap, sir,' said Frank quietly, 'All we have is that Grainne Riordan saw them together a few times. That's it!'

'And the fact that they were murdered within a few weeks of each other. *And* the fact that they both had business interests in South Africa.' Jack paused when he realised what he was saying, and the paucity of evidence to back up his theory, before saying quietly, 'Look, I know all this is a bit tenuous but this just *feels* right, Frank, while the whole racist thing doesn't, and never did. Even if it is a bit of a stretch of the imagination.'

Frank was silent for a moment before heaving a sigh of defeat, 'Well, you're the boss. We'll play it whatever way you say.'

'We'll investigate the case from both angles,' compromised Jack, 'We'll keep plugging away at the racist gang angle too, but we'll also investigate Crilly's death and see if we can shake anything loose there. After all, we're going nowhere anyway.'

'Alright,' said Frank, trying to raise some of his wonted enthusiasm, 'So what's our next move?'

'We talk to some of Crilly's old gang, see if we can get anything out of them. And his wife, of course. She lost the most, even apart from her husband, and is more likely to talk to us than a bunch of hardened crooks.'

'Okay,' agreed Frank, 'Shall I pick you up in the morning?'

'These are not morning people,' replied Jack dryly, 'You got any plans for tonight?' Frank answered in the negative and Jack continued, 'The new gang boss owns a snooker hall in Finglas, and that's where they mostly hang out. Feel like paying them a visit?'

'Oh, I'd love to!' responded Frank sarcastically, 'Just my idea of a fun night.' He paused before asking, 'When?'

'Whenever you're ready,' said Jack promptly, 'Come and pick me up, I'll be waiting for you.' He put down the phone, which instantly rang under his hand, making him jump. He picked up the receiver and said cautiously, 'Hello?'

'Jack? Eamonn here, how are you?' It was Rollins, to Jack's surprise, but he only replied, 'Fine, thanks. What can I do for you?'

Rollins barked a short laugh, 'Straight to the point, eh? Good, I'll get to the point, too. What the hell do you think you're doing, digging about in other peoples' cases?'

'*Excuse* me?' said Jack in a pained voice, not caring for his boss's tone at all.

'You know damned well what I'm talking about, Jack. I met Liam O'Malley earlier and he said you were trying to connect your case to the shooting of Sean Crilly. What the *fuck* do you think you're playing at?'

Jack heaved a sigh and explained his theory in some detail, at the end of which Rollins said contemptuously, and loudly, 'What a load of crap! I've never heard such rubbish in all my life. You must be more pickled in booze than I imagined. Either that or you've lost your mind! Look, Jack, let's cut to the chase; I took a big chance on you, giving you the Akima case. Alright, I didn't know there'd be any more of these racist killings, or all this Press coverage, but even so, it was still a big risk. Now, are you going to justify my support or do I have to replace you?'

'You didn't give me this case as some sort of favour,' retorted Jack, trying to keep his own temper, 'You gave it to me because you had no one else available, remember? And to buy off Seamus Carr without anyone knowing about it. And I don't see why you didn't expect more killings, considering the graffiti we found at the first scene. Anyway, I'm *trying* to justify your "support" by bloody well solving it!'

'Giving a washed-up drunk a second chance is one thing,' said Rollins coldly, 'Watching him waste police time and resources chasing red herrings is another. And I'll be honest, Jack; now that the Press are all over it I'm a lot more anxious to get a result than I was. Now, I'm giving you a choice; either get with the programme or you're out. I've got a whole division to run and I don't have time to run after you, holding your hand, trying to keep you on track. You're only getting one chance at this; either concentrate on finding these racist thugs and forget Crilly, or you're off the case! And the force too, because by God I'll *break* you!'

Jack was silent for a moment before saying, 'Will you at least give me a couple of days to look at the Crilly angle? Just in case there *is* a connection?'

'No, I won't! Stop pissing around, Jack!' said Rollins sharply, 'I don't know if you're drunk or what, but trying to tie Akima to Sean Crilly is ridiculous! I *knew* Crilly, back when I was with Serious Crime, and he had nothing whatever to do with Akima, or any other Africans!'

'Nothing?' said Jack, surprised.

'Nothing! He never met the man! And I'm not interested in the testimony of some dumb slut who's spent half her life either drunk or stoned and who is only just out of the nut-house! Now either forget it or you're out! Decide now!'

Jack took a deep breath, fighting to keep his patience, 'Look, I knew from the start that it was a long shot but what harm can looking into it do? It's only a matter of conducting a few interviews, poking around in Crilly's background?'

'I'm not discussing this at all, Jack. You're old enough to not need this kind of supervision. I'm a busy man and I thought I could leave you to get on with this on your own but apparently not. Apparently you still need me to hold your hand and wipe your nose and point you in the right direction. Now, what's it going to be?'

'You're not leaving me much choice, are you?' said Jack slowly, 'If you want me to forget the Crilly angle, I guess I'll have to obey.'

'Good!' barked Rollins, 'And don't have me speak to you about this again!' And with that he hung up, leaving a furious Jack to carefully replace the receiver rather than following his first instinct and hurling the whole thing at the wall as hard as he could. *What the hell had happened to Rollins?* They had never been close friends but Jack had liked him well enough back in the day, and had respected him as a pretty good copper. But he wasn't a copper any more; now he was a politician, pure and simple, and the power of his lofty position seemed to have gone to his head.

Jack shook his head in disgust and poured himself another drink, albeit an even smaller one than last time, thinking; *fuck him.* This was *his* case and he'd follow it wherever the trail led. And if Eamon Rollins didn't like it he could do the other thing.

Chapter Fifteen

When Frank's little car pulled up outside O'Neill's house the older man, who had been watching for him, exited his front door and walked down the path before Frank could get out. He climbed into the passenger seat beside him and said, without preamble, 'Tully Road, in Finglas. You know it?'

'Er, no, actually. I don't know that area at all.'

Jack nodded grimly, 'Find it. Start by driving up the M50 and taking the Finglas exit.' And with that he leaned back in his seat and stared fixedly ahead, his chin lowered onto his chest and his expression sourer than Frank had yet seen him.

Frank looked at him for a moment, but contented himself with merely saying, 'Okay,' before pulling away from the curb.

They sat in silence for ten minutes or so until Jack, after a sideways glance at his assistant, sighed and said, 'Sorry, Frank. I shouldn't be taking my temper on you but we've had a bit of a setback tonight.' And he proceeded to relate everything Rollins had said to him. After he finished there was a long pause before Frank finally said, 'Er, well, to be honest I can see his point.'

'Can you indeed? Cheers, partner,' said Jack sourly.

Frank laughed and, although his heart was warmed by that *partner,* said, 'Well, you have to admit that the connection between Akima and Sean Crilly is pretty thin. All we have is an unreliable witness who says she saw them together sometimes. Whoopee.'

Jack looked out the window and said moodily, 'I know. But another way of looking at it is that if there *is* a connection, however tenuous, then it's our job to look into it. Our *duty.*'

'Yes, sir,' said Frank simply, 'that's my view, too.'

Jack looked at him for a moment, studying the clean lines of his profile in the half-light thrown up by the oncoming traffic. At length he sighed and said, 'You're a good lad, Frank, you know that? But too trusting. You have a bright career ahead of you, but only if you stay away from the likes of me.'

Frank frowned, 'I don't get you.'

'I can afford to piss Rollins off,' explained Jack simply, 'My career is already over. Yours is only starting, so you can't. It isn't fair to involve you in my wild goose chases, so I'm not going to. I should have got a taxi tonight and left you out of this altogether but I wasn't thinking straight. However, that's soon remedied; you're not coming in there with me. You can park around the corner from the snooker hall and I'll walk the rest of the way. That'll keep you out of this altogether.'

'That's ridiculous!' exclaimed an incredulous Frank, 'We're in this together! You just called me *partner*, remember? Where you go, I go. Besides, Rollins might turn nasty with you, but he can't touch me; I'm only following your orders.'

Jack shook his head decisively, 'No. Sorry, Frank, but I've made up my mind. You'll only work with me on the racist gang angle of things. This is a sideline, a flight of fantasy on my part. I don't know why Rollins got so bent out of shape about me following it up, to be honest, but he did, so this side of the investigation I handle alone. Wherever it leads.' He gave Frank a rueful, slightly sour smile, 'Which I think we both know is probably nowhere. But one way or another you're out of it. This Sheehy guy is almost certainly under surveillance from the Serious Crime Task Force, so Rollins will probably soon find out about my visiting him tonight. And if there's any fallout I'm not bringing you down with me.'

'And if it's dangerous?' asked Frank mildly.

'Dangerous, my arse!' sneered Jack caustically, 'These guys aren't *that* stupid! They're not going to touch a cop in public, whatever I say and do, because they know that if they did their lives wouldn't be worth living for a very long time! They wouldn't be able to fart without getting arrested for polluting the environment! Besides, I haven't got a shred of proof to back up my theories and they'll know that too. Also, my going there alone could be a set-up, with an Armed Response Unit waiting outside. They're bound to know that the place is being watched most of the time by Serious Crime.'

Frank made a noncommittal sound and Jack shot him a sharp look, 'I mean it, Frank, I want you out of this side of the investigation. Either you give me your word that you won't interfere or we turn around and go home right now. Alright?'

There was a long pause before Frank, very reluctantly, said, 'Okay, sir, if you insist. I'll stay in the car.'

'Good lad!' said Jack with satisfaction; so long as Frank was covered Rollins could do his worst; much he would care. They drove in silence until they entered Finglas, whereupon Frank stopped and asked a pedestrian the way to Tully Road. He was careful, however, not to identify himself as a Garda; apart from the fact that such were unwelcome in this area, no policeman could ever admit to being lost. The directions he received brought them close, at least, and at last Jack exclaimed, 'Hey, there's the street! Pull in here; I can see the 147 Club at the end of the road!'

Frank did as he was told and the older man climbed out, rather stiffly. Jack was about to close the door when a sudden impulse made him lean over and hiss urgently, 'And if I don't make it back...*avenge my death*!'

Frank rolled his eyes and stuck up two fingers at him, and Jack laughed and slammed the car door shut. He walked off towards the club, feeling pleased with himself and with life in general; it felt good to be on the hunt again, tracking down dangerous prey. It also pleased him to reflect that Frank was safe from prying eyes simply because no one, cop or criminal, would ever believe that the *Ka* was a Garda vehicle.

West Finglas was not known as the Wild West for nothing, and Jack was well used to its dirty and often dangerous streets. Even by the hardly fastidious local standards, however, the 147 Club was a dingy hole, and Jack surveyed the shabby, peeling-paint exterior with disfavour as he approached it. It had once been some sort of shop but the glass windows had been boarded up and painted black, though not any time recently. The local kids had also had a hand in decorating it, though their compulsion to construct crude sexual portraits, and to write their names and tags in letters a foot high, had not been beneficial to the club's overall appearance. He also surveyed the disparate groups of youths hanging around on the street outside it, and noted one teenager eyeing his approach thoughtfully before disappearing into the club ahead of him to spread the glad tidings.

Jack grimaced to himself; some things never changed. Why did so many kids hang around criminals, running errands and generally wanting to be like them? The movies were to blame, no doubt, filling their heads with a glamourised version of what was really a sleazy, nothing sort of life filled with violence and fear. And long stints in prison, of course. Easy money was a myth; if nothing else he had learned that nothing in life comes easy, everything must be earned. And criminals earn their thrills and 'easy' money with long periods of their lives wasted behind bars. Assuming, of course, they aren't killed by rivals, or their own friends.

He banished these glum thoughts with a slight shake of his head and brushed through the group of teenagers who were blocking the doorway, all of whom were staring at him with hostile, defiant expressions intended to show they knew what he was and weren't impressed. Jack was even less impressed with their pretence at toughness and simply ignored them, though he knew any one of them were probably capable of attacking him. And possibly even stabbing or shooting him; violent crime had been on the rise in Ireland for years, but even more worrying was the seemingly unstoppable rise in juvenile crime. Even Jack had noticed this trend from the bottom of the bottle he had been living in, and it filled him with sick horror to think that kids, *children,* often no more than twelve or thirteen, were quite capable of maiming or even killing for no reason other than innate viciousness.

After shoving his way through the mass of kids he paused just inside the door. The interior of the club appeared slightly better than the outside, though possibly only because it was so dimly lit that little could be seen. It was also, in spite of the law, filled with cigarette smoke, and Jack could see that most of the dozen or so players in the big room were smoking. This did not interest him; the knot of men sitting at a small in one corner *not* playing snooker did. Even as he looked the teenager who had spotted him outside walked quickly away from the group, confirming Jack's suspicion as to their identity.

There was a counter to his left, behind which a bored looking teenage girl was staring at him apathetically. 'Well?' she said indifferently, 'Yeh want a table or wha'?'

Jack approached the counter and said in a hard, confident voice, 'Those men over there, which one is Mike Sheehy?'

The girl's eyes shot in their direction before looking back at him expressionlessly, chewing gum with an open mouth as dully and mechanically as any masticating cow. Although her lack of response was an answer of sorts in itself she was not about to overtly help so Jack abandoned her and made directly for the group in the corner, who appeared to be playing poker for money. Before he even reached them the man in the centre of the group sneered at him, 'What do you want, *copper?*'

'You're Sheehy?' Jack made it a statement, and the other's expression never flickered as he answered, 'What of it?'

'I want a word,' said Jack, showing his warrant card, which by the grace of God he had managed to find earlier, tucked away in a cupboard drawer months ago and forgotten about. 'In private.'

Sheehy looked him up and down, 'What about?'

'You may have noticed my use of the word "private",' Jack replied sarcastically, 'I'll tell you what about when we're somewhere prying ears aren't waggling.' The other made no move or reply so he continued, in a bored tone, 'You know the way this goes; you can either give me five minutes now or we can both waste the whole night down the local station. Either way you *are* going to talk to me.'

They stared at each other, a sneer on Sheehy's face, and Jack knew he had to allow him some leeway, some way of saving face in front of his cronies by not taking orders from a cop. And never willingly talking to one. He glanced around conspiratorially and moderated his tone, 'Look, I'm not looking for your life story, just a quick word. Five minutes and I'm gone. Otherwise it's an all-nighter in the cells.'

Sheehy heaved an exaggerated sigh and got to his feet, 'Alright, cop, I'll give you five minutes. I wouldn't want to keep you in the cells all night when you could be at home fucking your mother.' The others in the group laughed uproariously at this sally as he led the way to an unmarked door in the corner. Jack followed, his expression neutral. He was untroubled by the insult, caring nothing for the opinion of scum like these, and knowing that it was not personal anyway; Sheehy had to protect his tough guy image in front of his men, and possibly even in his own eyes too. It was all part of the game these fools played; it was as if they all believed they were characters from The Sopranos or something. Or wanted to be.

The door led to a small office not unlike Jack's own, containing only two chairs and a desk, behind which Sheehy sat. He leaned back and looked at Jack with an habitually blank face, saying, 'Well, what do you want?'

Jack sat on the other chair and looked at him; Sheehy was a big man and powerfully built, with a shaven head and heavy, bristly jowls. His brown eyes were small and close-set, and showed little in the way of intelligence. He was a stereotypical thug, in fact, walking muscle, and Jack would have bet he worked out in a gym, though not enough; there was also plenty of fat sheathing the muscle. Too much easy living since he had taken over as Boss, perhaps. What he didn't give was an impression of any brains, or even street-smarts. Nor had he any trace of charisma or personality. Jack stared at him, puzzled; far from running an international drugs ring, this guy looked like might have trouble with an international phone call. What was the deal here?

Sheehy lit a cigarette and blew the smoke across the desk into Jack's face. Then he looked at his watch and said, 'The clock is ticking on your five minutes. You now have four.'

The policeman said nothing, simply continuing to stare at him steadily. Silence was a weapon Jack had used on suspects many times before, knowing that many people feel compelled to break it, to fill the dead air by saying something, *anything,* especially when dealing with the police. And the longer it went on the greater the tension would be, and the greater the chance of the crook making a slip-up when he *did* start talking. It worked better with smarter and more imaginative people than Sheehy appeared to be, though. Still, dull or not, he would certainly have a guilty conscience about *something,* and this -or at least what passed for a conscience among his type- would be starting to move into hyper-drive about now.

In spite of his tough guy act the silence was clearly getting on Sheehy's nerves and he now drummed on the table with his fingers and said irritably, 'Your five minutes are nearly up, copper, and I'm a busy man, so either ask your questions or fuck off.'

'Alright,' said Jack agreeably, 'Here's a question for you; did you kill Sean Crilly?' He was watching Sheehy carefully as he spoke, and although the big man's facial expression was carefully wooden, Jack thought he detected something under the initial surprise; something moved in his eyes, like a rat scuttling about in the shadow of a wall. And suddenly Jack was certain that even if *he* hadn't done it, he knew who had.

Sheehy blew a cloud of smoke in Jack's direction, 'No, I didn't.' He didn't try to be convincing, or put any inflexion in his voice save boredom which, oddly, made Jack more inclined to believe him.

'Who did, then?'

'Who knows?' shrugged Sheehy, betraying the lie, however, by averting his eyes for a split second. 'With a popular bloke like Sean it could've been almost anyone in Ireland. Maybe even one of you lot; yeh certainly hated him enough. But a rival gang, is the word on the street.'

'Hm,' mused Jack, 'that's right, you wouldn't know, would you? Being just a water-carrier in his crew, I mean.'

Sheehy frowned and growled threateningly, 'Are you calling me a nigger?'

Jack frowned at him, puzzled, before saying coldly, 'You're thinking of spear *thrower,* you ignorant ape.'

Sheehy curled his lip at him, 'You're ignorant one. It's in the Bible. When Elijah got drunk his good sons turned their faces from his nakedness. But his wicked children looked upon him, so God made their faces turn black and condemned them to be forevermore hewers of wood and *carriers of water.*'

Jack looked at him, astonished at this evidence of education and in no position to challenge the accuracy of the quotation, before finally saying, 'How the bloody hell do you know that?'

Sheehy said nothing but his sneer deepened; he could have enlightened Jack about the number of religious bodies who flood prisons with tracts and religious lessons –and the fact that if a man is confined to a cell twenty-three hours a day he'll read almost anything, even the Bible- but he just couldn't be bothered. Besides, he liked the amazed look on Jack's face.

After a moment spent gaping at him Jack recovered and said, 'Anyway, don't use the N-word again; using it is a criminal offence in Ireland these days. It's called incitement to hatred. Besides, it's offensive. What's the matter, don't you like black people?'

Sheehy shrugged again, 'No, I don't. Does anyone? Are these questions going somewhere? I'm a busy man, yeh know.'

'It means that someone who doesn't like blacks killed two of them recently,' said Jack quietly, his eyes boring into his quarry.

Sheehy's face had been carefully immobile from the beginning and now his eyes froze over too and became lifeless. 'I don't know what you're talking about,' he intoned flatly. 'I thought you were looking for Sean Crilly's killer?'

Jack nodded, now certain he was lying; he knew something about Akima, and Daniel Wistarra too. He reverted to his earlier line of questioning, 'A water-carrier is someone without the brains or the balls to be a boss, someone who takes orders rather than giving them. Someone like you. So tell me; how did a dumb fucking nobody like you get to be boss of this crew?'

Sheehy refused to rise to the bait. He got to his feet and said quietly, even resignedly, 'Fuck off, copper. Either arrest me for something or get out; I'm through talking to you.'

Jack nodded, but made no attempt to move, 'So, why did you kill William Akima?'

Sheehy shook his head, 'I told you, I'm through talking. Arrest me for something or get out. I'm missing my card game.'

'What about Daniel Wistarra?' asked Jack, knowing he wouldn't answer but still hoping to rile him into some sort of reaction; even a negative reaction might tell him something. 'I can think of a few reasons for killing Akima, but why a kid like Wistarra? And a pouffe, at that?'

'Arrest me, or get out,' repeated Sheehy with infinite patience, though he sat back down again as he said it. His tone told Jack that he would just keep repeating it like a mantra, over and over, without deviating and without cracking; no doubt he had played this game many times before. And yet he hadn't carried out his threat and simply walked away. Why not? A guilty conscience, was Jack's guess; he had attended the psychology courses and knew that a certain type of person, when under pressure, simply digs their heels in and stonewalls rather than taking any positive action. But not the alpha-male Sheehy would have to be to take over a tough crew like this one; an alpha-male will always act, or react, rather than simply endure, even if action is not the wisest course. It's their nature. Once again it seemed Sheehy had no great decision or force of character; not even bad character. It was odd; Jack had met many gang leaders over the years and they had all had a hell of a lot more personality than this great lump. Even if this personality was so vile you wanted to kill them on sight they all had *something* about them.

'Alright, I'll go,' he said suddenly, getting to his feet, 'but I'll be back, Mike. I'm not giving up on this. I'm going to find out who killed them all. I think it was you,' he added softly, 'and if it was I'm going to put you away forever.'

Sheehy grinned at him, sneering openly and apparently genuinely amused, 'I'm shaking in me boots. The door's behind yeh.'

Jack nodded and turned away, thinking furiously; something had happened there at the end, something he didn't understand. Sheehy had seemed *amused* by Jack's threat. Did that mean he *hadn't* killed them? Or that he just wasn't worried by having O'Neill on his trail? No doubt he was used to the police pursuing him and had become *blasé* about it, but the secret amusement seemed oddly out of place in such a lumpen oaf. Jack paused, doorknob in hand, before turning back to say, 'I'm going to keep asking questions, Mike, and eventually someone will answer them. If not you, then Crilly's mother. Or his wife. Or *someone*. This is not over; it's only just beginning. You can trust me on that.' And with that he walked out of the office and on out of the club, knowing that if nothing else he had shaken the branch, and could only hope that something would fall out.

Many eyes followed him as he exited the club and began walking down the dark, dirty street; he could feel them burning into his back like so many lasers. But no one moved to follow him and the tension slowly eased out of his belly as he walked down to where Frank was parked and, after a quick glance behind him to make sure he was no longer being observed, got into the *Ka*.

'About bloody time!' snapped Frank, forgetting the respect due to a superior in his relief, 'I was just about to call for back-up and go storming in. What took you so long?'

'You know how it is with such hospitable people,' grunted Jack, putting on his seatbelt, albeit a tad stiffly; he had arthritis in both shoulders and the left one was giving him gyp at the moment. 'It's hard to drag yourself away. Don't drive past the club, go back that way.'

'Why, do you think you're being watched?' asked Frank, nonetheless obeying by performing an illegal U-turn across an unbroken white line.

Jack snorted, 'No, because they'll never take me seriously if they see me in a *Ka*.'

Frank lapsed into amused silence and Jack, with a sideways glance at his tight-lipped face, sighed and said, 'It's other Gardai I'm worried about seeing us. I told you I wanted to keep you out of this and I meant it. I admit it's unusual to be worried about being spotted by the cops rather than the bad guys, but if there *is* a surveillance team watching that place I don't want them to see you. I can handle Rollins finding out I was here; you can't. Not at this stage of your career, anyway. Oh, I know you have good political connections but even you can't afford to have the Assistant Commissioner as an enemy.'

'Even me, eh?' Frank sighed, his vanity ruffled; this was not the first time it had been made clear to him that within the police force his politician uncle was considered the main reason for his career progress to date, and he doubted it would be the last. Not that anyone seemed to think any the less of him for it; nepotism appeared to be rife in the Gardai. It irked him, though, and he tried to fight this assumption when he met it, though he was aware there was at least an element of truth behind it. This time, however, he let it go and asked, 'Okay, so what did you learn? Or am I not allowed to hear that either?'

Jack smiled internally at the bitterness in the young man's voice; the boy was made of the right stuff, no doubt about it. He really cared about the job. But he only said, 'Well, I'm more certain than ever that Sean Crilly was killed by his own people, and probably Sheehy himself. The trouble is it's just a feeling, an instinct; God knows where we're going to find the proof. I asked Sheehy straight out if he did it, to unsettle him, and although he denied it something about the way he answered made me certain that if he didn't do it himself, he knows who did. He said it was a rival gang but he was laughing at me, Frank, daring me to prove him wrong. Which I will, by the way,' he added grimly.

'So we're not really any further on, are we?' said Frank unthinkingly.

'Exactly what the bloody hell did you expect?' Jack blasted him, 'A confession? What we've done is tell the whole gang, including Crilly's murderer, that we suspect them, and that we're watching them; that we're not looking at rival gangs or whatever. It might just frighten someone into a mistake, or an enemy of the killer into giving us a tip-off. You never know. Plus I'm going to question Crilly's friends and family, and just hope that something breaks. Surely someone cared enough about the bugger to want to see his killer caught?'

'As you said earlier, his wife would probably be our best bet for that,' pointed out Frank.

Jack nodded absently, 'I'll talk to her tomorrow; it's a bit late for house calls tonight. The trouble, of course, is that all his mates were criminals, and the code states that you don't help the cops, no matter what. If someone hurts you or yours you take revenge yourself. Even his wife could feel that way.'

'What about his kids?'

'Good thinking,' said Jack approvingly, 'but apparently they're only six and eight, too young to know anything even if they wanted to help. Which I doubt; even by that age they have hatred and suspicion of the Gardai bred into them.'

'I don't want to upset you, sir,' began Frank cautiously, 'but even if you're right about Sheehy being responsible for Sean Crilly's death, it still might have nothing to do with Akima and Wistarra. It still *probably* has nothing to do with them.'

'You're starting to sound like Rollins,' replied Jack sourly. 'Don't worry, I told you I'm only going to look into this as a sideline. Officially we'll still be looking for a racist gang. That way I should be able to fob Rollins off. He can't pull me off the case for investigating another murder in my own time. Him and his "wasting police time and money". Ha! He'll sing a different tune when we solve this *and* our own two murders.'

'I hope so, sir,' said Frank, though less optimistically, 'After all; *"I cook for you the sourest dish, your own words forced to swallow! When I, maligned, am proven right, my greatest joy will follow".*'

Jack heaved an exaggerated sigh, 'It's been a long and difficult day, Frank; please stop making it worse.'

'Er, sorry, sir,' said Frank, crestfallen, 'I was just trying to comfort you with the thought of you eventually being proven right.'

'And I appreciate the thought,' Jack replied, leaning back and shutting his eyes tiredly, 'believe me, I do. But if you just take me home a large whiskey will have a very similar effect without saying a bloody word.'

Chapter Sixteen

It was still relatively early when Frank got home so, after some thought, he finally gave in to a temptation that had been tugging at him all day and rang Kate Bennett's number. As he had hoped it was Grainne Riordan who answered, her throaty greeting causing a slight catch in his own voice as he replied, 'Hi, Grainne, it's Detective Frank Carr here. I was, ah, just wondering how Ms Bennett was doing?'

'Oh, she's great!' gushed Grainne excitedly, 'She had her baby, and the two of them are just fine! He's lovely, actually, a beautiful little baby boy! They're going to call him Charlie. She had a pretty easy time of it in the end...well, relatively speaking, but it still exhausted her so I decided to nip home for a few hours once she fell asleep. I'm afraid you won't be able to talk to her until tomorrow at the very earliest.'

'Er, I don't want to talk to her,' said Frank awkwardly, grateful that the phone could not betray the fact that he was blushing like a schoolgirl, 'Er, to tell the truth it was you I wanted to talk to.'

'Oh yes?' Grainne's excitement disappeared and her voice became guarded and infused with apprehension, 'I told you everything I could remember earlier, and I'm afraid with all the excitement I haven't given it any further thought.'

'No, no!' Frank assured her, 'I didn't ring about the case. I suppose I rang...well, just to talk to you.'

'Oh? Just to talk to little old me?' Grainne's apprehension vanished, being replaced by a cool amusement which did nothing to ease Frank's confusion, 'What about?'

It was clear that she knew very well why he was calling, had known since puberty the effect her looks had on men, and in spite of his embarrassment Frank laughed at her archness and said, 'Good question! I'm afraid I didn't actually have a specific topic in mind, I was more after a general chat?'

'A *chat?*' Grainne's tone was now openly mocking but not unfriendly, 'That's not a very official-sounding term. Don't you mean you want to question me? *Interrogate* me, in fact? Or...no, wait, surely you didn't want to talk to me on a *personal* matter?'

'Most amusing,' replied Frank, trying to sound sarcastic but grinning in spite of himself and feeling much as he had back when he was fourteen and had asked out the prettiest girl in his school. Without success. 'I think you've been around Ms Bennett *way* too long. Prepare yourself for a shock but it *was* a private chat I was after. Worse, I was going to ask you out on a *date.*'

'Ah, well,' said Grainne, her tone suddenly serious, 'that's a very different matter, I'm afraid.' She was silent for a moment and then she sighed, 'I don't think that a date would be a very good idea at the moment. In fact it could be a spectacularly *bad* idea. I won't lie to you or play games, Frank; I like you, and I felt attracted to you the moment I set eyes on you. By the "Rules" I suppose I shouldn't admit that but honesty is one of the things I'm trying to cultivate in my life, and you're the first man I've liked for a very long time. But...'

'Yes, I thought I felt a "but" coming,' interjected Frank ruefully.

'*But,*' she continued firmly, 'things are never as simple as they seem. You know that I've got some personal problems, and I need to sort these out before I can,' she hesitated, 'you know, get on with a normal life.'

'I do know,' replied Frank carefully, 'better than you might think. Er, I don't know how to bring this up without upsetting you, but as I told you already I know all about your background. I wasn't prying, you understand; it came up in the investigation, before I even met you. And I sympathise with you for all you've been through. Er, nothing that has happened in the past has...put me off you, if I can put it as crassly as that. Quite the contrary, actually; I admire you all the more for surviving what happened to you and overcoming the problems it caused. So if you were turning me down because of the baggage you're carrying...don't. The only effect it has on me is to make me want to help you. Er, not that I feel sorry for you or anything,' he added hurriedly, 'God, no! Quite the opposite, in...'

'Frank, stop!' interrupted Grainne, trying not to laugh, 'You're babbling! Listen, I take your point, and I'm flattered, but you have to understand that I'm trying to rebuild my life from scratch. People who've been through...*stuff* like I have tend to have very low self-esteem. And when you feel worthless you tend to be jealous and possessive and attach yourself like a limpet to the first person who shows interest in you.'

She sighed, 'It would be the easiest thing in the world for me to grab on to you now and use you to assuage my insecurities, but that's just what I *mustn't* do. It's all a bit complicated but the therapy I'm doing with Kate is designed to allow me to become healthy and to *like* myself again. To respect myself, and to become strong and self-reliant. And until I do that I have no chance of happiness with someone else, or of a fulfilled life. Can you understand that?'

'All too well,' said Frank, trying to keep his tone light in to cover his disappointment, 'But are you sure you aren't, er, *there* yet? You seem pretty healthy to me.'

Grainne uttered that husky chuckle that made his stomach flip and said, 'Alas, no. At least I don't think so. I mean, what if we started a relationship and it all went wrong? I'm not strong enough to take the rejection of being dumped, and I'm probably still too needy to dump you, even if it wasn't working. Either or both of us could end up trapped for the next couple of years in a relationship we don't want but can't get out of. I'm sorry but that's a complication I don't need and don't think I can handle.'

'Fair enough,' said Frank softly, 'I hadn't thought of that. But I think you're under-estimating yourself. You're too smart and too self-aware to fall into these traps you're afraid of. I mean, seeing pitfalls is half the battle in avoiding them, isn't it?'

There was a silence and then Grainne sighed, 'I dunno, maybe I'm just scared and using my illness as an excuse to not take a chance. When you start analysing every thought and deed you can end up paralysed into inaction, unsure of your own motives for *everything*. It's easier to sit here with people I know and trust than to plunge back out into a world full of strangers.' A wistful tone entered her voice, 'And it would be nice to do something simple and ordinary, like going out for a meal, or to the cinema. I can hardly imagine how it would feel to go dancing in a club again. And it's been a long time since I felt the excitement of going out on a date.'

'Look,' said Frank, 'Forget what I said about a date. Why don't we just do something together as friends? Have a meal or go to the cinema, like you said. I can help you feel your way back out into the bigger world, but without the pressure of us trying to start a relationship. If something happens between us in the long run...great. If it doesn't, well, I'm big enough and tough enough to handle the rejection. And if nothing else we'll both have made a friend. What do you think?'

Grainne was silent, mulling this over, and Frank added, 'And if you think this is some sort of charity thing, me doing you a favour, you're wrong. I'm from Carlow and I don't really have any friends in Dublin yet, so if anything you'll be doing *me* the favour. Trust me, I have *no* social life, and I'm tired of sitting here every night looking at the walls.'

Grainne laughed and said teasingly, 'You're probably lying through your teeth. I bet you're a member of a dozen social clubs and football teams and all sorts. Come to think of it, with my luck you're probably married with eight kids.'

'I'm not!' protested Frank earnestly, 'Honest! Only seven. No, seriously, I had a casual sort of girlfriend until recently but she ditched me, and the only club I could go to is the Garda Social Club. And I'm not *that* sad. Not yet, anyway.'

'You know,' said Grainne thoughtfully, 'I think I will have to go out with you, if only because teasing you is such fun. And so easy. That *has* to help boost my self-esteem.'

'Fine by me,' said Frank softly, *'The harp doesn't care, that the harpist loves him not! By plucking on his strings, she frees the music in him caught.* A not very elegant way of saying that we can use each other, to our mutual benefit.'

'Are you sure, Frank?' she asked fearfully, sudden vulnerability naked in her voice.

'Positive,' he said confidently, knowing that he could be agreeing to far more than was being said, that he was shouldering a part of the responsibility of helping her rebuild her life. Far from being daunted by the prospect, he felt excitement flare up within him.

'Alright, then,' she said slowly, through numb lips, 'I'd love to go out with you so.'

'Great,' he said simply, hiding the elation filling him, 'We'll take it slow at first, and keep it simple, so how about a pizza and a movie on Saturday night?'

'Great indeed!' Grainne laughed suddenly, her fears forgotten as unwonted excitement suffused her, 'God, it seems like *years* since I went out on a Saturday night; I'm as excited as a kid! I can't wait to tell Kate! I can just picture her face!'

'Yes,' said Frank unenthusiastically; he too suddenly had an image of the redoubtable Ms Bennett's face, and it was snarling. Still, she'd be safely out of the way in hospital for another few days at least, and it was possible that motherhood would soften her. Or at least distract her for a while. 'Er, suppose I pick you up at seven?'

'Great,' repeated Grainne, her voice resonant with a mixture of nerves and simple pleasure, 'I'll see you then.'

'Okay, I'll talk to you then. Bye,' said Frank, hanging up with more than a trace of reluctance; in spite of her feminine propensity for teasing he found Grainne remarkably easy to talk to. On the phone, anyway; face-to-face her ridiculous somehow unreal beauty confounded him, and his flow of words could easily run dry. He stared at the wall for a long moment, wondering to himself just what he had done, and whether he would come to regret it. Perhaps. Was it the Marilyn Monroe thing, being attracted to vulnerability, to blatant need? Didn't every man feel that his love could have saved Norma Jean? On the other hand, if it was a mistake, why did he suddenly feel like the king of the whole damned world?

The heady elation lasted through the night, and when he arose next morning Frank found himself whistling cheerfully as he carried out his ablutions, and even occasionally bursting into snatches of song. His good mood lasted all the way into the office in Harcourt Square, where he found Jack already in residence, and very far from sharing his mood.

'You're early,' growled the older man as Frank entered the office, making it sound like a crime and apparently seeing no irony inherent in this statement. He was holding a Styrofoam cup full of coffee and as he spoke he took a long and noisy slurp before leaning back in his chair and fixing Frank with a basilisk glare.

'Well, I thought I was, sir,' ventured Frank, 'But not as early as you, it seems. What's wrong, couldn't you sleep?'

Jack lowered his gaze, slightly thrown by the direct question. 'Not really. At least, not very well. Booze knocks you out, coffee keeps you awake, and I had more coffee last night than whiskey. For once. I suppose it's the price I'm paying for changing my lifestyle.'

'A small price, I think,' said Frank softly, 'in view of what you stand to gain.'

Jack chose to ignore this, instead continuing, 'Besides, I kept replaying my interview with Sheehy over and over in my head, wondering if I'd missed something, or if there was some way I could have gotten more information out of him. It kept me awake half the night, worrying about it.'

'I didn't sleep much myself,' said Frank cheerfully, 'though the cause of my insomnia was far prettier and more pleasant to think about than Mike Sheehy.'

Jack eyed him suspiciously, 'Oh yes? A woman, I take it?' Frank nodded but volunteered no further information.

'Women are the cause of all evil,' uttered Jack speciously, shaking his head in sorrow at his assistant's downfall, 'Well known fact. It's in the Bible somewhere. Or possibly Shakespeare. In fact, I think he wrote a poem to that effect.'

Frank laughed but refused to rise to so obvious a bait. Instead he changed the subject, 'What's the plan for today, sir?'

'Plans,' replied Jack broodingly, draining the last of his for once unfortified coffee with a grimace; he had almost forgotten what it tasted like *sans* alcohol. 'I told you I'm going to interview Mrs Crilly today about her late husband, to see if she wants to co-operate with us in trying to catch his killer. But I've got a few other things in mind for you to do at the same time.'

'She didn't at the time,' said Frank dubiously, 'Co-operate, I mean.'

'Yes, but she's flat broke now, and back living with her mother in a Council house. If she's angry enough at his killers, and bitter enough, she might help, however obliquely.'

'Maybe,' shrugged Frank. He hesitated, 'Er...'

'No,' interrupted Jack baldly, 'you can't come with me.' He held up a hand to forestall any argument, 'We've been through it already, Frank, and I gave you my reasons for keeping you out of this side of the case. That still goes. You'll push on with the Akima case while I follow the Crilly angle alone. Though even if Rollins finds out I was out there I'm sort of covered by the fact that Crilly and Akima were friends.'

'Yes, sir,' said Frank resignedly, knowing that this was not true, 'What do you want me to do while you're gone?'

'You could solve the case,' grunted Jack, flipping open the folder containing their case notes, 'That would be nice! Actually, I'd like you to call around to all the premises surrounding the alleyway where Daniel Wistarra was murdered. I know the uniforms already canvassed the area but if you had photos of Sheehy and his merry men you might find someone who saw one of them in the area that night. Or all of them, if Jesus loves us. But that's not really sticking to the Akima case though, is it? I've just finishing rambling on about keeping you out of the Crilly angle of things and now I'm pulling you straight back into it!'

He drummed his fingers on the desktop and Frank urged him, 'Let me do it. I don't see how anyone can complain if I conduct follow-up interviews with possible witnesses. After all, who's to know I'm also showing them pictures of Sheehy's gang? If Rollins or anyone else asks I'm just questioning everyone the uniform boys missed when they did their sweep of the area the other day.'

Jack thought briefly and then nodded, 'Okay. I don't like you exposing yourself even to that extent but I could do with your help. Here's the list of the names of his gang I got from O'Malley; you can print pictures off the computer. Try the pubs and shops in the area as well, in case they were hanging around somewhere local waiting to attack him. I mean, they were hardly lurking in that alley all night, now were they? They probably followed him but still, it's worth a try. When you're finished there you might as well drive out and show Akima's neighbours the photos, too, though I doubt if it'll help since they're all blind and deaf, apparently. You *did* interview all Akima's neighbours, didn't you?'

'Yes, sir, save for a few I couldn't get hold off. I can talk to them today too, kill two birds with one stone. Anything else?'

'We never heard anything back from our Crimeline appeal, did we?'

'No, sir, not a sausage.'

'Well, get onto the Press Office and see if they can get them to run a follow-up next week.' Jack shrugged, 'It's a longshot but you never know.'

Frank made a note in his notebook, 'Okay. Anything else?'

'You tell me. Can you think of anything we haven't done that we intended to? Or that we should have done?'

After a pause Frank replied, 'We haven't spoken to anyone in that sports shop where the baseball bats were bought. Or rather,' he corrected himself, 'where we *think* the bats were bought. Now that we have suspects, and photos, we really should interview the staff there.'

'Good thinking,' said Jack approvingly; he had forgotten about Julie tracing the bats, 'Get onto it. Blanchardstown Shopping Centre, wasn't it? While you're out there talk to the security people and try to get a look at the tapes from the security cameras; we might get footage of whoever bought them. They usually co-operate but if they don't we can get a court order. Anything else?'

'We still haven't talked to the people I found with a history of violence against black people.'

'No,' said Jack heavily, 'but you'll hardly have time to do it today. Keep it in mind, though. Anything else?'

Frank hesitated, 'How are you going to get out Finglas to see Crilly's wife?'

Jack thought for a minute, 'I could use a staff car but if I get nothing out of her I'd only be giving Rollins ammunition about wasting Garda resources on wild goose chases, wouldn't I? Besides, the less anyone here knows about what I'm doing the better.'

'You can borrow the *Ka*, if you like.'

Jack laughed at the idea, 'Your pride and joy? Perish the thought! Suppose I scratched it? Or crashed? It would break your heart and I'd never live it down. Besides, it's a pretty rough spot I'm heading for and it would probably be stolen or vandalised.'

'Only if they knew it was a police car,' protested Frank, 'Which they won't.'

'You must be joking,' said Jack darkly, 'Benbow Avenue is Apache country, and *any* stranger is fair game, not just cops. Besides, that *Ka* is so stupid looking it just begs to be vandalised.'

Frank shot him a hurt look, making the older man laugh and say, 'I'm only winding you up, boy! God, you're easily roused.'

'That car is the apple of my eye,' said Frank, only half-joking, 'and I don't appreciate these witticisms at its expense.'

'Yeah, well, that was sort of my point; I couldn't deprive you of it. I can get a taxi.'

'I could give you a lift?' offered Frank.

Jack looked at his watch and got to his feet, 'No, it's miles out of your way. And it would defeat the whole bloody purpose of splitting up, wouldn't it? If I leave now I should be there by ten or so. I'll probably be back by lunchtime so if you're around I'll meet you here. If you're still out and about I'll call you on your mobile and let you know how I get on.'

'Right you are, sir.' Frank rose to his feet as well, 'I'll get cracking on the mug-shots of Sheehy and his cronies.'

'Good lad.' They exited the room together and Jack was already halfway to the staircase when he suddenly roared out, 'Let young Frank have your computer, Julie! And don't give him any of your crap about it, either! I know you're only pretending to work half the time!'

Julie was startled by this sudden assault on her senses but never missed a beat, instantly turning and responding with a crude gesture of her right hand. Jack just laughed and then surprised them both by blowing her a kiss in reply before vanishing up the stairs, taking them two at a time in spite of his rickety knees.

Frank shook his head as he watched him go, thinking that his pursuit of the fair Grainne was in away paralleled by Jack's slow and ponderous flirtation with Julie. The only difference was that Frank's pursuit was open and honest, while Jack refused to admit his interest in the secretary even to himself.

Chapter Seventeen

In spite of what he had said to Frank, and his years of working in the rougher areas of Dublin, Benbow Avenue still came as something of a shock to Jack. Hardly a house in the little cul-de-sac was without a wrecked car or van propped up on bricks in front of it, three of the fourteen houses were boarded up and derelict, and another had recently been burnt out, which gave the street a suitably war-torn atmosphere. The taxi driver had not known the area well, which is probably why he had accepted the fare in the first place, and there was more than a hint of relief on his face as he dropped Jack off and exited the street rather faster than policemen generally care to see people driving in a built-up area. On this occasion, however, Jack could sympathise with him, and as he looked around the little street with distaste it occurred to him that what the area needed was a convoy of bulldozers and a few lorry-loads of concrete. Or possibly some sort of small tactical nuke. It also occurred to him that he should have made the taxi wait for him; there was little chance that one would make a pickup from this address.

As was not uncommon in the poorer quarters of any city, the small street was teeming with dirty, unkempt children, all of whose interest had instantly zoomed in on Jack the second he alighted from the taxi. A hurried calculation on his part estimated an average of three kids per occupied house, scattered in separate gangs according to size down the length of the Street. In spite of his vast experience as a police officer Jack felt just the slightest touch of panic as he realised that he was suddenly the focus of the attention of them *all*, and that the whole swarm were rapidly descending upon him en-shrieking-masse. He grimly froze his face into an expressionless mask and grimly set a course for number fourteen, pretending that the mob flocking around him in a riotous circle, all squealing either questions or abuse at him at the top of their voices, simply did not exist. Slightly to his surprise -and sneaking relief- they allowed him to pass and he marched up the path and rang the doorbell with no more than a dozen of them at his heels. There was a brief wait for the door to be opened -during which a dozen questions were fired at Jack on such varied topics as his age, business there and sexual preferences- before an elderly but vocal woman opened the door. Ignoring him entirely, she descended upon the mob with a course of threatening gestures and several banshee-like screams. They fell back several feet and a few even left the little garden so, her work as complete as could be accomplished without violence, she jammed her cigarette back into her mouth and turned an unimpressed eye on Jack. 'Well,' she grunted, 'What do you want? You're not the new insurance man, are yeh?'

'No,' replied Jack sourly, 'I'm bloody well not! Are you going to let me in away from these little savages or do you want to discuss your business in public?'

'As if I've got anything to hide!' she sneered. She eyed him up and down before announcing, in a loud, unimpressed tone, 'Cop!'

'Yes, I am,' gritted Jack, aware that their audience had taken note and were expressing their own disapproval of his vocation, 'Now will you let me in, woman?'

With a sour *moue* she turned and walked down the little hallway, leaving Jack to follow and close the front door behind him with a relieved bang. Then, resisting the impulse to mop his forehead, he followed the old lady into the kitchen.

To his surprise the house was spotlessly clean, if untidy, with the kitchen table and most of the chairs being buried under mounds of clean clothes which the old lady was in the process of ironing. Wrinkling his nose in disfavour at the warm, damp smell and the clouds of steam billowing about his face, Jack said, 'I'm looking for Jacintha Crilly. Is she about? I'm assuming you're not her.'

With a sour, world-weary glance at him the old lady opened the back door and called out, 'Jacintha? Someone to see yeh, love.' She turned back to Jack and snapped, 'She'll be here in a minute, she's just hanging up some washing. That's how we make our living, washing and ironing clothes for people with more money than time. I'm her mother, by the way, Sara Byrne. D'yeh want a cuppa tea?'

Jack nodded, 'That'd be great, Mrs Byrne. Thanks.'

The old lady put on the kettle and Jack stood in the centre of the crammed kitchen, rather nonplussed, until finally she shifted some stacks of folded clothes and unearthed a chair for him to sit on. As he dropped gratefully onto it the back door opened and a woman entered carrying an empty clothesbasket. She dropped it to the floor and eyed him in disfavour before saying flatly, 'Yeah? What do yeh want?'

Jack returned her look far more appreciatively; although somewhat hard-faced, and a bottle blonde with black roots, Jacintha Crilly was a fine looking woman of no more than thirty-five or so. She had big blue eyes and full lips and even now, soured and embittered by life though she undoubtedly was, Jack had no trouble at all seeing what had attracted Sean Crilly when she was young. Even wearing just a cheap tee-shirt and black leggings she was a knock-out, for both were too slightly small for her and clung tightly to a full, shapely figure in a way that amply repaid his scrutiny.

Aware of his gaze, and irritated even more by it, Jacintha pursed her lips sourly and folded her arms, 'Well, yeh'll remember me next time you see me, won't yeh? Who are yeh and what do yeh want?'

'I'm a policeman,' said Jack solemnly, 'and therefore I've been trained to observe. Of course, sometimes it's a pleasure as well as a duty.' He tried a smile but got not a flicker in return so, with a sigh, he abandoned any attempt at friendliness and said gruffly, 'I want to talk to you about who killed your husband.'

Jacintha's face closed as quickly as a slamming door, and she turned away to busy herself with the washing again. 'I've nuthin' to say to yeh,' she said, keeping her back to him, 'about Sean or anytin' else. Now fuck off!'

In spite of her words she didn't sound angry, merely resigned, tired even, and Jack, untroubled by her reaction, merely sat back on his slightly damp chair and said to the mother, 'No sugar for me, thanks, but plenty of milk.'

Jacintha turned around to glare at him, her arms full of clothes, 'Are yeh deaf or sumtin? I said I've *nuthin'* to say to yeh!'

Jack looked at her in mild surprise, 'Oh, I heard you, all right. I just thought I'd have a cup of tea before I face those little hooligans again. It isn't a holiday or anything, is it? I'm sure most of them are old enough to be in school.'

'They are,' said Mrs Byrne without turning around from the sink, 'but their parents don't bother sendin' them. It's too much trouble to get them up and out in the mornin'.' She stubbed out her cigarette before turning and adding, 'Half the kids around here grow up hardly able to read or write, so what chance have they of gettin' a job? And when they fail and end up turnin' to crime people call them scum and want them locked up. But what else are they to do? What chance have they got of a future that *doesn't* involve crime? They don't all start off bad, yeh know.'

Jack nodded in sombre agreement and shot an inquiring glance at Jacintha.

'No!' she instantly snapped back, 'My kids aren't out there, for your information! *They're* in school. I make bloody sure they go every day! I might be stuck in this hole but they won't be. I won't let them make the same mistakes I made.'

'I'm glad to hear it,' said Jack, meaning it. Hearing the sincerity in his voice, Jacintha subsided with a shrug and a sneer before half-turning to stare moodily out of the window. Jack, waving a hand towards the front door, said, 'If they get an education they might escape from all this. *Permanently*, I mean,' he added, causing the sulky look to return to her face.

'I told yeh I wasn't goin' to talk to yeh,' she said wearily, 'and I'm not goin' to change me mind. So why don't yeh just piss off?'

'Why are you protecting the man who killed your husband?' asked Jack in a puzzled but still conversational tone, 'He left your kids fatherless and you a widow at what, thirty or so? You had a nice house and car, plenty of money; a nice *life*. And some swine took it all away from you. Yet you're protecting him. Why?'

'Protectin' *who?*' she said bitterly, 'It was you cops what took me house. CAB, to be precise, the rotten bastards. And don't yeh read the papers? A rival gang killed Sean, and that could mean anyone!'

'I don't believe that,' said Jack softly, 'I think someone in his own crew killed him to take his place. And I think you know full well who that someone is.'

Jacintha lit a cigarette and drew on it heavily, staring at him silently and without any expression, or any sign of replying. After a minute or two Jack asked, in the same soft tone, 'Are you scared of him?'

Jacintha tapped her ash into the ashtray and said, with a sigh, 'Why don't yeh promise to protect me? And when that doesn't work, you can turn nasty and start in with the threats. *They're* never far away with a cop, are they? Did it ever occur to yeh that I might not *know* who killed him?'

'No,' said Jack simply, 'it didn't. Oh, you might not know who actually pulled the trigger, but I'm sure you have a pretty good idea who ordered his death. Who profited most by it. I think we both know it was Mike Sheehy, the man who took his place.'

She shot him a sharp glance but said nothing, instead smoking so furiously that clouds of smoke wreathed her face and the glowing tip of the cigarette quickly burned halfway up to the filter. Jack watched her silently, hoping that the seeds he had planted would grow sufficiently for her to at least point him in the right direction. Mrs Byrne plonked a steaming cup of tea in front of him, though with no great grace, and Jack took a grateful sip; it wasn't whiskey but it was better than nothing. He gazed steadily at Jacintha all the while, refusing to concede defeat. She lit a fresh cigarette from the stub of the old and watched him back, obdurately silent and with seemingly limitless patience.

Jack's patience was anything but limitless, and now his lips tightened in frustration and he slammed his tea down onto the table, exploding, 'Look, I *know* that Mike Sheehy was behind Sean's death! For the simple reason that no one else had any real motive to kill him, and no one else profited as much by his death! All right? I *know* it was him! So why the silent treatment? Don't you *want* to see him punished?'

Jacintha gave him a look of contempt and sneered bitterly, 'Yeh think I didn't love Sean? Yeh think I don't hate them bastards for killin' him?' She waved her hand around the tiny kitchen, 'Even *apart* from what they did to me and me kids?' She leaned forward and jabbed her cigarette at him accusingly, 'But even if I helped get 'im locked up, where will yeh put 'im? And his mates? The black hole of bleeding Calcutta? He could still reach us from prison and you bleedin' well know it! Half the murders in the country are ordered from the Joy; how long do yeh think I'd stay alive if I helped put him away? *If* I even made it to the trial. You *know* how it works, you *know* what he'd do to me or me kids, *and you couldn't stop him!* He'd give the order from Mountjoy or wherever yeh put him, or his friends or family would do it for revenge, and you wouldn't be able to do a *ting* to stop it. And even if yeh could, how long would he get for killing another crook? Ten or fifteen years is the most you get for murder these days, so he'd be out in eight or nine. And I'd be the first person he'd visit!' She sat back and raised her cigarette with a trembling hand, 'Not that it would come to that 'cos I'd be dead long since!' She stubbed out the butt of her cigarette and immediately lit another one, drawing in the smoke in a huge, shaky gust.

Jack watched her with irritation tinged with a touch of compassion, frustrated by her refusal to help but understanding it too. Dublin had changed so much since he had first become a Gardai, and now gangland killings were routine, a near daily occurrence in a city awash with drugs, pushers and junkies. Violence was an accepted part of life for many now, and the thugs had far more power than the police. They were certainly more feared; rather than a symbol of authority a police uniform had in many ways become a target, and the idea of police protection a joke. Jack sighed and, resisting the impulse to take a fag himself, said softly, 'We might not be the F.B.I. with their witness protection program, but we can help all the same. I could see that you get a new name and a new home, far from here. Cork, maybe, or Donegal. Somewhere no one will know you, where you'd be safe from these scumbags. We could even send you to England, if you want. Think about it, a new name and a new start in life for you and the kids.'

Jacintha shrugged and looked at him tiredly, 'Maybe yeh mean what yeh say, maybe yeh don't. It wouldn't be the first time a cop promised someone protection and left them in the lurch after they testified. But it doesn't matter because I'm not testifyin'. I'll look after me own kids, thanks, me own way.'

Jack looked at her thoughtfully, 'I see.' He paused, then said, 'Well, you're still a fine looking woman, no doubt about that, so maybe you will. Sean's killers get off scot-free and you find another man to look after you and your kids. So, if you're lucky, the best you can hope for is that your kids end up like you and Sean. Great.'

She shot him a glance of pure malice, which he held before saying roughly, 'Wake up, girl! This is a chance for you and your kids to climb out of the sewer, to live amongst decent people instead of the scum round here! Don't waste it. Not to mention helping to punish your husband's murderer. At least think about it.'

She shook her head, 'There's nothing to think about, I know what I'm doin'. Besides, even if I know in me heart and soul who killed Sean, that's not evidence. I can't *prove* anythin', it's just a feelin', the whisper from one or two of his mates, that sorta thing.'

'Well, what is the word?' asked Jack impatiently, 'If you can't -or won't- give me a statement, then at least point me in the right direction.'

She was silent for a long time, then, 'Alri', I'll tell yeh what I know, which isn't much. Sean was clever, see, too clever for his own good really, and when he took over Benny Carter's old gang he really went places. He had his fingers into everythin' and the money *poured* in like water. He used to boast about how powerful he was, and about how the cops couldn't touch 'im. Ha! He used to say he *owned* the cops, that he owned *Dublin*. He certainly paid off enough of yeh. But he was always a greedy bastard, and no matter how much he got it was never enough.' She lit another cigarette and looked at Jack with hard, knowing eyes, 'I used to beg him to pack it in, to take the money he had stashed away and start a new, legit life somewhere else; a lot of his mates moved to Spain. He used to just laugh and say no one could touch him. Got a bit above himself, did our Sean. He used to say that if Cahill was the general, then he was the King.' She smiled wryly and shook her head, 'I don't know why he was so confident, because he wasn't stupid, but he really seemed to think he could get away with *anythin'*. Anyway, he always took the lion's share of everythin' goin' and gave the lads as little as he could get away with, and the word is they got more and more sick of it until finally Mike Sheehy topped him and took his place. No one complained too much because Sean had been so tight with the cash for years, and Sheehy gave them a bigger cut.'

She stubbed out her fag with an air of finality, 'And that's all I know.'

Jack stared at her in disbelief before protesting, 'Is that *it?* Jesus, I could have told you that much myself! Why else would Sheehy kill him if it wasn't for the money? Tell me something I *don't bloody know!'*

She gave him a look of dull surprise, 'Wha', did yeh think I'd have the shootin' on fuckin' camcorder or somethin'? I kept well out of Sean's business so I only know what I heard. And that's it. I *told* yeh I didn't know much. And even that's only rumours.'

Jack sighed and pinched the bridge of his nose, trying to be positive; all right, it was a disappointment that she had no real evidence for him, but at least now he *knew* he was on the right track. Though Jacintha Crilly's unsupported word wasn't going to get him far.

She was glaring at him, an angry expression twisting her lips, and now she said sourly, 'I don't know what *your* fuckin' problem is. If anyone found out I've told yeh even tha' much I'd be found floatin' in the Liffey within a week.'

'What? Oh, yes, sorry,' said Jack despondently, 'I appreciate that your talking to me at all is dangerous, it's just that I was hoping for something a bit more concrete. I'm no further on than I was, really. I've no evidence at all of who murdered your husband, and no idea where to start looking.'

Jacintha shrugged, 'You're wastin' your time. Sheehy was behind Sean's death, all ri', but it's not certain that he pulled the trigger himself. Or even got one of his lads to do it. He might have hired a professional from outside. Or an ex-IRA man, or one of the other lot, the UVF or whatever.'

Jack raised his eyebrows sceptically and she nodded in affirmation, 'Yeh'd be surprised. There's not much any of those bastards won't do for money, especially now they've all packed in the terrorism. Supposedly. Less funds comin' in, yeh know? Don't be fooled by all that political bollocks either; they were in it for the money, same as everyone else. Pay them enough and they'll work for anyone, and do anythin'. But there are plenty of others who'll kill for money too. And if you pass the word in the right places you'll find them. Well, maybe *you* couldn't, being a cop, but anyone dodgy could. Easy.'

Jack nodded gloomily and finished his mug of tea before saying, 'Don't I know it. I've always hated professional hits; they're even harder to solve than political killings. If a hitman did it I might never find him, and even if I do Sheehy might never serve time for ordering the murder. Is that what the word on the street is saying? That it was a professional job?'

Jacintha curled her lip and said sarcastically, 'You are jokin', aren't yeh? Since his death I've heard it on good authority that *everyone* was responsible for it, from Sheehy to the IRA to *you* lot. Every pub in West Dublin is crawling with rumours, spread by gobshites with nothin' better to do.'

Jack grinned ruefully, 'Try being a copper, trying to sort though a dozen contradictory stories at once.' He sighed, 'Well, I'm sorry we couldn't help each other, Mrs Crilly. I really hoped that together we might put his killer behind bars for good. Sean wasn't the only one murdered, you see; I have an idea that Sheehy was involved in the deaths of two other men as well. And while I'm on the subject, have you ever heard the names William Akima or Daniel Wistarra?'

Jacintha pursed her lips in thought, 'I don't tink so. But Sean never talked about business to me. Didn't even trust me, the mother of his children. Were they darkies? They sound African or sumtin'.'

Jack glared at her –his tolerance for racism had lowered somewhat of late- and said stiffly, 'They were *black*, yes. And African.'

Jacintha nodded, 'One thing I do know about Sean's work is that he used to do business with at least one African. A pouffe, accordin' to him, but he never mentioned 'is name. Sean was always careful wha' he said, even to me.'

'Pity,' muttered Jack. He shrugged and said, half to himself, 'Still, it's another piece of the jigsaw. Proves we're on the right track, if nothing else. But it isn't evidence.' He got to his feet and said, 'If you decide you want your husband's killer punished let me know.' He turned, 'Thanks for the tea, Mrs Byrne.'

As he made his way out into the hall Jacintha said abruptly, as if the words were torn from her against her will, 'Talk to Georgie Trinder!'

Jack turned back, 'Sorry? What was that?'

'Georgie Trinder.' She repeated patiently, 'Have yeh never heard of 'im?'

Jack shook his head, 'Can't say I have. Should I?

Jacintha lit yet another cigarette, the last in the box, and said in a staccato tone, 'Yeah, if yeh really are a cop. He was a friend of Sean's. His right hand man, actually. He was a friend of Sheehy's too, until about a month ago. That's when he was shot five times, supposedly by Sheehy.' She shrugged, 'You know what I think about rumours but I *heard* it was because he was shaggin' Sheehy's missus. But who knows?'

Jack mulled this over before nodding, 'Okay, I'll look into it. I'll talk to whoever is investigating his murder.'

She uttered a short laugh, a world of bitterness in the sound, 'Murder me arse! He survived! Five bullets in him, includin' two in the bleedin' head, and the prick didn't die. And there's my Sean, tough as they come and wiped out in a second by just one bullet.'

The naked pain and loss in her voice left Jack feeling embarrassed and inadequate, as if he were responsible for her troubles, or had somehow failed her.

'I'm sorry,' he said awkwardly, but she waved his apology away, 'Go on, get out. Talk to Georgie. He's in the Secure Ward in St. James Hospital in Blanchardstown. He's the only man in Dublin that knows Sheehy who might talk to yeh. And I do mean *might*. Personally I wouldn't fuckin' bet on it.'

Jack nodded and turned to leave, but almost immediately he stuck his head back into the kitchen and said, 'Er, do you think I could use your phone? I need to ring a taxi. If one won't come in here it can pick me up out on the main road. Call me a wimp if you like but I'm buggered if I'm going out there and waiting for a bus in front of that shower of little savages.'

Chapter Eighteen

When the taxi finally arrived -and Jack had to walk nearly a quarter of a mile to an acceptable pickup point before the cab would agree to go out that way- the detective climbed in and sank gratefully into the back seat with a little grunt of pleasure; the weather had turned chilly and he had been waiting for nearly twenty minutes.

'Where to, guv?' asked the driver. Jack opened his mouth to say Blanchardstown Hospital but at the last second asked the driver to hold on a minute. He bit his lip, quickly debating whether or not he should go back to the office first. Eventually he decided to return to Harcourt Square first, in an attempt to hook up with Frank and see what, if anything, he had learned. He would have preferred to ring him but couldn't; firstly because he was probably the only adult in Ireland who did not own a mobile phone, and secondly because he had not brought Frank's number with him. With a mental note to buy himself a cheap, ready-to-go phone at the first opportunity he finally gave the patient driver -the meter was running, after all- his instructions and sat back to reflect on what Jacintha Crilly had told him.

Although the driver was just as keen as the first taxi-man to shake the dust of Finglas off his heels the chronic congestion soon brought him to a grinding halt, leaving Jack plenty of time to think. However, he found it difficult to concentrate, and in the end spent most of the journey trying not to notice the contrast between the amazing speed the meter turned at, and the amazing *lack* of speed they were travelling at. Part of the reason for his being distracted, of course, was that since his visit to Jacintha Crilly was unofficial he couldn't even claim the fare back as expenses. It was a long time since he had privately hired a cab and he could hardly believe how expensive it had become. It also struck him as odd that not only was his driver black but the driver of almost every other taxi on the roads was black too; a couple of years back there was not one black taxi driver in the whole of Dublin, as far as he was aware.

When he finally reached headquarters he was torn between outrage at the cost and time the journey took, and sympathy with anyone forced to sit in that bloody awful traffic all day. Outrage won in the end and he launched into a bitter diatribe against the driver about the cost of the fare, though he also made a mental vow to shoot himself rather than ever own a car again. *Who could sit through that every day, to and from work?* He finally let the unfortunate driver go and walked up the steps into the offices, shaking his head in disbelief at the traffic chaos and wondering how people tolerated it sitting in it day after day on the work run. Thank God he lived on the Dart line.

Frank had not returned but, to balance this out, Jack found the business card containing his mobile number lying on his desk. He promptly dialed and after a long pause Frank, in the guarded, almost suspicious tone many people adopt when answering the phone, said, 'Hello?'

'Frank, it's Jack. Where are you?'

'Blanchardstown shopping centre, sir. You'll never guess what I've found out!' Frank was clearly bursting with news so Jack, grinning maliciously to himself, interrupted, 'Never mind you, wait till you hear what *I* found out.' And without giving the younger man a chance to speak he launched into a detailed account of everything Jacintha Crilly had told him. He concluded by saying, 'So I think we can now say for definite that Sheehy killed Crilly. We just have to prove it. And, of course, link him to the Akima and Wistarrra killings too.'

This touch of humor went unnoticed as Frank exploded with excitement, "I *have* linked Sheehy to them! Well, maybe not to Daniel Wistarra's death but definitely to Akima's.'

Jack held the receiver away from his ear, a pained expression on his face, before putting it back rather gingerly and saying, 'Start at the beginning, Frank. What did you do after I left the office?'

'Well,' -he could almost hear Frank marshalling his thoughts- 'I printed off photos of Sheehy and his mates and I took them down to the Abbey Street area, to see if anyone recognised them. Unfortunately the pubs and cafes around there are always so busy the staff probably wouldn't realise it if the Queen of England walked in, so no joy there. Anyway, most of them don't speak English, and the few that understood me seemed afraid they were in trouble of some sort once they heard I was a Garda. After that I tried the offices above the shops and stuff but I got nowhere there either so I gave up and came out here to the sports shop, to see if any of the staff recognised the man who bought the baseball bats.'

Frank paused, possibly for effect, and Jack, starting to get excited in spite of himself, grated, *'And?'*

'And nothing, sir,' replied Frank, and Jack could swear he could *hear* a grin in his voice, 'The shop assistants are just as thick as Julie said, and even less useful. None of them recognized anyone in my photos, and the guy who sold the three bats to one customer, which is hardly a usual order, had no clear recollection of even making the sale, much less of the customer who bought them.'

'Frank,' said Jack wearily, 'I'm sorry I cut you off earlier. It was just my bit of fun. I'm a bitter, broken old man and I have to take my amusement where I can find it. Now you've had *your* fun, but if you don't get to the sodding point...'

'Sorry, sir,' laughed Frank, 'I couldn't resist winding you up; the "biter bit" and all that. Anyway, I went to the security centre and asked to see the C.C.T.V. tapes for that day. And what do you think I saw on one of the tapes? Martin Leary strolling out of the shop with three bran-new baseball bats under his arm!'

'Well, well, well,' said Jack, boundless satisfaction in his voice, 'Now *there's* a turn-up for the books.' Martin Leary was a member of Mike Sheehy's gang, a man with a long criminal record and a history of violence.

'We've got him, haven't we?' said Frank in delight.

Jack laughed ironically, 'We sure have. We can arrest Leary as soon as buying baseball bats is made a crime. Sorry, Frank, but it means nothing on its own. Still, as part of a chain of evidence it might be useful.' He thought swiftly, 'Get back down to the sports shop and find out everything you can about that shipment of bats. Make, model, order numbers, shipment numbers; get everything you possibly can that might prove that the bats Leary bought are the murder weapons.'

'Already underway, sir,' said Frank, slightly breathlessly, 'I've got the shopping centre security tapes of him walking into the store empty-handed and walking out with them in his arms, so we can prove he bought them there. The tapes even have the time and date on them; the Sunday before Akima was murdered. And now I'm on my way back to the shop to see if I can get the internal, store security tape of him actually making the purchase. I couldn't get it earlier because the video recorder is locked in a sort of cabinet, as a security measure, and the staff have no access to it. But I've got the head of the shopping centre security team here with me, and he's going to open the cabinet and let me have a copy of the tape.'

'Hmm,' said Jack, still lost in thought, 'unless we can prove they're the same bats we still have nothing, really. Him buying three bats is suspicious but purely circumstantial. We never got a report back from forensics on the bats, did we?'

'Yes, sir. That is, when I rang they said they dusted for prints but didn't find any.'

'But they never sent us the actual report?'

'No, sir. But, er, what else would forensics be looking for on them except prints?'

'Never mind that now,' replied Jack thoughtfully, 'You just get that tape and find out where those bats came from. I'll go on out to the hospital and see this George Trinder guy. Talk to you later.' He put down the phone and walked to the office door, saying absently, 'Julie, you got a minute? I need a favor.'

'Well, that depends on what it is,' she said archly, moving into the doorway as Jack retook his seat, still deep in thought, 'If you're desperately stuck for a dinner partner this evening, for example, I might just be able to help.'

In spite of his preoccupation Jack laughed, 'Oh yes, and how could you help?'

'Well,' replied Julie, deadpan, 'I might be able to get you a date with my mother. She's nearly eighty now and getting desperate.'

'Oh, most amusing!' growled Jack, trying to scowl but unable to prevent a smile from cracking his lined features. 'Listen, Julie, I have to go out again and I need you to do something for me.' He paused but instead of agreeing to help she cocked her head to one side and said consideringly, 'You know, you're a different man lately, Jack. Rushing around, all caught up in your work. I'm glad, because it seems to suit you. Even apart from your not drinking, which has to be good news on its own, you seem a lot happier. You even look younger.'

He blinked at her, dumbfounded by this parenthesis into the personal. 'Er, thanks,' he said at last, uncertainly.

She flashed him the briefest of smiles, 'Don't mention it! Now, what was it you wanted me to do for you?'

'I want you to get onto the Technical Lab.,' he replied, all business again, 'I want the report on the baseball bats used in the Akima killing. I know they didn't find any prints, but our suspect handled all three bats the day before the killing, and I want to know if they checked for traces of moisture or skin particles or anything like that. Find out if it's possible that sweat from the killers' hands could have soaked into the wood. And if so, can they take a shaving and check the wood itself for DNA?'

'Okay. Anything else?'

'Er, yes. Rather a big job, I'm afraid. Can you get on to the lab and the manufacturer and try to narrow the murder weapons down to a particular batch or order? Then can you trace the whereabouts of the rest of that batch? And then can you ring the shops they went to, and try to trace them? How many they've sold and who to? Hopefully we'll be able to trace most of them through credit card receipts, though some will have been bought with cash. But even then the vendor might know the purchaser.'

Julie was gaping at him, open-mouthed at the sheer size of the task he was giving her, and he laughed and told her about the security tapes and Martin Leary. 'So you see,' he concluded, 'if the murder weapons and the bats Leary bought are from the same batch -and we can account for the *rest* of the batch- it'll prove that the ones Leary bought are the murder weapons. You with me? It's a process of elimination. I know it's a long-shot, and a big job, but will you give it a go?'

She nodded, 'All right, I'll do my best. Anything *else*?' she added ironically.

Jack laughed and got to his feet. 'I think that'll probably do for the moment! Thanks, Jules, I know it's a pain in the arse, and probably pointless, but we have to try it. Just in case we get lucky. And if we have to try and build a case against someone on purely circumstantial evidence it might prove vital. Look, I have to go out now but I'll check back later to see what the lab boys have to say.'

Julie stared at him speculatively; he really *did* seem like a new man, so much so that she was unsure what to make of him these days. She certainly preferred him this way, and was even starting to wonder if he was potential husband material. Or, at worst, father material.

She didn't particularly fancy raising a child on her own but if it was that or nothing she'd take a donor, thank you very much. He didn't have to be willing, either. To have a child, that is; he'd certainly have to be willing to bed her. But would Jack be on for it? All this time she had overlooked him on account of his drinking; was it possible that the object of her long quest had been right in front of her all along?

Jack was -perhaps fortunately- unaware of the trend of Julie's thoughts, but he saw the speculative look on her face and turned and walked away in something of a huff, believing that she suspected he was heading for the pub. He had forgotten his ire by the time he reached the front door, however, and exited the building with a purposeful air and a brisk gait. Neither lasted long. Getting a taxi out to Blanchardstown was -incredibly- an even worse nightmare than his earlier journey, with this one made even worse by gnawing hunger pangs and the growing awareness that he had not yet had lunch; since he had cut back on the booze his appetite was starting to return.

Interminable though it seemed the journey did end eventually, and Jack ill-temperedly hurled a -it seemed to him- vast sum of money at the driver, who was yet again both black and African. He slammed the car door shut and stalked into the hospital vestibule, wondering to himself just how many people lived in Dublin these days, and how many drove cars. Millions, and all of them, were the answers, if the ubiquitous traffic jams were anything to go by. He also spared a thought for the deterioration of taxi cabs since deregulation; he had ridden in three separate cabs that day and each one had seemed smaller, dirtier and dingier than the last. Whatever had happened to the days when taxis were large, luxury cars like Mercs, in which it was quite a treat to be conveyed around town? Being driven about in a filthy, -inside and out- battered old Toyota Corolla or Hyundai Accent just wasn't the same, somehow.

Morbidly aware that he was daily growing more and more like Victor Meldrew, he shook off his depressing train of thought and made a beeline for the receptionist, asking as politely as he could manage for directions to the Secure Ward. No help was forthcoming until he explained his errand and showed his warrant card, whereupon he was finally told the way. Which, the receptionist informed him, was deliberately not signposted for security reasons; Trinder was not the first at-risk patient they had harbored.

In spite of her instructions he eventually managed to find the locked glass door that led into the Secure Ward, and another explanation and flash of his credentials to the receptionist there -this one protected by a reinforced glass screen- eventually produced a doctor who listened to his story before finally letting him in.

'You have to understand,' the doctor, who looked at least twelve years old, explained, 'that we have to be really careful who we let in here. This ward is actually for patients with psychiatric problems *and* physical ailments. We have an arrangement with your lot, however, to also treat patients who are considered to be in danger from, shall we say, outside elements.'

'I didn't know that,' admitted Jack, slightly shamefaced at his own ignorance.

The doctor smiled, 'Well, we've been doing it for ten years now so you really should. Though if you're with the murder squad,' he added as an afterthought, 'I suppose your, er, clients are no longer in need of our services here.'

Jack laughed, 'That's one way of putting it, doc. How is this George Trinder anyway?'

'Lucky,' replied the doctor succinctly, 'He was shot five times, three times in the back as he ran away from his assailant, and twice in the back of the head as he lay on the ground. Yet he survived.' He sighed and shook his head, 'I've seen eighteen-year-old athletes die from falling off a chair, yet another man can be shot twice in the head and somehow survive.'

'Was there a medical reason he survived?' asked Jack curiously.

'Yes,' said the doctor dryly, 'I already told you; sheer-bloody-luck-itus. Whatever way the bullets struck his skull they bounced off it instead of penetrating the bone. A combination of a thick skull, a light caliber weapon, and the angle the pistol was held at all helped, but it was still astonishing luck. The bullets in his torso caused more damage, but less than you'd expect. Mind you, he's a big, powerful brute and the gun was only a .22, fired from a distance. Apparently he saw the guy waiting for him behind a hedge and ran for it. The guy shot him three times in the back before approaching to administer the *coup de grace.*' He sighed again, 'I sometimes think medical school was a waste of time, to be honest. It seems some people are destined to die young while others are damned near invincible.' He stopped for a moment, 'He's in this room here. You won't need me to get back out when you're finished with him; Brenda can buzz you out.

'Thanks, doc,' said Jack, and entered the room. It was surprisingly small and contained three beds but only one occupant, whom Jack assumed to be his quarry. George Trinder was indeed a big man, and powerfully built. He had strongly-marked features and a great shock of black hair, which sat oddly as the back of his skull was still shaven. The black hair wasn't just confined to his head, either; his stubble was dark enough to make the lower half of his face look almost blue. Like many Dubliners, he had bright piercing blue eyes to go with the black hair and sallow skin, and these fixed Jack with a flat, hard stare as he entered the room. He was sitting up in bed and Jack perched on the bed next to his and calmly returned his gaze.

'Well?' challenged Trinder, turning his head, which squatted on a massive body-builder's neck, only with difficulty. He eyed Jack up and down, 'Haven't *you* got anything you want to pry and poke me wi', or maybe stick up me arse?'

'Don't tempt me' responded Jack dryly, 'I'm not a doctor, I'm a policeman.'

Trinder rolled his eyes dramatically, 'Look, I already told that bastard Prendergast that I don't *know* who shot me! He was wearing a fuckin' *mask!* Do you people think I've got x-ray eyes or somethin'?'

'Ah, yes, that'd be Superintendent Prendergast, Serious Crime Squad,' nodded Jack, 'I know him well. I suppose I should have talked to him before having this little chat with you, but there wasn't time. And I'm not really interested in who shot you, to be honest.' He shrugged, 'If the shooter was a pro you probably wouldn't have recognised his face anyway. But what about the man who *sent* him? What about Mike Sheehy?'

Trinder's face closed shut with an almost audible *snap* and he said flatly, 'Who? Prendergast asked me the same question, and got the same answer; I never heard of him.'

Jack shook his head slowly, 'Come on, George, I'm too old and cranky to play these games. I *know* you were part of his crew. And we both know that Sheehy set up the hit on you. I've heard it was over his wife,' he added interestedly, 'Is that true?'

Trinder gave him a cocky smirk but made no reply. Jack waited a moment or two before saying, with a sigh, 'I have to admit I'm disappointed. Jacintha Crilly told me you were Sean's friend, maybe his only *real* friend. She said you'd help me catch his killer.'

'Bollocks!' sneered Trinder, his brows knitting, 'She knows better!'

'Does she?' inquired Jack, 'Well, maybe she does and maybe she doesn't. But she told me that Sheehy was responsible for Sean's death as well as your shooting. And she seemed to think you'd want revenge on the man who killed your friend, and tried to kill you. *Don't* you? You don't seem the forgiving type.'

Trinder's countenance darkened still further into a thunderous scowl but he made no reply. Jack leaned forward, his own face darkening, and said roughly, 'Come on, George, wake up! This guy tried to *kill* you! Don't you want revenge? Wouldn't you like to see him getting life in Mountjoy?'

Trinder's lip curled, 'Life's not long enough if yeh grass someone like Sheehy up, believe me. And him being in the Joy wouldn't protect me. I'd be looking over me shoulder the rest of me natural and you know it.'

Jack nodded and assumed a conspiratorial look, 'And if he got three life sentences, say, for *three* murders? For killing Crilly and two black men? Murders that had nothing to do with you? Would that make you feel safe? Especially if there was no mention of his trying to kill you? He'd never even know you'd spoken to me.'

'Mike Sheehy's a mate,' said Trinder in a bored voice, lying back with a grimace of pain and looking up at the ceiling, 'Not only did he not shoot me, but he even sent me flowers. Wasn't that nice of him?'

Jack nodded, 'Funny, that, since you never heard of him a minute ago.' Trinder made no reply and the two men simply sat in silence, the policeman fixing Trinder with a basilisk glare and Georgie trying to pretend he wasn't even there. In spite of his answer, and tone, Jack got the idea that he was considering the offer, so he waited patiently to let the notion sink in. And at length Trinder sighed and asked, 'Exactly wha' *do* yeh want, copper? A witness in court? Me to turn State's evidence and send Sheehy down? Santa-fuckin'-Claus to come early? *Wha'?*'

'Nope, you wouldn't have to do any of that,' said Jack briskly, trying to hide the sudden hope flaring up in his heart, 'Your name need never even be mentioned. I want him for the killing of two black men recently, not for your shooting or Sean Crilly's death. Come to think of it, you might even have known Akima since he was a friend of Crilly's?'

Trinder's expression never flickered for as much as an instant and with an inner sigh Jack continued, 'You don't have to testify or even make a statement. No one will ever know you even spoke to me. All you have to do is give me a clue, just point me in the right direction and I'll take it from there.'

Trinder cast a distrustful glance at the door, as if someone might be lurking behind it, and said, 'Is this in strict confidence? And without prejudice?'

Jack nodded, his suddenly gleaming eyes boring into the other man's.

'I'll deny it later, if yeh try to make me testify,' warned Trinder.

'Look!' said Jack, losing patience, 'stop fannying around and tell me what you know! I don't need much, just give me a head-start and I'll put him away!'

'Right,' began Trinder, 'Where do I start? First of all, I don't know anything about the two darkies that got stiffed. Rumour has it that Sheehy did them both but I dunno if it's true, or why he's supposed to have killed them. I was in here when it happened, see, and I'd already fallen out with Mike by then anyway.'

'You heard a rumour like that in *here*?' said Jack sceptically.

Trinder nodded, 'From me brother, Shane. He visits nearly every day. He's not one of Sheehy's boys but he knows people, know what I mean? He sez Martin Leary was boastin' about it to him in the pub the other night, pissed out of his head, and saying that I'd be next. Shane told him to fuck off, that it was all sorted out with Sheehy, and the heat was off. Which it is. Supposedly. Like I'd ever trust that fuckin' snake again. Anyway, it all calmed down and they ended up having a drink together, but when Shane asked him about the blackies Leary wouldn't say any more, only that he didn't know why they killed them; they were just following Sheehy's orders. Leary hates blacks anyway, so he enjoyed it, and he told Shane he sprayed "Niggers Out" and some other stuff on the wall beside the first darkie they stiffed.'

Jack froze, his mind in a whirl; this was the first concrete evidence they had against anyone, as information about the daubed slogan had not been released into the public domain. Surely his knowing of the writing was proof positive against Leary? Along with the footage of him buying the baseball bats? Jack bit his lip and came back down to Earth with a bump;

that bloody story in the paper had mentioned the graffiti and even carried a picture. The fool hadn't even got the bloody words right. Unless, of course, Trinder's brother had heard it *before* Wistarra's murder, before the paper got a hold of it?

'When did Leary say all this to your brother?' he asked carefully.

Trinder thought about it for a moment. 'Um, musta been Tuesday, 'cos he told me about it Wednesday.'

'You're sure it was Wednesday, not Thursday?' asked Jack sharply.

Trinder shook his head, 'He didn't visit me Thursday.'

Jack nodded in satisfaction; that private knowledge, before the newspaper reports, was proof positive of Leary's involvement in the murder of Akima, at least. Unfortunately he could never prove it in court. 'I don't suppose your Shane would testify to hearing this confession, would he?' he asked gloomily, already knowing the answer.

Trinder made a face, 'Yeah, right. Anyway, it'd be inadmissible in court. It's only hearsay, see, Shane's word against Leary's. Know what I mean?'

Jack gave him a look. Or maybe a Look. It never ceased to amaze him that criminals often knew more of the law than the average policemen. Though perhaps it wasn't that surprising; the desire to stay out of prison gave them a more powerful incentive to read up on the law, including the Rules of Evidence. He shook his head incredulously and said, 'Is that it? Is that all you know?'

Trinder looked sour at this ingratitude. *'All?* Tellin' yeh that much is enough to get me back on Sheehy's death list. If I really am off it.'

'Why did he want you dead in the first place?' asked Jack curiously. *'Was* it because of his wife?'

'What, me and Maggie Sheehy?' laughed Trinder, 'Give me a break. Yeah, I heard that story too; Shane thought that was hilarious. I bet even Mike laughed when he heard that one. Maggie Sheehy is a bleeding bucket; I'd say even Mike is reluctant to shag it, and he's married to her! No, we fell out about,' he hesitated, 'the sale of some goods. Let's just say I got a better price for them than I let on to him.' He shrugged, the movement causing him to wince with pain, and added, 'The cunnin' bastard never let on, never said a bleedin' word to me, but he must have found out because why else would he order the hit?'

'And that's how your brother sorted it out,' guessed Jack, 'by paying Sheehy off?'

Trinder nodded, 'Yeah, that and the fact I'd been shot. Mike didn't really need to kill me; just havin' me shot was enough to send out a message. And to save face.' He saw Jack's expression and added, 'If yeh want to be the boss people have to know they can't fuck with yeh. Mike was steppin' into some big shoes after Sean got topped, and he needed to prove himself. He needed to gain some respect straight away.' He shrugged, and then cursed as the movement sent arrows of pain all through his body. 'I'll tell yeh one thing for nuthin',' he said through gritted teeth, 'Hurtin' your back buggers up your whole body. You can't move *anything* without it hurtin'.'

He was silent for a moment and then continued, 'Lyin' here, thinking it over, I reckon he might have set me up for it.'

'What, he *deliberately* gave you the opportunity to cheat him?' asked Jack in surprise, 'Why would he do that?'

Trinder rolled his eyes, 'I *told* yeh; to make an example of me. And get me out of his hair.' Trinder sighed and added, 'It all goes back to Sean getting topped. I was his friend, and kind of his right-hand man. I was the only one who could stand him, really, so straight away that made me a target. Not that Sean ever told me anything; he was a right devious bastard and never told anyone anything. But I was as close to the cunnin' swine as anyone ever got. Plus I would have been the natural choice to take his place, so maybe Mike wanted me out of the way cos' a that too. Partly because I was a threat and partly to send a message to everyone, to show them he was just as tough and smart and ruthless as Sean Crilly ever was.'

'He kills people just to let the world know he's arrived, but your brother bungs him a few quid and you're all sorted out with him now?' said Jack sarcastically, 'Just like that?'

Trinder looked surprised, 'Yeah, why not? Mike got his money back, with interest, and I've been put in me place, so why wouldn't he take me back? He's shown everyone who the man is, and he's not likely to give me a chance to get me revenge on him, now is he? Except I'm only pretendin' to go back. I'm off to London as soon as I'm well enough. Apart from not trusting Sheehy anymore, after what happened I'd be a bleedin' laughing stock; no one would have any respect for me. It'd be a nightmare tryin' to get me name back, and without a reputation you're nobody; every clown in Dublin tryin' to make a name for himself would be after me.'

Jack sighed and rubbed his face, trying to fit all the bits he had learned into a cohesive whole. And what use any of it was, if any; well, that was anyone's guess. 'I take it there's no question that Sheehy killed Sean Crilly?'

'Not to me,' replied Trinder, 'Why? Yeh don't believe that oul' bollocks about the Ra killin' him, do yeh?'

Jack shrugged, 'Well, no, actually. You clearly don't, either.'

Trinder shook his head, 'It was obvious it was him, though he never let on. The day after Sean was topped Sheehy turned up at the club and tells everyone that he's taking over, just like that. He said if anyone had a problem with it he'd be glad to discuss it with them outside. Since he had a bleedin' Browning 9mm in his hand at the time no one took him up on the offer, know what I mean? We all just sat there lookin' at each other. We couldn't *believe* it at first. He wasn't exactly known for his brains, oul Mike, or ambition, and he was the last person yeh'd think would try to take over. Would *want* to take over. But he did. While we were all sitting there lookin' at him with our mouths hangin' open he tells us he has a big deal set up and we were all goanna get a decent share of it for once. Because Sean was always pretty tight with the readies.'

Trinder shot Jack a cautious look, 'So he tells us about this big shipment of…stuff, and says we're goin' to get fifty grand out of it each. And we did, too.'

Jack nodded, 'And that was him elected.'

'You could put it like that. No one was goin' to make a move on 'im until they got their money, for a start, and when we did get paid he had *another* deal set up.' Trinder gestured with his hand, which caused him to wince again, 'And that was that. He was the new boss. And no one had liked Sean enough to do anything about it. I still can't believe it, I mean, old Thick Mick runnin' the whole show? It's a joke! But he must be smarter than anyone ever thought cos' he's doin' it.'

'And no one argues because the money keeps rolling in,' said Jack thoughtfully.'

'That's it,' nodded Trinder, 'And he makes me an example of wha' happens if yeh mess him around. Yeh gotta hand it to him, he certainly has it sussed.'

'Yeah,' said Jack vaguely, 'he certainly has.' He looked around, preparing to leave, 'Is there anything else you can tell me?'

Trinder looked at him incredulously, 'I've practically told yeh me whole fuckin' life story! What else do yeh want?'

'Well, you haven't really told me anything very useful, have you?' said Jack irritably, 'I mean, all this is interesting enough but it isn't getting me anywhere! Give me something I can *use!*'

Trinder slumped back in his bed and said bitterly, 'That's the thanks yeh get for tryin' to help a bleedin' cop.'

'Come off it!' said Jack scornfully, 'You're trying to use me to get revenge on Sheehy, so less of the 'helping the police' crap! And while I actually *do* appreciate the effort, none of what you've told me is evidence. And it doesn't seem to be pointing *towards* any evidence. I was hoping you might be able to tell me where a body was hidden, or where to find the gun that killed Crilly or something. Think, man, isn't there *anything* that might incriminate him? In any of these killings?'

'Well, yeh'll never find the hitman,' said Trinder sulkily, 'or the gun. So no. Go after the guys who killed the darkies. Leary's a bit of a mouthpiece; lean on him. He talks tough but he never had much in the way of balls so he might crack. Especially if yeh have anything on him.'

'Great, I'd never have thought of that myself, ' said Jack sarcastically. He got to his feet, 'Thanks a bloody bunch! Anything else?'

'Yeah,' replied Trinder, 'I'll give ye one last little titbit. Sean was always boastin' that he had half the Met in his pocket.'

Jack chewed his lower lip thoughtfully, 'I suppose he never mentioned any names?'

'Nope. You weren't on his payroll, were yeh? Yeh have that look.'

Jack smiled humorlessly and approached the bed with one hand raised, 'You know, since you've been so helpful I think you deserve a great big pat on the back.'

Trinder sneered up at him, unafraid, 'Suppose you kiss me arse instead?'

Jack laughed and patted him on the head instead, before turning and leaving the room, no closer to an arrest than when he had entered it, but a lot happier. They still had no evidence against anyone but, on the plus side, his theory that Sheehy was behind all the murders seemed to be holding water. Why he had killed the two Africans was still a total mystery – unless he was a racist as well as a thug- but Martin Leary might help them with that, if they could only add some hard evidence to the circumstantial net they were starting to weave about him.

Chapter Nineteen

After yet another taxi ride -this one through the rush hour traffic- Jack arrived back at Harcourt Square fed up to the back teeth with the sight, smell and sound of cars but with his mind still buzzing from everything he had learned. And yet, as he had said to Trinder, he really wasn't any further advanced with the investigation. A line from a song -to the effect that the more we learn the less we know- rambled through his head, giving him quite a shock; if that sort of thing kept up before he knew it he'd be swapping poetic quotes with Frank. What he really needed was a drink, and he was marching purposefully towards the remains of the bottle of Jameson he kept hidden in his filing cabinet when he was waylaid by Julie. She greeted him with a broad smile and said, 'I've got some good news and some bad news.'

He stopped, albeit reluctantly, and said, 'Oh yes?'

'The bad news,' she said briskly, 'is that the bats were coated with varnish, meaning no...er, bodily fluids could soak into it, so no DNA for comparison. The good news is that they had a small crown burned into them at the top, meaning that they were made by King Sports Equipment, Ltd. The better news is that, in the whole of Ireland, only Marathon Sports sell that brand and yes, the three bats Leary bought were from the same batch as the murder weapons. To identify them as the actual bats themselves we'd need the bar codes, which were on the plastic outer wrapping, which was *not* found at the crime scene.'

Jack sighed; he hadn't known the bats had an outer wrapper. That was why Leary hadn't left prints or DNA on the bats when he bought them, even though he hadn't been wearing gloves in the shop. *Shit.*

'Apparently,' continued Julie, ignoring his glum expression, 'there were one hundred and forty bats in that particular batch, only thirty-two of which have been sold. Unfortunately, fifteen of those sales were cash, but their head office is cooperating with us in producing the receipts for the laser and credit card sales. They're gathering the information for us but obviously they can't release information on their customers, addresses and so on, without a court order. The three bats sold in Blanchardstown were a cash sale, of course, and they have confirmed that that was the *only* multiple sale from that batch.'

'That's great, Jules, thanks,' said Jack without much enthusiasm, 'I really appreciate all your effort.'

She looked crestfallen, 'You aren't pleased? I thought that was pretty damning stuff. Isn't it proof that Leary bought the murder weapons?'

He made a vague gesture with his hand, 'It's still only circumstantial evidence. And even if we're sure they're the same bats, it isn't proof. And even if we *can* prove it later on, proof that he *bought* them isn't proof that he used them. He could say he lost them or had them stolen from him or anything; even the worst lawyer in the world could get us laughed out of court with that sort of evidence. Not that we'd ever *get* to court with rubbish like that.'

Julie was watching him closely and thought, with a pang, that he was looking tired and beaten. Looking old again, in fact, all his recent energy and enthusiasm drained away. Resisting -barely- the impulse to pat him encouragingly on the shoulder she said consolingly, 'Well, maybe Frank will have some good news for you. He's waiting for you in your office.'

'Thanks, Jules,' he said with a smile that was part grimace. He started for his office but then stopped and shot her a glance from under his eyebrows before adding, 'You've done marvels and I'm grateful, really I am. If I seem less than thrilled it's just because I'm tired. It's not *damning* evidence but hopefully it'll become a nail in that scumbag's coffin.' Without thinking he leaned forward to kiss her cheek in thanks but caught himself just in time, jerking his head back in horror. He turned and proceeded into his office with a stiff, stilted gait and an embarrassed expression on his face that ill-suited his craggy features. He didn't know quite what had come over him there; certainly the last thing he needed was a sexual harassment complaint.

Frank was updating the daily Chronological Record when Jack's entrance caused him to look up from the desk. The expression on his face did little to assuage Jack's downbeat mood and in fact the first thing the younger man said was, 'I hope you got a lead from Trinder, because what we've got from the baseball bats is far from conclusive.'

Jack nodded wearily, wondering if he was ever going to get the shot of whiskey his whole body craved, but still reluctant to reveal to Frank the extent of his feet of clay. 'I know, Julie told me. Still, it might be enough for us to bring Leary in for questioning, and maybe even to get a search warrant for his house.' He sat behind his desk and, after a brief internal struggle, opened the top drawer of his filing cabinet and lifted out a bottle of whiskey. 'Drink?'

Frank shook his head, 'No, thanks, I'm driving.' Although his face and voice were carefully neutral, disapproval radiated from every pore and he pointedly glanced at his wristwatch, a cheap Timex.

Jack couldn't help but grin, 'Relax, I'm only having the one. And it *is* after five-thirty, you know; I'm on my own time now.'

'Yes, sir. But, er, you don't answer to me in any case, you know.'

Jack poured a small drink into an empty Styrofoam coffee cup and sipped at it before replying, with a sigh, 'No, I don't, but you work with me, and if I'm a hopeless drunk of course it affects you too. But I'm not drinking the way I used to, and I want you to know that. In fact, I'm probably down to about a third of what I used to drink. I'm not sure *why* I want you to know that, but I do.'

'These things I do, I know not why! My deeds directed, at an uncaring sky.'

Jack chose to ignore this, instead continuing, 'And for me three or four drinks a day is practically teetotal. I'm not going to get drunk during working hours and screw up this case, Frank, I promise. I won't let you down, and more importantly I won't let down the people who really matter here; the victims. So relax, okay?'

'Okay, then,' muttered Frank, a little embarrassed by the older man's openness about his weakness and not sure where to look; heart-to-heart chats and emotional revelations are not traditional strengths of the Irish male, and the preferred Irish way of dealing with personal problems is to ignore them and hope they go away on their own. 'Er, did you learn anything from Trinder?'

'Oh, yes, lots of things. Though what we're to do with any of it I don't know. Nor am I entirely sure any of it is anything to do with our case.' Jack finished his drink in one gulp and began recounting everything Trinder had told him. When he had finished he gave the whiskey bottle a longing look but then resolutely put it away before saying to Frank, 'And if you can make anything out of that lot you're a better bloody detective than I am, lad.'

'Yes, sir,' replied Frank, lost in thought, 'It's all very interesting but without hard evidence it really isn't of much practical use to us, is it? *These dreams I lose my way in, the fog of might have been! Where confusion wreaths my compass, and my eyes are stopped with sin.*'

'What,' asked Jack coldly, his patience exhausted by his long day, 'the ruddy hell are you talking about?'

'Sorry, sir,' mumbled Frank, reddening, 'I get a bit carried away sometimes.'

'No, I'm the one who's sorry, for snapping at you like that,' said Jack slowly, rubbing his forehead, 'I know it's just your way of getting your mind working, of getting the juices flowing. The mental equivalent of assuming the lotus position and saying 'Om' over and over. I'm just a bit tired. And frustrated. We think we know who killed these men but we're no nearer proving it than we were in the bloody beginning. Not unless Leary cracks under duress and confesses everything. How likely do you think that is?' He got to his feet, 'I'm going home. I'm old and tired and I need a lot of drinks.' He noted Frank's disapproving look and managed a grin, 'Which is why I'm going to have a Chinese takeaway and an early night instead. You're awful easy to get a rise out of, Frankie.'

Frank smiled ruefully, 'I suppose so. I think I told you that "Steve Naïve" was my nickname in college? Well, back home in Carlow my friends used to call me the Pike, because I'd swallow anything they floated in front of me.' He got to his feet, 'Can I offer you a lift home, Jack?'

'*Sir* to you, sonny,' growled Jack automatically, suppressing a shudder at the thought of another car journey that day. 'Thanks, but I'll be quicker getting the Dart. Besides, the walk to the station will clear my head. And possibly maintain my sanity.' He paused in the doorway, 'Did you take the photos of Sheehy's men out to Akima's place, to show his neighbors?'

'Not yet, *sir*, I haven't had time, *sir*. I could do it now, if you like, *sir?*'

'At this time of night? Am I that much of a slave-driver?' asked Jack whimsically, 'No, tomorrow will do well enough. When you went door-to-door none of them had seen anything suspicious anyway, had they? So those photos aren't likely to help.'

'Well, you never know,' Frank suggested optimistically, 'Besides, not everyone was in when I called round last time. I mean, I phoned those I missed, later on, but people only half listen to you when you ring because they're trying to get back to the telly, or their dinners. Besides, a photo jogs people's memories better than any number of words.'

'Fine,' said Jack, marching purposefully towards the stairs. He was halfway up them when he called back, 'But do it tomorrow...you still have to update the murder book, and the computer records. And I'm not approving any bloody overtime!'

He still had a half-smile on his face as he exited the building and walked down the front steps; when it came to encouraging and energising him Frank was a better tonic than any booze, and working with him was almost like being young again himself. *Almost.* A big, big word.

The walk to the Dart station may or may not have cleared his mind but it was certainly better than being in a car, and the joy of striding past frozen lines of traffic fizzed in his veins almost as effectively as alcohol. Again, *almost.* Some things cannot be substituted, and youth is only one of them.

When he reached his house Jack, as promised, ordered in Chinese food and, after checking that there was nothing on telly -for a change- went to bed. And if he had another whiskey to help him sleep, it wasn't a very large one.

It was perhaps just as well that O'Neill got an early and relatively sober night for he was awoken at what seemed to be the crack of dawn but was, in fact, just before six o'clock, by the ringing of his phone. When he answered it Rollins' strident tones cut into his early morning brain-fog like a steam whistle, 'Jack? Rollins here. Get up and get dressed. I want you in my office ASAP. Young Carr is on his way over to pick you up. And make damned sure you don't stink of whiskey when you get here!' And with that he hung up, leaving Jack staring at the wall in bleary-eyed surprise; what the hell could he want at this hour? Nothing good, that was for sure.

Amazed though he was by this wake-up call, Jack shook himself out of his torpor and began his morning ablutions, wondering profitlessly what this early morning call could possibly presage. No doubt the Assistant Commissioner had heard the direction Jack's investigation was still taking, in spite of his warnings.

Rollins had clearly rung Frank even earlier than Jack, for he had barely begun drinking his morning coffee -unfortified, for once, in view of Rollins' warning- when he was disturbed by a ring on the doorbell. He gulped down a couple of scalding mouthfuls to try and kick-start his brain into life and hurried to open it.

'Sorry to disturb you so early, sir,' said Frank diffidently, looking as neat and as spruce as ever, and certainly not as if he had been dragged out of bed before dawn, 'but Mr. Rollins rang and told me pretty peremptorily to come and get you. Are you ready to go?'

For an answer Jack pulled the door closed behind him and started down the steps, wondering a little at the "peremptorily" at this hour of the morning. Still, that's education for you. 'Do you know what this is all about, Frank?' he asked, preceding his assistant down the path.

'Not a clue, sir. I just know that Mr. Rollins was pretty brusque. Didn't he tell you what was going on?'

'No,' replied Jack heavily, getting into the *Ka*, 'but I think we can be sure it's nothing good.'

Neither man spoke for the duration of the startlingly brief, traffic-free journey to headquarters, but both had formed a pretty shrewd idea of what awaited them, and dreaded their arrival, making the unusually empty streets a curse rather than a blessing. To voice their suspicions seemed a bad omen, however, so both stayed silent for fear of acting as a jinx. The receptionist was not yet on duty at the front desk, and in fact the place was so deserted they had to be admitted by a cleaner. In the lobby Jack paused irresolutely before saying, 'You go on down to the office and make sure the Murder Book is up to date. I forgot to tell you to include all media reports in the file so check the morning papers and cut out anything relevant. This is probably for my ears only, anyway. If Rollins wants to see you as well he'll soon let you know.'

Frank hesitated before replying, reluctant to abandon his senior to what he privately feared might be his doom. 'Er, perhaps I should go up there with you? I mean, Mr. Rollins didn't specifically say he wanted me too but we *are* working this case together and...'

Jack held up one hand to interrupt him, 'Stop right there. I appreciate the sentiment, Frank, but I'm a big boy. I can take whatever's coming, and if it's a bollocking I'd rather not receive it in front of you, okay? Besides,' he added, almost as an afterthought, 'I haven't done anything wrong.' He turned and walked away to forestall further argument, the butterflies in his stomach belying his words. He held himself in iron control as he stood in the lift, and only a deep, compulsive breath before he knocked on Rollins' door betrayed his inner feeling of dread.

'Come!' snapped Rollins instantly, and Jack composed his features into stolid immobility as he entered the room. 'You wanted to see me, Eamonn?'

Rollins looked up from his desk, fixing him with a cold stare. 'Yes, I did. Sit down.' In spite of the early hour he was chewing one of his humbugs, which caused Jack's stomach to turn a little; he couldn't even bear food in the morning, much less a sticky, minty sweet. But perhaps Rollins preferred to freshen his teeth by eating one rather than simply brushing his teeth; they were certainly rotten enough.

After a pause enlivened only by the sound of crunching Rollins finally said, 'Do you remember me ringing you at home, Jack, and *ordering* you to stick to your own last, and to not get sidetracked by wild goose chases?'

'It'd be odd if I didn't,' said Jack ironically, 'since it was only a couple of days ago.' It might be an uneven contest but he wasn't going down without some sort of fight.

Rollins' glare became even colder, as did his tone, 'But you didn't obey me, did you, Jack? Instead I find you went straight out and did quite the opposite of what I told you to do. You went running off to question this Mike Sheehy guy and, incidentally, interfere with a long-term surveillance operation being run by the Anti-Drug Task Force. I have the written complaint here on my desk if you'd like to see it.'

'Oh, come off it,' snapped Jack, getting irritated himself, 'Do you think Sheehy doesn't know he's under surveillance? Every crook in Ireland knows all about Operation Anvil!' – this was a major police crackdown on all suspected gang members in Dublin, putting as many as possible under surveillance to disrupt their criminal activities- 'And what did I do, exactly? I went to a snooker club in my spare time! What's that got to do with you, or anyone else?'

'You also,' continued Rollins, ignoring this even though both knew perfectly well that fraternising with known criminals was strictly forbidden to serving Gardai, 'went to see Sean Crilly's wife, though what she has to do with William Akima's murder is something of a mystery to me. But at least she hasn't written in a complaint. Yet. Unlike Detective Inspector Prendergast of the Serious Crime Squad. He claims you've barged in on his investigation into the attempted murder of one George Trinder, and in fact interviewed him in hospital without so much as a by-your-leave, much less his permission. Not even a phone call out of common courtesy. Is that true?'

'Yes, well, I was in a hurry,' muttered Jack, 'And it's not like Trinder was going to be his star witness or something. He isn't going to tell Prendergast a damned thing about who shot him, because if he did he'd be sounding his own death knell.'

Rollins sighed and leaned back in his swivel chair, 'I warned you, Jack. I told you to stick to the case you were given. But you just couldn't do it. I gave you the chance to rebuild your self-respect, and your reputation, but you just couldn't do what you were told, could you? You always have to be cleverer than anyone else, you always have to see what no one else can. Jack always knows best.'

'Oh, give it a rest!' snapped Jack furiously, all the more stung because there was a grain of truth in Rollins' words. But only when he was younger. And what talented young man isn't a little cocky and arrogant? Ability is no use without the confidence to actually go out and use it. 'I'm tired of hearing about the big favour you're doing me by giving me this case! Just who the hell do you think you're talking to? I'm not a schoolboy, and you're not my headmaster! Do you have any idea how many murder cases I've investigated? Forty-four, not including this one. And I've cleared forty-two of them. That's the best record for a detective in Ireland *ever* and you know it, so I'm damned if I'm going to have *you* telling me how to do my job.'

Rollins blinked in surprise at this outburst; he had not expected such spirit from Jack. He began, 'Now...'

'I don't want to hear it,' Jack angrily interrupted him, 'This is my case and I'll follow it wherever I think it leads, and I'll question whomever I see fit! You have the power to remove me from this case, yes, but until you do don't *dare* question my methods! You wouldn't believe how much I've learned about Sheehy and his gang!'

'Great!' snapped Rollins, 'And what have you learned about the racist gang that is killing black men in Dublin?'

'It was Sheehy and his thugs who killed them!' shouted Jack, 'There *is* no racist gang! That's all just a cover. Akima and Wistarra were lovers, and they were involved in a drug-smuggling ring with Sean Crilly until Sheehy killed them all and took over the gang!'

Rollins went very still, his expression blank as he thought about this, until finally he asked, 'Do you have any evidence of that?'

Jack made a gesture of frustration, 'No, not yet. But by talking to people I've discovered all this, and now I just need some time to prove it.'

Rollins pursed his lips, 'Let me get this straight. George Trinder told you that Sheehy killed them all? Killed Crilly and our two black friends?'

Jack nodded and Rollins sneered, 'Why would a hardened criminal like him tell you all this, when he won't even tell us who shot *him?*'

'He told *me* that Sheehy had him shot,' retorted Jack, 'but strictly off the record. He won't testify to that effect because if he does he's a dead man, okay? So he told me about Sheehy killing the others –also off the record- in the hope that I'll put Sheehy away without involving him at all. That way he gets his revenge for the shooting at no personal risk, and without getting the name of being a snitch.'

Rollins was nodding his head, though not in agreement, 'So all you've got is the word of a man who admits he has a huge grudge against Sheehy? A grudge he daren't try to avenge himself?' He allowed a moment to let this sink in before asking, 'You don't think he could be just using you, Jack? Making it all up out of spite, to get his own back on Sheehy? Without any risk to himself? Hmm?'

'Of course he's using me,' admitted Jack, grudgingly, for it had not occurred to him that Trinder was lying; everything he said had had the ring of truth about it, 'but I don't think he's making it up. If he was he would have dreamed up a motive for killing them too; it was me who came up with the drugs angle and it's just a guess; Trinder said no one knows why Sheehy killed the two black men. That doesn't sound like an orchestrated pack of lies to me.'

'Does it not?' said Rollins softly, 'Well, it does to me. You're playing right into his hands by trying to make this complicated, Jack. Racist thugs killed Akima and Wistarra, but you won't admit it because you can't find them. And all this running around looking for conspiracy theories isn't just wasting valuable time, it has also allowed Trinder to play you for a fool.'

Stung, Jack glared at him, a look Rollins returned unmoved. Then, with utter contempt, he said, *'George Trinder told you.* God, you're like a wet-eared kid running around in circles chasing your own tail, and all because a known liar, thief, drug dealer and all around violent scumbag *told* you so? Do you have any idea how pathetic that sounds?'

'I believe him,' mumbled Jack doggedly, though an icy sliver of doubt had entered his mind. *Was* Trinder trying to use him for revenge? Well, yes, of course he was, but was he *lying* to do it? It was certainly possible, much as he hated to admit it. But why would he lie? If he just wanted to shop Sheehy he could do it for shooting *him.* And if it was all a fabrication surely he would also have made up a plausible reason for the killings? He shook his head, 'I'm sorry, I just don't think he was lying.'

'Yes, well I do,' said Rollins dryly, 'and here's why.' He picked up a sheet of paper and flung it across the desk at Jack. It missed him and fluttered to the floor. Startled, he picked it up and began to read.

'It's a police report,' said Rollins with quiet venom, 'Reporting how the body of a black man was found lying in the hallway of his house in Castle Riada in Lucan a couple of hours ago. He was beaten to death, Jack. Want to try and guess what was written on the wall beside the corpse? *WELL?'* he suddenly roared, half-rising to his feet, *'Do* you?'

Jack shook his head, stunned, 'This doesn't make sense...'

'Shut up!' snapped Rollins, sitting back down, 'Just *shut up.* Look at me, Jack. Look at me, and listen very carefully. I gave you this case because I was desperately short-handed. And yes, because it was a low profile crime and I didn't much care about it. I do now, though, because now it's a *triple* murder, and you haven't got a bloody *clue* who committed any of them!'

He held up one hand to forestall Jack's incipient protest and said dismissively, '*Don't*! Don't even mention Mike Sheehy because I don't want to hear it. While you've been wasting your time running after him another man has *died.* Because of *you.* Because you were wasting time on the wrong track!'

The icy hand of guilt gripped Jack's heart at these words, though a touch of anger heated it back up a little as Rollins continued, 'Have you any idea of the field day the Press is going to have with this? There's no containing it now; I'm going to have to get involved myself, call a Press conference of my own and come clean about this racist gang, these "Sons of Cuchuaillainn" or whatever they call themselves. People in the black community need to know about the danger they're facing, and we're going to be *crucified* for not revealing all this sooner. And all because you were busy running around in circles, chasing your own tail.'

There was just enough fight left in Jack for him to curl his lip a little at this; it was typical of Rollins to care more about public relations than lives. But even as this thought crossed his mind Jack deflated again; he was trying to work up a little self-righteous anger against his superior to assuage his own guilt, and to his credit he instantly realized it.

Meanwhile Rollins was silent, breathing stertoriously through flared nostrils for some moments before he finally shook his head and said simply, 'This is it, Jack, the last chance you're ever going to get. Find these arseholes, and find them quickly.' His face and voice took on a bitter tone as he added, 'And before you ask, Sheehy and his men were under observation all last night, while the murder was taking place. And if you as much as glance at him again, or mention his name, you're *out!* Got it? Off the case and out of the force too, for gross incompetence, drunkenness, dereliction of duty and whatever else I can think of. I have the power, and by God I'll use it if you try my patience any further!' His voice rose to a shout as he concluded, 'DO YOU UNDERSTAND?'

'Yes,' replied Jack through numb lips, too shell-shocked to protest at the other man's tone. Besides, he deserved it. 'I understand.' He rose to his feet, 'I'll get right onto it.' And he walked from the office like one in a trance, hardly able to believe what had just happened.

Chapter Twenty

Jack walked very slowly towards the lift, the report in his hand and nothing on his mind beyond the need for a very large whiskey, an image of which was before his mind like a beacon, which would restore the world to sanity. The fact that it was hardly breakfast time yet for normal people meant nothing to him; he had long ago accepted that his job made him anything but normal. Working odd, anti-social hours was for Jack like coming home, and even before his alcohol problem taking a drink in the morning was nothing new, though back in the old days it had only occurred after he had worked an all-nighter. But circumstances alter cases, and this circumstance had flattened his new found self-control and determination like a steamroller.

By the time he reached his office, however, he had recovered enough equilibrium to grimly –and only with an effort- banish thoughts of booze from his mind; tempting though it was, he had too much work to do to get drunk.

Frank was waiting on tenderhooks and when he saw Jack's pale, stunned countenance his own face immediately fell in sympathetic response. 'What is it? What's wrong?'

'I'll tell you in the car,' replied Jack glumly, 'Come on, we're going out to Lucan.' He turned and walked away, leaving Frank to grab his jacket and hurry after him. When the younger man caught up he said bleakly, 'I take it there hasn't been a breakthrough then, sir?'

'Oh but there has,' said Jack grimly, 'of a sort.' He took a deep breath and told Frank of the latest development, as well as the gist of what Rollins had said to him. By the time he had finished they were in the car and underway, and for several moments Frank was silent, concentrating on his driving and on trying to absorb the news. At length he shook his head and said, 'I just can't believe it. It doesn't make any sense. We were so sure...'

His voice trailed off and Jack said grimly, '*I* was so sure, you mean. *You* tried to talk me out of my wild theories, as I recall. It was just that all my instincts told me that the racist thing was bullshit, that Akima had been killed by professionals carrying out a hit disguised as a hate crime. And then when I spoke to Trinder...'

'Rollins is right, though, isn't he?' said Frank reluctantly, 'Trinder *could* be just stringing you along for his own ends. Must be, I suppose.' He paused for a moment and then said, 'Is it possible that this new victim is *also* part of the drugs ring? That it's another gangland killing disguised to look like a racist attack?'

'I doubt it,' said Jack dryly, raising the Report Sheet Rollins had flung at him, 'This guy was a doctor.' He waved his hand and sighed, 'And when you think about it, why bother inventing a racist gang? I mean, if you murder someone the evidence will either lead to you or it won't. Why go so far as to invent a racist group at all?'

'Because they knew they wouldn't leave any evidence,' replied Frank promptly, 'They knew the only way they could be traced was by motive, so they obscured the motive.'

Jack shook his head, 'Well, that was the theory, anyway. But it's not working out like that, is it? Maybe we were looking at the wrong motive. And Trinder seemed to be saying that Leary painted the "Ireland For The Irish" thing more or less as a joke.' He darted a sideways glance at his assistant, 'If I suggested that Sheehy and his mates murdered this new guy as well, to try and throw us off their scent, would you think I'd finally gone mad?'

'Well, it *is* a little far-fetched,' said Frank diplomatically, his expression, however, suggesting a more emphatic negative, 'Not that I think that the likes of Sheehy would have any scruples, mind, but they'd be taking a hell of a risk. We might find some forensic evidence at this new crime scene that incriminates one of them, or we might find a witness to this killing. Even aside from murdering an innocent man for no real reason, they'd be taking an awful big risk just to get us off their backs.'

'It worked, though, didn't it?' Jack pointed out, 'We *are* off their backs, and if we as much as look their way again we'll be off the case too. And in my case, off the force too. And some of these arseholes will kill a man as soon as look at him.'

He sighed and shook his head before glaring out of the window, unseeing eyes taking in none of the passing scenery. Then he said, half to himself, 'It *is* all a bit far-fetched, isn't it? As you said, they're risking an awful lot for very little gain. Why would they care if we suspect them, as long as we can't prove anything? I mean, it's not as if they have public reputations to consider or anything. Everyone already knows they're scum, so a bit of scandal won't hurt them. Quite the opposite, if anything; a few murders would make people more afraid of them than ever.'

'Yes, sir,' agreed Frank. 'Sorry.'

'Not as sorry as I am,' said Jack bleakly. 'Especially if I find out we could have prevented *this* killing by pursuing the racist angle more vigorously. I mean, we never even chased down the guys you found with a record of assaults on immigrants, which we would have by now if I'd really believed the whole racist thing.' He sighed again, 'Maybe I just didn't want to believe that otherwise normal Irish people had that much hatred in them for people whose only crime is to be a different color from them.'

There was no answer to this, and Frank maintained a silence until they reached the address typed on the Incident Report Sheet. Castle Riada was one of the new-ish suburbs that had mushroomed up all around Dublin during the property bubble and, while the houses themselves were appealing enough, the whole Lucan area was now so large and sprawling that driving through the endless estates engendered a slight feeling of desolation. There was a sameness about all the houses, the avenues and cul-de-sacs, that left a dreary impression on both men, and caused Frank to quietly murmur, '*Mirrored maze of deception that lures the traveller astray! The desert of Suburbia, that bleeds life and colour away.*'

When they arrived at the victim's home, however, they found it standing out from the crowd in the most unfortunate manner, differentiated from its neighbors by the blue and white Crime Scene tape sealing it off, and the white Garda Technical Bureau van parked outside. A uniformed Gardai was standing at the entrance to the short cul-de-sac where the victim had lived, and after showing him his Warrant Card Frank parked the car as close to the house as he could get. With a depressing sense of familiarity the two detectives donned blue plastic booties and rubber surgical gloves before walking into the house. After showing their credentials to a second Gardai posted at the front door, and signing the crime scene log, they made their way through the organized bedlam that constituted the forensic part of the investigation.

Once again the kitchen was at the back of the house, and once again it was here that the victim had been murdered. The body of Dr. Samuel Wilson was lying on the floor, in a wide pool of almost black blood that was drying into a crust on the laminated wood floorboards. The two policemen stared at the battered body -which was being attended by Ryan yet again, increasing the sense of *déjà vu*- before lifting their eyes to the hateful but by now familiar slogan daubed on the pale yellow wall. This time it *was* printed in blood rather than paint, and a discarded brush on the floor was creating another, smaller pool of its own. As they entered the kitchen Ryan glanced up, and sniffed audibly, 'Oh, it's you two.' *Laurel and*

Hardy. 'Here's another one for your collection. Three stiffs...they're really mounting up. Any chance of you actually catching the bastards that are doing this?'

Jack made no reply, though his grim expression lowered even further, but Frank burst out hotly, 'We are trying, you know! But there are only two of us, after all! And you haven't exactly showered us with useful information either, have you? What about all the wonders of modern science? For all your sneering you haven't been much help yourself!'

'Shut up, Frank,' said Jack vaguely, struck by a sudden thought; why *were* there still only two of them on this case? It was inching into the realms of mass murder, yet Rollins still hadn't given them a proper task force, or even a few extra bodies to help out with the routine stuff. Surely he couldn't be so short-handed that he *still* couldn't spare two or three more men? Especially in light of the growing media interest –indeed, *frenzy*- about the killings? Filing this away as a point to raise the next time Rollins voiced any complaints about his handling of the case, he looked around at the busy throng of men working the scene and asked, 'Who found the body?'

'I did, sir,' came a voice from the hallway, 'Garda Brennan.' The young uniformed Gardai who had let them into the house walked through the open kitchen door and said, 'That is, I reported it in. A colleague of Dr. Wilson made the actual discovery and rang 999 at about four this morning. I was on patrol nearby so I responded.'

Jack turned to him, 'And where is this colleague?'

'Er, in hospital, sir. She got a bit hysterical when I broke in and we saw the body, so I had my partner take her to Blanchardstown Hospital.'

'Nice,' muttered Jack, remembering how revolting the place had appeared on his visit there. 'Did they work there?'

'No, sir. They both worked at Tallaght Hospital but that's further away. She only lives up the road and they were on the same shift so they were car pooling. It was her turn to drive but there was no answer when she knocked so she peered through the letterbox. It was still dark of course but she thought she could see a foot lying in the kitchen doorway so, after banging and shouting on the front door for a bit, she called us. I broke a glass pane in the door to get in and...well, found him like that. Dr. Hennessy, the colleague, went a bit mental when she saw him, and we had to get her out and calm her down before we rang our Inspector, and he rang Harcourt Square.'

'Well, of course she got upset!' snapped Jack, 'You shouldn't have bloody well let her in to begin with!'

The young Gardai looked abashed and dropped his gaze, 'Yes, sir, sorry about that. It's just that she pushed her way in. And she *is* a doctor, after all, and we thought he might need medical attention. We didn't know he was dead at that point, you see, and we never dreamed he'd been murdered. Sorry, sir.'

Jack shook his head, 'Never mind, son, I'm just being cantankerous; of course you didn't know he was dead, much less a murder victim. You did the right thing. Did you disturb anything, apart from breaking the pane of glass in the front door?'

'No, sir. We took a quick look round the house, to make sure it was empty, but we were careful not to touch anything.'

'Did you find out anything about this guy from Dr. Hennessy?'

'No, sir. Er, it was all a bit manic, what with her screaming and crying and all that. Like I said, she was so distressed that Dave...that is, Garda Pearse, my partner, took her to the hospital while I sealed off the house. She might have talked to him on the way, of course. He's back here now, if you want a word. He's blocking off the street to all non-residents.'

Jack nodded, 'You go and take his place and send him in here to me. And watch out for the Press guys; they're bound to be here soon and they're bloody ruthless about getting into crime scenes to snatch photos.' He turned to his assistant, 'Frank, start poking about and see what you can find out about the victim.' He turned to examine the sliding patio door that led to the garden; the lock had clearly been forced. Unlike at Akima's, no finesse had been used, and he wondered if that meant anything. The officer in charge of the Technical Team, Sergeant Collins, was in the garden taking casts of footprints, and when he saw Jack inspecting the door he called out, 'Crowbar, sir. Popped the lock open in about a millisecond, I should think.'

Jack nodded as if this answered an unasked question, 'Any idea how many attackers there were?'

'There were just the two sets of footprints. And we only found two weapons inside.'

'Oh.' This too was different from the other killings. 'What were they?'

'The crowbar and a hurley. We've bagged them for examination so keep your fingers crossed; we might just get lucky.'

Jack nodded, although luck had been in short supply so far on this case. For them, at least; the murderers thus far seemed to be leading charmed lives. 'Did you notice anything else?'

The sergeant considered for a moment and said, 'Well, it wasn't a robbery because they never left the kitchen. They burst straight in the back door, killed the occupant while he was eating his dinner, and left again. Never went into any of the other rooms. Or at least,' he corrected himself, 'they didn't leave any muddy footprints in the rest of the house. I suppose we shouldn't make assumptions.'

'No,' said Jack heavily, 'you can leave that to me. That's my area of expertise.' He glanced at the small glass-topped kitchen table and saw the half-eaten meal resting on it. The plate as well as the table it sat on was flecked with blood, and to control his sudden nausea he looked back out into the back garden. 'Was the back gate forced too?'

Collins nodded, 'Yeah. It has a small mortise lock rather than a bolt. Burst open just like the lock on the back door, and with what appears to be the same implement. And before you ask,' he added, 'that gate backs out onto the main road. It isn't overlooked, either; the houses on the other side of the main road face each other, not the road. And with these high fences the only people who might have seen the intruders would be the immediate neighbors and any passersby on the main road.'

Jack nodded with interest, though he intended to check all this himself anyway, 'So all they had to do was wait till there were no cars passing and they were straight in, with no danger of being seen except by what, two or three of the neighbors?'

The forensics expert nodded glumly and Jack stepped gingerly out onto the patio, careful not to touch anything, and made his way to the back fence. He turned and looked at the neighbor's house; the victim had lived in the last house in the row, so really he was only overlooked on one side. But, high as the fences were, anyone looking out the upstairs back window of any of the houses in the terrace would certainly have seen the intruders opening the back gate and making their way up to the patio door. It would only take a couple of seconds to get there, however, so they would have to be damned unlucky to be spotted. Especially at dinnertime. Though the meal the victim had been eating might not mean anything, not if he was on shift work; dinnertime might be noon to him, or midnight. Jack had to assume that they hadn't been seen, since no one had dialed 999, but obviously they would still canvas the street; some people were quite capable of seeing two figures walking up the path but persuading themselves that they were the owners, or that they had imagined it, rather than checking, or ringing the police to have them check it out.

He re-entered the house and glared at the young Gardai nervously waiting for him, 'Are you Pearse? Good. What did Dr. Hennessy tell you about our victim?'

Pearse visibly composed himself under O'Neill's glare and gathered his thoughts before replying, 'Well, I didn't really like to question her properly, sir, because she was so upset, but she did tell me a few things. Like, she was saying, *oh, he was only thirty-one and had everything to live for,* that sort of thing. You know what I mean? Anyway, I gathered that he was just out of a relationship with some nurse so he was single, he'd lived here for two years and loved it, and well, I think Dr. Hennessy was hoping to get together with him, if you know what I mean.'

'Yes, I do know what you mean,' said Jack irritably, 'In fact I speak English quite well so you don't have to keep asking if I *know what you mean.* Let's just assume that I understand every word unless I say different, okay? Now, where was he from?'

'Dundalk, sir. Like I said, he'd only lived here for two years.'

Jack gave him a hard look to see if he was taking the piss; apparently not. He took a deep breath and said, 'I see. And was he Irish or an immigrant?'

'An immigrant, sir. From Zimbabwe originally.'

Jack sighed, 'This is like pulling teeth. All right, anything else?'

Pearse thought hard, 'I don't think so, sir. Like I said, she was so upset I didn't like to interrogate her; I just let her ramble on, if you know what... Sir.'

'Right, here's what I want you to do,' said Jack, 'Knock on every door around here and question all the neighbours. I want to know if anyone saw or heard anything out of the ordinary yesterday afternoon or evening. Get all their names, addresses and telephone numbers. Most of them will have left for work by now so you'll have to find out where they work and contact them there. Got it?'

'Yes, sir,' Pearse looked uncomfortable, 'Er, I've been working all night and I was supposed to go off shift at seven...'

'Shut up,' said Jack briskly, 'For today you're working for me. This is your lucky day, lad; lots of lovely overtime. Think of all the extra cash you'll rake in to spend on your girlfriend. Or whatever. Tell your mate outside to stay on roadblock duty while you're chasing up the neighbors. Anyone not home you'll have to come back and talk to tonight. Go on, then, move it!' He turned away and called out, 'Find anything interesting, Frank?'

Frank was on his knees in the sitting-room, working his way through an old biscuit tin full of documents. He looked up and answered, 'Not yet, sir. At least, not much.'

Jack nodded, 'I'm letting the uniformed boys do the door-to-door because I don't believe anyone saw anything. This isn't Darndale or somewhere; if the neighbors round here had seen anyone breaking in they would have rung the police. I think. Still, we have to check. You keep at it down here, and keep out of the forensics boys' way. I'll take upstairs.'

As he walked out into the hallway a thought struck him and he roared out the front door, 'Pearse! Come back here! Write down Dr. Hennessy's address and phone number for Detective Carr here.' He began walking up the stairs, noting that while the house was bright and clean the decor was all magnolia and beige. It was all a little bare and impersonal, reminding him a bit of Akima's apartment, though it wasn't half so extreme. Even the windows had blinds on them rather than curtains. It didn't take much of a detective to deduce that Wilson was a bachelor, or that he lived alone; there were no feminine touches anywhere. Upstairs Jack noticed, in spite of the Technical officers swarming through the bedrooms, that it was the same; it was a neat, clean house devoid of most of the decorative touches that make a house a home. All three of the bedrooms were decorated; one as Wilson's master bedroom, one done out as an office, and the third as a guest bedroom that was frugal even by Wilson's apparently Spartan standards. Apart from a fair number of what appeared to be family photos on the walls –quite a few of them of a white family- there was little in the way of ornamentation, though at least the office had all Wilson's degrees and diplomas framed and hanging on a vanity wall. He even had his Inter and Leaving Certificates hanging there. Along with the photos, this was pretty much the only vestige of personality the late owner had stamped on the place, which struck Jack as being oddly sad. He hadn't lived here long enough to make this place truly his, to make it a home, and now he never would.

An hour or so's patient digging through old boxes and suitcases unearthed nothing of interest, even in the attic, and a dusty and disgruntled Jack returned to the ground floor in search of a cup of tea and inspiration, in that order. A scandalized Sergeant Collins ran him out of the kitchen before he could touch the kettle, so he called Frank out to drive him up to the Eurospar beside the Penny Hill pub, where they could at least get a takeaway coffee. Once this was achieved they sat in the *Ka* in the pub car park, drinking the scalding, plastic-tasting brew with distaste and comparing notes. In Jack's case this did not take long, but Frank's search had proved more fruitful.

'He was an orphan by the age of six,' he informed Jack, not without sympathy in his voice, 'His parents were murdered trying to defend the farm they worked on from government sanctioned land grabbers, and Wilson, like most orphans in Zimbabwe, was left to starve to death. Mugabe doesn't give a damn about his own people so there are no state orphanages, no welfare workers, and no charities either. The only people who do anything for anyone out there are the foreign aid groups, and Wilson was lucky enough to be picked up on the streets by one of them. He was one of a group of homeless children living in a skip, apparently, though I can't even begin to imagine what he ate or how he survived. Anyway, he was brought to Ireland on an aid program, and he was fostered to a family in Cork. He was an exceptionally bright kid, it seems, and got ten A1's in his Leaving. He studied medicine at U.C.C. before doing his internship in Cork General Hospital. Then he had three years at Dundalk before getting his current job as registrar in Tallaght…'

'Great,' interrupted Jack gloomily, closing his eyes, 'Why do all these victims seem to have survived bloody awful horrors in their own countries, only to be murdered in Dublin?'

'Er, because quite a few of our immigrants are only here *because* they're fleeing from bloody awful horrors in their own countries, sir,' replied Frank.

Jack opened his eyes, 'Actually, it was a rhetorical question.' He shook his head angrily, 'It doesn't seem possible, does it, that life could be so cruel? That *people* can be so cruel. You'd think these poor buggers had suffered enough, wouldn't you?'

Frank had no lack of sympathy for desperate immigrants but he contented himself with saying, 'Er, was that another rhetorical question, sir?'

'Oh, never mind!' said Jack crossly, 'Do you have the name and address of his foster parents? Good. Someone will have to inform them of his death. We'll need one of them to ID the body too. Get onto headquarters, will you? Have them contact Cork and send someone around. I know it's our job, really, but a round trip to Cork would take up an entire day we just can't spare.'

'Er, now, sir?'

'Do you have other, more pressing business to deal with?' asked Jack sarcastically, 'Yes, now! You have a mobile, don't you? Well, get on with it! It's a miracle the Press aren't here already, but I'm sure they'll turn up soon enough, and we don't want his family finding out he's dead by opening the front door to some nosy bloody vulture of a reporter!'

While Frank used the phone Jack concentrated on thinking about the kind of people who could murder so casually, so senselessly, and carefully *not* thinking about how he might have prevented this death if he had not been so wrapped up in his own theories. If only he had not been so convinced that Sheehy had been behind it all. And yet that still made more sense to him than believing these killings to be the work of a random group of neo-Nazis. *That* made no sense to him at all. Though, of course, every day people perpetrated bloody awful acts that made no sense to him. A thought struck him and when Frank was finished on the mobile he said, 'If you wanted to murder a black man in safety and privacy you could hardly have picked a better candidate in all of Ireland than Dr. Wilson here, could you? I mean, he had no family nearby, lived alone, and had no girlfriend anymore, so it's unlikely he'll have visitors with him when you burst in. And then there's this house; end of terrace, corner site. The only way you could be spotted breaking in is from upstairs by the neighbors on one side, and even then only after you were in the garden, and only for a second or two at that. In the dark, what are the chances of you being seen in those couple of seconds?'

'Very low, sir,' obliged Frank, 'So you think his killers knew him?'

Jack rolled his eyes, 'They bloody well had to know him or they wouldn't have known where he lived, would they?'

'I meant knew him *personally,* sir' responded Frank with a touch of irritation of his own.

Jack pursed his lips, 'I suppose they must have. They had to have known some stuff about him, at least. I mean, how else could you pick such a perfect victim? Go around peering through windows till you see a black man alone in a room?'

'You have a point, sir,' said Frank thoughtfully, 'It *is* all a bit coincidental otherwise, isn't it? I mean, he could have had a wife and kids in there with him. Or be sharing the house with other doctors or something. I think you're onto something here, sir. You think that if we look hard enough at his background we should find our killers?'

Jack shook his head, 'Never mind his background, if we look hard enough at his *neighbors* we should find either one of the killers or someone connected to them. Someone who set up Wilson, either deliberately or without realizing that talking about their black neighbor to a friend would get the poor sod killed.'

'Where shall we start, sir?' asked Frank, brightening up with anticipation.

'Not we, *you.* I have other fish to fry. Start with the neighbors, obviously. Get a list of the names of everyone on this road and do a background check on the lot of them. Run them all through the computer and see if any of them are connected in any way with those anti-immigrant people. Even if *they're* not members, a relative might be. A record of violence would be nice, particularly against immigrants, but as much as an angry letter to a newspaper would be a start. Any criminal connections would be a bonus, too. If you don't find anything gradually expand your search into the whole of the Castle Riada estate. And don't have a fit, but I want you to see if you can tie in any of the neighbors with Sheehy and his mob. Any sort of connection will do.'

'Oh, Jack, is that wise?' groaned Frank, rolling his eyes to heaven.

Jack grinned, 'Probably not, but do it anyway. Suffering is good for the soul, laddie, and your soul will get a real spring cleaning if Rollins finds out what you're doing! I'm sorry, Frank, but I don't believe it was just coincidence that Akima and Wistarra were lovers, and both just *happened* to be murdered in separate attacks by some sort of fascist group. That's ridiculous, whatever Rollins says. And I don't believe it was *another* coincidence that Akima was connected with Crilly, who in turn just happened to be murdered by Sheehy! I'm sorry but that's all just too much to swallow, so check out everyone around here, and everyone Wilson knew, to see if you can tie any of them to Sheehy. I don't care how tenuous the link is; if there is one, find it.'

'Yes, sir,' said Frank reluctantly, 'but the bottom line is that we still only have Trinder's word for it that Sheehy killed Crilly. And what if Mr. Rollins finds out what we're doing?'

Jack shrugged, 'Then my head will roll. But it's not as if I've got a long, glittering career ahead of me anyway. And don't worry; if I sink I'll make sure you don't go down with me.'

'That wasn't my concern, sir,' said Frank a little stiffly.

'I know, but it is mine. One of my concerns, anyway. You think I want to you to ruin your career out of mistaken loyalty to a drunken has-been whose career is already pretty much over?' Jack shook his head, 'I won't allow it. Now, do you think you can get all that done today?'

Frank puffed out his cheeks, 'Well, I can try. I can certainly do all the computer cross-referencing today, especially if I can rope Julie in to help on a second machine. It's only a quarter past nine now and it shouldn't take more than four or five hours. I doubt if I'll get to talk to them all today, mind.'

'No,' said Jack briskly, 'Well, I wasn't expecting you to. Nor do I want you to, even if you get any likely leads; not without me. Meanwhile, I'm going to go to the Hospital to talk to Dr. Hennessy, see if I can get a statement from her. You never know what I might learn.' His face hardened, 'And since I'm going to be in the same hospital I'll also have another chat with our favourite grass, Georgie Trinder, to see if he sticks to his story. I doubt if I'll be back in the office today so, if you do get finished, is there anything you can occupy yourself with for the afternoon? Something innocent that's not connected with Sheehy and won't upset Rollins?'

Frank thought for a moment, then said, 'Do you want me to chase up the thugs with a history of violence against foreigners?'

'Not alone, I don't. You're still pretty inexperienced and I doubt you'll pick up on a lie as quickly as I would. I've heard millions more of them, for a start. Is there anything else outstanding?'

'Well, I still haven't shown the photos of Sheehy's gang to all of Akima's neighbours. A couple of them *never* seem to be in. I could do that, if you like?'

Jack let out a groan and held his head, '*Not* connected with Sheehy, I said! All right, do it if you get time, but if anyone asks, say you're just taking witness statements, that you never spoke to all of the neighbors initially.'

'So you want me to just lie to my superiors?' asked Frank.

Jack considered this, 'Yes, that seems to describe it perfectly.'

Frank laughed, 'Fair enough! Anything else?'

'Yes, get me to a taxi rank before any reporters show up. I just can't face the barrage of questions they'll have for me.' *Nor the accusations,* he thought but did not say. *Particularly because any mud they sling at me will be perfectly justified, and indefensible.*

Chapter Twenty-One

It took Frank several hours of file surfing to find what he was looking for, and when he finally came across it he leapt up out of his chair in triumph and engulfed the watching, rather sour-faced Julie in a bear hug.

'If you've *quite* finished,' she said acidly, refusing to be mollified as she was displeased at having had her computer usurped for so long, 'perhaps I could have my station back?'

'Just a few minutes more,' Frank promised, hurriedly sitting back down at her desk, 'It's just that this is really, really important!'

'And my work isn't?' she snapped, but without any real rancour; though she knew just how little regard the policemen had for her work, she couldn't whip up any genuine anger. After all, next to pursuing murderers her filing duties were pretty low-key and it seemed churlish to insist on her rights. Besides, -even aside from having a soft spot for attractive young men- she liked Frank, and his enthusiasm for his job; it was just that after being banished from her desk for the entire morning her patience was wearing a little thin. In spite of Jack's cynical view of his co-workers Julie was a natural doer and liked to keep busy. Now, her stock of gossip had been exhausted, she was bored stiff and wanted to get back to work. She glared at the back of Frank's head but bit down the caustic words fighting to get out. Then she turned and stamped away to the canteen for a soothing cup of tea, and an even more soothing coffee slice.

Frank never even noticed her departure, glued as he was to the computer screen. As he worked he fought to suppress a rising tide of savage glee at the thought that they might finally be closing in on their quarry. For most of the morning he had gotten nowhere with his careful cross-referencing of the names and addresses of Wilson's neighbors, and frustration had started to grip him. It was only when he had widened the search field to include everyone in the whole of the Castle Riada area that an ex-convict had finally popped up; one Michael Lynch. Lynch lived in Castle Riada Crescent, just three streets away from where the unfortunate Dr. Wilson had lived, and must either have known him or at least known of him. Lynch was a career criminal and life-long loser with a history of violence, but that was only the start of the good news; he was also a long-time associate of a certain Michael R. Sheehy. Here was yet another connection back to the gang once run by Sean Crilly; yet another unlikely coincidence, if you happened to believe in such things. Frank didn't.

He began trawling through Lynch's record for confirmation of his "known associates" but there was no mistake; on at least two occasions Lynch had actually been arrested in Sean Crilly's company. Moreover on another occasion, years before, he had been arrested in the process of robbing a post office in company with Mike Sheehy, among others. Frank rubbed his hands together in glee and leaned back in the swivel chair, almost chuckling to himself in his delight and wishing he could contact Jack to share the good news. He would really have to get the old man a mobile phone and drag him, however unwillingly, into the twenty-first century. Or even the twentieth. He twirled the chair around in a celebratory pirouette that was brought to a sudden halt by his spotting the glare that the returning Julie was directing at him. Slightly shamefaced, he got to his feet, 'Sorry, Jules. I got a bit carried away. Anyway, I've finished for now. Finally. Thanks for the loan of your machine. Er, could you print all these pages out for me?'

Julie sighed dramatically and took over at the computer, saying with resignation, 'Sure. The printer's over there. Go and wait; they'll start feeding out in a minute.' She waved her hand in the direction of the communal printer set over in one corner of the open-plan offices, and Frank almost skipped his way over to it, rubbing his hands in glee. Okay, it wasn't proof of anything, but it was yet another connection back to Sheehy and his mob. It *couldn't* all just be coincidence, which meant that they -or at least Jack, he mentally amended- had been on the right track all along. *And be damned to both Rollins and the* Sons of Cuchuaillain!

He retired to Jack's office with the printed sheets to consider his next move. Although it was hardly lunchtime it had already been a long day but Frank had no intention of even slowing down, much less stopping; he was way too psyched-up for that. In fact, even just sitting still was something of a struggle. But what to do next? It was a matter of prioritizing, of balancing the importance of his next task against the need to have O'Neill in tow. There was no urgent need to interview any of Castle Riada's inhabitants now that he had found the link to Sheehy -he hoped- and one of the uniformed Gardai was already busily checking the neighbors in a probably fruitless search for witnesses to the break-in. What else could he do? He looked at his watch, reminding himself to ring Garda Pearse that afternoon to see how he was getting on. However, there was no point in seeking him out now as he could hardly have spoken to all the neighbors yet, especially as, it being a weekday, most of them would still be at work. Or maybe not; the recession was biting everyone pretty hard.

Dare he interview this Lynch guy alone? No, best not; Jack would go mental. Besides, Frank well knew he had neither the experience nor the gravitas to conduct that kind of interview. Even a rookie like him knew that police interviews with suspects came down to force of personality, that whoever could dominate and outwit the other would emerge victorious. And he wasn't ready yet to tackle hardened criminals. One day, though...

With an inward sigh Frank decided to go out to Phibsboro and trawl through Akima's neighbors with photos of Sheehy and his band of uglies, to see if he could jog any memories. It was dull, routine work but Frank knew that only by paying his dues and serving his time could he become a good detective; he had to learn how to crawl before he could walk, much less run. And he was happy to pay the price, for right now becoming a good detective was the most important thing in the world to him.

Two weary hours later Frank was beginning to regret ever joining An Garda Siochana, much less coming out to Foster Road. Of the residents who were home few were inclined to give him the time of day, even when they discovered his errand. This baffled Frank; he could understand people being short with him when they thought he was a salesman, or a mendicant for a charity, but how could anyone show such a lack of interest in catching *murderers?* Murderers, moreover, who had brutally killed one of their own neighbors? Yet everyone he spoke to was brusque to the point of rudeness, and fobbed him off as swiftly as possible. Most hardly glanced at the pictures before declaring the subjects to be total strangers. With these people Frank, becoming angry but maintaining his polite demeanor even after his naturally good manners had started to fray, kept insisting they look again and again until they actually gave the photos more than a cursory glance. But even then no one recognized any of the men or remembered seeing any of them in the vicinity. Or at least, so they said.

After finishing Foster Road Frank moved onto Foster Terrace, which was behind and parallel to the street on which Akima had lived, and resumed his weary round. It was starting to get dark and lights were beginning to come on before he worked his way down to number 98, where he hardly had time to knock before the door was whipped open and an enormously fat middle-aged man practically leapt out onto the porch. When he saw Frank he recoiled in evident surprise and snapped suspiciously, 'Yes?'

Frank's jaw had dropped at the sudden emergence of this apparition, clad in a dirty tracksuit and with a shock of gray hair standing up off his head like the poll of a parrot, but he recovered enough to start into his by now routine spiel about being from the Gardai and conducting a murder inquiry. He had hardly got his name out and the fact that he was a Garda before the fat man, his eyes lighting up, threw the door wide and exclaimed, 'Come in, come in! I've been expecting you.' He led the way into a rather dusty, untidy sitting-room and said, 'Sit down. Would you like a cup of tea? Or coffee?'

'No, thank you, sir. As I was saying, we're conducting some routine inquiries in the area and we wondered if you might be able to help us.'

'Is it about those bloody kids?' asked the fat man, thrusting his chin -or rather, chins- forward aggressively, 'What have they done this time?'

'Er, no, sir, your children haven't done anything,' Frank began, but the man interrupted him with a roar, 'They're not *my* bloody kids! I don't have any. I'm not married, as it happens. I'm talking about the bloody kids in that school next door. The little hooligans are always in trouble, always committing some sort of vandalism!'

'I don't know how many times I've rung your lot but you never do anything,' he added bitterly, 'I've complained to the school dozens of times, too, but they don't take a blind bit of notice either. What do they care what the little savages do? Oh no, they're just their responsibility, that's all! In *law.* I've told that poxy headmaster over and over that while they're wearing his uniform they're *his* responsibility but he just keeps wittering on about what they do inside school hours and outside of school hours being different things. Hah! Pansy! No wonder the kids ignore him and run riot.'

The fat man paused to draw breath and Frank, in a desperate attempt to seize control of the situation, said sharply, 'Sir! Please, let me speak. This has nothing whatsoever to do with any children. In fact this is about a...'

'I've rung Dublin Bus, too,' continued the fat man grimly, effortlessly steam-rollering Frank's attempt to steer the interview back towards sanity, 'Them and their bloody bus stop! Who the hell do they think they are, putting a bus stop outside my house? Hey? Who asked them to put it there, that's what I'd like to know! What gives them the *right* to put it there? *I* didn't give permission, and it's my bloody house!'

Frank stared at him in a kind of dull horror, wondering what he had gotten himself into here, and if he were going to make it back out alive. Was he some sort of nut? Clearly he had stuff on his chest that he had needed to unload for a very long time, and fate had decreed that Frank be the lucky recipient.

'Sir,' he began again, weakly, 'I really have no idea what you're talking about. I am here as part of a *murder* investigation. I know nothing whatsoever about any schoolchildren or vandalism or...'

'No, well, you wouldn't, would you?' said the fat man bitterly, shaking his head in disgust and sending a gentle shower of dandruff floating down onto his shoulders in the process, 'Who cares about my garden and all the rubbish the little bastards throw into it? No one, that's who! Every day I come home and pick up the litter they throw into my garden, and every day I come home to see new graffiti on my front wall. And all because of that bloody bus stop! Well, if the school won't do anything about it, I bloody well will! I've been keeping a log of everything that gets thrown into my garden, and everything that gets written on my wall! I'm taking photos, too; not just of the graffiti but of the damage to my plants as well. Here, look at these!' He got to his feet and picked a handful of Polaroids from the mantlepiece, 'Go on, have a look at what the little bastards write!'

Hating himself for his weakness in not slapping this guy down but trapped by a mixture of natural courtesy and sympathy for the older man's obvious distress, Frank accepted the handful of photos and gave them a glance out of politeness. The man's front wall was indeed daubed with slogans, many sexual in nature but a fair proportion indicating what the local kids thought of a certain Mr. Blobby; precisely who this was Frank was careful not to ask. There was also a large degree of damage to the man's otherwise well maintained garden and Frank's smidge of sympathy for him grew stronger.

'It must be awful to have your plants and flowers crushed and broken like that,' he said at last, flicking through the photos with a touch more interest, 'Why do they do it?'

The fat man shrugged hopelessly and sat back in his armchair, his anger suddenly spent. 'Because they're little shits, that's why,' he said quietly, 'Because they have no respect for anyone or anything. Personally, I blame the parents. They spoil the little pukes rotten and never discipline them until they end up running wild, doing whatever they like without a thought for the consequences, or for who they might be hurting. So what can you expect? It's the same in the schools; the teachers don't dare as much as raise their voices to the kids, and if they do the parents are round the next day screaming blue murder and threatening to sue the school.' He shook his head in despair, 'Where will it all end? I just don't know, I really don't.'

Frank could have told him precisely where it ended, in extreme cases; in violence, in crime, in drug abuse that spawns yet more crime, in alcohol abuse, in prison and in death. Any and all of these things, singly and combined. And even outside the criminal classes it ends in boorish, anti-social behavior from ignorant louts that are little better than animals and constitute a blot on society. But he only said, 'This is criminal damage and trespass, and you shouldn't have to put up with it. I'll see what I can do.'

'Every day,' replied the fat man, eyes downcast and his pendulous jowls dropping in a mixture of sorrow and self-pity, 'every bloody day.'

'I'll have a word with the local station,' said Frank uncomfortably, 'they might send someone to have a word with the kids in their classes, or have a Garda walk by every day at letting-out time. To keep an eye on them and keep them in line.'

The fat man's head lifted again in renewed, angry animation and his upper lip curled in contempt as he replied, 'You must be joking! You think they're afraid of the cops? Don't make me laugh! They know the cops can't touch them so they openly defy them, sneer at them! God, some of the estates these kids live in the cops don't dare drive into!'

Frank had no answer to this and a moment's uncomfortable silence fell before the fat man said, with a gleam of defiance in his dark, piggy eyes, 'Well, I'm not giving up! I'm keeping a daily log of everything the little shits do and I'm going to take legal action for damages against the school, and against Dublin Bus! I'll show them who they're messing with!'

Frank turned an incipient laugh into a cough, 'Yes, sir. Er, the best of luck with that. Though I didn't see any litter in your garden today, as it happens. Or any graffiti on the wall. Anyway, I...'

Before Frank could finally resume his mission the fat man bounced to his feet and cried, 'Do you bloody think so? Wait right there! I'll show you.'

He shot out of the room, leaving Frank to close his eyes and fight the impulse to laugh; oh, he had an air of natural authority to go with his badge, no doubt about that! But although he doubted that Jack would have allowed himself to be railroaded thus, he really didn't see how he could have wrested control of the interview from his new best friend without committing an act of violence. Within seconds his host was back, carrying a large plastic sack full of assorted rubbish. Frank watched in disbelief, wondering if other detectives had to put up with this sort of thing, and trying to ward off the surreal sensation that he was actually at home in bed dreaming it all.

'I wasn't doubting your word in the slightest,' he protested as the fat man grimly shook open his sack and offered it for inspection, 'and I don't wish to be rude but really I'm here on a very important matter...'

He stopped suddenly, transfixed by what he could see lying amongst the rubbish. It was a long, wrinkled tube of clear cellophane. There was a paper sticker affixed to the outside which bore the legend "The L'il Slugger Genuine American Baseball Bat". Below was written, in smaller letters, King Sports Equipment, Ltd. There was even a little crown logo underneath the name. Wondering if he really *was* dreaming, Frank reached out and took the sack from the fat man's hands and stared at its contents. As if from far away he heard his own voice asking, 'When did you gather all this up, sir?'

'Over the last couple of weeks,' replied the fat man, gratified but more than a little surprised by the effect his little collection was producing.

Careful not to touch anything, Frank pointed at the bat wrapping and said, 'And this long piece of plastic, sir. Do you have any idea when you picked *that* up?'

The fat man considered for a moment before saying, 'Oh, a few days ago, I suppose. Monday, I think. Why?'

Monday, the day Akima had been murdered. 'Can you be more definite, sir? It could be very important,' said Frank softly.

The fat man leaned over to peer more closely at the tube of cheap, wrinkled plastic. 'Really?' he asked doubtfully, 'it doesn't look it.' He thought for a moment, 'Yes, it was definitely Monday afternoon. I remember it distinctly because I remember thinking that the last thing any of the little shits need is a weapon like that in their hands. Most of them are already thugs; they oughtn't to be allowed to own things like that. Besides, I remember it because it annoyed me more than usual, because it was a Bank Holiday and the school was closed. I mean, usually weekends and Bank Holidays are the only times I get a break, the only times the little brutes *don't* persecute me, so I was doubly pissed off.' He shook his head and sighed, 'Never live next door to a school, Garda, and never buy a house with a bus stop outside it.'

Frank gazed at him almost in reverence, blessing his anger and his petty little mind. 'Would you be willing to make a statement to that effect, sir? I mean, to its having been dropped there on Monday afternoon?'

'Yes, I would,' said the fat man sharply, 'It definitely wasn't there when I left at nine that morning, and it *was* there when I got home at five-thirty. I had to work that Bank Holiday, which is bad enough without coming home to...' He paused in his diatribe before saying, 'Come to think of it, that was the day my plants all got trampled, too. Hang on a minute.' He went to a cabinet in the corner of the room and shuffled through a sheaf of photos before saying, 'I have a digital camera and you can print the time and the date and... Yes, there we go; Monday the 15th at 17:51pm.'

Frank surveyed the photo excitedly, then looked at the previous one on the roll; it too was dated and showed the garden the day before; no plastic tube. Other debris, yes, including crisp packets and empty cans, but no baseball bat wrapper. He shook his head in disbelief; the photos didn't mean much but they did tell him that the wrapper hadn't been left out overnight...so, was it possible that there were prints on it? There had been none on the bats Lynch certainly hadn't been wearing gloves when he bought them. So -he could hardly bring himself even to think it, the mere possibility was making his hands shake- *was it possible that there were prints on the wrapper?* It hadn't been left out overnight and there had been no rain that day; indeed it had been warm and sunny. And it had been safely tucked in this bag with the other rubbish ever since. And you couldn't ask for a better depository for fingerprints than a cellophane wrapper. *It was possible.* It seemed almost too good to be true but it *was* possible. He looked up at his host and, resisting the impulse to kiss him, said, 'Do you think I could have a smaller plastic bag, and some gloves? Rubber, if possible. We don't need all this stuff as evidence. Just the tube.'

'Of course,' said the fat man, bustling off to get them. When he had returned, and the potentially priceless wrapper had been safely bagged, Frank said to him thoughtfully, 'Your name is Collins, isn't it? Yes, 98 Foster Terrace. I remember. I rang you at your workplace last week, remember? I told you about the murder that took place on Foster Road, and asked if you had any information. Why didn't you mention any of this *then?*'

'Oh, was that you?' said the fat man interestedly, 'Well, I wasn't going to waste your time with my little problems when you were busy looking for a *murderer,* now was I?'

'No, I suppose not,' said a wondering Frank, reflecting that angels can come in the unlikeliest guises.

'I mean,' said Mr. Collins reasonably, 'if I went on about litter when you were searching for a murderer you would have thought I was some sort of nut.'

'Yes,' said Frank solemnly, 'Quite possibly. I'm going to need this piece of plastic as evidence, if that's all right with you. And would you mind coming down to headquarters with me, to be fingerprinted and to make a statement? We're going to need your prints for elimination purposes anyway.'

The fat man shook his head, 'Oh, no, no, no, I don't know about that, I'm afraid. I'm a very busy man and I haven't had any dinner yet...' His voice tailed off as the penny finally dropped, 'That black fella from behind who got killed? You think the murder weapon was in this tube? Wow! They never said anything on the news about a baseball bat being the murder weapon or I would have twigged!' And he subsided onto the couch in open-mouthed astonishment.

'You,' said Frank softly, gazing up at him in unaffected awe, 'may single-handedly be responsible for the arrest of a gang of vicious murderers. A gang who have committed not one but three brutal killings.' It was astonishing but true; this slightly pathetic man's running battle with a bunch of schoolkids might well be the difference between a group of multiple murderers being jailed and going free. *Awesome.* And he said a silent prayer to the god of policemen that the cellophane held the prints of at least one member of Sheehy's gang, if not those of the ringleader himself.

The fat man swelled even further, with self-importance, 'Well, if you put it that way, of course I'll come with you and make a statement. After all, it's my civic duty to help the Gardai in any way I can. But I was in the middle of a sandwich when you knocked...er, do you think I could just finish it before we go?'

Chapter Twenty-Two

By the time Frank had shepherded the invaluable, if reluctant, Collins back to Headquarters, taken his statement and fingerprints, and delivered the latter -along with the potentially equally priceless wrapper- to the Forensics Lab. for analysis, it was after nine and he was utterly exhausted. He was also, however, more than content with his day's work. Before he could knock off for the night there was one other, highly pleasurable, task ahead; that of telling Jack what he had unearthed, and seeing the older man's expression when he heard the two bombshells he had to throw at him. *Not that anything was certain*, Frank hastened to ward off bad luck by presumption; *there might be no prints on the wrapper at all. But oh, if there were...*

The delivery of such electric news warranted the personal touch so, in spite of the hour, and his tiredness, Frank pointed the *Ka* in the direction of Glenageary. When he rang the bell and Jack answered, Frank was horrified by the change in his appearance; no oil painting at the best of times, tonight he suddenly looked twenty years older. *And* ill. His news momentarily forgotten, Frank asked in concern, 'Are you all right, Jack?'

Jack stared at him for a moment as if he had no idea who he was, then he blinked and animation suddenly returned to his features, his jaw firming up and the sharpness Frank had come to expect returning to his eyes. It was a bit like watching a toaster warming up. And at last he said, with a frown, 'Frank, what the hell are you doing here? And at this time of night?'

'I had some news that I thought you'd want to hear straight away,' replied Frank, relieved by this return to something like normality, 'But never mind that for the minute, are you feeling okay?'

'No,' said Jack heavily, 'I'm not. Come on in.' He led the way into his small, rather dark sitting-room and said, 'Sit down, sit down. Drink?'

'No, thanks, I'd better not; I'm driving. You aren't ill, are you, sir?'

'Not physically,' came the somewhat cryptic reply. When it became clear that this was the full extent of his answer Frank asked wonderingly, 'What happened at the hospital today?' Meaning; *what happened to you?*

'Eh? Oh,' Jack made a visible effort to gather his thoughts, 'nothing much. I got a statement from that Dr. Hennessy. For what *that's* worth. She didn't have much to add to what young Pearse told us, though I got a bit more background on our Dr. Wilson.'

His face hardened all the way back to its usual craggy demeanor as he said grimly, 'And I had another word with Trinder. I told him I was going to let it be known on the street that he was a grass, that he had spilled everything to me. Then I threatened to get him shifted out of the Secure Ward -at which he nearly had a fit- but he never budged an inch from his story. Either he's decided to call my bluff and tough it out or he really believes what he told me about Sheehy.' Jack subsided into silence for a moment, lost in thought, and then he shook himself and asked, 'What about you, did you dig up anything?'

'Actually, yes, sir, quite a bit,' said Frank, brightening up again as he proceeded to tell Jack all that had transpired that day. When he was finished he looked eagerly at Jack's face, anticipating excitement and, perhaps, a few words of praise. Certainly vindication.

Instead Jack remained preoccupied and said unemotionally, 'Well done, son. If Lynch *is* connected to the Wilson killing -and it's another bloody funny coincidence if he's not- then it looks like we were right and it was Sheehy and his boys all along. Maybe we'll pull Lynch in tomorrow and see if we can sweat anything out of him. Like why they killed them all. We still have no proof against anyone, mind, so if he doesn't talk -and he probably won't- we're back to square one. And why they would have murdered a kid like Wistarra, or a doctor like Wilson, is beyond me. Unless they really are just racists as well as criminals. But we'll find out. Trust me on that. Good work with that wrapper, too; with a bit of luck we'll get prints of at least one of his men. That would finally be a bit of real, tangible evidence. Who knows, we might even get Sheehy's own prints?'

'That's what I thought, sir,' said Frank, a little deflated by his superior's marked lack of emotion, much less the elation he had expected. 'If there *are* prints on it we've enough to pull in their owner for questioning, at least. And we might shake enough information out of him to implicate the others. It's all still a bit circumstantial, though.'

'Yes,' said Jack vaguely, 'but even circumstantial evidence can lead to a conviction, if it's strong enough. Pray for prints, boy, pray for prints. Even if they belong to someone outside of the gang; well, at least we'll finally have a suspect.'

'Yes, sir,' replied Frank, not saying; *as long as they have a criminal record.* 'Of course, we still have to prove that the wrapper we have is from the murder weapon, but surely either the manufacturer or Forensics will be able to help us out there?'

Jack made no reply and eventually Frank said, 'Er, did anything else happen today? Like, did you receive bad news or anything?'

Jack looked at him blindly, 'Did I offer you a drink?'

'Yes, sir, I refused it.'

Jack nodded absently and gave him a tired smile, 'I forgot to get myself one. *Not* like me, I need hardly say.' He got to his feet and poured a -to Frank- frighteningly large glassful of whiskey before retaking his seat before the ashes of a dead fire. He noticed Frank's alarmed look and gave him another absent smile, raising his glass in salute, 'Don't worry, lad, this isn't enough to hurt an old drunk like me. In fact it's hardly a nightcap. Besides, a whole bottle wouldn't get me drunk tonight. Do you ever get like that, Frank? Where you could drink any amount and still stay stone cold sober?'

'Er, no, sir. I'm afraid I don't have a very good head for spirits. Or any alcohol for that matter. It doesn't really agree with me.'

Jack gave a mirthless laugh, 'Oh, a tolerance can be developed! It just takes time and perseverance. Though I don't recommend it. Look at me; up to a week ago I was putting away a full bottle of whiskey a day.'

He noticed Frank's horrified expression and nodded grimly, 'Hard to believe, isn't it? That a man could drink so much without killing himself? But you'd be amazed what the human frame can tolerate. For a time. It crept up on me bit by bit, and I developed such a tolerance that I could drink that amount and still function. More or less. My consumption was spread out over the whole day, you see, so I didn't really get dead drunk until eight or nine at night, by which time I was safely back here and could crash out.'

He gave Frank a penetrating look, 'Am I making you uncomfortable, Detective Garda Carr?'

'No, sir,' replied Frank simply. He looked a little surprised himself and added, as if by way of explanation, 'It's not as if your drinking was a secret, or anything. Everyone in the Metropolitan Division knows about it. And the reason for it,' he added softly.

'Ah yes,' said Jack, regarding his full glass thoughtfully, 'the reason for it.' He raised the glass to the light, as if seeking something hidden within, and then slowly and with great deliberation he put it to his lips and drained it all in one long swallow.

'God Almighty!' cried Frank, jerking upright in his seat, his eyes wide with shock, 'Stop! You'll kill yourself! What the hell do you think you're doing?'

Jack gave him a small, humorless smile, 'Didn't I tell you that tonight I could drink any amount without it affecting me?'

'It'll affect you, all right!' said Frank roughly, 'Right into the morgue.' Nobody could drink neat whiskey like that without disastrous effects. *Nobody.* 'Are you actually *trying* to kill yourself?'

Jack regarded him thoughtfully, 'Possibly. I think for a long time that's *exactly* what I was doing, though in rather a half-hearted manner. Much more honest, don't you think, to just swallow a bottle of pills. Or a bullet? Wouldn't you say? But in the beginning I had my work, you see, and that kept me going. And then I had the outward *structure* of work, even after I had stopped caring. And lately,' he said with a sigh, 'I've hardly been drinking at all - by my standards, at least- because I started to care again.'

'And then today?' prompted Frank, almost fearful of the answer but knowing he had to ask, had to know.

Jack surveyed his empty glass for a moment before placing it carefully on the mantelpiece. He sighed and said softly, 'Tonight an old friend rang me with some news. He was a good friend, once, and he wanted to warn me that Rollo Walker is being released from prison next week.' He glanced at the bemused Frank and added steadily, 'He's the man who killed my wife, and my daughter. He was pissed and speeding and he took them away from me.'

Something in the controlled, dignified way he spoke twisted Frank's heart, and he felt a flood of sudden sympathy for the older man. He opened his mouth to utter soothing words, perhaps even to use poetry as he had always used it, to brighten dark spots in his life, and even to offer wisdom. But he closed his mouth again, the platitudes unvoiced. This was too solemn a moment for mere words, however consoling they were intended to be.

Jack sat up straight and said, with a sort of artificial brightness, 'So I've been sitting here thinking about things! And I have a choice to make.' He fixed Frank with a look filled with grim humor, 'There's always a choice in life, lad, even if it's only between bad and worse. And I suppose my choice is between life and death. Because what I've been doing these last few years is neither really living nor being honest and outright killing myself. I've been in limbo but I've known for some time that it couldn't go on. I think that's why I had that drink earlier; to say goodbye. It's my last one, you see, because I've decided to choose life. Life in its beauty and its ugliness, its pain and its joy. I've decided not to let that man kill me too.'

He looked at Frank with eyes that were somehow clear and sober in spite of the huge draught of whiskey he had taken, and added, 'I thought about killing *him,* you know. Rather than myself.' He sighed, 'But apart from the moral issues, it's serving the Law that has always given structure and meaning to my life. To break the cardinal law now would make a mockery of everything I've ever believed, and everything I've ever worked for. And I'm not yet so dead inside as to want that. Besides, it wouldn't bring either of them back, would it?'

Once again Frank wanted to speak, to offer words of sympathy and understanding, but he had none. There was nothing he could say that would not cheapen his friend's suffering. But then a thought occurred to him and he said softly, 'I suppose you're saying that when it comes right down to it you're neither a good man, nor a bad man, but simply a policeman.'

Jack considered this briefly and then grinned, causing the years to dissolve away and reminding Frank that, in spite of his battered appearance, he was only in his mid-fifties. 'Yes,' he nodded, 'that's exactly it.'

'I suppose most people would think it a small thing,' he added apologetically, 'but it's who and what I am. Being a cop has kept me alive, and it's kept me more-or-less honest, and there are worse things in life that a man can be. So I'll continue to serve the law, even though it means leaving that swine alive. Besides, there's always the chance that the bastard is genuinely remorseful for what he did. And if so I'd rather he remained alive; after all, I wouldn't want his suffering to end too soon.'

Frank was surprised into a scandalized laugh, and he shook his head and said reprovingly, 'You really are incorrigible. That's not a very Christian attitude, if I may say so.'

'No,' replied Jack, not without a certain satisfaction, 'but then I never claimed to be a good Christian. Or even a good man. Like you said; I'm just a *policeman*. And policemen believe in punishment the way born again Christians believe in Jesus.'

He got to his feet, 'Come on, get out of here. Go home and get some rest, or go and see your girlfriend or something.' He cocked a knowing eye at the younger man, 'Have you *got* a girlfriend?'

Frank reddened slightly and said, 'Not as *such*, but let's just say I'm not entirely without hopes in that direction. It's a work in progress.'

Jack nodded and walked him to the front door, 'Well, whoever she is, give her a call. Don't be alone if a little effort, and courage, will bring love into your life. When you get right down to it we human beings have nothing else, and only a short time to enjoy it. Go on, get out!' A thought struck him and he became serious again as he asked, 'What time does the Forensics Lab. open at these days?'

'It doesn't shut at all,' replied a surprised Frank, 'Oh, we're all very modern and high tech these days! Twenty-four hour service, if you please, courtesy of the night shift. Though how long that'll last in the current recession is anyone's guess. Sergeant Bryson said he'd have something for me first thing.'

'Good,' said Jack dryly, 'We have a very busy day ahead of us. But you can give it to me *second* thing.' With a smile he added, 'I'm only kidding; don't be afraid of waking me up. I'm an early riser.'

It occurred to Frank that the older man said this because he was not expecting to sleep much that night, which caused him another pang, but, containing his sympathy, he just nodded and said, 'Okay, sir. Goodnight.'

'Goodnight,' said Jack gruffly, 'And thanks for listening to a babbling old fool, Frank. We all need someone to talk to sometimes.'

To forestall further remark he shut the door with a bang, leaving Frank to make his way home in a slightly melancholy mood that lay somewhere between sorrow and hope, and which contained elements of both. And when he got home, late though it now was, he rang Grainne Riordan. Not for any particular purpose, merely to hear her voice, and perhaps feel a connection with another human being. And if it happened to be a young and beautiful female member of the species he was connecting with; well, that was just a bonus, not the object of the exercise. Perhaps most of all he wanted to indulge himself with a little touch of hope of his own.

Chapter Twenty-Three

Frank woke very early next morning despite having suffered a restless, disturbed night. He had been too excited to sleep properly, too wound up by the possibility of finally breaking open this case, and too anxious lest the wrapper contain no prints. And he had also given more than a passing thought to the growing bond he was forging with Grainne Riordan. They had talked for over an hour the night before, swapping war stories and comparing wounds, though Frank was of course seriously outclassed in this department. They had also discussed their tentative hopes and dreams for the future before Frank had finally managed to tear himself away and go to bed, glad that he had heeded Jack's advice about ringing her. But although she was starting to occupy an increasingly large portion of his mind, his last thought the night before had still concerned the State Forensics Lab, and that was where his mind flew the instant his eyes opened the next morning. And his very first act upon waking, before washing or even brushing his teeth, was to pick up his bedside phone and dial the Lab's number. Bryson, the technical officer, had not yet arrived for work, but the wrapper had been examined for fingerprints by the night staff, and an anxious Frank was informed by one of the clerical staff that two different sets of latents had been lifted. Unfortunately, the clerical people at Forensics had no access to the police database containing the prints of convicted criminals, nor were they in any case allowed to compare the prints they found with those stored on the national database; many of the Lab workers were civilians rather than Gardai, and as such were forbidden access to confidential Garda files. All of which meant that Frank would either have to wait until a technical officer got around to running a comparison on the prints, or he could get a copy sent over and try to find a match himself. Unsurprisingly, he asked that a copy of the prints be faxed through to Harcourt Square and leapt out of bed, almost beside himself with anticipation as he indulged in some loud and largely tuneless singing in the shower. All right, nothing was proven yet, but at least he knew now that there *were* prints, and his excitement rose to giddy heights. And surely two separate sets of fingerprints must surely bode well for their investigation? One of them almost certainly belonged to Mr. Collins, as they knew he had handled the wrapper when he picked it up and bagged it, but there was a good chance that the others belonged to one of Sheehy's men. But even if the prints did not belong to one of Sheehy's gang –Frank didn't dare dream they might belong to Sheehy himself- they still might belong to someone with a criminal record. They had not had much luck so far with this case but he was hopeful that at last some sort of breakthrough was in the offing.

Skipping breakfast, Frank hurried out of his flat and drove in to town as fast as the traffic allowed, his urgency making him uncharacteristically impatient with other road users, and even occasionally rude to anyone who held him up. He arrived in the office before any of the clerical staff and, with a feeling of excited glee mingled with a sinking fear that they might come to nothing, collected the fax sheets sent from the State Lab. He settled down in front of Julie's computer and, after a silent prayer to the unfortunate, overworked deity who looks after policemen, scanned in the two sets of prints, one of which had been found literally all over the wrapper. Then he scanned in Collins' prints and ran a comparison program. Within a minute the computer confirmed that the less widespread prints did indeed belong to the fat man. This was expected and Frank, nodding silently to himself, started searching for a match to the second set. Generally speaking a fingerprint comparison search could take hours but in this case they already had a list of suspects, and Frank was able to call up the prints of Sheehy's associates and order the computer to run a comparison check with the latents he had scanned in. After almost an hour's wait, during which Jack arrived and Frank almost lost his mind with frustration, the computer finally shared its findings with them; they had found a perfect match. The prints found on the wrapper shared fourteen points of similarity with those of one Martin Leary, lifelong criminal and long-term associate of Crilly, Sheehy and Lynch *et al*, and most recently caught on tape emerging from Marathon Sports carrying three baseball bats. Eight points of similarity was enough to make the prints admissible evidence in court, and the two detectives shared a long look of satisfaction before Frank, fighting to stay calm, said briskly, 'Well, that seems to be that.'

Jack nodded and grinned wolfishly, rubbing his hands together, 'Well, we've got Leary, anyway. With the CCTV footage from the shopping center it's enough to pick him up, and hopefully enough to send him away for a very long time. Get me a warrant for his arrest, Frank, and we'll go and get him. Put down Store Street as the holding center.' In spite of his air of calm Jack was bubbling over with excitement inside; by God they had got the bastard, and he couldn't wait to get him into a cell and start sweating him.

Frank sprang to his feet, 'On what charges, sir? Murder, I presume, but which victim?'

Jack barked out a short laugh, 'Murder, my arse! No, make it for littering, damage to property, and criminal trespass. I'm sure your new best friend, Collins, will swear out a complaint if you ask him.'

Frank goggled at him in comical disbelief and Jack explained, 'We probably won't *charge* him with those offences, but we need an excuse to pick him up and we don't want to show our hand too soon. If we arrest him for murder Sheehy will have a lawyer down here within ten minutes of our picking him up, and any chance of squeezing a confession out of Leary will be out the window. We need a bit of time to sweat him, to get him to open up and talk to us, and we won't do that with a lawyer butting in all the time. Now go type up a warrant and look for a judge.'

'Yes, sir!' Frank shot out of the basement as if catapulted, knowing that Jack had no warrant forms of any sort in his desk, not having needed to arrest anyone or even search a premises in quite a long time. His footsteps were echoing back down the stairs as Jack took his place in front of the computer and grinned amiably at the disgruntled Julie, who had just arrived and was hovering slightly aimlessly in the background. 'Morning, Jules,' he called over cheerily, 'Any chance of a coffee?'

Her reply was characteristically terse and to the point but after a few moments of indecision she actually acceded to his request, fetching not one but two cups, and joining him at the desk on a borrowed chair. Although no expert, all Gardai are required to take basic computer courses and Jack was just about able to order the computer to conduct a nationwide comparison search on both sets of latents. This had to be done for elimination purposes and while they awaited the results they sat sipping the steaming brew in companionable silence for some time, neither feeling any great need to speak. Long before the younger man returned to the office the result came out; aside from Martin Leary the closest match was two points of similarity. Although expecting nothing else Jack nodded in satisfaction and returned Julie's computer to her before taking his turn at fetching the coffees.

When Frank finally returned he charged into the basement like a rampaging Viking and, waving the warrants he had prepared, said in suppressed tones, 'Got 'em! Come on, let's go!'

Jack laughed at his eagerness before saying, 'Calm down a minute. I'm just printing out the official search results to shove into the murder book. We need written confirmation of who the prints belong to in case this goes to court.' He saw the look on Frank's face and smiled grimly, 'Yes, *if*. There's many a slip, Frank, and we've still got a long way to go yet before any of them do time. Here, shove these into the file and we'll go talk to Leary.'

'Er, what about Mr. Rollins, sir?' asked Frank hesitantly, reluctant to give his superior tips on official protocol, 'Shouldn't we inform him that we're about to make an arrest?'

Repressing his first instinct –which was to shout *fuck him*- Jack shoved out his lower lip and thought it over; Rollins would likely cut up rough if he were left out of the loop. At last he said, 'Yeah, I suppose we'd better. We're supposed to keep him informed anyway and, more importantly, I just can't resist telling the swine that I was right and he was wrong. About *one* of the gang, at the very least. And that, against all the odds, we're about to make an arrest. Just as long as he doesn't talk to the Press yet; I know he's champing at the bit to give them something.' With a slight but smug smile on his face he picked up the phone and rang the Assistant Commissioner, telling him in a few short sentences about the fingerprints and what they planned to do next. Rollins' reply was even shorter and Jack hung up and said to Frank, with a grin, 'Bastard was pretty well speechless. For the first time in his life, I should think. No congratulations or anything, mark you; just told me, none too politely, to go and pick Leary up ASAP.'

'Is that it?' asked Frank in surprise, 'After all the fireworks and drama, after threatening to sack you if you didn't abandon the whole Sheehy line of inquiry, he just casually told you to pick Leary up? No congratulations, no apology for trying to force you off the right track onto the wrong one?'

Jack shrugged disinterestedly, 'He never could admit it when he was wrong. I think he was in shock, actually. He certainly sounded like he couldn't believe his ears. No protests, no arguments, just said to pick the man up.' He hauled himself to his feet and said, with boundless satisfaction, 'So let's go do just that.' As he put on his coat he said to Julie, 'Thanks for everything, Jools. I really owe you one.'

'Yes,' she replied tartly, 'you do. But when are you going to give it to me?' She saw his quizzical look and raised brows and snapped, 'The favour you owe me, I mean! Dirty-minded beast!'

Jack laughed, giddy with triumph, and pursed his lips, noticing but choosing to ignore the almost frantic Frank as he said thoughtfully, 'How about dinner tonight at the best restaurant in Ireland; Shanahan's on the Green? Work commitments permitting, of course.'

Julie, though surprised, was not one to turn down a free dinner –especially at Shanahan's, which was way beyond her civil service pay cheque- and opened her mouth to accept. Some deep feminine instinct wouldn't allow her to comply that easily, however, and she automatically replied, 'Sorry, I'm busy tonight.' However, in case he cried off, she quickly added, 'You'd never get a reservation at such short notice anyway. Make it tomorrow night. Work commitments permitting.'

He nodded, 'You've got it. And don't worry; I'll get us a reservation all right. Yes, Frank, I'm coming, keep your hair on.' And, well pleased with the way his day was going, he followed his junior out of the office.

Even without the rush hour gridlock the journey would have seemed interminable to Frank, so keen was he to make his first arrest of a killer, but as the entire population of Dublin seemed to be in front of them he found the slow grind out to Leary's house almost unbearable. And in spite of his years of experience Jack wasn't much better, for it had been so long since he arrested a murder suspect that it was like his first time all over again. However, he was better able to contain his excitement. Or at least conceal it.

When they finally reached the part of Blanchardstown where Leary lived Jack sniffed in disapproval, not so much at the sight of the cheap, close-packed Council houses as at the condition most of them were in. And although he had never been in this estate before the graffiti-stained walls and the burnt-out wrecks of cars lying everywhere gave him a strong sense of *deja vu*. What was it with these people that they all looked alike, acted alike, and lived in much the same sort of areas? You could practically tick off the requirements on a list; graffiti, litter, burnt out cars, and boarded-up houses. Yet another area of Dublin that needed to be bulldozed into oblivion, in his opinion, though he conceded that it was at least a step up on Jacintha Crilly's home in Finglas. But that wasn't saying much.

As they turned into Kingfisher Terrace Jack –in spite of the fact that his own heart was pounding and the butterflies were dancing in his stomach- warned the younger man, 'Now remember, low-key is the way to go. This isn't a bust on CSI or whatever cop show you watch on TV; we're just picking this guy up for questioning. And yes, on littering and trespass charges, including damage to Mr. Collins' beloved plants.' Jack was grinning as he continued, 'He'll think we're just hassling him because of his gang activities, -in fact he'll probably recognise me if he was in the snooker hall the other night- and he'll come with us without a fight, albeit loudly demanding a brief all the way. Got it?'

Frank grinned back, his adrenaline pumping and his hands starting to sweat, 'I admit I had something a little more Miami Vice than that in mind, but since there's only the two of us I suppose I have to go along with it.'

Jack shook his head in disgust, 'Jesus, you kids! Look, we don't need backup, and we don't need to go in like gang-busters. This is all routine to an old lag like Leary. I'm sure the organised crime boys pull him in for questioning every time there's a major heist in Dublin. One of the few pleasures of a copper's life is making a scumbag whom you can't arrest very uncomfortable on a regular basis.'

Frank nodded solemnly, 'I'll remember that, sir, for when I'm old and bitter and have abandoned hope too.'

Jack refused to rise to this, merely grunting, 'Laugh all you want. You just wait. You'll be old and disillusioned yourself some day. Far sooner than you'd believe possible, in fact. Though I don't think you're really the type to lose hope. Okay, there's the house, pull in.'

They parked and walked up to Leary's front door and rang the bell, with even Frank fully expecting a long wait before the door was opened; no criminal either man had ever met had been an early riser and it was still only ten-thirty. To their surprise, however, the door was opened by a woman whom either could have described without ever setting eyes on; a short, over-weight, peroxide blonde with a hard face and still harder eyes. It was uncanny how criminals all seemed to marry the same woman, with only the weight and degree of attractiveness varying. In this case the level of attractiveness was not high, and surely few women of any class would have chosen the violent purple dressing gown favoured by this particular specimen.

'Mrs. Leary?' asked Frank politely, 'We're Gardai from the Detective Bureau, Metropolitan Division. We need to talk to Martin.'

'Ye needn't tell me yer gards, I could fuckin' smell ye cumin' before ye got here!' she loudly sneered in reply, leaning against the doorframe to block ingress. Wha' d'ye want?'

Jack's small stock of patience quickly evaporated, 'He just bloody told you; we're here for Martin! We have a warrant for his arrest and a search warrant so either get him for us or get out of the way!'

'I don't give a fuck *wha'* sorta warrant yev got, pig!' she screeched in reply, 'Yer not settin' foot in my fuckin' house and that's it! He's not here and he's not coming back either. So hard fuckin' shite!'

At this point Frank thought it best to intervene and quickly, so he interposed himself between them and said pleasantly, 'Now, Mrs. Leary, there's no point in being difficult. We have our warrants and we *will* have Martin. Why don't we just do this quickly and easily, and without giving the neighbours a show?'

The redoubtable Mrs. Leary answered this by stepping out onto the path and screaming in the direction of her lucky neighbours, 'Are ye fuckin' deaf or sumtin! I told ye he's not fuckin' here! And I don't give a fuck about the neighbours! Let them fuckin' look and good luck to them! D'ye think I fuckin' care wha' any of them think? Fuck them all!'

Rather than reply Jack simply stepped through the doorway she had unwisely vacated and began searching for Leary, for whom he was starting to feel a touch of reluctant sympathy; whatever else he might be he was certainly unfortunate in his choice of a wife. On seeing him enter her domain Leary's better half shot into the house after him, screaming abuse at the top of her voice but stopping short of the actual violence she clearly longed to inflict. However, this merely gave Frank the opportunity to slip into the hall behind her and quietly make his way upstairs. The house was not a large one, and a few short minutes were enough to establish that –almost unbelievably- Martin Leary really was not there; against all the odds the old harpy was telling them the truth. In spite of this –and in spite of Mrs. Leary's showering them with invective, abusing them each in turn- they poked around for a while in a rather desultory search for anything incriminating. There was no trace of weapons or drugs or large amounts of cash and the two men finally gave up and left the house empty handed, scurrying to the *Ka* in ignominious defeat with Mrs. Leary screaming triumphantly after them, 'I fuckin' told yiz he wasn't fuckin' here! Now fuck off!' And with that she slammed the door.

'Thanks for fuckin' nothing!' muttered Frank without humour, getting in and starting the engine. They began driving back to Headquarters in dull, disbelieving silence, each too dispirited to speak until Jack finally said, in a low voice, 'This sodding case. I can't believe it. Every time we think we're getting somewhere we run head-first into a brick wall. At full speed.'

'He'll turn up,' offered Frank optimistically, trying to make himself believe it, 'His wife never asked what we wanted him for he won't be afraid to come back, and his sort never stray far from home for long.'

'What, with a wife like that?' asked Jack caustically, 'Would *you* go home if you escaped from her?'

Frank managed a small smile in spite of their shared gloom and said, 'Well, no, but it's possible *he's* fond of her. He did marry her, after all.'

Jack shook his head, 'Didn't you notice? All the drawers still filled with men's clothes, and empty suitcases on top of the wardrobe? He left in a big hurry, carrying bugger all, which means he knew we were after him, which means he won't be back any time soon. Actually, give me your mobile and I'll ring HQ, get them to issue alerts at the port and Dublin Airport in case he's trying to skip the country.'

'We have to cover every eventuality, of course, but he *can't* have known we were after him,' reasoned Frank, handing over his phone, 'We didn't even decide to arrest him till a couple of hours ago.'

'Did you see the blue Focus outside the house?' asked Jack, 'His. Says so in his file. So he just took off without his clothes or his car, which means he was panicking. Someone came and picked him up and took him to a safe house or the airport or something.'

'But he *can't* have known we were coming for him,' argued Frank, 'Maybe he's just gone off for a few days, to get away from that bloody awful wife of his.' Neither man uttered the obvious and Frank continued, 'He could be off fishing, on a job, anything. Hell, maybe he just went to the shops to get a paper.'

'Maybe,' replied Jack, unconvinced, 'Took his time about it though, didn't he? We were there a good hour. And it's a bit of a coincidence that he just happened to pop out while we were on our way to pick him up. Besides, Ma Leary back there seemed to me to be expecting us. I was surprised she was even up so early. After all, their kids are all grown up and gone, and that type are rarely early birds. And in any case I got the feeling from her that she wasn't expecting him back any time soon. Maybe George Trinder warned him that we were asking questions and he panicked and legged it. Or maybe he found out we were snooping about in the shopping centre where he bought the baseball bats. Hell, half the staff there could be friends or relatives of his.'

Frank shook his head doggedly, 'Sorry, I don't believe a word of it. Er, *sir*. I bet we'll find out there's an innocent explanation, and his being gone is just a coincidence. He's probably off playing cards somewhere with his mates, or done up on drink and drugs lying on someone's couch somewhere. *The dissolute in soul are dissolute in all/ and vicious are the habits, of the wicked till they fall.*'

'Perhaps,' shrugged Jack, noting without any great joy the return of his assistant's poetry after a recent hiatus, 'Hopefully you're right and he'll turn up sooner or later. But I can't help but wonder why that old bitch back there never even asked us what we wanted him for.'

'Occupational hazard?' offered Frank, 'She must be well used to this sort of thing. Operation Anvil, remember?'

Jack shrugged again, 'Maybe. Tell you what, let's swing by that snooker club of theirs, see if your all night card game is happening there.'

Frank eagerly complied but a second disappointment awaited them, as the club contained only a couple of diehard snooker fans practicing on the tables and an old man serving at the counter who genuinely seemed to know nothing of Leary's whereabouts. Nor Sheehy's either, since he was conspicuous by his absence. Not that it meant anything; they wouldn't have expected him to be around that early anyway; laziness and criminality go hand in hand.

In moody silence and bitterly conscious of defeat they returned to Harcourt Square to regroup and plan their next move, both knowing that the Assistant Commissioner was waiting for them, and waiting for an arrest, and would not be pleased at their failure. Nor was he likely to keep his displeasure to himself.

After they parked the car and were unenthusiastically approaching the main entrance their miserable morning was made complete by the sight of at least a dozen reporters, each with a photographer in tow, standing on the steps outside. Any faint hope that they were interested in some other case vanished when they surged around Jack as soon as he appeared and began peppering him with questions about the racist organisation currently whittling down Dublin's black population.

Jack teetered on the verge of telling them all to sod off but restrained himself with an effort; taking such liberties with reporters was no longer possible. These days the Press knew exactly how much power they wielded and, having no scruples or conscience, and no great respect for the Gardai, they were all too willing to use it. And even aside from the fact that it didn't take too many attacks in the papers to end a Garda's career, no one likes being mauled and abused in public.

So, with a sigh, he stopped and said wearily, 'Look, I'm not going to answer your questions out here on the steps but we will issue a statement shortly. Okay?'

'Is there any update on yesterday's statement concerning the group of neo-Nazis murdering black men in Dublin?' asked one reporter breathlessly, not even seeming to hear

Jack's refusal to answer questions. 'Have you identified this group or any of its members? Have you any suspects for the killings?'

Jack hesitated, unwilling to be drawn into an *ad hoc* Press conference but aware that if he didn't throw them a bone they might print some of the wilder rumours currently circulating the streets and pubs. And some amongst their ranks wouldn't be above inventing their own. At length he reluctantly replied, 'All I can tell you now is that the three recent murders of black men *are* connected, and that we are pursuing a definite line of enquiry.'

In response to another question he said, 'No, we haven't *yet* found any evidence of a neo-Nazi gang operating in Dublin.' And, after another question, he responded rather sourly, 'No, no arrests have been made yet, but we hope to make one soon. As I said, we are pursuing a definite line of enquiry, and we have a suspect in mind. You know I can't say any more than that. What do you want, the suspect's name and address? Now that's it, anything else will have to wait until we release a statement or call a press conference later on in the day.' And with that the two men pushed their way into the building, ignoring the questions that continued to rain down on them in spite of Jack's final remark. Once safely inside the front doors Jack stopped and said reluctantly, 'I'd better go up to Rollins, tell him what's happened.'

Frank grimaced in sympathy, 'He'll just love it, won't he? Especially after you rang him earlier to tell him we were about to make an arrest.'

Jack shrugged and said sourly, 'It's got to be done. And even *he* can't blame me for Leary taking a powder. And if nothing else he'll have a suspect for the Press, if he cares to name him. Go on downstairs and get the coffees in, I shouldn't be long. You can start drafting some sort of Press release. Basically you can repeat the stuff I just said outside, with a few frills added to keep the buggers quiet.'

And with that he squared his shoulders and almost marched over to the lifts girding himself for the ordeal. In the event neither of them need have worried; when Jack reached his office he found Rollins in an understanding mood about the setback they had received, and even sympathetic.

'Not to worry, Jack,' he said encouragingly when he heard the news, 'He'll turn up sooner or later...his kind always do. Criminals tend to be territorial so I don't see him straying far. We'll just keep ours eyes peeled and nab him as soon as he surfaces.'

Jack nodded dully and asked, 'Can you issue an All Points Alert for him? I've already alerted the airport and harbour police myself, in case he's trying to get out of the country.'

'Sure,' said Rollins, making a note on his pad, 'I'll get onto it right away. I'll do a nationwide all points, and I'll contact the PSNI in Belfast in he heads north to slip into Britain through the back door. Plus I'll have a 'Be-On-Look-Out-For' issued to all patrol officers in Dublin.'

'What about surveillance?' asked Jack, rubbing his face tiredly and trying to think; there was still alcohol in his system from the evening before but it was years since he had gone without a whiskey breakfast and he was starting to feel a bit odd. He pushed away an incipient headache with an effort; he wanted to milk Rollins for all he was worth while his mood was still conciliatory. 'We need a twenty-four hour watch on his house, and on his wife. We'll have to look at his kids too, in case he's shacked up with one of them. I know it's a long shot but you never know. We should be watching Sheehy too, and his snooker hall, since Sheehy's the obvious person to be hiding him.'

Rollins nodded, 'Now that you have some concrete evidence I think we can stretch to two two-man surveillance teams on the house, each working a twelve hour shift. We can't spare anything for the snooker club and Sheehy but we don't need to. I'll talk to Sheehan over in organised crime; they're watching him already so they can keep an eye out for Leary.'

'It's our arrest though, if he turns up?' said Jack immediately, forgetting his pounding head for a minute, 'Me and Frank's?' Although more concerned with justice than glory, like all policemen he very much believed that to the victors belong the spoils.

'Of course,' agreed Rollins, 'though I'm going to instruct Sheehan to pick him up if the surveillance unit spots him. If we're lucky enough to find him a second time we're not going to lose him again just to pander to your vanity, Jack.'

O'Neill gave him a dirty look; as if he'd risk losing him just to personally execute the arrest. His ego wasn't *that* bloated.

Rollins leaned back and unwrapped a humbug. Inbetween disgusting sucking noises he said, 'What else have we got to go on? I mean, have you any other suspects?'

'Depressingly little,' replied Jack in surprise, 'but obviously my other suspects are the rest of the Crilly gang. Or rather the Sheehy gang, as it is now. After all, aside from the evidence we amassed, Leary's married to Sheehy's older sister. And a right piece of work *she* is,' he added feelingly. 'The problem is that we have no hard evidence against any of them. Not even enough to pull one of them in and lean on him a bit. Though a known associate of Sheehy, Michael Lynch, lives in the same estate as the unfortunate Dr Wilson and probably set him up. We'll question him but we've no real evidence so I don't see him talking.'

Rollins lip curled and he said dismissively, 'Are you *still* on that? Listen, you got lucky once, with Leary, but I doubt if Sheehy's mob are the killers. Face it, man, these killings are racially motivated! Okay, so Leary's a crook as well as a racist. Well, that's no big surprise; ordinary citizens don't usually go in for violent murders! But you're wasting your time with the rest of them. We've already established that Sheehy and his crew were under surveillance when Wilson was murdered so none of them were involved. This was probably Leary's private gig, like a hobby.'

A hobby? Jack looked at him wonderingly; *did the man really say* hobby? He shook his head before replying, in a carefully neutral tone, 'Maybe, but in any case the rest of the gang have to be checked out. He certainly wasn't acting alone.'

Rollins nodded, 'Of course you have to look at them. But don't waste too much time on it, Jack; I'd bet that of the whole gang only Leary was in this Nazi group. There's a gang of racist thugs out there somewhere and we need to find them before they strike again.' He saw Jack's sceptical look and said angrily, 'Don't start that crap again about these being gang killings disguised as race murders! Wilson was a doctor, for God's sake! Was *he* part of the gang? It's just a coincidence that Leary is one of Sheehy's mob. You just got lucky with him. It just so *happens* that one of our racist killers is also a criminal…big surprise! The other killers could be anyone!' He leaned forward, giving Jack a blast of minty breath, 'Honest citizens, racist or not, rarely murder people! So yes, we need to look at crooks first but I'm warning you, Jack, don't neglect the neo-Nazi gang angle. They're out there somewhere; find them! The press are asking more and more questions every day and I want answers for them.'

Jack was suddenly too weary to argue anymore. He nodded and replied, 'Aside from being a mate of Sheehy and Leary I'll be starting with Michael Lynch because he was a neighbour of Dr. Wilson. But don't worry, I don't plan to leave any stone unturned.'

Rollins' eyes bored into his for long seconds before he finally nodded in return, 'Make sure you don't. I'll be watching.'

And with that Jack got up and quietly left the room.

Chapter Twenty-Four

For the rest of the morning the atmosphere in the little basement office was funereal to say the least, as Jack's efforts to locate the missing Leary –or to catch him in attempted flight from the country- all came to naught. With a carefully bland statement issued to the Press, and every alarm raised that could be raised, he and Frank busied themselves updating the mound of paperwork the case had generated thus far, both carefully avoiding talking to each other, and both desperately trying to think of a new direction for their stalled investigation as they filled in report after report. Even the usually insouciant Julie stayed out of their way, knowing that neither was in the mood for sympathy, or for her particular brand of humour.

The morning dragged itself into afternoon without any further progress, except of the negative kind, and the two detectives finally set out for Lucan and an interview with Michael Lynch in a sombre, even grim mood that contrasted harshly with the excitement of their morning trip to Blanchardstown. As they drove Jack felt himself break into a sweat and produced a voluminous handkerchief to mop his face. Under his jacket his shirt was sticking to his skin and he loosened his tie and opened the window to let in a blast of cold air, wondering if this was the start of the DT's and if so how he could fight it. And he told himself, though without any real conviction; *probably just a touch of the flu.*

When they got to Castle Riada they found, somewhat to their surprise, Michael Lynch at home and apparently expecting their visit. And their surprise intensified when he invited them into his home as if they were welcome guests.

'So, gents,' he said when they were comfortably seated in his living-room, 'What can I do yeh for?'

Jack eyed him with disfavour; in his admittedly jaundiced view the "Long Good Friday" had a lot to answer for. Lynch seemed to be modelling himself on the archetypal cockney wide-boy, with the same expensive but casual clothes, gold medallion and flashy wrist jewellery. He even had the offensively chipper, friendly manner, and Jack sourly wondered if he should point out that the "Del-boy" look -and act- was about thirty years out of date. However, reflecting Lynch had probably grown up on re-runs of "Only Fools And Horses" Jack contented himself with a disparaging sniff and said, 'What can you do for us? Well, you could start by telling us where Martin Leary's hiding?'

'Who?' asked Lynch, with what he probably thought was a cheeky but endearing grin that in fact simply enraged the two detectives.

'We're not here to play stupid games,' replied Jack, his head pounding, starting to actually hate Lynch, 'We all know what we're talking about. You and Leary and Sheehy killed Wilson, Akima and young Wistarra. But here's the problem,' Jack leaned forward to glare at Lynch, who maintained his friendly mien without flinching, 'With Leary in hiding all the heat is going to come on you, Michael. You see, he was our target, but if he's taken a powder, you'll do instead. Get it?'

Lynch spread his hands out wide while widening his little grin, which never once touched his eyes, 'Sorry, guv, dunno what you're talkin' abou'. I heard about those darkies getting stiffed but it's nothin' to do with me.'

'No?' said Jack, unimpressed, 'So who did it, then?'

'Sorry, don't know. Come on, guys, you know the score! I'm no grass.'

'Why not?' asked Jack interestedly, 'After all, you are just scum. A thief, a liar, a drug-dealer, a murderer, a racist... Actually, I think grass would be a step up for you. A big one.'

Lynch's grin had long since vanished and his cheeky chappie mode of speaking vanished too as he mumbled, 'Look, I don't know anythin', and even if I did I wouldn't tell you lot a fuckin' thing. If yeh've anything on me, arrest me. Otherwise get out. I'm not talkin' to you any more without me lawyer.'

'I believe you,' said Jack solemnly, 'About you not knowing anything, I mean. You certainly appear to be an ignorant arsehole.' He got to his feet and leaned over Lynch with all the considerable menace he could still muster, 'Just remember this, boy; from now on every time you take a shit I'm going to be close enough to wipe your arse for you. One false move for the rest of your life and you'll be *doing* life. Know what I mean...*guv*?' And with that he pretty much stormed out of the house, closely followed by a Frank who appeared to be struggling not to laugh.

Once back in the car Frank said, 'I'm impressed, *guv*. Best Clint Eastwood impression I've seen for a while.'

Jack mopped his face with his now sopping hankie before inclining his head modestly, 'Why, thank you; my "Dirty Harry" always did go down a storm at Christmas parties.'

'Aside from venting your frustration,' said Frank more seriously, 'Did we actually achieve anything there?'

'Not,' replied Jack positively, 'unless we've spooked them enough to stop them attacking any more black people. That was the object of the exercise, and on its own would be a considerable achievement, in my view at least. But are we any further with the case? No. He was never going to talk and we have nothing on him except that he lives near Dr Wilson. I really just wanted a look at him. And to let him know I was looking. Now he knows he's under the microscope he might just crack and do something foolish. He's going to imagine coppers everywhere, watching him and following him, and the strain might get to him eventually.'

'You think he might talk?' asked a sceptical Frank.

Jack shook his head, 'Not if he was one of the killers. He's not *that* daft. But if he was only peripherally involved, if he only told them he had a black neighbour, then we might turn him eventually. They're all sewer rats, Frank; if he thinks he's taking the fall for one or all of the killings he'll grass the others out, no question.'

'And if he *is* one of the killers?'

Jack sighed, 'Personally, I think he was. Which means he won't talk. Which means we need to find some evidence against him. But not tonight, Frank; I'm too tired and defeated to even look. I hate these gobshites who treat crime like a game, as if they were living in a movie. Well, this isn't "Heat" and I'm not Al-fucking-Pacino. I don't respect criminals as my professional opponents; I hate and despise them for the sneaking, cowardly, thieving, murdering scum that they are. All of them. And I hate them even more for the damage they do to ordinary people; the hurt and pain and fear and loss they cause to people just living their lives as best they can without hurting those around them. That's what made me a policeman in the first place; these people and the crimes they commit *sicken* me. All I ever wanted in life was to protect the decent people and punish the scum who want the good things in life but are too stupid and too lazy to go out and earn them. The selfish pricks who don't care who gets hurt or killed as long as they get what they want. That sense of outrage is what kept me going in the Gardai all those years and that's what'll keep me going now, even after our latest setback. I've failed on cases, Frank, but I've never given up on one yet and I don't intend to start now. We'll start again tomorrow.'

Frank's sombre expression and gleaming eyes clearly showed that he felt the same way but he made no reply; they understood each other well enough that he didn't need to. He just nodded his agreement and started the car. But for all the fine words and grim determination failure hung heavy over the two detectives and they departed to their respective homes with hardly another word; Frank to a movie date with Grainne Riordan, and Jack to an evening of largely futile thought, and a harder but less futile struggle with his eternal thirst.

The next day started off little better, with no recorded sightings or rumours of Leary's whereabouts, much less reports of his capture. Both men were at the office early after troubled nights, Frank being able to sleep properly for fretting about the case, and Jack unable to sleep because he had been shaking and sweating and shivering all night, as his body demanded the alcohol it had become used to. A very long, very hot shower followed by two pints of water had restored him enough to allow him to get dressed and go to work but even so his hands were shaking pretty well constantly and hot flushes and cold sweats were taking turns to rack his body. Frank was no fool and guessed the cause of Jack's ills –the nicks on his face where he had cut himself shaving were a dead giveaway just for a start- but, although he thought the older man should really be in bed, he had sense enough to keep this opinion to himself.

Several cups of coffee helped Jack a little and eventually he said, 'I've been racking my brain to try and come up with something we might have missed, and I've realised that I made a mistake.'

Frank raised his brows before nodding in agreement, 'I know. We never interviewed the guys I found who were guilty of racially motivated assaults.'

Jack shook his head impatiently, then winced as bolts of pain shot through it. 'Not that! I haven't forgotten them; I just haven't gotten around to them yet. Besides, whatever that idiot Rollins says we *know* who committed the murders; we just need to find some more evidence against them. We got lucky with Leary's fingerprints, now we need another break like that against one of the others. No, I was thinking about what Rollins told us, about Sheehy and his boys being under surveillance by the Serious Crime Taskforce. If he's right, how could they have committed the murders?

'Well, they couldn't,' replied Frank promptly, 'So either they didn't commit them, or they somehow evaded the surveillance at the times of the murders.'

Jack nodded, 'Right. So they would have to know they were being watched, for a start. And they'd have to know the limits of the surveillance operation. Trinder reckoned Crilly had bent cops in his pocket; I wonder if any of them were on the Serious Crime squad? Maybe Sheehy is paying them off now?'

He thought for a minute before saying, 'We need to find out the extent of the surveillance op ourselves, and check if they really were all being watched while our murders were being committed. If the bloody Garda are giving them an alibi we're sunk, but if the log shows they *weren't* being watched at the relevant times, or evaded pursuit during the right time frame, then it's another strand of circumstantial evidence against them.'

Frank shook his head, 'I wouldn't call it evidence. It might be useful as negative evidence, to eliminate them from our list of suspects, but even if they weren't being observed while the murders were being committed…well, so what? It's not evidence.'

'It *sir* to you, by the way,' Jack pointed out irritably, mopping his face with his hankie; he had brought six with him that day, and was starting to fear that six might not be enough. 'And I was more thinking of convincing Rollins than a jury. And if they know exactly when they're being watched, and not, it could mean a bent copper is feeding them information. If so, and if we can find out who, we might get them yet. And their pet policeman.'

Frank, not pointing out that Jack only insisted on *sir* whenever he disagreed with him, said, 'Well, you're right about one thing; even if it's only negative evidence it has to be checked out anyway. Sir.'

'Get onto it,' said Jack abruptly, 'But don't approach the top guy, Sheehan; I believe he's pissed off with me for barging into the snooker club the other night. Talk to an underling.'

Frank dived for the phone and Jack returned to the murder book, angry with himself for missing something so obvious. And what else had he missed? Being ring rusty was no excuse, and neither was having the whiskey horrors. *Not with lives at stake.* He dug out the three estimated times of death and wrote them down for Frank, who was all the while talking rapidly and persuasively into the phone. Then, conscious of the hand of tension gripping the back of his neck and knowing that he needed a drink, he headed for the coffee machine yet again instead, ruefully reflecting that this was about the only task left he trusted himself to perform. And even at that his shaking hands were causing him to spill quite a lot out of each cup. He gripped his hands into fists as he waited for the dispenser to fill the plastic cup; *was there yet worse to come? Christ.*

Twenty minutes later Frank put down the phone and puffed out his cheeks, 'I don't know if it's good news or bad. There's a twenty-four hour watch on the snooker hall because it's open twenty-four hours, but the personal surveillance is only on Sheehy, and not even all the time at that, for budgetary reasons. Turns out he wasn't being watched when Akima was killed because he's not watched during the morning or afternoon. He was *supposed* to be under observation when Wistarra was murdered but gave the surveillance team the slip, but he *was* being watched when Wilson was killed, and never stirred from his house.'

Jack's eyes lit up, 'So much for Rollins and his surveillance bullshit! So neither Leary nor Lynch were being watched while all *three* murders were committed, and even Sheehy could have been involved in the first two! And, if you remember, Forensics reckoned only two men killed Dr Wilson. Leary and Lynch, I'd bet.'

'You'd win, sir. I don't think there can be any doubt now about who killed our three victims.'

Jack tugged at his lower lip, 'Yeah, but it's not evidence. We'll have to talk to Sheehy and Lynch but I'm sure they're smart enough to have cooked up alibis for the times of the killings.' He sighed, 'What it comes down to is that without Leary we've got nothing. We need is a whole new approach to this case, Frank.' He darted a sidelong look at his assistant, 'Trouble is, I've been racking my brain all night trying to come up with a new angle, and so far I haven't got zip.'

Frank nodded wearily, 'Same here, sir. I'm afraid I'm stumped too.' He pursed his lips and Jack, recognising the signs, steeled himself for a touch of the younger man's poetry. He was, however, literally saved by the bell as at this point his phone rang.

'Jack O'Neill?' came a loud, too-hearty voice, 'Detective Inspector Mick Prendergast here, Serious Crime Squad.'

Jack's heart sank; *thank you very much, God, this is just what I needed right now.* 'Well, Inspector,' he began, 'I'm sorry if I trod on your toes by interviewing George Trinder without asking your permission first but…'

'Forget it,' interrupted Prendergast crisply, 'I'm not ringing looking for an apology. I *was* a bit pissed off when I heard you went steaming into the hospital without talking to me first, but I found out later that you weren't interested in our Georgie, or who shot him, and that you interviewed him about something else altogether.'

'I gather you weren't thrilled that I confronted Mike Sheehy at his snooker club, either,' said Jack with the morbid persistence of one poking at a loose tooth with their tongue, 'though that wasn't about the Trinder shooting either.'

'Not my problem,' came the reply, 'that's Organised Crime's operation. Though I hear Superintendant Sheehan has it in for you over that. But anyway, for me the bottom line is that we're all on the same team, with the same overall goal; putting the bad guys away. If we're fighting one another, or protecting our own little patches of turf, we all lose, and only the perps profit.'

Jack closed his eyes; Prendergast was right, of course, but inspirational talks about teams and goals and even bottom lines, or any other form of cheerleading, left him cold even at the best of times, which this very much was not. And the less said about the word "perps" the better. Trying to swallow his nausea he said patiently, 'Well, if you're no longer pissed off at me, and don't want an apology, what *can* I do for you?'

'Ask rather what I can do for *you*,' replied Prendergast cheerily, 'I'm ringing to offer my help. My team and I have had many a run-in with Crilly, Sheehy and the others over the years, and there's not much we don't know about them. Plus we often pool knowledge with Organised Crime since our cases often overlap. The upshot is that I have a list here of what we believe are some of their "safe" houses. All are unoccupied, and all are owned by overseas companies, but over the years little birdies have whispered rumours about who really owns them, and who uses them now and then for nefarious purposes. If it's true –and if Leary hasn't fled the country- there's a chance he's hiding in one of them. In the past we've had a hundred such tip-offs that proved to be false, mind. And even if these are genuine I'm sure they have others too, that we don't know about, but still, it's a start.'

Jack sat up straight and grabbed a pen, fully alert now, 'You're damned right it's a start! And a lot more than we have now! Fire ahead.'

Prendergast slowly read out four addresses and Jack hastily scribbled them down, his heart beating a little faster. 'That's great, er…Mick, isn't it?' he said at last, 'And many thanks for the call.'

'Any time,' came the reply, 'I'd rather put them away myself, of course, but when it comes to the crunch I'd rather you made the pinch than have these scumbags still infesting the streets. Do you want any help checking out those addresses? My men are involved, after all, if only peripherally.'

'No, I think we can manage,' said Jack slowly, knowing it to be the literal truth that Prendergast would rather put them away himself; politics formed a large part of police work, and whoever was making the big, high profile arrests was liable to get the lion's share of the far from abundant available cash at budget time. This unfortunately but naturally led to inter-departmental rivalry and jealousies that only helped the bad guys. He was no longer a part of any of this in-fighting and he added truthfully, 'But if we need any help we'll certainly give you a shout. And again, my thanks.' He put down the phone and rapidly passed on to Frank the gist of the call.

The younger man rubbed his hands in excitement, 'Great, where do we start?'

'With the address nearest to his house,' replied Jack promptly, 'If he legged it in as big a rush as I think he did he'll probably have bolted to the one closest to him. One of these addresses is in your home town, Carlow, and another is in Cork, so I think we can rule them out for the moment and concentrate on the two in Dublin.'

Frank jumped to his feet, 'Lead on, Macduff!'

'*Sir* to you,' growled Jack, but his heart wasn't in it; he too was filled with sudden, unlooked-for hope.

'Lead on, *sir*!'

Jack frowned, 'Hang on a minute, shouldn't it be "*Lay* on, Macduff"?'

Frank recoiled as if stung, then pushed his lower lip out thoughtfully, 'Do you know, I think you're right?'

Jack grinned in satisfaction as he slowly got to his feet, feeling better than he had all day, 'Well, well, well; so the old philistine isn't quite as ignorant as you thought, eh? Fancy me catching you with your quotes down!'

Frank rolled his eyes but said only, 'Where are we going, anyway?'

'Would you believe Finglas again?' Jack shook his head, 'What is it with criminals that they seem to spend their whole lives within the same square mile? Excepting trips to prison, of course. It's like the possibility of straying more than a few yards from their birthplace never even occurs to them. Even when they're on the run, for God's sake.'

'*The ground the branch shadows, is where the seed falls/And when the motherland sings, men heed her calls,*' quoted Frank, 'Besides, I wouldn't complain if I were you. After all, the well-known homing instinct of the common criminal plays right into our hands. We'd find them a damn sight more difficult to pick up if they were constantly on the move. Isn't that the whole point of probation and reporting in to your local Garda station and all the rest?'

Jack was looking at him rather thoughtfully so Frank beamed at him to wash away any possible ill-feeling about his smart-aleckery and said, 'To the *Ka*, is it?'

Jack sighed, 'To the *Ka*, God help me! Tell me, Frank, have you ever published any of your poems?'

Frank blushed, for here Jack had touched on his most tender nerve, and his fondest dream. 'Er, not as such, sir,' he said apologetically, 'That is, not yet. I've never had the nerve to try. But perhaps some day. Why?'

'Hmm,' replied Jack, 'Well, I was just thinking; don't give up your day bloody job.' He smiled to rob the words of their apparent malice and continued, 'I don't know anything about poetry but I do know a bit about policing, and you have the makings of a damn good copper in you. For all I know you could be a good poet too, but I wouldn't like the Garda to lose you to the literary world.'

Frank blushed again, speechless for once, and Jack waved his hand impatiently, a lurching wave of nausea in his stomach restoring his ill-humour, 'Come on, let's go catch a scumbag.'

The first address on their list proved a blank, with the house in question being boarded up and empty, and a quick but thorough examination showing them it clearly had not been used in a long time; the boards had all been nailed into place from the *outside*. And had then turned rusty, staining the surrounding wood a dirty red. However, perseverance was the watchword of both men and, brushing aside legal quibbles like a warrant, they forced an entry. Frank was not keen on this gung-ho approach but Jack overruled him, saying that if he thought for one second Leary was actually there he wouldn't be doing it; they were only crossing the "t"s" and dotting the "i"s". After a brief but thorough search confirmed what they already knew –that the place was inhabited only by rats of the four legged kind- they moved on to the next address, in Walkinstown, which at least made a change from Finglas.

42 Davitt Close was neither detective's idea of a safe house in any sense of the word, being on a busy road in a far from salubrious estate, but no doubt a man on the run would view these things differently. They parked some way down the road from the house –which was not boarded up, or so obviously derelict- and sat in silence to watch for signs of life. After a couple of hours, however, it became obvious that if anyone was in there they were keeping a very low profile, and were not about to give themselves away. Eventually Jack, who had drunk a two-litre bottle of water and who was sitting hugging himself and trying not to vomit, grimly rocking back and forward without even realising he was doing it, broke the silence by saying, 'What do you think, son? Should we walk straight up and knock on the door? See what shakes loose?'

'Er, if he's on the run won't he be watching and leg it away out the back as we approach?' came the reply. 'Shouldn't we call for back-up if we're going in?'

'For one man?' asked Jack scathingly, ignoring the fact that he felt as weak as a kitten and was in no state to be handled roughly, 'I don't think so! If he's even here, which I doubt, I'm sure we can handle him. Come on, I'll knock on the front door while you cover the back.'

'We don't actually have a search warrant, sir,' Frank pointed out, far from sharing his superior's confidence in their ability to "handle" a man they knew to be a violent killer. Frank could take care of himself in a melee but then so too no doubt could Leary, and he could see that Jack was not well enough to be of any help.

'For God's sake, Frank,' said Jack impatiently, 'I'm only knocking on the door, not kicking it in! We won't go in unless we're pretty certain he's not there or we see something to give us cause, anyway.'

'Yes, sir,' said the reluctant Frank, who was not really scared but was nervous; this was all new to him and his inexperience left him unsure of what to expect. And the last thing he wanted was for this swine to escape. 'But, er, what if he's armed? He *is* known to be violent, after all.'

'Welcome to life in the Met,' replied Jack with either real or well assumed indifference; this was old hat to him and although the adrenaline was pumping –which was actually helping to counteract his withdrawal symptoms- and he was breathing heavily he wasn't particularly worried about being shot. Being unarmed usually worked in the Gardai's favour in these situations, as even hardened crooks will rarely shoot an unarmed cop. They know well that even liberal justice systems ensure that cop killers never again see the light of day. He paused, realising that this was new and therefore intimidating to Frank, and said, as reassuringly as his pale, sweating face would allow, 'Look, Leary's an old pro who's been arrested dozens of times. He's been in and out of prison all his life and trust me; even if he's armed and we corner him he won't panic and start shooting like a scared kid. I can understand you being nervous but it's just one of the things you have to get used to. If we find he *is* there, armed, and he won't come out we'll called in an Armed Response Team.'

Some inner demon prompted him to add dryly, 'Provided he doesn't kill us first, of course. Now go on, get round the corner and cover the back door. I'll give you *exactly* five minutes before I go up and knock.'

After glancing at his watch Frank slid out of the car and made his way around the back of the grimy, mustard-coloured house. Jack checked his own watch, counting off the time to the second before getting out himself. And even though he wasn't exactly new to this sort of thing there were butterflies fluttering in his own midriff as he walked up the little path through the wildly overgrown patch of garden. He knocked loudly on the battered, peeling front door and then listened intently. With the heightened awareness and drawn nerves that had been stretching thinner all day he became aware of every little noise on the street and from the neighbouring houses, but from 42 came only deafening silence. He knocked again, louder, and then again, not expecting the door to be opened but rather listening for any furtive noise within, and watching for any stealthy movement at a window. But nothing stirred and Jack, his always meagre supply of patience quickly wearing out, began pounding on the door, pausing only to roar through the letter-box, 'Open up, Leary, I know you're in there!'

He began banging on the door again, sending a gentle rain of green paint flecks floating towards the ground, and was opening his mouth for another bellow when, to his amazement, the door actually began to open. His amazement increased when he came face-to-face with not Martin Leary but Frank. Jack's mouth fell open in astonishment and he roared, 'What the hell are you playing at? I never told you to enter the house! Without a warrant anything we find is inadmissible! Any judge will boot us out of his court in a heartbeat!'

'I think you'd better come in, sir,' said Frank glumly, 'I've got something to show you. Er, you're not going to like it. But at least I think we have enough probable cause to not worry about judges kicking our case out of court.'

With a sinking stomach Jack followed his assistant down the hall to the kitchen, listening as Frank explained how, on hearing how the knocking and shouting on the front door produced no result, he had slipped into the back garden and peered through the kitchen window. 'When I saw *that*, sir, I broke in through the back door to let you in.'

That was the body of a thickset, balding man in his early forties. He was lying face-up on the kitchen floor with two bloody holes on the chest discolouring his once white tee-shirt. A further pool of blood on the floor by his ruined left temple showed that the executioner had left nothing to chance.

'Jesus Christ,' uttered Jack wearily, feeling shaky again and looking around for a place to sit down, 'another bloody corpse.' He parked himself on a hard pine chair and said, 'What do you think are the chances of his being Martin Leary?'

'Pretty good, I should think,' said Frank dryly, 'Do you want me to search him for ID.?'

Jack nodded, 'But carefully. For God's sake don't disturb the body. Is he cold?'

Frank touched the corpse's bare arm before nodding in distaste, 'Icy, sir. There's nothing in his jeans pockets.'

'Okay,' said Jack briskly, crossing the kitchen to gingerly examine a tan coloured leather jacket thrown onto the counter-top, 'Use your mobile to ring it in, Frank, and get a Technical Team and the Pathologist's office out here ASAP.' He rummaged through the jacket pockets before raising his hand and saying in a tired voice, 'Bingo. The driving licence of Martin Lucas Leary. Big fucking surprise.'

Frank, his phone to his hear, nodded sympathetically; he had never heard the older man swear like that before but he certainly couldn't blame him. He felt like cursing blue murder himself. And he wondered if this was the final straw for their investigation, the final dead end. Would they even be allowed to continue working it? And if so, in what direction could they possibly go now?

Jack, now conducting a cautious and slightly dispirited search of the house, was wondering the same thing. Although he hadn't exactly covered himself with glory during the investigation he wasn't sure he had done anything very much wrong, but of course his superiors might not take the same view. Not with four corpses and no suspects, no leads, and no evidence. If they did replace him at this point he couldn't really blame them. Much.

By the time he returned to the kitchen Frank was off the phone and poking through the cupboards and drawers with no very hopeful expression. 'Did you find anything, sir?' he asked, looking up as the older man entered the room.

Jack shook his head dolefully, 'Not a sausage. There's bugger-all furniture in the house. Two armchairs in the sitting-room, one bed upstairs. No sheets, pillows or blankets, just an uncovered duvet. Not even a telly. And our friend here had only a holdall with him, containing one change of clothes and two pairs of socks. And nearly five grand in cash.'

Frank lifted his head, 'Are the notes new? Any chance they have consecutive numbers?'

Jack shook his head, 'All old and tatty, as was the bag. Muddy, too. Looks like they were buried in the ground somewhere. For a rainy day, no doubt.'

Frank scratched his head, 'Well, there are no more rainy days for him, anyway. Though this one's not exactly sunny either. For him or us.'

'Don't worry, he'll be warm enough where he's gone,' said Jack callously, 'and good riddance to the bastard. The world's a better place without him.'

Frank gave him a somewhat shocked look and Jack smiled wryly, 'Never fear, I'll still do all I can to catch his killer. Because the world will be a better place without *him* running around loose in it, too.'

Frank smiled back in spite of himself; the old man really was incorrigible, and Frank didn't see him changing his ways this late in the day. And he said, 'Well, I'm glad you're not planning to give his executioner a medal or something! But seriously, what's our next step now?'

Jack sat back down on the wooden chair he had occupied earlier and rubbed his wet face with trembling hands before replying, 'I don't know, son, I just don't know. Every avenue we explore turns into a dead end. *Literally* a dead end, with a corpse at the end of it.'

A long silence ensued before Jack raised his head and said slowly, '*Executioner* is exactly the right word; someone snuffed Leary out because he feared what he might say to us. But why? Sheehy must have had as much on Leary as Leary had on *him*! And by talking he'd only be implicating himself. So why kill him?'

'I suppose it doesn't make much sense,' said Frank blankly, 'Do you think someone *else* ordered the hit?'

There was another long pause before the furiously thinking Jack lifted his head and said, 'Not only ordered it; carried it out.' Frank raised his eyes quizzically but Jack refused to elaborate, instead continuing in the same slow tone, 'Our next step is to persuade our good friend Doc Ryan to take this body away and do the autopsy today.'

'Is it that urgent, sir?' asked a puzzled Frank, wondering to himself if the DT's were affecting Jack's mind a little.

Jack nodded, lost in thought, his blind gaze looking straight through Frank and seeking something far away, 'I think so. We need to get at least one of the bullets over to Ballistics as soon as possible. I have a feeling the gun that killed Sean Crilly will also be the murder weapon here.'

Frank frowned, 'You think Mike Sheehy did this?'

Jack shook his head, 'Nope. And I don't think he killed Crilly either. Not any more. Though he *did* kill our three black victims. With a little help from his friends. He carried out the first two murders and ordered the third.' He pointed a toe at the corpse, 'Chummy here took care of Dr. Wilson.'

'We already know that, but how do we prove it?' asked Frank, thrown by Jack's odd demeanour.

'I think we can,' said Jack softly, 'You see, I've finally started thinking instead of running around like a headless chicken, and certain things are finally starting to make sense to me.'

'Well, not me!' protested Frank, 'I'm more lost than ever. Tell me what's going on!'

Jack stared at him blankly for a moment before shaking his head, 'I'm not sharing this particular theory. Not yet. It's pretty wild but it's the only solution I can come up with that makes any sense at all. But I have a few enquiries to make before I say anything. But I think I finally understand it all.'

In spite of his words there was no triumph on his face, and no joy; the ill look had been replaced by a look of fierce resolution that boded ill for someone, and had the strange effect of making his face look harder and sterner, yet younger. And full of grim purpose.

Chapter Twenty-Five

That evening Jack was sitting alone in his front living-room, staring at the small coal fire smouldering in the grate, a fire that was more smoke than flame and which he made no effort to improve. Indeed, it was doubtful if his blank gaze even registered it. There was a large whiskey glass in his hand –though in fact it currently held only ginger ale- and a pensive look on his face. Although it was currently the furthest thing possible from his mind, tonight was the night he was supposed to have taken Julie out for dinner, a fact which that redoubtable lady at least had not forgotten. In view of the day's events, however, even her courage had failed her, and she had not reminded him of their arrangement when he had finally –and briefly- returned to Harcourt Square. But even had he remembered he would not have gone; aside from anything else his body was reacting very strangely to the lack of alcohol –though there were probably traces still left in his system, with worse effects to come over the following days, when he was fully purged- and he didn't trust himself more than a few yards from a toilet. Besides, there was nowhere else on this planet he would rather have been this evening than right there.

A ring on the doorbell interrupted his rather black train of thought and he rose swiftly to open the door. On his doorstep stood a soaking wet and grim-faced Assistant Commissioner for Crime (Metropolitan Division), Eamonn Rollins. Autumn had finally arrived in its full fury and it was a wild night, with heavy rain being driven by a bitter, blustery wind, and in spite of his heavy overcoat Rollins was drenched and bedraggled-looking. Jack looked past him for a moment into the cold dark night; so *much for Global bloody warming*. Yet the weather was apt for this meeting, somehow, and perfectly matched his mood. He stood to one side and jerked his head towards the sitting-room, 'Come in, I've been expecting you.'

'I bet you bloody have!' almost snarled Rollins, brushing past him, 'After your phone call from earlier I can only assume you're drunk, but drunk or sober even you would have to expect this visit if you're going to throw insane accusations around the office.'

'No accusations, insane or otherwise,' replied Jack mildly, following him inside, 'I went up to your office to see you, but since you were in a meeting I rang your mobile. It was off so I left you a message. No big drama.' He resumed his seat before the fire and picked his drink up without offering one to his uninvited guest, or a chair either. Notwithstanding, Rollins dropped into the only other armchair in the room, the coat still wrapped around him dripping water onto the upholstery and the carpet. Jack eyed him with disfavour and said, 'What do you want, Eamonn?'

Rollins looked at him in disbelief, 'What do I *want*? You ring and accuse me of murdering a man and you ask what I *want*? You *are* drunk!'

There was a silence broken only by the wind howling around the house before Jack shook his head and replied, 'I've given up the booze.' Then he added, in a wondering tone, 'Was it only two nights ago? Seems longer.' *Like a year.* He fixed his superior with a bloodshot but contemptuous stare and said, 'There's no doubt about it. You killed Leary, Eamonn, and you're going to go down for it.'

Rollins laughed, loudly and naturally, 'I take it back, Jack. You're not drunk…you're mad! All those years of soaking up whiskey have finally turned your brain to mush.' He shook his head, still chuckling to himself as he reached into his pocket and withdrew one of his ubiquitous humbugs, slowly unwrapping it and popping it into his mouth with a voluptuous motion that showed his enjoyment of the humble sweet. Watching him, Jack suddenly grinned, then chuckled himself.

'What the hell are you laughing at?' snapped Rollins, suddenly nettled.

Jack slowly shook his head, 'You have your own addiction, Eamonn, though I dare say a far healthier one than mine. You just can't lay off those sweets, can you? You should have stuck to smoking, you know. Believe it or not, it would have been better for you in the long run. No matter where you are or what you're doing, you're always munching on those damned humbugs. It's got so you don't even realise you're doing it.' He reached into his own pocket and pulled out a clear plastic evidence bag with a handwritten tag on it; inside it was another, smaller piece of equally clear plastic. 'Even when you went to that derelict house to murder Leary, you had to have one of your sweeties. It's comical, when you think of it; a grown man hooked on sweets. And I suppose there's a certain comic irony in your being convicted and sent to prison because of your childish little habit. But there's nothing comical about the Rules of Evidence, and this little wrapper is going to send you away for a very long time.'

'Bullshit!' exploded Rollins, 'Jesus, I used to think you were a decent detective, Jack! You think you can convict me of murder because you found a sweet paper the same as my brand at the scene? Talk about circumstantial…you *are* drink-addled. Or senile!'

'And if your fingerprints are on it?' asked Jack softly, 'As I think they *must* be? Because when you're going anywhere you like to put a handful of them loose into your pocket for easier, quieter access, don't you? No embarrassing rustling in the plastic bag by a grown man. I've seen you do it a hundred times. I'm quite sure you wore gloves when you killed Leary, but I'd bet anything you like you weren't wearing them when you filled your coat pocket with sweets last night in your office, *before* setting off to murder him. Now, you're the senior officer here so tell me; are *fingerprints* found at a murder scene just circumstantial evidence?'

There was a long silence, which Rollins eventually broke by saying quietly, 'More bullshit. If there were prints on that wrapper you would've arrested me straight away.'

Jack smiled; a quiet, vindicated smile as his last, lingering doubts were laid to rest. Then his smile faded; in a way he would have preferred to be wrong. In a low voice he said, 'Apart from the fact that you've just as good as admitted your guilt, we'll know tomorrow, won't we? First thing in the morning we'll have this down to the lab for analysis. Then we'll see what's what. Who knows, there might even be traces of saliva on it; I've seen the way you bite the sweets out of the wrapper when you're eating them one-handed. If you're holding a gun in the other hand, say.'

Oddly, Rollins seemed to relax for the first time, settling back and unbuttoning his overcoat as he asked, 'Who else have you told your ridiculous theories to, Jack? That half-witted young assistant of yours?'

Jack frowned, 'I haven't told anyone, as it happens, but Frank Carr is far from half-witted. In fact, he's got the potential to be one of the best assistants I've ever had, though I'm sure you didn't realise that when you assigned him to me. That was the plan, wasn't it? Saddle the useless old drunk with the raw, useless new boy, who's only a detective because of his TD uncle anyway, right? We were never supposed to get anywhere from the very beginning. Oh, how you must have laughed to yourself when you lifted me out of the gutter and dusted me off and *so* generously offered me one last murder case, one last chance of redemption. On paper you were giving the case to a senior, experienced detective so your arse was covered if anyone got curious, but you must have thought that you were as safe as houses, that you'd never be found out.'

Rollins shrugged at the bitterness in Jack's voice and said, 'Well, if so you proved me wrong, didn't you? So you've no cause to complain. *I'm* the one who should be bitter. I thought giving you the Akima case was like putting the file in the bin but you fooled me, Jack; you weren't washed up after all.'

Jack frowned, 'But you must have known that a string of murders, racist or otherwise, would eventually turn into a media circus, maybe even lead to a public enquiry. Sooner or later it was going to blow up in your face, and if I failed someone else would eventually have taken over.'

'Ah, but that was the beauty of using you on the case,' explained Rollins coolly, 'After the shit hit the fan I intended to use you as a scapegoat and throw you to the wolves. Accuse you of incompetence and boot you off the force. You see? And by that stage any trail leading to the killers –and I knew there wouldn't be much- would have gone cold. And any evidence you *had* found I could dispose of, and blame the drunken old fool in charge of the case for losing it. You have to admit it was beautiful.'

Jack shook his head in bemusement at the other's duplicity, 'I always figured you were a bit of a rat, Eamonn, but I think I was being unfair to rats. You're about as low as it gets.'

'The *stakes* weren't low,' Rollins pointed out, 'My whole world was on the line. And after all, as far as I was concerned your career was already over, so what did it matter? You hadn't done a stroke of work for years, and were pickled with booze; if you were sacked it would be no loss, even to yourself. You don't have a life, you care about nothing, and you literally have nothing to lose. Who would have thought you were still up to leading a murder investigation? Or that you'd bother even trying to clear it?'

It was Jack's turn to shrug, 'Old habits die hard, I guess. Apart from whatever pride I have left I guess some deep corner of my soul must still consider human life sacred, because by God I wanted to solve this case. Besides, you made a couple of mistakes. Even so, it took me long enough to get around to you. The problem was always motive, and I certainly never dreamed that *you* had one. But although I finally figured out *what* happened I still don't understand *why*? What turned you bad, Eamonn?'

'It isn't rocket science,' sneered Rollins defiantly, 'Money, of course! What else? I spent years tracking down criminals and trying to put them away -and earning a pittance for it- while lawyers earned fortunes keeping them on the streets. Or some senile old fool of a judge would throw a case out of court because a secretary put a comma in the wrong place on a warrant! *You* know what it's like, Jack. Any long-termer does. The justice system's a joke, and I got sick of watching scum get rich while I had to watch every penny, and watch my kids go short. And for what? A fourth-rate salary and a fifth-rate pension.'

'So you took a bribe,' said Jack softly, 'I figured that must be how it started.'

Rollins sighed and rubbed tiredly at his face, suddenly looking like an old man. 'Yes,' he said at last, the anger and bile leaking away, 'I took a bribe. But it wasn't just on a whim. This bloody recession wiped me out, Jack. You've no idea what a struggle it's been, trying to maintain a decent lifestyle *and* put the kids through private schools and all the rest of it. I managed it somehow, though it was always a struggle. And I did it honestly! I never took a damned penny from anyone, though I was offered fortunes, over the years. A few years ago I would have laughed at the idea of taking a bribe. I know it's hard to believe now but a more honest copper never lived.'

He shook his head sadly, 'The property boom fucked me. All of a sudden house prices shot up so much that my house was worth the best part of a million euros!' He shook his head again, this time in amazement, 'We couldn't believe it, Jack! Suddenly we were millionaires, in equity at least! It was like a gift from God. We took out a big mortgage, and then another, but it didn't matter because the prices kept going up and the interest rates kept going down! I invested the money I borrowed in property, and everything I touched made money because the house prices just kept rising! You can call it greed if you like but suddenly I saw a chance of a better life. Not so much for me as for Mary and the kids. I bought old houses and turned them around, selling them on for a quick profit. I even bought bits of land and built a house on them here and there. And the money rolled in for eight, ten years! Oh, not the millions some people made, but big bucks for someone like me.'

He sighed and rubbed his face with both hands before continuing, 'Then came the big one. I was offered the chance to invest in a big housing development and I jumped in with both feet! I put in everything I had and everything I could borrow! And why not? House prices had been rising for years and I thought I couldn't lose, even though the land was costing us a fortune. It was going to be the making of me, and set my kids up for life. I was going to be a millionaire in *cash*, not just equity, and I was going to get the retirement I deserved.'

'And then came the crash,' said Jack softly.

Rollins shrugged in something like despair, 'More of a slump than a crash, at first. House prices just started to drop. Only trouble was, we'd already bought the land and hired the builder. So we had to plough on, even though our projected profit margin was dropping by the week. We couldn't build the houses fast enough, and by the time they were up the entire world economy had collapsed, and the housing bubble, and nobody wanted them. At *any* price; we couldn't even sell the fucking things at a loss. So there I was, in debt up to my eyeballs, stuck with houses we couldn't –and still can't- sell, and with the banks screaming for the money we owed them. I was going to end up not just broke but homeless and bankrupt.'

Jack was watching him carefully, and not without a touch of sympathy, and now he said, 'So who threw you the lifeline?'

'I had a rubbish "possession with intent to supply" heroin case against Sean Crilly, which probably wouldn't have got a conviction anyway, but he didn't want the hassle and somehow he knew I was in the shit and he offered me fifty grand to bin it.' He sighed again and lifted his hands in a gesture of defeat, 'It was stupid, and weak, but I saw the chance to stave off bankruptcy for a little while longer while I prayed for a miracle to save me. I took the money, and from that moment my life stopped being my own. It was only a temporary respite, of course; I was still up to my eyes in debt, and Crilly strung me along like a puppet, doling out small amounts of cash to me whenever he needed a favour. Just enough to keep me afloat, you understand, but not enough to actually get out me of trouble. He had me by the balls, Jack, and he made sure I knew it. I was that scumbag's dog and he never passed up a chance to rub it in. But at least he kept it quiet. For all his lording it over me privately he never told anyone else about our association. Not for my benefit, I may say; he was just naturally secretive. And he knew he couldn't trust any of his people to keep it quiet. Anyway, after I got made Assistant Commissioner I eventually started to get my head back above water. I was still broke but there came a time when I thought I could survive, just. So the next time he came looking for a favour I told him to shove it. I guess you're not the only one who still has some pride. And that's when I learned just how deep I was in.'

He shook his head angrily, and gestured helplessly with his hands, 'I'd always made sure I couldn't be tied to anything illegal, that I was always in the shadows, but guess what? That Finglas scumbag had videotaped me taking money from him.'

'Tut tut,' said Jack sardonically, hiding the treacherous trickle of sympathy he actually had for his old comrade, 'You just can't trust anyone these days, can you?'

Rollins didn't even seem to hear him. His eyes were fixed on some private, inner hell as he continued, 'He laughed when I told him I was finished with him, and showed me the tape. He told me I was his bitch, and said I was stuck with him for life. Can you imagine that, Jack, the likes of him calling me his *bitch*? Can you imagine how that felt?'

Jack nodded, though he couldn't, not really, and didn't ever want to. But he wanted to keep the other man talking and so said, 'And that's when you decided to end your bondage by ending his life.'

'I *had* to, Jack, I was desperate! There was no other way out.'

'Maybe not,' said Jack, sympathetic to the reason he had killed Crilly but knowing it was not the whole story, 'but it isn't quite as simple as that, is it? You weren't just saving yourself from a scumbag's clutches. Mike Sheehy is just a cipher, without the brains or ambition to run his own outfit. You're the real power behind his throne, aren't you? The real brains? Because when you killed Crilly you saw the opportunity to rebuild your finances. So you took over his operation.'

Rollins' head dropped, 'I got greedy, I admit. Padraig was just starting university and the girls' school cost…oh, what's the use? You'll never understand the pressure I was under. And I admit, I had gotten used to the good life and wanted more of it. I suppose that's the long and short of it. So that night, after I'd shot Crilly I rang Sheehy –anonymously- and told him how it could be. He was sceptical at first but he came out to meet me and I told him how it could work, and gave him the details of a deal Crilly had set up. He went for it, and once that initial deal went well he was accepted as the new boss. At least as long as the money kept rolling in. And it did, thanks to me.'

'Why Sheehy?'

Rollins shrugged, 'He was dumb, but more trustworthy than the others. He's the only one out of the whole gang whose word could be trusted. The only one who would keep his mouth shut and not get greedy, not get ideas above his station. That much at least I learned from Sean Crilly.'

Jack shook his head in disbelief, though in fact he had figured out much of this already, 'I never thought much of you as a detective, Eamonn, but I thought better of you as a man. You crossed over and became the evil we've always hated, and fought against, and for what? *Money.*'

There was a whole world of contempt injected into that single word and Rollins flinched a little before dully replying, 'It wasn't just the money. I couldn't face the disgrace, Jack. Mary and the kids would have been so humiliated, so ashamed of me. And then later… Well, I was in too deep to turn back. You know what life is like inside for ex-cops.'

'No, I don't,' replied Jack caustically, 'you can tell me all about it when I come to visit you in Mountjoy.' A lengthy silence followed his words until he finally asked, 'What about Akima? Why did you kill him?'

Rollins had been looking Jack in the face but now he dropped his gaze again as he replied, 'Akima and his boyfriend, Wistarra, were the ones who videoed me taking the first bribe. Crilly used them because he didn't trust any of his own people and didn't want them to know what he was up to. Akima was perfect because he didn't know who I was, or why Crilly was paying me off.'

'So why kill him?'

'I didn't know at the time, obviously, but Crilly left a letter with a solicitor in case anything ever happened to him, telling Akima who I was and what to do with the tape. He wanted me exposed but Akima didn't play ball. He had other ideas. When he got the tape he started thinking and decided he wanted the same deal Crilly had.' Rollins' voice dripped bitterness, 'So now I was to be a dogsbody for a nigger drug-dealer.'

'Akima was a drug-dealer?' It wasn't a major shock but it was a let-down; Jack believed in the sanctity of life, and liked the idea of being an avenging angel of justice, but somehow championing drug-dealers and suchlike scum just wasn't the same. Maybe it should be, but to him it just wasn't.

Rollins nodded, 'He was part of the supply chain, growing the poppy in Africa and transporting it to Afghanistan for conversion into heroin. He laundered money for Crilly, too, through more-or-less legitimate businesses in South Africa.'

Jack sighed and shook his head; the whole sordid story and everyone in it was making him feel unclean, 'So now you had to murder Akima, or work for him.'

Rollins spread his hands helplessly, 'That's what happens when you leave the path of righteousness, Jack; you sink deeper and deeper into the mire. And the worst part is that there's no way back; all you can do is flounder about trying to stay afloat in the shit. Akima had to go, and I used Sheehy to get rid of him. I knew all about the surveillance on him, of course, and planned the first two killings for when I knew he wasn't under observation. I came up with the racist angle to try and divert suspicion away from Akima's real activities, and the real motive, but I wasn't as clever as I thought because you didn't fall for it for a minute, did you? Right from the beginning you refused to believe in the racist gang.' He stopped suddenly and shrugged, 'And there you have it. And here we are.'

'What about young Wistarra?' asked Jack curiously, 'Surely you weren't afraid of being blackmailed by a kid like him?'

'I was watching Akima, that's how I knew about the kid in the first place,' explained Rollins, 'He had to go because I couldn't be sure what Akima had told him. Besides, I had an idea that the video might be at his place. Which it was, by the way; I picked the lock on his apartment the night Sheehy killed him, and lo and behold…there it was on his bookshelf. Anyway, I needed another victim for my racist gang, to help muddy the water.' He leaned forward suddenly, 'Look, Jack, I don't regret killing any of them; these people were all criminals, scum. We've spent our lives putting them away. I just went a bit farther. Armed Response Units kill people all the time. Is my killing them really that different to locking them up forever?'

Daniel Wistarra was just a kid, you utter shit! Struggling to keep the rage from his face Jack, keeping his voice steady only with an effort, said through gritted teeth, 'And our doctor friend in Lucan? *He* wasn't scum, was he? He was a healer. Why kill him?'

Rollins shrugged indifferently, 'Sheehy picked him out. But because of the way you barged into his snooker club and confronted him he was starting to get cold feet about the whole thing, and wouldn't handle that killing personally. All he knew was that I wanted a nigger killed, someone without a record. I needed someone totally removed from criminal circles to get you off the right track, and he was convenient.' He sighed heavily, 'Didn't work, though, did it?'

Jack's rage at his callousness, his difference to another human life, was so great that for some moments he couldn't see properly, his vision blurred by the blood pounding furiously through his brain. But at last he got his emotions under control and was able to say, almost calmly, 'And then, when we got lucky and found some evidence against Leary, you decided he had to die, too.'

'He was a loudmouth, and chicken. With the fingerprints on the wrapper and those security tapes you would have broken him, Jack, and got the confession. He would have given the others away. And Sheehy would have given *me* away. I mean, he was loyal but only up to a point. He would have shoved all the blame onto me to get a lighter sentence. Ironic, isn't it? I had to kill Leary to protect Sheehy.'

'Why did you kill him yourself? Why not get Sheehy to do it?'

Rollins shrugged, 'I tried but he wouldn't do it. They were best friends, and married to two sisters. In fact, Leary was his best man at his wedding. He wanted to let him take his chance on escaping to England. I knew he was going nowhere so I was stuck.'

'It's terrible,' marvelled Jack, 'that all these people forced you to murder them! God, I really feel sorry for you. Let's hope the judge does, too.'

Rollins simply looked at him, no expression on his face. Then he shook his head, 'I thought I was safe with Leary dead. I can't believe a fucking *sweet paper* has stirred up the whole can of worms again.'

'It wasn't just that,' Jack contradicted him, 'I knew anyway. It came to me while I was searching the house where you murdered Leary. You were too hasty, Eamonn, and you panicked. Yesterday, when we went to pick Leary up, he had just legged it. I mean, we missed him by *minutes*. So why did he run so suddenly, without packing properly or anything? Why did he literally leg it out the door and fly to the safe house while we were driving out to pick him up? Because he was tipped off that we were coming to get him, that's why. And the only person I told we were going to pick him up was you.'

There was a momentary silence before Rollins nodded wearily, 'Of course. How stupid of me. But that's not evidence and you know it. Circumstantial at best.'

'Yes, but tonight after you'd gone home I accessed the phone log at Harcourt Square. And guess what? After I rang you yesterday morning to say we were about to pick Leary up, you immediately telephoned a mobile number. That's not evidence either, but the fact that the mobile phone is registered in Mike Sheehy's name, *is* evidence. And I bet we'll be able to prove that the call was answered in his house. Plus, I rang Telecom, and *his* phone record shows that after you rang him, he immediately rang Leary at his home. All circumstantial, I know, but still pretty strong. Strong enough to ruin you.'

Rollins nodded, 'In conjunction with the sweet wrapper it is anyway. *If* it has my prints on it.' He held his hands out to Jack, palms up, 'What do you say, Jack, can we work this thing out? Bury it? You know I have the money to make it worth your while. And after all, they were only criminals that died, not civilians, and the scandal will only hurt An Garda Siochana. I know we were never close friends but we do go back a long way. What do you say, Jack, you want to hand over that evidence bag and forget the whole thing?'

Jack's lip curled in utter contempt, 'Trying to bribe me? Pathetic. I'm not for sale, Eamonn; you shouldn't judge everyone by your own standards. And Crilly and his ilk might be scum, but I'm content to be just a policeman; I don't want to be judge, jury and executioner too. Making others obey the law is what our wholes lives are about, and it's all meaningless if we don't do the same.' He paused and then shook his head, 'Besides, the others might have been criminals but Daniel Wistarra was just a kid, and guilty of nothing but being Akima's boyfriend. And Wilson was a *doctor*, for Christ's sake! Someone has to answer for their deaths. You.'

'But I didn't kill any of the niggers,' protested Rollins, 'That was all Sheehy!'

Jack paused, fighting his rage; *if Rollins used that word just once more...* Finally he nodded, 'Yeah, Sheehy killed them, but on your orders. Well, he and his mates can go down with you.'

Rollins nodded too, as if this merely confirmed something he already knew, and with a quiet, unobtrusive gesture he produced a black automatic pistol from inside his overcoat and laid it on his knee. 'I'm sorry about this, Jack,' he said quietly, 'I really am. But I need that bag.'

Jack's sneer deepened, 'So now you're going to murder me too? A fellow cop? No doubt I'm *forcing* you into this, too. Is that the gun you used to kill Leary?'

'Yeah'... Rollins started to reply but froze as the sitting-room door flew open and two armed Gardai burst into the room from the kitchen, weapons raised and pointing straight at his head. Amid loud, urgent shouts for him to drop the gun Rollins simply sat and stared, bemused by this sudden turn of events. His stunned, trapped eyes met Jack's for a split second before he jerked his pistol up with a swift gesture that was curtailed by the two armed Gardai simultaneously shooting him through the heart.

Epilogue

Frank was not far behind the armed officers, his own heart almost stopping as the deafeningly loud gunshots rang through the little house. When he burst into the room and saw Jack standing unharmed, if a little shaky, in the center of the room he shut his eyes and let out a great gusting sigh of relief, hardly sparing a glance for the blood soaked corpse that O'Neill was standing over.

Jack stood staring down at the body for some time, an unreadable expression on his face. Frank crossed the room to stand beside him, saying nothing but examining Jack's face with anxious eyes. He knew what the Garda meant to the older man, and feared lest this betrayal by one so high in their ranks would prove too much for him and his new, still tenuous grasp on sobriety. At last he took Jack's arm and gently led him into the kitchen to make him a cup of tea.

Frank stayed at Jack's side throughout all the chaos that ensued, including the arrival of Doc Ryan to pronounce Rollins dead, the arrival of a technical team, and the subsequent removal of the body to the morgue. And at the end of all this activity he helped usher his weary mentor through the throng of shouting journalists that had gathered outside the house into the comparative peace of his little car, stolidly ignoring the hurled questions and flashing cameras en route.

Once safely in the *Ka* Frank simply drove slowly forward into the reporters surrounding them, trusting to their sense of self-preservation to make them get out of his way but not greatly caring if they did not. He only remembered to breathe when they were through the throng and speeding down the street towards Harcourt Square once more. As they drove he found time to shoot a glance at Jack and say, 'Are you sure you want to make your formal statement tonight, sir? If you like I could just take you to a hotel or something and you could do it tomorrow? You could even doss down at my place if you don't mind sleeping on the sofa.'

Jack shook his head with immense, soul-sick weariness and replied glumly, 'No, I might as well get it over with. I want to keep tomorrow night free to take a certain lady out to dinner. If I'm well enough. I forgot I was supposed to take her out tonight.' He gave a slight smile, 'I'm going to have some serious grovelling to do tomorrow, I can tell you. Though to be fair, our arrangement was *work permitting,* and work didn't really permit.' Then, half to himself, he added, 'And somehow I don't think I'll be sleeping much tonight anyway.'

Frank darted him another sideways glance, 'No, I suppose not. Um, you probably don't want to hear this but I think what you did was immensely brave. You deserve a medal for it, you really do.'

Jack shrugged, a sneer on his face, 'I wouldn't call it brave; I was scared alright but there really wasn't that much danger. I knew that once they heard the word gun those armed response lads would be in like a flash. To be honest I was more worried that he wouldn't confess on tape. We *do* have the recording of everything he said, yes?'

Frank laughed, 'We have two separate recordings of everything that was said, sir, don't worry about that! With a bit of luck they'll convict Sheehy and his mates, too. *If* they're admissible. I'll get on to the Director of Public Prosecutions about it tomorrow. And I still think you deserve a medal.'

CPSIA information can be obtained at www.ICGtesting.com
Printed in the USA
LVOW102014050313

322843LV00026B/926/P

'Spare me the hero worship, Frank,' said the older man irritably, 'I've done nothing to be proud of tonight, merely what I thought was necessary.'

Frank's mouth dropped open in amazement and he protested, 'Are you kidding me? This was like the impossible case, with your own boss planting obstructions at every turn, and you still cleared it! I'm awestricken!'

'I did nothing clever, or praiseworthy,' replied Jack sombrely, 'I simply did what I felt I had to. Eamonn made a couple of stupid mistakes, that's all, and I tricked him into paying the full price for them.'

'Tricked? Yes, and why not? He was a *murderer!*' almost shouted Frank, 'And he got exactly what he deserved!'

'That's more or less what *he* said about the people he killed,' said Jack thoughtfully, 'I suppose it's all a matter of perspective.'

'Except that you didn't kill him,' Frank pointed out more calmly.

'Didn't I? I wonder. You didn't see the look on his face just before he lifted the gun. I still don't know if he meant to use it on me or himself. But I do know that I had a fair idea of how things would turn out, and I'm not proud of tonight's work. Apart from anything else there's Dr Wilson, you see. I couldn't have done anything about the first two killings, but Wilson was murdered for *my* benefit, to throw me off the scent. And I can't help feeling that if I'd been a bit smarter, or worked a bit harder, he might still be alive. I threw the whole burden of the investigation on you, Frank, at least for the first day or two. But if I'd put in a bit more effort initially we might have got Leary's fingerprints a day or two earlier. And Wilson would still be alive.'

Frank refused to accept this and put up an argument but Jack tuned him out, simply not listening as he removed from his pocket the evidence bag containing the damning sweet wrapper, that vital piece of evidence that Rollins had known would destroy him. He stared at it for a while, lost in thought. And his musings were less than pleasant. He was going to have to "lose" the wrapper, for he had never gone for a dirty conviction in his life and never would. The sweet paper would not be entered as evidence, and he had never intended that it should. He had always intended it merely as a tool to trick an old colleague into damning himself out of his own mouth. Or, if he was honest, into using the gun on himself. For that had been in his mind all along rather than a conviction. A neat, clean solution that saved the Gardai the embarrassment of the trial of one of their top men. And the possible complications of an entrapment plea. It wasn't clean but it was a legitimate *ruse-de-guerre,* alright. If your morals have a touch of elastic to them, that is. And his morals had been battered and distorted by so many years of beating his head against that same brick wall Rollins had spoken of, a wall all long serving cops know too well, to be over-nice now. For the wall was comprised of the law, in all its complications, while Jack cared only for justice.

But however low his morals sank, to say nothing of his morale, he would never tell Frank the whole truth; that the sweet paper had not come from the Leary murder scene at all, but rather from the waste-paper bin in Rollins' office. He would never admit to his idealistic young assistant that he had lied to a man and tricked him into taking his own life because he had no actual evidence with which to convict him. Considering the paucity of the evidence against Rollins it had been a necessary evil, perhaps, but an evil nonetheless. An evil he would not share with the still innocent Frank. That particular burden of guilt and shame he would carry alone. He deserved it.

The End